THE FOURTH
TIME IS
MURDER

Previously published Worldwide Mystery titles by
STEVEN F. HAVILL

THE FOURTH TIME IS MURDER

STEVEN F. HAVILL

W★RLDWIDE®

TORONTO • NEW YORK • LONDON
AMSTERDAM • PARIS • SYDNEY • HAMBURG
STOCKHOLM • ATHENS • TOKYO • MILAN
MADRID • WARSAW • BUDAPEST • AUCKLAND

For Kathleen

Recycling programs
for this product may
not exist in your area.

The Fourth Time is Murder

A Worldwide Mystery/May 2017

First published by Poisoned Pen Press

ISBN-13: 978-0-373-28406-1

Printed in U.S.A.

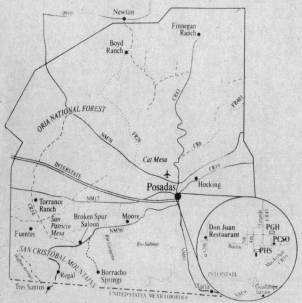

Posadas County, New Mexico

ONE

UNDERSHERIFF ESTELLE REYES-GUZMAN regarded the lengthy e-mail message, again finding herself intrigued. At the same time she wondered why, three weeks before when the message had first arrived from *A Woman's World* magazine, she hadn't just tapped the delete key. Since the day the e-mail had arrived, she had read the full text a dozen times, and repeatedly opened the four attachments that had arrived with it.

The first was a photograph of herself, taken three years before by *Posadas Register* publisher Frank Dayan. In that photo, Estelle was a bloody mess, standing with several other officers at the edge of the county's landfill pit. She held a blood-soaked handkerchief to her upper lip. The photo of that night's crime scene was dramatic and harsh, and Estelle had cringed when it appeared on the front page of the *Register*...and again when the image had blossomed on her computer screen as an e-mail attachment.

Another attachment included a brief interview with current Posadas County Manager Leona Spears, an interview that had appeared in an Albuquerque newspaper the year before. The article was as much about Estelle as anyone else, but at the time Estelle had been unable to contribute. Instead, she had been under intensive care in a metro hospital, tubed and drugged. Mercifully, there were no photographs of that, but the undersheriff remembered the intensive media coverage the case had generated. Of the shooting that had put her in the hospital, she remembered little. *Not a very good track record,* she thought.

The third and fourth offerings were single photographs, and one of them she glanced at only in passing—it was the official county portrait of Estelle as undersheriff that hung in the hall of the Public Safety Building along with the gallery of all the Sheriff's Department staff.

The last photo, obviously taken by a professional, had been shot from backstage at the Cultural Center in Las Cruces in November. Her eight-year-old son sat at the keyboard of an enormous grand piano, the spotlights shooting reflective stars from the piano's polished lacquer finish. His body leaned to the left, one hand poised over the bass keys, index finger targeting a single note to finish his presentation at the college recital. It was a gorgeous photo, dramatic, flattering, even exciting. Her son was impossibly handsome, caught in a shining moment as he and his audience were captivated by his music. The presence of that photo in company with the others had made her uneasy when it had first arrived, and did so again each time she opened the file.

She leaned back and rested her chin on steepled fingers, looking at the photo of her son until the screen saver preempted it. Touching the keyboard, she brought the picture back, then called up the e-mail again, reading it carefully as if it might somehow include messages that she had missed the first dozen times, messages concealed between the lines. The reporter's interest had progressed beyond the idle curiosity stage—she had done some research, and her request for interviews was courteous and professional.

A week after that initial message and its attachments had arrived, Estelle had typed a careful response to the magazine reporter, heavy with bureaucratic disinterest.

Dear Ms. Bolles:

You are welcome to pursue any articles you wish about the Posadas County Sheriff's Department, and we will be pleased to cooperate as time and policy permit.

Although we are a public agency and our work is a matter of public record, details of ongoing, open investigations are not routinely available for inspection or review by the public or the press.

Also, articles about individual employees are undertaken with the voluntary cooperation of each employee. Employees are under no obligation to discuss their work or their private lives with the press, although they may do so if they wish without review by, or permission from, department supervisors.

Due to the nature of our work, it is impossible to set a schedule of appointments. While we encourage civilian "ride-alongs" with patrol officers on an occasional basis, we do require that participating civilians obtain a waiver of liability from County Attorney John Sherman. We are in business 24/7, and staff will always be here to meet with you, workload permitting.

She grinned at the last sentence. "Most of the staff," she amended aloud. She found it impossible to imagine "himself," Posadas County sheriff Robert Torrez, agreeing to an interview with a reporter for *A Woman's World* magazine…or any other magazine, for that matter, with the possible exception of *Solitary Hunting*. The *Woman's World* reporter had a challenge waiting when she tried to interview the taciturn sheriff.

Predictably, the magazine's interest would focus on the women in the department, but unless the reporter's approach was just right, she wouldn't have much more success with Deputy Jackie Taber than with the sheriff himself. Taber, an ex-military loner, preferred working the graveyard shift, where most of the time she was left alone with her own thoughts and supervision.

What photographer Linda Real would say—with her own hefty baggage of memories—was unpredictable. Chief Dispatcher and Office Manager Gayle Torrez, the sheriff's wife, might be a useful ally for the reporter.

County Manager Leona Spears had made them all aware of the power of positive publicity, regardless of how it might be skewed. Estelle was sure there would be plenty of magazine copy to be generated by the flamboyant Leona. With her relentless promotion, more funding than ever before had been pried loose from the county legislature, and garnered from carefully authored grants. There might be still more to gain from coverage in a national magazine.

Still, Estelle had hesitated before sending her original e-mail reply, looking again at the photo of her son. The implications of that photograph being included were clear, she decided. But whatever the magazine editor's real agenda was, it would not include little Francisco. That was certain. At age eight, the little boy didn't need national media exposure, regardless of his prodigious talent.

Finally, after taking a week to let things settle and sift, and satisfied that her reply said what she intended, she had tapped send, with a copy of the original request and her response sent to the sheriff, who wouldn't read it, to the county manager, who would bubble with enough relish and anticipation to make the county commissioners nervous, and to each member of the department.

That had been two weeks ago. Estelle had heard nothing from the magazine writer since then, and had even wondered if the idea had been abandoned. But that Friday morning, the second message arrived.

Good Morning, Undersheriff:

I'm delighted for the opportunity to talk with you and your staff. I plan to arrive in Posadas tomorrow, Saturday, Feb. 9th, and will touch base with you when I'm settled.

I realize that this doesn't give you much notice, but your response indicated that would not be a concern. We have had some scheduling issues at the magazine, and this window of opportunity recently opened for us.

I look forward to meeting you. If you have any further questions, please don't hesitate to contact me.

Madelyn Bolles, associate editor

Estelle typed a brief, polite response acknowledging the message, then shut down the computer, unplugged it, and tucked it into its slim black nylon case. Taking a moment to survey her pleasantly cluttered desk, she ran down the mental list of things pending.

As Friday evenings went, this one was an interesting mix. At 6:30, the February sky was already dark, with heavy clouds to the southwest, obscuring the peaks of the San Cristóbals. No precipitation was predicted for the prairie, but in the mountains anything was possible.

Even though the temperature held at fifty degrees in the village, the evening appealed to Estelle as a perfect time to curl up with her husband under a down comforter and watch the fire.

They would have an hour or so while Francisco finished up his homework, but then his piano would beckon. Little brother Carlos, still spared the affliction of homework, would be deep in his constant passion, great heaps of modeling clay that he shaped into the wonders of the moment.

The evening wouldn't be as serene for other members of the Sheriff's Department. She glanced at the clock. An hour before, the school bus from Lordsburg had arrived in Posadas via the interstate, carrying the junior varsity and varsity basketball teams for a late season game. Tip-off for the JV game was now minutes away, and two deputies, Tom Pasquale and Tony Abeyta, would work the raucous crowd at the school. As a routine precaution, the officers would escort the bus out of Posadas after the game, seeing it safely onto the interstate for the trip home.

For whatever reason, a game between the evenly matched teams always lowered the common sense quotient of the crowd by several dozen points. Bearing that in mind, Deputy Dennis Collins would patrol the central portion of the county, including the village itself, staying only seconds away from the school if his backup should be needed. Captain Eddie Mitchell had planned to work late in his office catching up on paperwork and would swing by the school about the time that the final game buzzer sounded.

Briefcase in one hand, laptop in the other, Estelle walked out of her office and paused at the magnetic whiteboard behind dispatcher Ernie Wheeler's console. The list of working deputies was short, and would be shorter still when the graveyard shift began. Jackie Taber and Mike Sisneros would cover the whole of Posadas County, and the village of Posadas as well—7,500 souls, plus or minus.

On Sunday, coverage would drop again, leaving one deputy for each shift.

Ernie was talking either to himself—boredom could do that to a person—or into his headset, and he turned to catch Estelle's eye, holding up a single finger in the "wait a minute" gesture.

"And where are you now?" he asked, and paused again, finger still poised in the air. "All right, we'd appreciate that. Someone will be out there. Stay on the line for a moment, please." He swiveled to punch a button on his console, and then turned back to Estelle. "One of the highway department patrols is on her cell phone from just this side of the pass. She's reporting a motor vehicle is off the road, way down in the rocks. Just short of mile marker four."

"Anyone around it?"

"She can't tell, and doesn't want to climb down to look. She's all by herself."

"I can understand *that*," Estelle said. The climb down and back would be ghastly enough without the added possibility of bashed and mangled victims. "Is there a state officer handy?"

"Nope. One's got a vehicle down, and the other is thirty miles east on the interstate with an accident."

"If he's clear, Dennis can head that way, then," she said.

"He is. I told him to stay central, but he can break away."

Estelle nodded. "I'll be home if you need me." Ernie nodded and turned back to his radio.

The undersheriff left the building, greeted by cold, moist air.

A heck of a time to walk Regál Pass, she thought—dark, cold, wet, probably a biting wind thrown into the bargain. As she juggled the remote and pushed the button to unlock the door of her county car, she heard the deputy's vehicle before she saw it. Collins' unit turned south on Grande, grill lights pulsing. She watched until he was out of sight, under the interstate and headed southwest on State 56.

His adrenaline would be pumping, she knew—any young kid with a hot car and twenty-nine miles of open road would be just as eager, provided that collecting a deer or peccary or armadillo in his patrol car's grill at 90 miles an hour didn't blunt his enthusiasm.

As she turned onto Bustos from Grande, she saw the wink of lights from a southbound ambulance.

A left-hand turn to South 12th Street put her in view of her home, and she could see a curl of smoke from the chimney. Her husband's SUV was parked in the driveway, and Irma's Toyota sedan was at the curb. With a wonderful predictability, a world of aromas would waft out the door as Estelle entered. Irma Sedillos, nana for the two boys, talented chef of the best Mexican food on the planet, a source of good cheer during the black moments, had become a family fixture, bringing some order to the chaotic nonschedule of a family that included both the undersheriff of Posadas County and her husband, a busy physician and surgeon.

She parked beside her husband's vehicle, and winked the red lights in the grill briefly at the face peering out through the living room window. With everything in order, she keyed the mike. "PCS, three-ten is ten-ten."

"Three-ten, stand by." Ernie Wheeler's tone was crisp. He didn't sound the least bit understanding that the undersheriff was now home, parked in her driveway, anticipating hugs, hot food, and a long, quiet evening. Estelle waited, engine idling. Deputy Collins had had time to cover perhaps ten miles. Over at the high school, the basketball game was seconds from tip-off.

Her cell phone rang, and Ernie's familiar, low-key voice was urgent. "Estelle, the gal from the highway department says that a trucker stopped and they both climbed down to the wreck. There's at least one dead. You want me to call the sheriff?"

"No. I'm already set to go." As she backed the county car out of her driveway, she could see her younger son, Carlos, standing in the front door, hands on his hips. She blew him a kiss, and then dialed the phone as she accelerated back up 12th toward Bustos. Irma answered on the second ring.

"We've got a fatal down on Regál Pass, Irma," she said.

"Well, you *almost* made it," Irma's voice replied. "We'll save some posole for you."

"Thanks."

"Do you want to talk with your hubby? He's on the computer in the back room with Francisco."

"No. Just tell them I'll be back late."

"You got it."

And so it goes, Estelle thought. She forced herself to concentrate on one challenge at a time, switching back to the radio. "PCS, three-ten is en route. ETA about thirty minutes."

"Ten-four, three-ten."

"Three-oh-four copies," Collins said, his voice oddly detached over the electronic airwaves. "ETA ten." Ten minutes was a long time to wait if you were lying bleeding and broken down in a mountainside gorge...but that was only if the Good Samaritans were mistaken.

TWO

THE SAN CRISTÓBAL Mountains created an effective border fence between old Mexico and Posadas County, New Mexico. The ragged, rotten granite peaks were inhospitable enough that even the most determined illegal immigrants sought other routes to wealth. Presumably, they thought it more pleasant to die of thirst or snakebite farther west in the Arizona desert than to plunge into a jagged, skin-tearing, bone-breaking crevasse high up in the San Cristóbals, to be soaked, baked, or frozen until the hungry spring ravens arrived to clean up the mess.

State Highway 56 dove south through a dramatic saddle in the mountains at Regál Pass. The highway ended at the village of Regál and the days-only border crossing a hundred yards south of the Regál church. A dozen feet into Mexico, the highway faded into the gravel road that passed as the highway southbound to Janos, Buenaventura, and Chihuahua.

Estelle let the heavy sedan settle in at 85, with the spotlight playing ahead to catch the reflection from startled eyes.

The highway through Regál Pass was the best that modern design could manage. In fact, the current Posadas county manager, Leona Spears, had been instrumental in the redesign of the route while employed by the state highway department. Still, despite the highway's wide, paved shoulders, bright lane markings, and rumble strips on both sides and down the center, motorists found a way to vault off into space.

Five miles east of the Broken Spur Saloon, Estelle saw the flashing lights of the ambulance ahead, and she overtook the vehicle by the time they passed the bar's parking lot.

Beyond the intersection with County Road 14, the highway swept south and began to climb in earnest, widening to include a passing lane that continued all the way to the summit, where the third lane switched sides.

Despite the broad right-of-way, the road became a tortuous serpent as it climbed, including one switchback across a jagged ravine where the highway was posted at 15 miles an hour.

"PCS, three-oh-four is ten-six just south of mile marker zero-five," Collins radioed. "I'll be with two civilians. Three-ten, what's your twenty?"

"Three-ten is just coming up the hill. ETA about five minutes."

"Ten-four. PCS, ten-forty-five, one and one as far as I can see. Ten-twenty-eight New Mexico Sam Lincoln Charlie two-seven-seven. I think it's a Chevy S-ten, color white."

"Ten-four," dispatcher Ernie Wheeler responded. "Three-ten, did you copy?"

"Affirmative." One vehicle, one victim. A pickup truck with New Mexico plates could be a local, someone from Regál even, perhaps headed into town to see the basketball game. For more than a mile, the highway headed due west, climbing the flank of the mountain. Then another switchback sent Estelle east, and the highway snaked sharply upward. At regular intervals, the guardrail was scarred with blackened dents and scars, moments of panic when the drivers strayed or slid or swerved from the marked lanes and kissed the steel rail.

The last time she had responded to an MVA on Regál Pass, it had been a trucker who had allowed his rig's rear tandem duals to catch the end of a guardrail section. The rails had vaulted the trailer up and then refused to let go, the rig riding along like a wild locomotive, pinned to the wrong set of rails. By the time the thirty-ton load of scrapped automobiles jack-knifed and buried the cab under a pile of smoking junk, there wasn't enough driver left for the EMTs to patch together.

Mist now hung over the peaks, reaching down to the 8,000-foot level, just low enough to blanket the 8,012-foot pass. Estelle snapped on the fog lights, and seconds later the kaleidoscope of emergency lights broke through the mist. She slowed the car to a walk, easing past the bulky propane delivery truck that was parked along the guardrail off the oncoming lanes, its flashers bright. Just behind the big rig, a bright orange State Highway Department truck was marked with its yellow beacon pulsing in the mist.

They were a quarter mile north of the pass itself, and even in clear weather, oncoming traffic would have had little warning when they came upon the scene. Fiery phosphorus flares were stabbed into the shoulder every dozen feet, so bright they hurt the eyes. A few yards up-hill from the state truck, and on the other side of the road, Collins had parked his county unit tight against the steep bank. A dead deer lay in the ditch in front of his vehicle.

A bulky figure wearing a bright orange safety vest over his down winter coat approached from behind the delivery truck. "They're down there," the man said, pointing over the guardrail. "It's a bad one."

Estelle stepped to the rail and looked down through the rocks, brush, and fill left by the highway's construction. She could see the beams of flashlights, and her own light reflected off the bent license plate. She played the light along the scar left by the truck's hurtling trajectory. It appeared that this time, luck was not on the driver's side. The likely scenario was a swerve followed by overcorrection. But when he had lost control and plunged his truck off the road, he had done so right at the beginning of the guardrail. The curved rail had acted as a vault, flipping the truck up and over.

Tracks showed the truck had vaulted over a small hummock left by the original grading, then plunged down through the rocks, tumbling like a small toy. Unfortunately for the driver, it appeared that the truck went off the road with considerable momentum, ricocheting off boulders and trees, strewing parts along the way.

Estelle palmed her handheld radio. "Three-oh-four?"

"Go ahead."

"What do you have down there?"

"One vehicle. Looks like just the driver. I think he was ejected and then the truck got him. Maybe more than once."

The ambulance approached, adding another Christmas tree of lights.

"Is there anything I can do?" the trucker asked, and Estelle shook her head.

"I'd like you to move your rig in just a minute," Estelle said.

"You betcha."

"Three-ten, PCS."

"Go ahead," Estelle said, and then dispatcher Ernie Wheeler paused.

"Three-ten, be advised that vehicle is registered to Christopher Marsh, DOB six nine eighty-six. An address in Las Cruces."

"Ten-four. Ten-forty-six." It would be a challenge for the wrecker to winch this wreck up through the rocks, hoisting it over the guardrail. "And we're going to have a traffic problem. If you can find me another officer or two, I'd appreciate it."

Almost immediately, the radio responded, but this time with Sheriff Robert Torrez's soft voice.

"Three-ten, I'll be down in a few minutes. You got it until then?"

"Ten-four."

"You need Perrone?"

Estelle hesitated. The EMTs were as capable as anyone of determining whether the driver was dead—if the driver had been crushed by the flipping truck, odds were good that he was. But the emergency medical staff wouldn't give up easily. If there was a breath, a whisper, of life remaining, they'd find it and nurture it along until they could transport the broken victim to Posadas General.

"Hold on that call for a minute until we see what we have."

"Ten-four."

It appeared that the trucker was going to climb back in his rig, and Estelle took him by the elbow. "Walk with me for just a minute?"

The man bundled along beside the undersheriff as Estelle walked uphill beyond the big rig and the state pickup to the point where the crashed truck's skid marks were obvious on the damp asphalt. She aimed her flashlight at the deep gouges in the dirt mound where the pickup had catapulted off the pavement, ripping the rail from its supports.

"I bet he swerved to avoid that deer over there," the man said, nodding across at Collins' Expedition. "I counted fourteen on my way up the hill just a bit ago." He pointed into the mist. "Including a mama and twins back by the pass sign."

"Did the truck pass you coming up from Regál, sir?"

"No. I seen the highway department truck stopped, and the deer, so I pulled over. I figure that's what he did…clobbered the deer."

"Hard to tell. But that's most likely," Estelle said. She looked at the man, trying to remember his name. "You're working late tonight," she said.

"I'm runnin' so far behind I'm about to meet myself," he laughed. "This cold weather reminds folks that their tanks need toppin' off."

"So you didn't see any of this."

"Nope. I stopped 'cause the state truck was here and she was puttin' out flares. She wasn't about to climb down in them rocks without some company, but it ain't gonna be me. I don't need no broke leg just now."

"I don't blame you a bit, sir. If you'd move the truck on out, that'll help."

"You got it."

A car approached from the south, and Estelle watched it go by, tires hissing on the pavement as wide eyes peered at them.

The tanker started with a belch of fragrant propane fumes, and the undersheriff walked to the edge of the highway out of his way. She looked down at the lights far below. Switching the radio channel to local, she keyed the handheld.

"Dennis, what do you have down there?"

For a moment, she was answered only by silence, then Deputy Collins flashed his light up the hill at her. "Estelle, I think before we move the victim, Perrone should take a look. Matty agrees."

Matty Finnegan, the lead EMT, had voiced opinions many times before that Estelle valued.

"And you, too," Collins added. Estelle's curiosity was piqued, but the last thing she wanted was a discussion of the accident scene, and the accident victim, over the public airwaves, even if the local handheld signal was limited in its range.

"I'll be down in a minute. We need some coverage up here on the highway first."

"Connie is on her way up," he said, referring to the highway department worker. "Matty and Cliff will stay here until you say otherwise."

She watched the flashlight beam wobble its way up through the rocks, marveling again at the wild ride that the truck must have taken as it vaulted into space. In a few minutes, Connie Ulibarri reached the guardrail, grabbed it with both hands, and stopped, winded and red faced. She was a tiny girl, maybe twenty-five years old, her hard hat skewed back from her forehead.

"Dr. Perrone's not going to like that climb," she managed.

She walked uphill along the narrow lane behind the rail to join Estelle. "The driver's been dead awhile," she said.

"Just the one occupant?"

"Yes. He wasn't wearing the seat belt. The passenger side is retracted as well. He stayed with it for quite a ride," Connie said.

"Steering wheel is bent all to hell where he hung on. But then Dennis thinks that he went out the passenger side window."

"This evening sometime, you think?"

"Maybe. But he's stone cold, Estelle. That's why Dennis was thinking that you and Perrone should take a look."

"Okay. How'd you happen to stumble on this, Connie?"

Ulibarri took a deep breath and pulled her hard hat straight. "I saw the deer over in the ditch. She was out of the traffic lane, and I wasn't going to stop, 'cause I could see she was too big for me to pick up alone, but then I saw that she had a Game and Fish radio collar on. I thought I should retrieve that." She nodded toward her truck. "I got it in the unit. Then I started looking and saw the skid marks and the scuffed dirt by the rail." She shrugged. "What a mess."

"The propane deliveryman said he didn't see the wreck happen, either."

"No. He stopped after I did. I was settin' out the flares, after I called you guys."

Her handheld crackled again. "Estelle, when you come down, you might as well come down loaded," Collins said. She could sense the excitement in his voice. "I think we got something going on here."

"God, be careful," Connie said fervently. "We don't need you to take a header."

"No, we don't," Estelle said. She left Connie to flag traffic, crossed to her car, and hefted the black field case out of her trunk.

THREE

THE PICKUP LAY on its top, nose downhill. The twisted frame and torn bed had been mangled in every direction. A single stubborn bolt had refused to sheer, and the lightweight aluminum camper shell had been flailed into what looked like a white, rumpled sheet, still attached to the truck bed by that single bolt. The cab was crushed flat to the dashboard, having taken the brunt of the first somersaults over the guardrail.

The EMTs had covered the driver's body with a sheet of yellow plastic. Matty Finnegan and Cliff Herrera waited off to one side while Estelle surveyed the entirety of the catastrophe. The EMTs were well aware that adding their tracks to the scene only complicated matters.

"He stayed with it for a while," Matty said. She pointed up the hill. A hundred yards above, the guardrail was a faint glint in the lights of the parked vehicles. The scars where the truck had hit the ground were clear. Had the steep slope been covered with the characteristic runty brush of this rugged country, the little Chevy might have been snagged earlier, its crashing descent slowed. But the rocks hadn't provided anything other than a hard springboard for each amazing tumble.

Estelle nodded. The driver had stayed with the truck for most of the journey—unfortunately for him. What the crushing cab hadn't done to him, the rocks had finished off. He lay smashed between two large slabs of limestone, and Estelle approached the body from the side away from the truck.

She bent down and pulled the yellow plastic back. The young man—if it was his truck, he was just twenty-one—lay on his back. One leg had caught and twisted sideways in the dead stump wood of a gnarled juniper. His right arm, hidden under his body, appeared to have been broken so many times that the original line formed by the elbow's joint to upper and lower portions was lost.

"We haven't touched anything," Matty Finnegan said. "Just covered him up. I wouldn't be surprised if in a little bit this mist turns to rain...or worse."

Another vehicle stopped on the road up above, and Estelle recognized the sound of the sheriff's elderly pickup. "Weather isn't going to bother this young man much anymore," Estelle said. She knelt and stretched out a hand, feeling the side of the victim's neck. The skin was as cold as the February weather. The young man's features were surprisingly composed, the only injury to his face a single massive laceration through his right cheek.

"Any idea how long he's been here?" Cliff asked. "He's not rigored anymore."

"No telling," Estelle replied. "Connie called Dispatch to report the accident just a minute before Ernie called you guys out. As far as I know, he could have been here for a week."

"Well..." Matty said.

Estelle glanced at her and shrugged. "In a manner of speaking," she amended. She looked back at the victim's face. He stared straight up into the night sky, face surprisingly clean of dirt or blood. The ravens and coyotes hadn't found him yet.

A puddle of blood had formed and dried beside his

head, and Estelle bent down with her flashlight. The man's left ear had been terribly lacerated, gouged out of the side of his head by a raking blow—probably a sharp corner of boulder, the same instant that his cheek had been ripped open.

"He's local?" Matty asked.

"Don't know yet," Estelle said. "The truck is registered to Chris Marsh of Las Cruces, who should be twenty-one. That part fits." She looked at the victim's left arm, and saw that the unpredictable forces of the crash had broken it in several places above the elbow, including a catastrophic fracture of the joint of clavicle and shoulder socket.

She shifted position and realized that Deputy Dennis Collins was crouching at her right elbow, so close that she could hear his breathing and smell his aftershave. He reached out and laid his hand on her forearm. "This is what I meant," he said. "Look at this." He held his flashlight for her. The man's left hand lay palm up in a small clear spot between the two rocks, fingers gently curled. Estelle bent close, puzzled at what she saw.

"What have we got here?" she said, more to herself than Collins. But the deputy assumed the question was meant for him, and he used a ballpoint pen as a pointer. "I think these are boot marks," he said. "We got the heel right here, in this patch of dirt between the rocks. The ball of the foot rested right on his hand." The marks were clear, outlined in muddy dirt on the pale skin of the man's palm.

"What's with this?" Estelle whispered. "Move a little bit," she said to Collins, and he pushed himself away enough that, shifting her knees, she could scrunch down until the slope of one of the rocks cradled the side of her head.

"More light?" Matty asked helpfully.

"Please," the undersheriff said. "Don't step anywhere around his head. Come in from behind me." In a moment, the second beam from Matty's light flooded the grim picture. It hadn't been their imagination. Someone had planted a good-sized boot on the victim's left hand, pinning it in place.

"You want me to lift his hand up so you can see the back side?" Collins asked.

"No, no," Estelle said quickly, straightening up. "Whatever is there will wait." She nodded at the EMT and then turned to Collins. "But you're right, Dennis… that's going to be interesting. If this happened right here, then there'll be grit and debris pressed into the back of his hand. We need pictures before any of this is moved."

She straightened up and looked up toward the highway. In the glare of emergency lights, she saw the towering figure of Sheriff Robert Torrez, who only two years ago would have bounded down this rugged slope without a second thought. A hip injury that had demanded six months of convalescence and another half year of therapy had changed his outlook on indestructibility.

Estelle pulled her handheld from its belt holster. "Bobby, we need to call Linda on this," she said, then thought, *She'll love it,* and that prompted the recollection of the e-mail she'd been reexamining for the umpteenth time just an hour before. The reporter from the women's magazine didn't know what she was missing—the big, tough, macho sheriff up on the highway, who understandably hesitated to launch himself down the cliff, calling the cheerful young girl, the department's photographer, who would tackle the assignment without a second thought, even though she was blind in one eye, her depth perception far less than perfect.

"Got it," Torrez said. "What do you have?"

"One dead from multiple trauma. But someone else has been here."

"How's that?"

"We've got a boot print where it shouldn't be." She had tried to imagine how Chris Marsh—if this was in fact him—might have accomplished the boot track by himself…reaching down to his broken foot, hearing the sharp snap and pop of broken bones as he did so. Not likely. She flicked the yellow tarp clear of the victim's lower body. The victim was wearing what had been a tan jacket, a neatly pressed tan work shirt with matching tan trousers, and highly polished ankle-high black work boots.

"Ay," the undersheriff said. "What have we got here…?"

"That's what I thought," Matty said. "He a delivery-man of some sort?"

Estelle turned and played her flashlight over the truck.

Although not new, the pickup would have been a neat little unit, with its matching white camper shell. She got up and made her way farther downhill until she could see the driver's door. During one of the crushing land-ings, it had opened and then been smashed double, fold-ing forward against itself. Estelle could see there was no logo or sign on the door.

"Odd," she said, hefting her radio again. She rested the stubby antenna against her lower lip for a few sec-onds, deep in thought before she pressed the transmit bar. "Bobby, I'd really like Alan to take a look at what we have here, but getting him down here is going to be a stunt."

"He'll manage," Torrez said. "We'll come in from the bottom."

"How's that going to happen?" Matty asked. She played her light downhill, and Estelle could see the bottom of the canyon—perhaps only fifty yards farther down the hill.

"One of the old minin' roads cuts up the bottom of this canyon," Torrez radioed, as if he could hear Matty's question.

"I can get Alan in there."

"Linda, too," Estelle replied. "Is there room for the ambulance on that trail?"

"That's negative. But we can put the gurney in the back of my truck. Save a long climb."

"You got *that* right," Cliff Herrera said with relief.

"Be back to you," Torrez said, and his figure disappeared.

"Tell Cliff to come up and move his unit before someone punts it over the side on your heads. I'll show him where to park."

"*My* unit," Herrera said, and grinned at Matty. "Suddenly it's my unit." They held their lights for him, amplifying his own, until he had climbed far enough up the slope that they could hear his breath coming in ragged whistles of effort.

"Bobby," Estelle radioed, "see if you can find the exact spot where the driver lost it. When Linda gets here, have her take a complete series of photos of any skid marks that might be left. If the weather closes in any more, we're going to lose those."

"Yep," Torrez replied. "I was lookin' at the dead doe

in the ditch up here. Connie says she retrieved a transmitter. We don't know for sure if it's the same accident."

"No, we don't. But the condition of the deer fits. It's been there a day or two."

"More'n likely, that's where it started," Torrez said. "Look at the left front of the truck for hide and blood."

Over the years, Estelle had come close to clobbering critters on the highway half a dozen times, and connected twice—once with a mule deer and once with a Brangus calf. She knew how little it took for even seasoned reflexes to do the wrong thing. It was easy to picture the white pickup truck driving on the damp pavement, perhaps a shade too fast, cresting the pass and starting down the slight curve just as the doe stepped off the shoulder, intent on crossing the highway for no other reason than that it was there. The rush of headlights would make no sense to the animal. It would either freeze in place or bolt—and a driver could bet money on the critter bolting the wrong way.

Estelle took her time, sweeping the ground around the body for anything out of place. The muddy residue on the victim's left palm carried enough of the characteristic mold marks that there was no mistaking its origin. Why would someone do that? Did a passerby witness the accident, then clamber down the dangerous hill and, unable to stop the momentum of his descent, plant a foot on the victim's limp hand? Stranger things had happened.

She peered again at the mark. With a proper photo, they might be able to ascertain direction, but here in this variable light, it would only be a guess. Collins thought a deep imprint in the gravelly soil was a heel. He might be right, and that meant the boot that stomped the hand was pointing *uphill*. The owner of the boot would have been standing close to where she now stood.

Keeping to the hard surface of the surrounding rocks, Estelle made her way to a point uphill of the body, near the right side of his head. A large amount of blood had foamed up and out of the victim's gaping mouth, and she could imagine the young man struggling for his last breath as his flailed ribs moved in all the wrong ways. "Huh," she said, and tried to find a way to support herself on elbows and knees, ignoring the dull, naggy ache in her own bones, exacerbated by the climbing and bending. Past injuries had a way of reminding their owners, she thought.

The victim's head was turned slightly to the right, and she bent down close enough to smell the path of his last breath. The distinctive odor of beer clung to the body, and she imagined that she could see dried residue on his right cheek, as if the beverage had trickled out of his mouth during his final moments. Maybe it had.

Was Chris Marsh tipping a can of brew just as the doe bolted into the truck's path? Smashed and battered down through the rocks, crushed by his own somersaulting truck, he had come to rest here flat on his shattered back, staring at the foggy heavens, choking on a last mouthful of beer.

Were you dead when your friend stepped on your hand? she thought, and then aloud, she said, "And where did he go?"

"Who?" Matty said. The EMT sat quietly on a nearby rock, watching.

"That's what we need to find out," Estelle said. She pushed herself upright and turned back to the truck. Again picking her way using the rocks as her only path, she took her time, finally kneeling at the crushed door on the driver's side. Because the truck was upside down and twisted, the opening would have allowed a child to wriggle through, but not Christopher Marsh. The inside of the cab was a jumble, with all the trash that had been on the floor now tossed about the crumpled space in senseless disarray. A white plastic cooler was jammed between the crushed roof, the remains of the steering wheel, and the gear lever, jammed so hard that it had cracked open and molded itself around the bent lever.

The smell of beer was moderate, and she could see where some had leaked from the cooler and puddled on the head liner. In the far corner, about where the corner of the windshield had originally met the dashboard, lay a bent but still-sealed beer can, sprung loose from the cooler, no doubt.

"Okay," Estelle murmured to herself. She had seen hundreds of accidents similar in most respects to this one—crumpled and torn steel, crumpled and smashed drivers and passengers, all tainted with that familiar, depressing aroma potpourri of beer and blown bladders and colons.

She got up and brushed off the knees of her trousers. The accidents were all too familiar, and so was the notion that someone—some Good Samaritan—had stopped and gone to all the trouble of climbing down that forbidding cliff side. But then, instead of phoning 911 from that spot with the ubiquitous cell phone, at that moment he or she had left the scene.

And then what? Estelle thought. Who would stop, climb down, and then leave, panicked by the gurgling death rattles of Chris Marsh?

"Three-ten, PCS."

Dispatcher Ernie Wheeler's disembodied voice startled her out of her thoughts.

"Three-ten. Go ahead."

"Three-ten, be advised that both Dr. Perrone and Dr. Guzman have been called into surgery. The hospital tells me that it's going to be a little while before either one of them can answer a call."

"Ten-four. Keep me posted. The weather might force us to transport here in a little bit. I'm going to hold off as long as we can, though. As soon as one or both are out of surgery, get back to me."

"Ten-four."

She could feel the mist on her face like a cold, clingy veil, and she bent to pull the yellow plastic so that it covered the boot-marked left hand of the victim.

FOUR

By MIDNIGHT, photographer Linda Real had finished at the crash scene and Estelle was confident that they had a complete portrait of the accident. Pictures would show the wild skid marks on the highway, the battered guardrail, the various gashes and gouges the somersaulting truck had dug in the hillside rocks and in the victim himself. They had examined the carcass of the doe and found white paint flecks that no doubt would match the truck. There was blood and deer hair caught in the crushed metal of the truck.

Unless it had spun about at the last instant, the animal had been crossing from the truck driver's right, headed for the bank and brush on the left, or uphill, side of the highway. Other deer tracks marked the bank.

The skid marks suggested that the driver may not have seen the deer until the animal was about to leap into his truck's grill, just as he rounded the curve at the top of the pass—a sweeping right-hander that paralleled the flank of the mountain. Had the driver held the steering wheel motionless while he stood on the brakes, the doe might have bolted away unscathed.

But the wet pavement had conspired with driver panic. The skid marks showed that in concert with slamming on the brakes, the driver had twisted the steering wheel. The truck had rocketed first to the left, veering all the way across the highway toward the inside bank. With overcorrection, it had then spun right, its back tires actually cutting the gravel of the southbound shoulder of the highway. Had there been oncoming traffic, a head-on collision would have been likely.

The truck had smacked the doe, then plunged back across the highway and struck the first section of the guardrail with the left corner of its bumper while the right front tire vaulted up and over a hump of dirt and rock. That had sent the little truck airborne. The driver wouldn't have had time for more than a short scream during the 133 feet from first skid to bashed guardrail. On dry pavement, that distance would have been enough to stop even if he had been driving at 60 miles an hour, but not in the wet.

As the weather closed in, it was clear to Estelle that she could spend hours on this hillside in the dark without finding what she was looking for—and at this point, she didn't know what that was. The wrecked truck wasn't going anywhere soon, either. Short of hiring a helicopter and sky hook, there was no practical way of retrieving the wadded-up vehicle without doing more damage to the evidence. Taking the wreck downhill to the old mining road would require cutting numerous trees, and even then Stub Moore's tow truck wouldn't be able to back to within a hundred feet of the crash site. The most direct route would be to drag the wreck back up the rock-studded cliff side to the highway. That would wait for daylight, which was just as well, Estelle reflected. There were too many unanswered questions.

"Hey," Sheriff Robert Torrez said. So absorbed was she in her own thoughts that Estelle hadn't heard him approach from behind her. She snapped off her flashlight. "We're about to head out," he said.

By the glare of the spotlights on the roof rack of the sheriff's truck, she could see that the two EMTs had secured the gurney in the back of the pickup for the victim's short ride out to the highway and the transfer to the waiting ambulance. "Maybe with the light of day," Estelle said, and Torrez cocked his head. "I just don't know." She shrugged helplessly. "We need to take the truck apart. I agree with Dennis—there wasn't a passenger with Marsh. He was by himself, and I think it's as simple as a collision with a deer. That happens all the time. The *crash* is simple," she corrected. "What happened afterward..." She let the words trail off. "We need answers from Alan."

"Well, we gotta roll or that ain't going to happen," Torrez said. "You want Stubby out here with the wrecker, or you want to wait?"

Estelle shook her head. "I don't want the truck moved until we have a chance to scour this place. It's too easy to miss something."

"That's a fact. Take your time," Torrez said. "There might be a real simple answer." He almost smiled. "I can't think of one, but who knows."

"At this time of night, I'd *like* simple answers," she sighed. "And by the way, speaking of simple answers... we have a reporter from one of the national magazines coming for a visit."

Bob Torrez jerked as if someone had slipped a cattle prod down his trousers. "What the hell for?"

"Well, that's what they do, Bobby."

"When's this going to happen? Who thought this up?"

"She contacted me a couple of weeks ago, and I e-mailed a generic, bureaucratic response to her saying that we were a public agency, blah, blah. I hadn't heard anything, so I thought maybe the idea had been dropped. It hadn't been, I guess." She smiled at the thunderclouds on Bobby's face. "She's coming tomorrow sometime." She shined her light on her watch. "Today sometime."

"That's just what we need," the sheriff grumbled. "How come you didn't let *me* know?"

"Check your e-mail," she replied. "I sent a department memo and a copy of my response to everyone, including you."

"I didn't see that."

"You have to turn your computer on, Robert," she chided.

"Well, she don't need to talk to me."

"You'll be the challenge, that's for sure."

"Yeah, right." He looked up at the battered junk that had once been a truck. "You got someone to sit this for the night?"

"Jackie Taber is coming out to give Dennis a hand. I'll ask her to stick close so he can go back in and wrap up the preliminary paperwork. He was working a double shift, so he's about had it."

"Pasquale's workin' graveyard. He can help."

"I know he is," Estelle said. Pasquale had worked the game before his midnight-eight shift—he had the endurance of the young, and twelve hours once in a while was a matter of course.

"But I want Jackie's eyes and ears," Estelle added. She took a deep breath in frustration. "Somebody somewhere knows about this wreck, Bobby. Someone was down here. Maybe just looking, maybe we don't know what. I'll be interested to hear what Alan has to say."

"He ought to be free by now. Him and Francis got called to the hospital earlier. A kid collapsed at the school. Right before the tip-off. Pasquale was tellin' me that she was headin' out of the gym to the refreshment stand, and boom. Down she went."

"Really. One of ours or theirs?"

"Pam Gardiner's daughter."

"Kerri, you mean?"

"Yep."

"*Ay*, that's too bad. What happened, do they know?" She could picture Kerri Gardiner, vivacious, raucous, and nothing like the great doughy mountain who was her mother. Pam had been editor of the *Posadas Register* for a dozen or more years, but it would have surprised Estelle to see her at a sporting event.

The newspaper's publisher and business manager, Frank Dayan, covered all those, the modern technology of his little digital camera finally allowing him to take some in-focus pictures. He sold ads, covered sports, and chased sirens…all the things that Pam would or could never do. He was a frequent visitor at the Sheriff's Department, and Estelle had come to trust his judgment. She didn't worry about what he saw or heard.

"Don't know what happened. Gayle called me from home. She said Kerri was with a few friends and collapsed right there by the trophy case outside the gym doors." He shrugged. "Mears is with them."

"Okay. That's good." Sergeant Mears would have been at the game as a parent, more to listen to the pep band of which his daughter Melody was a member than to watch the basketball action.

"PCS, three-oh-three is ten-ninety-seven, Regál Pass." Deputy Jackie Taber's quiet voice broke the radio silence.

"You want to ride out with us?" the sheriff asked.

"I'll go up the hill, thanks," Estelle replied. The old

mining road angled out to meet State 56 almost a mile down the hill.

The two hundred feet up through the rocks to where her car was parked would give her more time to think and one more chance to scour the cracks and crannies between the rocks—looking for what, she didn't know.

By the time she had scrambled her way along the tortuous route back up to the guardrail, she could look down through the trees to the east and see the headlights of Bob Torrez's pickup truck still picking its way along the narrow, rock-strewn mining trail. If the victim's bones weren't in a jumble before, they certainly would be now, she thought, and shivered.

"Hand?" Jackie Taber's blocky figure appeared out of the dark, looming over the guardrail.

"Thanks," Estelle said. The young woman's grip was strong and sure, and Estelle eased over the rail with a loud exhale of breath. The steel rail was icy cold and sopping wet. "That is quite a climb."

"Bad night for it," Jackie said. "Last place you ought to be."

She wore a yellow slicker, and the plastic weather cover over her Stetson was dotted with water, the beads of moisture catching the flashing lights from the roof rack of her vehicle. Her admonition was gentle, and Estelle nodded her appreciation.

"Yes, I was just beginning to think that," the undersheriff agreed. Estelle knew that, without the added drain of the climb, her energy reserves were still less than optimum. The initial weeks of hospital convalescence following extensive surgeries had done nothing for muscle tone, and the slow months of recuperation and therapy at home had been tedious. Sometime during those months, she had begun working consciously to avoid the posture that initially had given her the most relief—hands tucked under opposite armpits, arms hugging her chest the way a heart patient hugs his post-surgery "cough pillow."

She had returned to work three months after the incident, and still ran out of gas—usually at the most inopportune moments. And she had returned to work fully aware that in order to be of any use, bulletproof vests needed to be between the bullet and the wearer.

"Dennis was saying that some things don't work out on this one," Jackie said.

"Let's sit in the Bronco," Estelle said, the chill of the dank night finally penetrating her clothing. A car whistled over the pass from the south, altogether too fast, tires hissing on the wet pavement. The driver braked hard at the sight of the flares and emergency lights. Deputy Taber stepped forward, pointing an index finger at him with one hand while indicating that he slow down with the other. He passed, brake lights bright.

"Morons," Taber muttered. She swung into the Bronco and slammed the door, picking up the radio mike at the same time. "Three-oh-four, three-oh-three."

"Three-oh-four."

"Ten-twenty?"

"Three-oh-four is just coming up on Moore."

"Ten-four." She hung up the mike. "If Denny wasn't so far on down the road, I was going to have him pull over for a minute and pick up Speedy Gonzales there on the radar. Anyway, another time."

"There'll always be one," Estelle said. "Look, I know it's a pain, but I need you to sit this until we can get back here in daylight. We're not going to move the truck until tomorrow, and I really want to go over the whole area again with some daylight. It's just too hard to see out there tonight. There's no way to get lights on that cliff from above or below."

"Roger that," Jackie said. "I was thinkin' that the forest road at the top of the pass would be a good place to camp out. I can see this spot from there. What was this about a boot print on the dead guy's hand?"

"We think so. But it's hard to tell for sure. The light plays games. Or *lack* of light, I should say. I'll be really interested to see Linda's pictures and hear what Alan has to say." She started to open the door of the Bronco. "Did you hear any more about the youngster at school? Kerri Gardiner?"

Deputy Taber shook her head. "Just a request for medivac to transport."

"Ouch. That's too bad."

"I'll stay in touch," Jackie said. She reached out and patted the radar unit mounted on the dash. "Good night to run a superblitz on the pass," she said with a grin.

"How many cars does it take to make a blitz?" Estelle asked, laughing. "You'll be lucky if five vehicles go by all night."

"And four of them will be speeding," Jackie said hopefully.

"Did you read your e-mail, by the way? I sent a memo around last week."

"About the magazine lady? Yes, I did. Thanks for your response, by the way. I appreciated that. In the army, nobody except the top brass does any talkin'."

"I just wanted to make sure everyone understands the ground rules," Estelle said. "Nobody needs permission from Bobby, or from me, to talk about anything they want. That's all. Or *not* talk to her, as far as that goes."

"She had an article last month about that woman aerobatic pilot who just won the national unlimited championship," Jackie said. "It was pretty good. I left my copy in the workroom, if you want to take a look."

"I'll do that," Estelle said, and slid out of the Bronco. The air was raw, and she ducked her head against the sting of the mist, driven now by the funnel of air through the pass. "She's coming sometime today, by the way. She should have been here for all this. She might have enjoyed clambering up and down that cliff."

"I bet."

"I'll be home if you need to reach me."

By the time Estelle walked back to the dry protection of her own unmarked county car, the mist had thickened. The cloud pressed the San Cristóbals down to the prairie, enough to obscure the sodium vapor lights in the parking lot of the Broken Spur Saloon. Another few degrees and it would be sleet, Estelle thought. The asphalt up on the pass would take on a dangerous sheen of black ice. The ambulance was just pulling out onto the highway as she passed.

A few minutes later, as she drove northeast on State 56 onto the flat of the prairie between the Rio Guigarro and the Rio Salinas, the windshield was dry. The mountain made—or at least captured—its own weather, letting hints of it fan out to evaporate over the lowlands. What had happened there in the rocks, moments after the crash, remained just as obscure.

FIVE

THE TRAFFIC LIGHT at Bustos and Grande turned, and Estelle braked the county car to a stop. Lights blasted in her rearview mirror as a late model pickup truck pulled in behind her, red and blue emergency lights in the grill wiggle-wagging. With a grin, she reached out and keyed the mike transmit button twice in greeting.

A right turn on Bustos and then a block past the Posadas State Bank she turned into the parking lot of the Public Safety Building. The pickup followed and pulled into the spot reserved for Sheriff Torrez.

Formerly a Posadas County sheriff himself, and now a New Mexico livestock inspector, Bill Gastner took his time climbing out of the shiny new truck, a mammoth thing sporting chrome grill guards, extra spotlights, and enough antennas projecting from the roof that it looked like an imitation of a mountaintop bristling with radio, cell phone, TV, and microwave towers. The New Mexico Livestock Board's shield was centered neatly on the door.

Estelle patted the hood of the giant truck, waiting for Gastner to climb down.

"Quite the heap," she said. "You've been promoted, or what?"

"'Or what,'" Gastner replied. "They thought the old one looked disreputable. Probably like its driver. You just getting in from the pass?"

"Yes."

"Just the one?"

"As far as we can tell, he was alone when he went off the highway. After that, we're not so sure, *padrino*."

"Local guy?"

"Las Cruces."

"Nasty," he said, and leaned against the fender of the truck, crossing his arms over his large belly. "Ready for some breakfast?"

"Because after all, it is after midnight," Estelle added dryly. "Technically morning."

"You're learning, sweetheart. It's Friday, or was, and the Don Juan stays open until two. We have an hour."

"Uh," Estelle groaned, thoroughly familiar with the old man's prodigious eating habits, at any time of day or night. Gastner combined eating—especially foods that were high octane with green chile—and insomnia as his secret for longevity. "I really don't, *padrino*. What I really need to do is go home to bed."

"Tough country out there, and a nasty night for mountain climbing. You did okay?"

"I did okay," she said, but sounded unconvinced. "The truck went off that really steep spot right at the top."

"That cliff on the east side of the highway?"

"Exactly. Right where the Mexican car hauler got hung up on the guardrail last summer. But there are some things that don't fit."

"That pass kills its share of people. What's not to fit?"

She grinned. Gastner's curiosity was easily whetted. "He might still be there if Connie Ulibarri hadn't been as sharp as she is."

"You ought to pillage the highway department and hire her away," Gastner said. "She saw the crash?"

"No, but the guy hit a deer, *padrino*. A doe wearing

a collar. Connie stopped to collect the collar, and saw the skid marks. The truck's down the hill, out of sight of the highway. It looks like maybe a day or two? The victim's a twenty-one-year-old boy. He's been lying out there all by himself, broken all to pieces, staring up at the sky. But…"

Gastner raised an eyebrow.

"But I think someone else was down there at the crash site. No…" She tapped the hood of the Dodge. "I *know* someone was. Whoever was there planted a boot on the victim's hand."

"What do you mean, sweetheart? Like *stepped* on him, you're saying?"

"Yes. I think so."

"Now why would he do a thing like that, other than tripping over his own clumsy feet?"

"That's one of our questions."

"Ah," Gastner said. "Well," and he pushed himself away from the truck. "You know how that goes. Someone witnesses the accident, climbs down to see, and sees too much. He doesn't want the complications of that, and just leaves. People do funny things. Sometimes damn unattractive things. Trippin' around in the dark, he might not have even known he stepped on the kid's hand." Gastner polished an insect speck off the hood's air dam. "Now, I had something to tell you, but damned if I don't remember what it was." He inspected the fancy grill of the truck. "Oh," and he straightened suddenly. "Had a call from some woman who wants to do a story on you. For *A Woman's World*. You read that rag?"

"No. But I got her e-mail a couple weeks ago requesting that she be allowed to spend some time with us. She's coming today."

"You agreed, you mean? I'm surprised. Goddamn delighted, but surprised, sweetheart."

Estelle laughed and shrugged. "What could I say, sir. We're a public agency. If she wants to come and see what we do, then fine. She's free to do that."

Gastner regarded her for a long moment. "It's not the department that she's interested in, sweetheart. It's you. Our star."

"Oh, please."

"I'm tellin' ya," he continued.

"And she called you?"

"Uh-huh. I'm to be the 'deep throat' in all this. She wanted to know if she could interview me for background…about your early years with the department." His flinty blue eyes twinkled. "What you were like before your meteoric rise to power."

"That should take a couple of minutes."

"I'll stretch it," Gastner said. "I just wanted to clear it with you. If you don't want to talk to 'em, I'll tell 'em to take a hike. The Constitution is a wonderful thing, you know. The press can ask to their heart's content. We don't have to answer."

Estelle frowned. "There is one thing, though."

"And that is?"

"She…the reporter…included some pictures from some of my misadventures that have been in the papers— I guess to show that she's done some research. I didn't mind that. But there was a photo of Francisco that was taken during his performance in Cruces at the Christmas concert with the university orchestra. I want to give anything that involves him a *lot* of thought. And I want to discuss it a *lot* with Francis."

"Could be a big deal." Gastner nodded. "That's the

temptation, of course. National exposure like that doesn't come along every day. That magazine has one of the largest circulations in the country. Hot stuff." He shook his head. "We all knew this time would come, didn't we. The coverage at the Cruces concert was a hint of that."

"*Por supuesto, padrino*, but it's coming too soon."

"Everything comes too soon. Christ, all this philosophizing is starving me. Anything I can do for you? You have someone sitting the wreck? They're not going to tow it up out of there tonight, are they?"

"No. Jackie's watching over it. You can cruise down that way and keep her company, if you want."

"Might do that. I saw you zipping up the street, and wanted to check with you about this celebrity stuff."

"*Ay*, celebrity stuff," she laughed.

"She wants to interview me at one o'clock," Gastner said.

"One? As in today at one? This afternoon?"

"That's it. Striking while the iron is hot sort of thing. Won't be long before your little one's mug is on the front pages of the newspapers in the grocery store checkout racks, right there with all the alien abductions."

"Stop it."

He laughed. "How's your mom, by the way? She recover from having a birthday?"

"Just," Estelle replied. Teresa Reyes had turned ninety-five years old the week previous, and had grumbled about the attention the special day had brought. A visit from Román and Marta Diaz and two of their children from Tres Santos had been an unexpected treat for Teresa. Román and Marta, her former neighbors in the tiny Mexican village where she had lived and taught school, had purchased Teresa's modest little home and the twelve acres surrounding it five years before.

"I wish I knew her secret," Gastner said. "I'm seventy-three and feel like crap most of the time. She's got me by twenty-plus years and seems to be getting younger every goddamn day."

"She's had her bouts," Estelle said.

"Well, yeah…she has. Anyhow, I'll let you go. I'm about to faint from hunger." He reached out and squeezed her arm.

"And I will swing by and chat with Jackie a bit later. This story lady is going to talk with her, too? That's the impression I got."

"*Sin duda.* And Linda. And Gayle. And Leona, I would imagine."

"Well, damn. And it's all my fault, isn't it. I started it all by hiring you. Look where it got us."

"Sure enough, sir."

He touched the brim of his baseball cap in salute. "Well, I did good, if I do say so myself. Behave yourself. You're sure there's nothing that you *don't* want me to tell the story lady?"

"Positive, sir. She'll find out for herself."

He waved a casual salute and swung up into the truck. She watched him drive off, the diesel engine emitting a low, guttural clatter.

Inside the Public Safety Building, the air was institutional, stuffy and tinged with disinfectant. The "fresh evergreen scent" advertised on the side of the jug of cleaner that the custodian dispensed into the mop bucket bore little resemblance to the real thing—the damp air of Regál Pass, tinged with piñon and juniper.

Dispatcher Ernie Wheeler had gone home as his shift

ended, replaced by Brent Sutherland. Brent looked up as Estelle entered, and lifted a hand in salute.

"How's it going?" he asked.

"It's going. Everything else quiet?"

"More or less." He leaned forward and looked at the log.

"Since I came on, I've had a handful of calls. Edith Mallory is still arguing with her husband, who is still drinking. The schnauzer over on Tenth Street is still barking, and Mrs. Sanchez is still irritated at *that*. And the clerk over at Portillo's called to say that he's got a bunch of rowdies who can't find anything better to do than gather in his parking lot. Abeyta is going to swing by there when he's finished with the Mallorys."

"Wonderful. Did Dennis go home yet?"

"I think he's still in the workroom."

The telephone rang and Brent reached up to swing the headset boom back into place. "Posadas Sheriff's Department. Sutherland." Estelle turned away, headed for her own office.

She heard Brent say, "We'll have someone swing by there in just a few minutes, Bernie." He listened for another minute. "No, don't do that. Just hang tight, all right?"

Estelle stopped with one hand on the doorknob of her office. At the same time, Dennis Collins appeared, a sheaf of papers in hand. He dropped several of them in the office in-basket, then headed for the bank of filing cabinets across the room.

"Just a minute," Sutherland said. "Estelle," he called, "this is Bernie Pollis over at Portillo's again. He's got a group of kids over there chuckin' rocks at each other."

"As long as it's at each other," Deputy Collins observed.

"Jackie's down in Regál, and Pasquale is way the hell and gone down by María."

Collins sighed and shoved the remaining papers into the file. "I go right by there on my way home. I'll stop by and send 'em all home. I don't know what the heck kids are doing out at one o'clock in the morning."

"Thanks, Dennis," Estelle said.

"You betcha."

As she closed the door of her office, she heard Sutherland back on the phone, assuring Bernie Pollis that an officer was en route. Tommy Portillo's Handi-Way convenience store was three blocks away. Had Estelle stepped outside to the front steps of the Public Safety Building, she knew, she would have been able to hear the kids yelling back and forth.

Settling behind her desk, she turned the police radio down, then out of habit more than anything else awoke her computer.

The list of e-mails included nothing that required immediate action, and most of them were taken care of with the delete key. With her office window closed, she could not hear the single gunshot that came from three blocks away, nor did she hear Deputy Collins' frantic ten-sixty call.

SIX

WITH THE RIGHT circumstances, a quiet little village could produce a huge audience out of thin air. Only moments had passed from the time she was alerted to Deputy Collins' call for assistance to the moment when Estelle pulled to a jarring stop in front of Tommy Portillo's Handi-Way convenience store, but she wasn't surprised that the crowds were gathering.

Parked askew just ramped up on the Grande entrance to the parking lot was Deputy Collins' Expedition, one of the newest in the fleet. A black-and-white State Police cruiser blocked the other parking lot entrance. Pulled into the curb, looking like an abandoned derelict, was Sheriff Robert Torrez's battered pickup.

As Estelle climbed out of her car, she saw that Richard Black, the State Policeman, had five youngsters gathered at a late model SUV on one side of the convenience store, while Bob Torrez was engaged in animated conversation with four other people on the opposite side of the parking lot by the fuel pumps. His audience included a middle-aged woman, two young girls, and Bernie Pollis, who appeared from behind the store, walking sideways like a crab, looking over his shoulder at whatever the shadows hid. Torrez appeared to be holding something against the woman's head. She leaned her rump against the back fender of the Volvo parked at the pumps.

Deputy Collins stood by his vehicle with one hand

on the right front fender. He appeared to be watching Officer Black.

"Dennis, are you all right?" Estelle asked, and as she stepped closer she saw that the Expedition's windshield had been one of the targets. Something had exploded on the glass in front of the driver, and the parking lot lights glistened on the liquid that had splashed across the glass, hood, and fender. From several paces away, she could smell the beer.

"Yeah," he said, but sounded far more subdued than he had before leaving the Sheriff's Department to respond to the call. Just beyond the Expedition's front wheel on the street side, she saw the neck portion of a broken beer bottle. Fresh liquid puddled around it. A large sunburst of cracks scarred the windshield.

"What happened?" She stepped close so that the deputy wouldn't need to raise his voice. Everyone in the parking lot was on his or her feet, and there was one officer with each group. Estelle focused her attention on Collins. He turned his back on the group with Black, and Estelle saw complete defeat on the young man's face. The deputy, just turned twenty-five and the department's most recent academy graduate, normally was not at a loss for words. He enjoyed the day shift, was adept at working with the media, and coordinated nearly all of the department's efforts in the various public schools. He never complained when overtime, or covering another deputy's shift, extended his workday, as it had now.

"As I came down the street, I could see those folks were over there by the Volvo getting gas," he said, and then took a deep breath before continuing his recitation. "Bernie Pollis was standing in the doorway of the store, and those punks..." He turned to nod toward the group corralled by Officer Black. "They were gathered around the Lexus. I drove wide to give myself some time to look the situation over, and then turned into the parking lot. That's when there was an explosion, and my windshield went opaque. My first thought was that someone had fired a shot at me. A little speck of glass winged off the steering wheel and hit the back of my hand." He held up his hand. "It's nothing."

Estelle looked at his hand, then turned and examined the windshield. The bottle had been an impressive shot, fired by someone with a better than average throwing arm.

She turned back to the deputy, whose story didn't jibe with the expression on his face. "And then?"

"I bailed out of the unit, and I don't even remember doing it, but I drew my weapon. I had to have done it as I was sliding out of the unit." Estelle glanced down and saw that the large automatic was holstered—hammer cocked, safety on, in exactly the condition that the deputy had been trained to carry it.

She held up a hand to stop the flow of words, a well of dread already rising in her gut. "Slow down," she ordered. "Is anyone else here injured?" She saw the woman across the parking lot wave off Torrez's attempts at first aid. "What's going on over there?"

"I think she cracked her head on the trunk lid," Collins said morosely. "That's what I think happened, anyway. The bullet didn't hit her."

"*You* fired a shot?" She glanced across at Black, who now had the five young people sitting along the sidewalk beside the store.

"I didn't mean to," Collins said. "That's what I was saying. I got out of the unit, saw that it was just a bunch of kids over by the store, and probably not an armed robbery or something. Then I saw the glass scattered all over the place and smelled the beer. I heard another vehicle, and that's when Rick Black pulled in. I holstered the weapon. I mean, I *went* to holster it, but I guess I fumbled it. I dropped the gun."

Silence hung heavily between them for the count of ten. "That's when it went off?" Estelle asked, incredulous. She didn't add, *That's not possible,* because she knew perfectly well that with the right combination of bizarre circumstances, nearly anything was possible.

"Not when I dropped it. It bounced off the side of the truck. You can see the mark right here." He turned and pointed at a tiny ding in the white paint just below the name badge on the fender. "I made a grab for it. You know…like anybody would. I caught it, and *that's* when it went off."

"Just once?"

"Just once. Christ, that's enough."

"Yes, it is. Where did the bullet go?"

"Bernie says that it ricocheted through the grill of his Cavalier, over behind the store."

Estelle twisted and looked back to the spot where Collins had to have been standing when he fumbled the gun, on the street side of his vehicle, close to the door. A straight line between there and the Cavalier, which Estelle couldn't even see from where she stood, would pass through the Expedition's fender, its engine block, and the opposite fender, then through the corner of the store itself. *Not* possible.

Before she could ask *Ricochet off what?* Sheriff Torrez caught her eye and beckoned. At the same time across the parking lot, Black pulled one of the youngsters to his feet, spun him around, and cuffed him. The bottle thrower had fessed up, she guessed.... Either that or in a moment of misplaced bravado the kid had said the wrong thing.

"Hang tight a minute," she said to Collins. "Stay right here." The sheriff met her halfway across the lot, and storm clouds touched his dark, handsome features. "Is everyone all right over there?" Estelle asked. She saw the woman pat her temple again with a folded handkerchief.

"She just cracked her head on the trunk lid," Torrez said. "That ain't the problem. Dufus over there," and he nodded grimly toward the deputy, "dropped his goddamn gun. The bullet hit the base of the gas pump and then ricocheted into Bernie's car.... At least Bernie says it did. I ain't looked at it yet. You can see a little dent and smear of lead on the lower skirt of the pump."

"Did you call Linda?"

"No."

"We need her over here ASAP," Estelle said. She knew that the sheriff understood the situation as well as anyone—that a discharged weapon, even an accidental discharge where the bullet struck no one and caused no serious property damage, was cause for serious concern. In this case, the repercussions could go far beyond the department having to pay for some broken plastic and a punctured radiator. The woman had apparently injured herself, perhaps when the gunshot startled her. This was not a situation where an *oops, sorry, folks was adequate.*

Estelle also knew—as did Bob Torrez—that if they interviewed each of the dozen people currently in the parking lot, and some of the curious spectators now gathered on the sidewalk across the street, there would be as many versions of the incident as there were people.

There were unlikely to be many versions that favored Dennis Collins.

Finally, beginning with these very first moments, when everyone was trying to sort out what happened and why, Estelle was determined that wheels would be set in motion to reduce the likelihood that something like this would ever happen again.

"You want to talk to her?" Torrez asked, turning to glance at the woman by the Volvo. "She's a little hot under the collar."

"As well she should be," Estelle said. "And yes, I want to talk to her."

"I'll see what Black's got goin'," Torrez said, and stalked off. He didn't look Collins' way, didn't say a word to the deputy. That in itself told Estelle that they were going to face another interesting challenge in the hours ahead.

As she approached the Volvo, she recognized the woman, who looked up at Estelle and shook her head in disbelief. The undersheriff recognized Marge Chavez, wife of the service manager at the Chevrolet-Oldsmobile dealership.

"Are you all right?" Estelle asked. She reached out and touched Marge on the cheek to turn her head slightly so that the glare of the parking lot vapor light caught her full on. A tiny nick marked her temple at the end of her right eyebrow.

"Oh, that's nothing," Marge said. She was a pleasant-faced woman, wearing a housecoat over what appeared to be flannel pajamas and loose slippers. "But my God, this whole thing just about did me in."

The two girls, one whom Estelle knew to be fourteen

or so, the other a bit younger, had slipped back into the car's backseat, where they sat silent and wide-eyed.

"I'd like to hear what happened, Marge."

"Oh my," the woman said. "Look, I don't want to get Denny in trouble, but my gosh."

"I understand that, and appreciate it, but I need to hear what happened."

"It happened so fast. Just unbelievable."

"That's how these things go. Tell me what you remember."

"I had picked the kids up after a little party that one of their friends was throwing after the basketball game. I told them *I'd* come and get them at midnight. It wasn't a stay-over or anything like that. But then Barbie called and asked for another hour or so. They were watching a movie, and wanted to see the end. And I said all right. Just this once. So I did that, and on the way home, I saw that I had forgotten to get gas....I'm *always* doing that, sheriff. Always. My husband has given up on me. He bought me a cell phone to keep in the car just for that reason. So when I run out, I can call for help." She smiled gamely and dabbed at her eyebrow again.

"Anyway, here I was. The two kids wanted to go into the store to get something, and I said no. For one thing, they don't need to eat any more junk this time of night, and for another, I was a little apprehensive about those kids across the lot. I knew they weren't local, and it didn't take rocket science to know that they were drinking."

"Where was Mr. Pollis during all of this?"

"Bernie was standing in the doorway of the store. I could see one of the other kids who clerk there behind him, standing behind the counter, I suppose. But Bernie—

he was standing there in the doorway, watching the group of kids. He had a phone in his hand. So I assumed there had been some kind of trouble. That's just about all I saw, until Denny arrived. I had just finished gassing up the car and was around back when he pulls in real fast from the south, there, and *boom*! I heard a loud pop and a tinkle, like breaking glass hitting the pavement."

"You were standing near the trunk of your car?"

"Yes, I was. I was rummaging to see if I had any windshield washer fluid. That's another thing I'm always running out of."

Why do people do these things at one o'clock in the morning? Estelle thought. Then again, Bill Gastner would be heading for his next beloved green chile burrito, an incomprehensible habit by most other people's standards. Compared to that, a little gasoline and windshield washer fluid wasn't so bad. "Did you actually watch the deputy pull into the parking lot?"

"Well, no. I didn't. My back would have been to him."

"But then you heard something?"

"Well, I turned when I heard the bottle—that's what it sounded like. A loud pop, and then glass spraying on the pavement. He stopped right in the driveway, there, and got out of the car. He had his gun in one hand, and my first reaction was to get back in the car and get the girls out of there. Then I heard another car coming really fast, and saw it was the state cop. That's when Denny fired a shot. My lord, it was loud. Something hit the pump island here and shrieked off that way." She first pointed at the pump island, and then waved a hand toward Bernie's aging compact car that slumped beside the building. "And my first thought was, *My God! He's shooting at us!*

I jerked around, lost my balance, and cracked my head against the corner of the trunk lid....It was still open."

She frowned and squinted against the harsh light. "And look now. They're arresting that boy."

Estelle glanced across the parking lot. Sure enough, Rick Black was escorting his charge toward the state patrol car, the teenager's hands cuffed behind his back. Three of the others still sat on the sidewalk, and a fourth was face-to-face with the sheriff, who towered over him by a full head. With good reason, the boy cowered. Torrez stood with feet planted and both hands on his hips. *Don't hit him,* Estelle thought. *We have enough problems.*

"Mrs. Chavez, you said that you thought you heard something strike the pump island here. Are you sure about that?"

"I'm *very* sure," the woman said. The car door started to open and she spun around. "You stay in the car, now," she said, and Barb, the oldest daughter, did as she was told. "I don't know exactly where it hit, but I'm sure it did. I mean, my gosh, sheriff, look at this. That's only a couple feet from where I was standing, or from hitting the back window where the girls were sitting in the car."

"Mrs. Chavez, we're going to need photographs, and I'll need to talk with you again. I'd like to take photos of this area right now, before you move the car. We need to take a measurement or two, then you're free to take the kids home. It'll be half an hour or so. If you want to call your husband to come and pick them up, that's fine, too."

"He's in Fort Worth for some kind of regional meeting," the woman said. "I'm not looking forward to telling him about this." She looked at Estelle expectantly, as if awaiting instructions.

"Is there anyone else at home?" Estelle asked.

"No."

"I was going to suggest that an officer take the girls home, but we don't want to do that if no one is there. Mrs. Chavez, I'll be as prompt as I can. I appreciate your patience."

Another Sheriff's Department vehicle approached from the south and nosed in behind Estelle's sedan. Deputy Tom Pasquale got out of his SUV, lifted a hand in greeting to Collins, and then sauntered across toward Torrez and the group of kids.

Estelle retrieved her camera and took several dozen photos of the Volvo and the pump island from every conceivable angle. She photographed the automobile's trunk lid, with close-ups of the offending corner. Marge Chavez wasn't happy about having her face photographed but grudgingly agreed.... The little nick would be difficult to see in the best of prints, and Estelle wished that Linda Real, with her amazing photographic talents, was driving the camera.

"Go ahead and take the kids home," Estelle said. "Someone will be in touch tomorrow for a written statement. You might want to stop by the emergency room and have that cut looked at."

"Oh, heavens no. It's nothing. My own clumsiness." Marge folded herself back into the Volvo and in a moment pulled away from the pumps.

The gouge and smear of lead on the pump island's lower concrete skirt showed that the fat .45 slug from the deputy's gun had hit a glancing blow just inches off the ground where the concrete began to curve around the corner. Estelle walked over to where Bernie Pollis' car was parked next to the building. Sure enough, centered neatly just under the Chevrolet logo on the old compact car's grill was shattered plastic, and an irregular hole the size of a quarter in the mesh of the radiator.

"You want me to open the hood?" a voice said, and Estelle turned at Pollis' approach.

"Yes, sir." She watched him fumble with first the cable release and then the safety latch. The engine compartment was dark and smelly, and Estelle played the beam of her flashlight down into the depths between engine block and radiator. The slug had punched through the radiator, nicked a fan blade, and then smacked into the water pump housing before dropping straight down. A large fragment of it lay on the asphalt under the car, in a puddle of antifreeze.

"I'd appreciate it if you wouldn't touch anything yet," she said. "I ain't touching a thing. Who's gonna pay for this?"

"I'm sure it will be taken care of," Estelle said. "Right now, it's important that nothing's disturbed."

"I ain't touchin' it."

Estelle heaved a sigh of relief. No one had been hurt, and she knew where the bullet had gone. Now it was just a matter of filling in the little details.

"Tell me what happened, Bernie," she said.

"Look," he said quickly. "I did not sell alcohol to those kids. I don't know where they bought it, but it wasn't here. They *wanted* to buy more, I can tell you that. That's what started the argument. Stuart didn't know what to do, and I'm glad that I was workin', because I stepped in and told 'em that it wasn't going to happen."

"Who was doing the buying?"

"The one in handcuffs, there," Bernie said, nodding at the state car, now with a backseat occupant. "Him and the one that the sheriff is talkin' with. The others were just buyin' snack stuff."

"You asked them to leave the store?"

"You betcha. They camped out there by their car, bein' obnoxious. I guess it was just to get my goat. Well, they did that, all right. So I called you guys. I wasn't going to go out and confront all five of 'em by myself."

"That was the wise thing to do, sir."

"Well, maybe. Maybe not, you know. I called your office twice, 'cause at one point I saw the kid who got himself arrested there throw something at a passing car. So I'm all, *This is just going to get worse, you know what I mean? That's what I thought* to myself. So I called again. Brent said he was sending Denny over."

"Did you see what happened then?"

"What, when he fired the shot? No, I couldn't see. He was behind the cop car, there. I heard this loud bang, and just about the same time a kind of a clang. *Jesus Christ,* I thought. *What the hell is he doing? Not that I wouldn't have liked to take a baseball* bat to that drunk kid myself. But I don't think I'd *shoot* him."

"Where were you standing when the shot was fired?"

"Right in the doorway of the store. I saw the state cop guy coming into the lot from Bustos, and that's when it happened.

Damn good thing Denny didn't shoot the state cop. I can see the newspaper headlines now." He managed a feeble laugh.

Given a few hours for frayed nerves to mend, there was a good chance that a lot of people would be laughing,

Estelle reflected. Two other cars approached simultaneously from opposite directions on Grande; and Estelle groaned inwardly. One was Linda Real's little red Honda, but the other was driven by Frank Dayan, publisher of the *Posadas Register*.

SEVEN

SATISFIED THAT NO person had been in the path of the errant .45 slug, Estelle turned her attention to the most seriously injured—Deputy Dennis Collins. During the various comings and goings of investigators, the young man hadn't moved more than a step or two from his position by the driver's door of his county vehicle.

Estelle was proud of him for that—it was exactly the right moment for silent restraint, to speak when spoken to. She knew this wasn't an easy moment for the normally gregarious, cheerful deputy whose ego, normally large and fully inflated, must have been withered like a shrunken pea. There was no handy excuse for dropping a loaded gun—Dennis knew that, and kept silent.

The last thing Collins needed at that moment was an interview, but it appeared that Frank Dayan was zeroing in on him. The newspaper publisher's step was slower than usual—he appeared weary and worried, and Estelle knew Frank's concern wasn't because of a ruckus in a convenience store parking lot. Even though there was no yellow ribbon to stop him, Dayan hesitated as he approached. He knew better than to cross into a crime scene, even with the absence of a yellow tape. Collins, obviously unoccupied, alone, and on the periphery of the action, was a logical target.

"Excuse me, Frank," Estelle said as she approached, and Dayan stopped in his tracks.

"Am I—" Frank started to say, but Estelle gripped him firmly by the elbow, and together they walked up the sidewalk, well beyond Bob Torrez's truck. Collins did not follow.

"You've been over at the hospital?" Estelle asked as they walked.

"Oh, you heard about that?" He stopped. "The most tragic thing, Estelle. Just boom." He chopped the air with his hand. "Kerri just dropped in a heap. Thank God there were people around who knew what to do."

"Is there anything that Pam needs?"

"I don't think so. I mean, but gosh. Who knows with a thing like this. She's still over at the hospital, of course. I think they're going to airlift Kerri to Albuquerque."

"A rough time."

He groaned a response, then straightened his shoulders and surveyed the parking lot. "What's going on here?"

"We have a situation at the moment," she said as they walked. "We're going to need your cooperation with this."

"Of course," Dayan said. "I was just on my way home and saw all the traffic. We have a robbery, or what?" The dapper publisher sounded hopeful.

"I wish it were that simple," Estelle replied. She weighed how much to tell Dayan, who over the years had proven himself to be discreet when necessary—his newspaper would publish the following Wednesday, and a lot could change in the next five days. Frank viewed any other media—the big metro papers and TV stations in particular—as competition, even though they probably didn't know his small town paper existed. "It appears that there was an assault on the deputy's vehicle," she said, choosing her words carefully.

"I saw the damage to the windshield. Somebody took a shot at him?"

"No. Someone threw a loaded beer bottle."

Dayan grimaced in disgust, and Estelle wasn't sure if the newspaperman was disappointed that the story was as insignificant as a chucked bottle, or if it was just his comment on rowdy youth. "That's it?"

"Well," Estelle said carefully, "we're continuing to investigate exactly what happened after that." Frank would be irked at her sin of omission when the full story came out. "There may be some public intoxication involved."

"Oh," he said. "These days, isn't there always. What's Marge Chavez's connection? I saw her pulling out when I was on my way down Grande. They throw bottles at her car, too?"

"No. We're always interested in what witnesses have to say. Apparently she was fueling her car at the time the incident happened."

"Oh," Dayan said again. "Any injuries? Collins looks all right."

"No injuries, Frank. I'll have something for you a little later, but right now I need to talk with the deputy. With juveniles, things aren't always clear-cut. Will you excuse me?" She touched him on the arm and he nodded vigorously.

"Sure, sure." He ducked his head and looked toward the State Police car. "You have someone in custody already, it looks like."

"More for you later, Frank," Estelle said again.

"Okay? And please...give my best to Pam. If there's anything she needs, have her call me. I'll stop by and see her in the morning."

He smiled at the undersheriff, holding up both hands in surrender. "You're the boss," he said. "I'm headed home anyway. It's been a long day. I'll talk to you later, all right?" He started back toward his car and then paused. Estelle saw him pull a tiny camera out of his pocket and snap several pictures, of what it was impossible to tell. Given his lack of photographic talents, it might be just as impossible after the photos were downloaded.

She returned to Collins, who stood quietly by the door of his truck, watching Dayan.

As she crossed back toward the deputy, she was intercepted by Linda Real. The young woman carried a bulky camera bag, with another camera slung over her shoulder. Linda half turned and aimed a cheerful wave at Frank Dayan, her former boss.

"Hey," Linda said. "How's it goin'?"

"It's going," Estelle replied. She quickly outlined the gist of the scene for the photographer, whose normally unflappable good cheer dissolved when she heard what had happened to Deputy Collins.

"Bobby's going to have a cow," Linda said in her habitual straight-to-the-heart fashion, and Collins winced.

"We'll just have to see," Estelle replied. The sheriff's initial choice of "dufus" as a moniker for his deputy didn't bode well. She could predict that whatever Sheriff Robert Torrez did, he wouldn't concern himself with politics or image. That in itself was something of a relief. Equally sure was that he wouldn't shrug his shoulders and say, "People drop things. Happens every day."

"Let me show you what we need," Estelle said, and then turned to the deputy. She looked hard at Collins. "And listen to me, now. After Linda takes a photo of that chip in your truck, the broken glass, and the beer puddles, I want you to go back to the office and write a detailed deposition for me. *Exactly* what happened, from A to Z. Leave nothing out. Take your time and do it right."

"Yes, ma'am."

"Don't make *anything* either less or more than it is. Do you understand what I'm saying? This isn't the time for creative writing. Right now I'm *only* concerned with the *what*, not the *why. Okay?*"

"Yes, ma'am."

Again, Estelle was impressed that she had heard no string of excuses from the young deputy.

She turned her attention to his Expedition. The chip in the white paint of Dennis Collins' county vehicle was tiny—a little, sharp-edged mark just below the right fender logo, immediately in front of the door. Estelle crouched down and trained her flashlight on the spot.

"Can you make a clear photo of that?"

Linda bent down beside her. "Oh, sure," she said cheerfully. "Holy macro."

Estelle laughed at the young woman's easy good humor. Maybe it was for Dennis' benefit, but it was welcome regardless. "And as long as you're doing that, I need a good, clear blowup of Dennis' .45. There may be some paint or scratches that will show in a print."

"Oh, it will."

"I'll bring the gun to the office in a few minutes. You can do it there."

"You got it."

"You want my gun?" Collins asked, and he made it sound as if Estelle were asking him to disrobe in public. He started to reach toward his holster protectively and she caught his wrist.

"Just unbuckle the whole belt, Denny." She could tell he was counting mentally to ten—maybe even twenty or thirty. Finally, he unbuckled the heavy Sam Browne belt, then refastened the buckle deftly and hung the entire heavy rig over Estelle's extended hand. She felt a pang of sympathy for his humiliation.

"I know you're off-shift, Dennis. It's been a long day, and is going to be longer before it's over. But wait for us at the office, all right? Finish up the deposition, make sure you dot every 'i' and cross every 't.'"

"The sheriff is going to fire my ass," Collins whispered, more to himself than to anyone else. That was conceivable, Estelle knew. Equally conceivable was that Deputy Dennis Collins would end up being an even better officer than he had been before the incident.

"One step at a time," Estelle said. "Don't start making assumptions. I'll see you in a few minutes in my office. All right?"

"Yes, ma'am."

"You're all right with that?"

"I guess I have to be," Collins said. He managed a rueful smile. "I'm just glad nobody got hurt."

"Exactly."

Linda finished a series of a dozen or more photos of the truck, then stepped back. "You can have it now," she said. Collins climbed into the Expedition without a word, started it, and backed out of the parking lot. As he drove off, Linda turned to Estelle. "Wow," the photographer said.

"'Wow' is right," Estelle replied. She opened the trunk of her car and laid the Sam Browne rig inside. Drawing her flashlight, she bent down to inspect what she could see of the officer's gun without drawing it from its holster. The white paint on the square, sharp corner of the back sight was obvious. "Right here," she said, and turned both gun and light so Linda could see. "Smacked it right on the back sight."

"No problems getting that," Linda said.

Estelle positioned the belt so that the gun was protected from touching anything in the trunk. "Just in case, can you take a picture of the gun now?"

"I can do that."

Linda tried half a dozen angles, frowning and grimacing as she worked. "We can do better in the lab with the tripod and easel, but this'll work for now as backup," she announced finally. When Linda was finished, Estelle shook open a black plastic bag and slid in the belt, heavy with its half-a-hardware load of gun and accoutrements. She slammed the trunk lid shut.

The sheriff and State Trooper Rick Black were conferring well out of earshot of the remaining four teenagers, who still sat like forlorn statues on the store's sidewalk. Linda headed off toward the fuel pumps to take photos there and at Bernie's car. The clerk had retreated back inside the store. Estelle wondered what version of the tale he and his teenaged assistant, Stuart Fernandez, were concocting. She shrugged off that thought, since it was something over which she had no control.

Rick Black laughed at something Torrez said, and the two men turned as Estelle approached.

"That one," Black said, nodding toward his car where a figure slumped in the backseat, "admits to throwing the bottle. All five of 'em have been drinking. Started during the game, is my guess." He handed Estelle a silver hip flask that had been sealed in a clear plastic evidence bag. "Pretty fancy, eh? That belongs to the driver."

"More likely to the driver's daddy," the sheriff muttered.

"All from Lordsburg?"

"Yup. The kid's name is Tyler Parker," Black said. "He turned twenty-one last week. So this ain't just the smartest stunt he ever pulled. He's so soused he can hardly stand. If he pukes in the back of my car, things are *really* going to get ugly." He grinned.

"The other four are minors."

"Whose Lexus?"

"Registered to Elliot Parker of Lordsburg. The daddy, I would guess."

Torrez beckoned Deputy Pasquale, who had been working with Linda. The deputy held another evidence bag with the single shell casing inside. "Take these three back to the lockup," the sheriff instructed, counting off the first three teens. "You take the last one there," he added to Estelle. "That'll keep 'em a little bit separated, not that it matters much. They can get comfortable in the conference room while they wait for their parents to get over here to check 'em out."

Estelle could see in the kids' hangdog expressions that they were past the defiant stage, ready now to accept the end of the world. Sheriff Torrez and Officer Black had intimidated them into compliant silence.

"I'll take care of Bernie," Torrez said after the three young men were secured in the back of Pasquale's Expedition, with the fourth in Estelle's unit. "I want that slug out of his radiator, too."

"It's lying on the ground right under the car," Estelle said. "Straight down from the fan housing. I asked Linda for photos before we move it."

"Well, that's easy, then," Torrez said. "I called Stubby to come get the Lexus, so I guess we're all set." He regarded the expensive SUV. "Maybe he'll put a few dents in it for good measure," Torrez added, although they both knew that Stub Moore, handling impounds for the county, would treat the suspect's vehicle with loving care.

Some parents in Lordsburg were going to be furious, Estelle mused. Arrested children, impounded vehicle… and it would all be the Sheriff's Department's fault, no doubt. The department could expect that someone—a parent, perhaps even Marge Chavez when she had some time to think on it—would make the most out of the accidental discharge. They could almost guarantee that would overshadow everything else. Five drunken youngsters driving an SUV on the interstate after midnight would pale in comparison to that single mistake.

Torrez turned to Estelle. "You're going to talk with Collins?"

"I had planned to."

"As far as I'm concerned, he can clean out his locker and be out of here."

"We'll want to think about that carefully, Bobby."

"Look, that slug missed hittin' one of Margie's daughters right between the eyes by about three feet. There was no reason to have drawn down on those pissants in the first place. A bunch of drunk kids?"

"He didn't know that at the time," Estelle said. "And I don't think he 'drew down' on them. I think he reacted with a mistake. He didn't see the kid throw the bottle, and for just a few seconds, he thought he'd been shot at. He drew his gun as he slid out of the vehicle, saw he was mistaken, and then, in the process of correcting that mistake, fumbled the gun."

"You sound like a damn lawyer."

"I'm sure we'll hear from them before this is all over. Right now, I'm puzzled why the gun went off."

"'Cause he had his friggin' finger on the trigger," Torrez said.

"Maybe so. If that's the case, then it's our training and proficiency program that's at fault. If it was a fault in the gun, then it's a problem for our equipment maintenance program." *Program?* she thought to herself. Like most small, financially strapped departments, the Sheriff's Department found it was all too easy to use equipment until it collapsed.

"He's got eyes and ears to use like all the rest of us," Torrez snapped, and his tone had sunk to little more than a whisper.

Estelle recognized the anger and had already decided to let the matter drop for the moment when Torrez added, "But hey. If you don't want to do it, I'll take care of it." He didn't explain what the *it* was but instead turned to the State Policeman, who had remained tactfully silent. "Thanks for your help, Rick."

"I'll get my deposition to you ASAP," the trooper said.

"You pulled in just as Collins got out of his unit?" Estelle asked.

Black nodded. "I did. I didn't see him fumble the gun, though. I was watching the kids. I was starting to get out of the car when I heard the gunshot. I could tell by the look on Denny's face that it had been an a.d." He shrugged. "I told him to stay put until I had a chance to make sure no one had been hit. The sheriff here arrived just a few seconds later." He held up both hands. "Not much, but it all helps."

"Thanks again for your help."

As Estelle walked back to her car, she saw that the sheriff and Bernie Pollis had the hood of the Chevy open and were bent over the engine. Linda Real joined them, and Estelle saw the flash of the photographer's camera light up the engine compartment. Estelle dug out her cell phone, pushed the auto-dial, and waited for two rings before the connection went through.

"Gastner."

"I hope I didn't wake you," Estelle said. She glanced in the rearview mirror at the youngster in the backseat, behind the security grill that separated front from back.

Gastner chuckled. "I've never fallen asleep as long as a green chile burrito is spread out in front of me. I'm still over here." He didn't explain where "here" was, but Estelle knew, to the exact booth, where he was sitting in the Don Juan de Oñate restaurant. "You hungry?"

"No thanks. You're closing the place down?" They were well past the 2:00 a.m. closing time for the Don Juan.

"Fernando and I were solving all the world's problems." Bill Gastner and Fernando Aragon, the longtime owner of the Don Juan, were perfectly capable of sitting and eating the night away—two insomniacs with the best restaurant in town right in the family.

"If you have a minute when you finish dessert, would you swing by my office?"

"Of course I would. But good God, you should be home by now, sweetheart."

"*Sin duda.* But we had a nasty little incident."

"Who?"

"Nobody hurt. I'll tell you about it when you come over. I'm ten-fifteen, one juvenile."

"I don't like the sound of that. I don't know what an old dumb guy like me can tell you, sweetheart. Especially about the younger generation."

"A second opinion, is all," Estelle said.

"Well, hell, I'm all opinions, as you well know. Give me ten?"

"That's fine. No rush, sir."

"Not in this lifetime," he said. "But I'm down to the last morsel."

"Thanks, *padrino.*" She switched off the phone just in time to swing the car into the Public Safety Building's parking lot. Pasquale had parked his SUV directly in front of the side door where they moved prisoners back and forth to the small booking room.

Everyone was inside, including Dennis Collins, whose nicked SUV was pulled in behind the fuel pumps, parked beside a damaged county pickup truck that had languished there for three weeks awaiting parts.

The last of the undersheriff's worries was a damaged truck. She sat quietly for a moment, mentally putting things in order on her list of priorities before escorting the youngster inside.

Perfect timing, she mused. Although she liked to think

that she didn't care what the media said or did not say, she drew a sigh of relief that the writer from the national magazine hadn't arrived a day early. The whole mess made her insides ache.

EIGHT

"MAY I?" Bill Gastner extended his hand and Estelle passed over the .45 automatic that had been holstered on Deputy Collins' hip…and that had then taken an excursion through space. Gastner laid the gun in his lap and took off his glasses, inspecting the lenses carefully. He wiped away a small spot on the sleeve of his shirt, then replaced the spectacles with care.

The slide was racked back on the handgun, but the empty magazine was in place. Gastner thumbed the release and let the magazine slide into his hand, then laid it on the desk.

"I lived with one of these for a long time," he said thoughtfully. "A very interesting, very old design." He turned the gun this way and that, as if admiring it just before a purchase. "Collins fumbled it somehow? Is that the story?"

"He says that he drew the gun as he slid out of his truck, and then when he saw that there was no particular threat, maybe seeing that it was just a beer bottle that hit his truck and not a bullet, he went to reholster it. That's when he fumbled it. The gun hit the truck—we have a chip in the Expedition's paint, and there was a tiny speck of paint residue on the back sight." Gastner held the gun in two hands and rotated it, imitating its flight toward the truck's fender. "And then he managed to grab it."

"Apparently. After it bounced off the fender."

"You sound skeptical."

"Well, I'm not, really. We do that all the time, after all. We drop something, and make a grab for it. Sometimes the catches are spectacular, sometimes we don't even come close."

"We just don't do it too often with a loaded and cocked gun," Gastner said. "Still," and he took a deep breath, "the gun didn't go off when it struck the truck." He turned the gun so Estelle could see the chamber clearly. "Nothing to feed it, nothing in its mouth," he said, and waited until she nodded. Then he thumbed the slide release, and the slide shot forward with a metallic clang, closing the gun, leaving the hammer cocked. He bent over with a grunt, and whacked the butt of the cocked automatic on the floor, then did it again. The hammer remained cocked. He straightened up, turned the gun over, and tapped the hammer spur itself sharply on the metal edge of Estelle's desk.

"Solid as a rock," he said. "See, there's just an infinitesimal chance that this gun is going to discharge when dropped." Gastner turned the gun, holding it by the barrel. "It's not like the old Colt single actions, where the only thing holding that hammer back was a thin little sliver of trigger steel. Drop *that* sucker on its hammer, and boom. But not this one. You have to be holding it so that the grip safety is depressed." He pushed that broad, contoured safety on the back of the handle that a shooter's grip on the gun would activate. "Unless he's holding it properly, this prevents a discharge. Supposed to, anyway."

He thumbed on the hammer safety on the side of the broad, flat slide. "You probably know all this better than I do," he added, then charged ahead. "And if he's carrying it with the hammer back, ready to go, he has to de-press the thumb safety—if he remembered to click it on in the first place the last time the gun was holstered."

Gastner snapped the safety up and down, and Estelle sat silently, watching him. "Ehhhh," he said, and snapped the safety some more. "That's a little softer than it should be," he said finally. "Let me see his rig. You got it here?"

"Sure," Estelle replied. She retrieved the deputy's belt and holster from the bottom drawer of a filing cabinet and handed it to Gastner.

For several minutes, he manipulated the gun and hol-ster, then sat back with a shrug. "It's conceivable that the thumb safety worked its way out of position against the leather of the holster," he said. "Especially sitting in a vehicle, with the added nuisance of a shoulder belt."

He held up the gun. "I think...you might want to have Robert look at it...but *I* think this thumb safety is a little softer than it should be. I wouldn't be a bit surprised that over time it worked its way down, into the 'off' posi-tion. When Collins grabbed the gun, he made one mis-take." Gastner held the gun up and his trigger finger lay along the frame, outside of the trigger guard, well away from the trigger. "Instead of having his finger like so, he curled it into the trigger guard...on the trigger. If the thumb safety had rotated down, guess what."

Estelle didn't see his finger move, but the hammer fell with a sharp snap. "Just like that."

"Exactly, just like that." He reached out and laid the gun on Estelle's desk. "That doesn't excuse the a.d.," he said. "No matter what the gun did or didn't do, his fin-ger had to be on the trigger. Period. End of story. We could argue physics working against us if the gun had hit nose first, and firing pin inertia was involved. Blah,

blah, blah," and he waved his hand in dismissal. "But that didn't happen."

"Mitigating circumstances," Estelle said, and Gastner laughed.

"Mitigate, schmitigate," he said. "If his finger hadn't been on the trigger, the gun wouldn't have discharged, sweetheart. I'm not saying it's impossible. Just very, very unlikely."

"And that means that his training wasn't adequate."

Gastner regarded her thoughtfully for a moment, and she waited. "It could probably be argued," he said after a moment, "that our training is *never* adequate, considering the job we do. Consider for instance last spring, when you scared the holy shit out of all of us. There are just those unfortunate moments when events conspire, no matter how adept, no matter how *good*, we are."

"Desperate" was the word Estelle would have chosen to describe the incident to which Gastner referred, and not just the moment itself when the two shots from a 9mm in the hands of a highly competent gunman had bludgeoned her to the ground. The surgery and weeks of convalescence afterward had been the worst moments in her thirty-eight years of life. But that was not the issue here, and she pushed the memory from her mind.

"Bobby wants to fire him, sir."

"His nibs will get over that. That would be a stupid overreaction. Tell him I said so. Hell, can that thought. *I'll* tell him I said so."

"That's the catch," Estelle said, and was about to add that *telling* Sheriff Robert Torrez anything was usually a waste of breath. "But it can be argued that the fault is not entirely the deputy's. More intensive training might have resulted in safer gun handling."

"Sure. He was rusty, like most of us. And it could be argued that his immediate supervisor should have inspected the firearms more frequently. Who's his shift sergeant?"

"We don't have a day sergeant," Estelle said, and by the trace of a smile on Gastner's face she knew that *he* knew that perfectly well. Both she and Captain Eddie Mitchell served as supervisors during the daytime shift, with Mears assigned as patrol sergeant for swing. Tom Pasquale worked graveyard with Mike Sisneros—with the sheriff and undersheriff on call if they were needed.

"What I want to—" and she was interrupted by the phone. Her husband's voice was like a welcome warm blanket, and she glanced at the clock.

"Querida," Francis Guzman said, "I just got back. How are you doing?"

"I'm sitting here in my office ruminating with *padrino*. How's Kerri?"

"Ah, you heard about that. Well, she'll be all right, I think. She's up in Albuquerque at University. Or will be shortly. The flight left almost an hour ago."

"What happened?"

"It looks like a mitral valve prolapse," he said. "Just like that. If she hadn't been surrounded by all kinds of people who just happened to do all the right things, she'd be gone. The athletic director was walking right behind her when she went down, and he's the hero of the moment. She's a lucky kid."

"She'll be all right, though?"

"I think so. Look, the reason I called, *querida*, other than needing to hear your voice, is to mention that Alan wants to talk to you about your car accident victim. He was going to keep him on ice until a more civil hour, but he and I ended up doing a prelim on him. Some interesting things you need to know about."

"Does Alan want me to call him right now?"

"If you can."

"Then I need to do that, and then I'll be home, *querida*."

"I'm on my way there now," the physician said. "Are you staying warm?"

"Oh, sure. I'm fine." She was amused and touched by her husband's gentle hovering, exponentially increased after her lengthy bout of recuperation.

"She needs to eat more," Gastner said loudly, and Francis laughed.

"He's right, you know," the physician said.

"I *am* eating more, *mi corazón*," Estelle said. "Just not in the middle of the night." She looked at the clock again. "How long ago did you talk with Alan?"

"About six minutes."

"Then I'll call now. Thanks, *querida*. We have a houseful of juveniles that we need to send back to Lordsburg with their parents, and then I'll be home."

"Take care. *Te amo*."

"Always." She rang off and, as she dialed medical examiner Alan Perrone's number, said to Gastner, "Kerri Gardner is going to be all right. Bad heart valve." He grimaced in sympathy.

On the third ring, Dr. Perrone found his cell phone. His voice sounded distant and tired.

"Alan, it's Estelle."

"Hi. Go home and go to bed," Perrone said without hesitation. "It's going to be a long day tomorrow."

"Francis said you might have something for me?"

"Well, it's preliminary, but interesting. For one thing,

I think that you guys are right. That looks like a boot or shoe print on the palm of his left hand. It's not very clear, but that's sure what it looks like to me. Your miracle girl spent a lot of time burning film…or digits, or whatever it is photographers do these days. The shoe tread looks like one of those waffle stompers, or even a running shoe with aggressive tread. There was enough mud that it left a pretty good impression. And that's consistent with the other."

"The other?"

"Look, this guy would have died in minutes or maybe hours at best. He was busted up so badly that any significant movement was out of the question. Multiple fractures and lacerations—just beaten to pieces. His right chest was so badly flailed that if he was breathing at all, it was just out of his left lung. Even if the EMTs had gotten to him seconds after the crash, he wouldn't have made it to the hospital. Four of his ribs lacerated the hell out of his liver."

"I don't understand why someone would step on his *hand*," Estelle said.

"Two explanations that I can think of," Perrone said, and yawned loudly. "Excuse me. First, it might have been an accident. The step, I mean. The Good Samaritan witnesses the crash and scrambles down the bank…and steps on him by accident. Or, as I think now, the Good Samaritan used his foot to keep the victim's left hand out of the way. That arm was busted in a couple of places, but the victim might have been able to move it some. He would have been convulsing, maybe. Flailing a little bit. Or, the killer might have thought that he *might*."

"You're kidding."

"You know I don't," Perrone said.

"That's grotesque. And you said 'killer'?"

"Well, think on this one, if you want grotesque, my dear. If you were lying on your back in a million pieces, and someone pours beer into your gaping mouth, drowning you in the stuff, you're going to thrash around a little bit...no matter how it hurts."

The line fell silent.

"That's what happened?" Estelle asked finally. She pictured a crushed and battered Christopher Marsh lying gurgling and moaning among the rocks, and then the shadowy figure looming overhead. If Marsh had been capable of cogent thought at all, he might have gasped a plea for help. Help was not what he got.

"I'm thinking so." Perrone let it go at that without further explanation.

Estelle sat motionless, staring off into space.

"You still there?" Perrone asked. "Let me take another gander tomorrow morning. You'll want to be here."

Estelle shook her head to clear the image. "Yes, I will. I have to hope that you're wrong."

"Hey, we'll see. I'll have more for you then," he said. "But I know I'm right with the preliminaries. There was beer in his esophagus, and in his windpipe, and aspirated into his lungs. A *lot* of beer. It isn't a question of having just taken a gulp an instant before his truck clobbered that deer. He choked on the stuff, and when he stopped breathing, whoever it was just kept pouring. Not a pretty picture. I'm not sure I'd want to meet up with this guy."

"And you're sure that Chris Marsh was alive at first?"

"I'm one hundred percent sure. A dead man does not aspirate beer into his lungs. Or lung, I should say. Only one of 'em was working enough to matter."

"Ay," Estelle whispered, and when she saw that Bill Gastner was watching her like an old basset hound, "I'll be in touch, Alan." She hung up the phone and sat back. "Our accident victim drowned."

NINE

THERE WAS NO point in scrambling up and down the rock-strewn precipices of Regál Pass in the dark, regardless of how Chris Marsh had died. In addition to being drowned in his own beer, the victim had been dead for at least twenty-four hours, maybe longer. Dr. Alan Perrone was sure of that. The killer wasn't still lurking at the scene. He was long gone, leaving nothing but puzzles behind.

Some of the answers, Estelle felt sure, would be found at the accident site, and that required a careful, methodical approach—not a fleet of big feet slipping and sliding, ruining evidence.

After a brief phone consultation with Deputy Jackie Taber, who reported that Regál Pass was so quiet she could hear the piñons grow, Estelle walked Bill Gastner to his truck, then settled behind her desk to read Dennis Collins' deposition. The brief document was a master-piece of garbled syntax. Estelle read it quickly, saw no gaping inconsistencies, and chalked up the lack of grammatical precision to exhaustion tinged with apprehension. Despite the young man's bravado that might come to his defense, Dennis Collins would suffer the awful bouts of self-doubt that churned the gastric juices into rebellion and drove sleep away.

Estelle saw that she had two arguments to use when she discussed the young deputy's future with Sheriff Robert Torrez. That conference would wait, however.

Torrez had gone home, as had Collins. Rest would do them both a world of good.

"Estelle?" The voice jerked the undersheriff out of her musings, and she turned to see Brent Sutherland standing in the doorway of her office. "Elliot Parker is on the phone from Lordsburg. He would like to speak with you."

"Do we know Mr. Parker?"

"He's the kid's father. The kid who threw the bottle?"

"Ah. That's good," Estelle said. "Even at two thirty in the morning, that's good." The boy's phone call had been straight to Dad. Deputy Tom Pasquale and Rick Black had taken care of booking Tyler Parker into the detention center's minimalist facilities. The four others, all minors, were waiting glumly in the conference room. State law prohibited incarcerating or even cuffing children unless they were an obvious physical threat to themselves or others, and Deputy Pasquale had confirmed that the county Juvenile Probation Office wanted the kids sent home with parents, the sooner the better. If there were to be charges against any of them, it would wait until the next day, or the next—on whichever mañana the JPO authorities chose to decide.

Mr. Parker was the first irate parent to contact the department—perhaps because his son, of age, had the most to lose. His case didn't fall under the providence of the JPO, but rather that of the district attorney and Judge Lester Hobart.

She picked up the phone. "Undersheriff Guzman."

There was a long pause, then, "May I speak with the sheriff, please. This is Elliot Parker." The man's voice was carefully modulated, as if he was putting great effort into self-control.

"Sheriff Torrez is not in the office, sir. May I help you?"

"Well, I guess so. Look, my son Tyler is with you folks? Do I understand that correctly?"

With us. Estelle smiled at the quaint phrasing. *Welcome to your local county B and B.* "Yes, sir, he is. The deputies are working on an arraignment schedule with Judge Hobart."

"He's all right, though?"

"Yes, sir."

"The four others are still with you as well?"

"Yes, sir."

"So they're *all* being detained. Do I have that right?"

"Yes, sir. They're all minors, all under the influence to one degree or another. They will be detained here until parents or guardians arrive to take them into custody."

"There's bond, I assume? For my son, I mean?"

"At the moment, no. He is being held pending arraignment."

"It's the middle of the night," Parker said. "The judge isn't going to like that much." Judge Lester Hobart didn't like much of anything that jarred his strict routine, Estelle knew...least of all being hauled out of bed to tongue-lash drunken youngsters. She offered no comment about what the judge might or might not do.

"Okay, look," Parker said. "After my son called, I spoke with some of the other parents. Is it acceptable if I pick the kids up?"

"No, sir. We will release them to parents or legal guardians. That's all the law allows us to do."

"How about if I have a signed note."

Anything for convenience, she thought. "No, sir."

"So each of these boys is going to have to be picked

up by his own parents?" A note of exasperation crept into the man's tone.

"That's correct, sir."

"That might not be until tomorrow sometime. I mean, later today. It's not a convenient drive over there, you know."

"I understand that, sir. I'm sure the boys will wait."

"My son's arraignment hasn't been set?"

"I haven't had a chance to talk with the officers handling that, sir. But it would be better for your son if the arraignment was later in the morning."

"Now why is that?"

"For one thing, sir, your son is intoxicated to the point that he isn't making intelligent decisions. I'm sure you noticed that when you spoke with him. It wouldn't be in his best interests to make an appearance before the judge in his present condition. Let him sleep for a few hours."

"Huh." The line fell silent for a few seconds. "Look, what was your name again?"

"Undersheriff Guzman."

"Okay, look. I'm going to bring the kid's checkbook over. He's going to have some kind of bond to pay, won't he?"

"That's a possibility."

"Any idea how much?"

"No, sir."

"And what's he charged with again?"

"At this point, assault on a police officer, battery on a police officer, public intoxication, supplying alcoholic beverages to minors, and four counts of child abuse."

"Jesus H. Christ. Child abuse? Where the hell did that come from? Are we talking about the same case here?"

"Your son is no longer a minor, sir. When an adult

commits a crime that either injures or has the immediate potential of injuring a child…a minor, if you like… that's the basis for charges of child abuse."

The phone went silent again except for a rhythmic tapping in the background, as if fingernails were drumming on a desk.

"Why the battery charge? Did he try and fight the officer?"

"It's possible that a piece of glass from either the windshield or the bottle struck the deputy in the hand. That's still under investigation."

A long, impatient exhale of breath greeted that. "We're talking felonies here, aren't we." Parker's tone was no longer as assured.

"Yes, sir." They wouldn't remain that way, Estelle was willing to bet, but she wasn't about to discuss or try to predict what Judge Parker and District Attorney Dan Schroeder would agree to.

"All right, then. I'll bring over his checkbook a little later. He's going to bail himself out of this one. Maybe that'll get his attention. He's working toward buying his own car, you know. This'll put a damper on *those* plans, let me tell you. He was driving his mother's Lexus this time around. Any damage to that?"

"No, sir."

"Well, that's something. Is he going to be able to drive home?"

"That will depend on Judge Parker, sir. My suggestion would be that the vehicle's owner comes and retrieves it."

"I guess. His mother's not going to like that." Parker waited an instant for another suggestion and, when one wasn't forthcoming, added, "I'll call the parents back and tell 'em that I can't play chauffeur."

"That would be good, sir. I appreciate that."

Parker sighed. "You have kids of your own, sheriff?"

"Yes, sir."

"Well, then you know all about it," he said. "May I give you my cell phone number, just in case you need to reach me?"

"Certainly, sir." She jotted down the numbers as he rattled them off.

"Any time day or night," he added. "Thanks for taking my call."

She hung up with a sigh, and made a bet with herself that Elliot Parker's show of cooperation and understanding would evaporate the instant he learned of the accidental discharge. It was interesting that his son hadn't mentioned it yet—a sign of just how drunk the boy really was.

TEN

ESTELLE OPENED ONE eye and stared at the alarm clock until it swam into focus. That focus came with a start as the numbers coalesced into 6:07 a.m. She wanted to leap out of bed, eager and ready for a new day, but her body expressed no interest in the challenge. A blink of the eyes and the clock skipped to 6:38.

A large, furry face loomed over hers. "How are you doing?" A gentle, soft hand brushed the hair away from the side of her face. "Mumfh," she managed. Her husband sat down on the edge of the bed. One hand moved to the back of her neck, gently massaging to find the aches and the tension.

"*Hijo* wants to know if you're awake," Francis said. "He's getting impatient."

"Is *mamá* up?" Her voice sounded far away.

"Oh, yes."

"Then I am, too," Estelle said. "Tell him to go ahead." She sighed deeply, enjoying the flood of warmth that Francis' strong fingers brought. "When did late nights become such torture?"

Her husband laughed. "The nights aren't so bad. It's the next morning payback that's a bummer."

"I need to find out if the Lordsburg gang made it home," she said, starting to squirm toward the edge of the bed. "And we have an arraignment this morning."

Her husband didn't move from the edge of the bed, effectively blocking her way.

"I'm sure your staff is perfectly capable," he said.

"I'm sure of that, too. But I have a dozen things to do besides all that. How's Kerri? Did you check this morning?"

"Yes, I did. And she's doing remarkably well. That was around five o'clock. The surgery went routinely."

"See?"

"See, *¿qué?*"

"See," Estelle said, "you got up and the first thing you did was go to work. In a manner of speaking."

"That's because I knew you'd ask."

From the living room came the first sounds of her older son's morning ritual, a methodical scale that sounded as if he was thinking hard about each individual note as the piano's hammers struck the strings. The penetrating aroma of coffee drifted in, along with the faint clank of dishes.

"Irma?"

Francis nodded. Irma Sedillos, Sheriff Bob Torrez's sister-in-law, had become an extension of the family, more than a dependable nana for the children. Irma was fond of referring to the household as the Guzman *corporación*, and she understood her role as corporate manager. In addition, Irma had become a companion and best friend to Estelle's mother, ninety-five-year-old Teresa. Estelle knew that the time would come when the twenty-six-year-old Irma would say yes to her longtime fiancé, beginning her own family. Until that time, they would continue to treasure the young woman's competence and friendship.

The pace of the piano scales increased as if the musician were turning a rheostat, and Estelle listened as she lay under the comfort of her husband's warm hand.

During the past months, a new aspect of her son's musical journey had manifested itself. Rather than continuing his joyful romping on the piano keys, often dissolving into the giggles and nonsense of a little boy, Francisco had crossed a threshold, embracing a new world of tightly disciplined practice. He could focus on something as simple as a two-octave scale for long moments, the metronome in his mind as unrelenting and exacting as the wooden and brass one that ticked away on the corner of the piano, a musical version of Chinese water torture for everyone else in the house.

As his fingers warmed up, so did the pace, and he shifted effortlessly from one key to another, this time alternating scales of sharps and flats as he worked his way around the circle. As his fingers warmed to the task, he pushed the tempo, always accelerating to the ragged edge of losing control and then remaining on that plateau until he was confident to push again.

Carlos appeared in the bedroom doorway. "Irma is making waffles," he announced, and then darted away, mission accomplished. "And of course, you're going to take some time to enjoy that," Francis said skeptically.

"Maybe a little bit." The idea of the thick, moist, golden brown waffles awash in richly fruited syrup made her stomach churn again—as had Bill Gastner's offer of a green chile burrito at two in the morning. She knew that Irma would have hot water ready for green tea and, along with several strips of bacon, that would have to do.

"You're headed down to Regál this morning?"

"Yes. This is a nasty one, *querida*. Jackie has been sitting the pass all night."

She twisted to look toward the window. "What kind of day do we have?"

"Brilliant," her husband said. He rose and opened the double shade, letting in a flood of sunshine, and then stood regarding her for long enough that she looked at him quizzically.

"You slept pretty well last night," he said finally. "Not so much tossing and turning."

"I'm fine, *querido*. Stop fussing." She reached out a hand, enjoying his grip. He eased her upright, and she swung her feet over the edge of the bed. Out in the living room, the piano practice continued unabated—and would until the waffles hit the plates. Her cell phone jangled, strident and off-key with the piano, and as she reached for it, Francis shook his head in resignation.

"The first thing to do is stomp all those into the ground," he said.

"And go back to smoke signals," Estelle added. "Then all the asthmatics would complain." She flipped open the phone. "Guzman."

"Good morning," Jackie Taber said. "I was hoping you'd be up."

"I am." She released her husband's hand, and he padded out of the bedroom. "What have you got?"

"It's been quiet," the deputy said. "The sun's coming right up the canyon, and it's exquisite." Jackie's appreciation didn't surprise Estelle. Deputy Taber was the only officer in the department who kept a thick sketch pad and a box of pencils in her patrol unit. More than once, it had been the young woman's recognition of pattern and contrast that had helped at a crime scene.

"What are you thinking?" Estelle asked.

"Well, first of all, I found *the* beer can. I think. About

a fling down the hill, over to one side in the scrub. Same brand as in the truck, everything else consistent. I protected it from the weather, and put an evidence flag to mark it."

Estelle felt her pulse kick up a notch. "Anything else?"

"The driver's name tag. I found that. It found itself a little home down between some rocks, but right in line with the crash trajectory."

"You recovered it?"

"Marked it. We need camera girl out here. I already told Brent."

"Good. Was the name of the company on the tag?"

"Yep. Global Productivity Systems. GPS. Does that ring a bell with you?"

"No, but there's no reason it should. There are a lot of companies out there. What was the name? Marsh?"

"Barry Roberts. How about that. We got two people in the truck, or what?"

"Ay," Estelle whispered. "Jackie, we'll be out shortly." She glanced at the clock, and closed her eyes, running down the list of names. "I'll get someone out there to relieve you."

"Not to worry," Jackie said. "I'm having fun. If someone wants to bring out some coffee, that would be nifty. Captain Mitchell is already headed this way."

"Ay, estoy torpe esta mañana," Estelle groaned. "I'm *sooooo* slow."

"The mountain will keep," Jackie replied. "Any word this morning on Pam's daughter?"

"Francis checked on her this morning. They think she'll be okay. The surgery went well." *Went well.* It was so easy, she thought. Crack somebody else open to repair defective parts, and it all goes well. Kerri Gardiner, fifteen years old and full of the self-conscious self-image that plagued the teen years, might not think so when she had her first look at the scar down the middle of her chest that the "went well" left behind.

"That's good to hear," Jackie said. "See you in a bit, then."

Estelle rang off and sat on the edge of the bed for another moment, deep in thought. Jackie Taber had already located two important bits at the crash site. More might surface. Christopher Marsh had not died alone. He'd been helped. Estelle pushed off the bed and headed toward the bathroom.

It took great planning and thought to move about this planet without leaving some kind of track, she mused. Marsh's crash had been an accident—a deer had waited until the wrong moment before crossing into the truck's path. What had happened next had been a crime of opportunity, and those so often left room for error.

The hot water felt good, and she stood under it with her eyes closed, letting the steam turn the shower into a sauna. In slow motion, she began the ritual of stretches that helped tame the ache in her right shoulder and side, bending with her arm arched over her head, letting the hot water beat her skin, then twisting carefully to full extension, locking her hands behind her back and tugging.

After fifteen minutes, she turned off the water and sucked in a deep breath. "*It went well*," she repeated aloud. "Oh, *sí*." The mirror was steamed over, and she didn't bother with it. She didn't need to see the massive scar that circled around the right side of her own torso, from armpit to the lower, medial margin of her right breast. The scar had faded over the months, from livid roadway to a narrow track, just as her husband had said it would.

If the memory of those moments would fade, all would be well. But just the reverse happened as her mind dredged up the details that she thought had been lost, re-running the tapes at the most inopportune times.

She dressed quickly, shook her short black hair into some semblance of order, and hurried out to the kitchen to begin the day with a moment, a concentrated shot, of normalcy.

Halfway through the first small square of waffle, a sweet chunk of magic about the size of a playing card that Carlos convinced her to try, Estelle's cell phone rang.

"I can answer that," Francisco chirped, and he started to reach for his mother's holstered cell phone. Estelle fended him off with a mock threat from her fork as she rose from the table. That earned a glance from her mother, who usually kept her thoughts to herself when the children were present. Tiny, wrinkled, and now so bent of spine that she sat no higher in her chair than did six-year-old Carlos, Teresa Reyes lifted an arthritic index finger for emphasis. "They ask too much of you," she said, and then nodded as if to add, *and that's that.*

"Sometimes they do," Estelle said, "but I'm late." She walked into the living room and opened the phone on the third ring. "Guzman."

"Hey," Sheriff Bob Torrez said, his soft voice carrying no urgency. "You okay?"

"Sure," Estelle replied, surprised that the taciturn sheriff would ask. But he was used to her being places before he was. "I conked out for a while."

"I'm headed out to the pass. You headed that way?"

"Yes. I just talked with Jackie. She's found a couple interesting things."

"Yeah. I talked to her, too. Linda?"

"She's been called."

"Okay. I'm headed to Regál right now," the sheriff said. "And hey… Sutherland's got a bunch of paperwork that came down from Catron County. They've got a situation goin' on up there that maybe has a tie with us. You want to stop by the office on your way and check it out?"

"What kind of situation? Are they asking for an assist, or what?"

"Little bit, maybe. If you think there's anybody we can break free, that'd be good. I'll see you in a bit, then." The connection broke.

ELEVEN

THE MANILA ENVELOPE from the Catron County Sheriff's Department was folded into the undersheriff's mailbox. With the time-consuming investigation pending down in Regál Pass and the sticky situation surrounding the accidental discharge of Deputy Collins' handgun, Estelle's first impulse was to leave Catron's problems for later. She already had the feeling of looking uphill at a huge snowball that was perched on the brink.

She pulled the envelope out of the box and was about to open it when she saw a civilian push himself out of one of the chairs in the foyer beyond the dispatch island.

"Undersheriff Guzman?" The man approached her, skirting Brent Sutherland's workstation and stopping by the electrically operated half gate that blocked access to the offices behind Dispatch. Neatly dressed in a dark business suit, he looked like a successful salesman who had had a bad night's sleep.

"Good morning, sir. How may I help you?"

He extended a hand, and his grip was perfunctory. "I'm Elliot Parker. I understand that my son's arraignment is this morning at nine?"

Estelle glanced at Sutherland, who nodded agreement. "Mike scheduled it," Sutherland added.

"Anyway, I'm here for that," Parker continued. "The sheriff was in here earlier, and was good enough to allow me to talk with my son. May I have a moment of your time? The sheriff suggested that I might talk to you."

The sheriff didn't suggest that to me, Estelle thought, but she was thoroughly used to Robert Torrez's ways. "It will have to be a brief moment, Mr. Parker." She had no trouble imagining what the abrupt sheriff had actually said.

"This is important, officer."

"I understand that you're concerned about your son, sir. But at the moment, there's nothing I can do about the schedule of the arraignment, or even about the fact that he's going to *be* arraigned." She saw the muscle of Parker's right cheek twitch.

"The others have all gone home. My son is still locked in that cell. Now I can understand you all being a little unsympathetic about this sort of thing, and no one wants to tolerate underage drinking, but—"

"It's not a question of sympathy," Estelle said evenly. "The others are all minors, Mr. Parker. They are under eighteen. For them, Juvenile Probation has jurisdiction. Your son is not underage. On top of that, there's more here than a question of underage drinking. Your son will be treated like any other adult."

"I think that we need to talk, young lady," Parker snapped.

Estelle stepped closer and rested her hand on the gate's polished wood. "Thank you for that thought, Mr. Parker. A forty-year-old mother of two always appreciates a compliment." She saw his eyes narrow a bit. "But at the moment, we have an active homicide investigation ongoing. Even if that were *not* the case, there isn't much that the sheriff or I can do for you until after your son's arraignment. Or even then, for that matter."

She tapped the edge of the manila envelope on the rail. "It's a matter for the district attorney now, not us."

"I assume you have an office?" Parker's tone was heavy with condescension, and Estelle did not reply, waiting for him to continue. "May we talk in private?"

Did you ask the sheriff if he had an office? she thought, but kept her tone civil. "Go ahead, sir. I'm listening." Parker looked across at Sutherland, who was doing a credible job of ignoring them.

For a moment Parker regarded Estelle, and she could hear his index finger tapping on the counter. "I spoke with my son," he said finally, as if that summed up the whole issue. When Estelle didn't reply, he added, "He tells me that the officer fired a shot from his weapon."

No question mark followed Parker's remark, and Estelle remained silent.

"Is that true?" he persisted.

"Like the rest of the incident, that is under investigation by both our department and the State Police."

"I want to know how this could happen."

"So do I."

"I should be able to talk with the officer," Parker said. "If what my son says is true, and I have no reason to doubt that it is, your officer's behavior put everyone in that parking lot in jeopardy."

"And that means that *you* should be the investigating officer?" Estelle snapped. "Is that what this all means? I don't think so."

Parker appeared to swell and Estelle watched the color wash up from his white shirt collar.

"Now look," he said, and then hesitated as he groped for words.

"Mr. Parker, unless there is something urgent that I

can help you with at this particular moment, I have other issues that I need to attend to. Your son's arraignment is at nine in the court chambers down the hall in the main building. I'm sure he'd appreciate you being there."

As if on cue, the door of the officers' workroom opened, and both Deputy Tom Pasquale and State Police officer Richard Black appeared. Black walked past them and nodded curtly at Parker. "Morning, sir."

Deputy Pasquale had a thick folder of paperwork in his hand, and paused at the dispatch counter. "Are you headed out to the pass?" he asked Estelle, and nodded politely but without any apparent interest at Parker, who appeared to deflate a little at the abrupt appearance of the two uniformed officers.

"Yes. I'm running behind a little," Estelle said.

"So all of this is just going to be swept under the carpet?" Parker said.

"No, sir," Estelle said, "I imagine it will be all over the front page of every newspaper that will carry the story. I'm sure it will be the lead story on *News at Five*. I'm sure it'll be the central topic of conversation for every group that gathers to discuss the behavior of today's kids, or the ineptitude of today's cops." She cocked her head, appraising Parker. "And you'll do your share, I'm sure."

His eyes narrowed still further. "And I'm not sure that I care for your attitude, young lady."

"Well, I tell you," Estelle said, "I'm tired, you're tired, and we're both asking for the impossible, sir. Go get yourself some breakfast, and take one matter at a time. Your son's arraignment is at nine. He'd appreciate your being there." She rapped the divider again with the folder. "Excuse me." Deputy Pasquale lingered near the door, and she nodded at him. "I'll be out in a couple of minutes, Tom."

Without waiting for a final parting shot from Elliot Parker, Estelle returned to her office and closed the door. Parker's reaction was predictable—a man grasping at something that might take the public spotlight off his son's behavior.

Settling into her chair, she opened the envelope and pulled out a sheaf of photocopied reports, along with a set of digital photographs that wiped Elliot Parker from her thoughts. Someone else had their own share of troubles, and Estelle was immediately curious about what tendrils might connect an incident in rural Catron County with her own border community.

The Catron County deputy's incident report listed the victim's name as John Doe. The death had occurred sometime Thursday afternoon, and had been discovered late in the day by a firewood contractor, Anthony Zamora. The preliminary report was handwritten in the investigating deputy's tight, angular script:

> Landowner Lucencio Zamora says that he gave permission to his brother Anthony and his crew to cut firewood on the Zamora ranch. Anthony Zamora states that he left the victim and another man alone to cut piñon and cedar in the woodlot near the ranch road off County 18-A.
>
> When he checked at approximately 4:15 p.m., Anthony Zamora discovered the victim dead, apparently as a result of bleeding to death from a chain-saw injury to his inside left thigh. It appeared that the victim had been limbing when the bar kicked back. The chain cut the victim across

the inside thigh on his left leg. It appears that the victim tried to stop the bleeding, but could not.

Anthony Zamora states that the second man was not in the area when he arrived, and might not have known about the accident. Mr. Zamora did not know the names of the two men, but states that he hired them in Reserve for day labor. He doesn't know where the other man went, but he likely hitched out of the area.

A search of the body shows no documentation; a scrap of spiral notebook paper with a phone number was also found in the dead man's jacket pocket.

Fidel Romero states that the men stopped at his store earlier in the day and inquired about work. He says that he believes the two were illegals, but didn't think much about it.

The incident report, signed by Deputy Albert Romero, included a series of photographs. Estelle read the report again. If deputy Albert and store owner Fidel Romero were related, that made life a little more interesting.

The photographs included one panoramic shot showing that when the gnarly piñon tree in question had been chain-sawed down, it had propped itself up on broken limb wood. Several other trees had been cut in the immediate area and the ground was a welter of boot-trapping slash. The bright scars of freshly cut limbs dotted the felled piñon trunk for a dozen feet, to a point where the tree trunk was suspended two feet above the ground by the remaining broken limbs.

A close-up view showed the stub of a dead limb low on the left side. The stub had been deeply nicked by the saw's chain, and a dark spatter of what could have been blood—there was too much for it to be bar oil—sprayed the bark and the ground nearby. The chain saw was still wedged upside down among the cut limbs, no doubt unmoved from where it had been flung.

Estelle shuffled the photos and looked hard at a third that showed the victim. He had crawled nearly a dozen feet, spraying the ground and himself with blood as he did so. Estelle grimaced, imagining the moments of panic. The young worker, perhaps twenty-five years old, had managed to prop himself up against a shaggy juniper. The wound in his leg, deep and ragged, would have been fatal in a few minutes at most. Blood loss must have been from a gusher, enough to render the victim immobile in seconds. By the time he had crawled even a few yards, he would have been dizzy and disoriented as his blood pressure plummeted. In a final slump, he had leaned back against the tree, both hands clutching his leg in a vain attempt to stop the pumping blood from his lacerated femoral artery.

"What a mess," Estelle whispered. Where had his partner been at that moment? Standing rooted in panic? Ready to faint at the sight of the spurting blood? Even if the second man had been on the scene with his wits about him, the situation would have been desperate. A tightly cinched belt might have worked to stem the tide, but the accident had happened so far from medical help that time was their enemy.

Other photos showed a faded yellow pickup truck fifty yards away, its bed a third filled with neatly stacked firewood. A gas can and a plastic quart bottle of oil rested on the tailgate, along with a small blue cooler and a second chain saw.

Estelle scanned the photos again. The other woodcutter had fled, but he had not run for help. He had not even made an anonymous phone call—if the two men had owned a cell phone, which was unlikely at best. The man had simply abandoned his dying companion. "Why would you do that?" Estelle wondered aloud. An accident was an accident. What did it matter if the pair had indeed been illegals? One woodcutter could have bundled the other injured man into the truck, and driven for help. Judging by what Estelle could see of the wound, a mad dash to the clinic in the nearest tiny village would have been futile. The injured man would have drained out long before they had driven the seventeen miles of rough roads to the nearest nurse-practitioner or physician's assistant. *But you didn't even try,* she thought.

Frowning, she leafed back to the photos of the tree and the offending limb. The saw would have been snarling full throttle as the young man touched the chain to the dead limb spar. The scene brought back memories of another incident to which Estelle had responded as a young deputy, when an older man had been building a stock fence south of Posadas. He'd been cutting railroad ties when the saw kicked and bit him savagely in the face, laying open cheek and jaw, shattering teeth, and coming a hair's breadth from the major arteries in the man's neck. He had managed to stagger into his mobile home, splashing blood over everything. That he was even able to dial 911, much less mumble a garbled message, had been remarkable.

In this case, the clear digital photo showed that the limb had been free of bark, the hard gray of seasoned piñon. The saw's flashing teeth had touched the wood, perhaps on the very tip of the saw's bar, and Estelle could imagine how the teeth had bitten deep and then kicked up and back. If the sawyer was standing astride the trunk, twisting with the saw to reach down awkwardly for the limb with his boots caught in the snarl of limbs on the ground, he was an easy target. It was a moment of in-attention, of carelessness, late in the afternoon after a full day of labor.

Estelle tapped the photos into a neat pile and sighed. From hopes and dreams, fueled by quick cash earnings and a pleasant day in the fragrant woods, to a moment of horror and total loss…not what the young man had had in mind when he and his friend had found their way across the border.

His friend. It wasn't hard to imagine the other wood-cutter fleeing. People panicked all the time. It was one thing to imagine heroism in the comfort of a living room chair, when no real threat actually loomed. When the moment came with all its ugly reality, there was no pre-dicting how people would react. In this case, the blood and gore hurled by the saw, the shriek of pain, the im-possible wound—all of that would have been enough to test the strongest nerves. Estelle suspected that the other cutter had run, too unnerved even to take the pickup truck. He had run out to the highway, run to hitch a ride, leaving his dying friend to be found by someone else.

"And now, the question is," Estelle said aloud, "why do we need to know about all this?"

A brief memo had been included with the photos, signed by Deputy Albert Romero, that requested a check of the telephone number found scribbled on the scrap of paper in the dead man's coat pocket.

Estelle frowned at the number, eyebrows arching up in surprise. Her mouth formed a silent *O* as she stared at the number, puzzled by its familiarity. The prefix indicated Regál, the tiny village just south of the pass that shared its name, a very long way from the piñons of Catron County.

She thumbed the Rolodex and stopped at a well-worn card. The phone number matched the one scrawled on the slip of paper recovered from the dead woodcutter's pocket.

TWELVE

COINCIDENCE MADE ESTELLE Reyes-Guzman uneasy. She had known the Contreras family for years—the elderly and crippled Emilio, who spent practically every waking moment working for the mission in Regál, Iglesia de Nuestra Señora; his wife, Betty, the energetic, bustling lady whose volunteer activism filled her days after a long career in the elementary classroom; even their three grown children, who returned infrequently to the little border village to celebrate the long string of birthdays and anniversaries.

But as Estelle drove south toward the pass, she considered the other odd pieces of this puzzle that had presented themselves. An unidentified man, odds strong that he was an illegal alien, had managed to lose control of a chain saw, which had then chewed him to death. His partner had vanished without lifting a finger to help the mortally injured man. All of this had happened 150 miles to the north, yet the sole documentation on the victim was a slip of paper with the telephone number of Emilio and Betty Contreras in Regál.

The radio and cell phone remained mercifully silent for the twenty minutes during which Estelle's car sped south on State 56 toward the looming mountain range that formed the southern border for most of Posadas County. During those twenty minutes, she relaxed back in the seat and let her mind roam through the possibilities.

If one were to dial the Contrerases' telephone number, odds were overwhelming that it would be Betty who answered. Her husband, 20 years older than Betty, was so lame that walking the 300 yards from home to the mission was a major penitence each day. Emilio did not belong to the twenty-first century. He and the little white mission continued on as he had for 88 years, and as it had for 219.

The mission had no electricity, no heating system other than the large potbellied stove that dominated the east wall. It certainly had no telephone. Emilio didn't carry a cell phone draped on his worn, hand-tooled leather belt. He needed no phone to keep in close contact with his God, with whom Emilio shared most waking moments of each day. If anyone else wanted to talk with him, well…they could meet him at the church, or pass a message to him through his good wife, Betty.

If a stranger carried the Contreras phone number in his pocket, then Betty Contreras would know why. That loose end was what the deputy in Catron County wanted tidied up, and was the sort of thing one county routinely asked of another.

Just before the beginning of the guardrail as the road started its long grade up the pass, Estelle saw the tracks cutting off to the left where the EMTs had pulled the ambulance onto the mining road the night before. Later this morning, the wrecker would unceremoniously bundle the smashed vehicle back up the rugged hillside. What information the little truck might hold needed to be gained before that happened, and Estelle knew that Deputy Jackie Taber, assigned to guard the site during the night, wouldn't waste any time. The deputy had a keen eye and would have made good use of the long hours during the night.

At one point as the highway swept through a long, graceful turn to the left, Estelle saw the wink of morning sun off vehicles parked down below on the mining road—more just an overgrown path than anything else. In another mile she passed the accident site, then using the turnout just beyond the Forest Service sign that announced the 8,012-foot elevation of the pass itself.

Pulling as far off the pavement as she could, she eased the county car in behind Jackie Taber's white Bronco.

"I'm coming up." The disembodied voice crackled out of Estelle's handheld radio.

"Take your time," Estelle replied.

"Tom and the sheriff are down below," Jackie said, and Estelle could hear the young woman's labored breathing.

"Not to hurry," Estelle said. She slipped the clip of a small digital camera on her belt, and as she got out of the car, she saw Jackie Taber reach the guardrail and pull herself over.

"Interesting stuff," the deputy said as she heaved a deep breath. "Let me show you." She retrieved a large sketch pad from the Bronco and spread it out on the hood of the truck. Her drawing of the accident site was from a raven's-eye view with the trees in perfect perspective from overhead. The measurements had been neatly penciled in.

"My first thought," Jackie said, "was that a little truck like that wouldn't be cookin' along too fast after climbing a mile-and-a-half grade…and the south side of the pass is the steeper one. But the skid marks say maybe sixty, even a little faster. The truck's a V-six, so that's possible. He sees the deer at the last minute," and the deputy traced the route with the eraser end of a pencil, "swerves, crosses the highway, *recrosses* the highway, and vaults over at that mound of dirt near the beginning of the guardrail." She pointed over Estelle's shoulder with the pencil. "Another foot or two, and he might have just bounced along the rail and never gone over at all." She shifted the drawing.

"First impact after the jump was right here, downslope just shy of eighteen feet. That hump of rocks and dirt launched him up a bit, but the truck kind of rolled. Like a barrel roll to the left? When we go down the hill you'll see this set of rocks. The marks are really clear. A nose-dive, an impact right there left fender first, and then the truck somersaulted. The driver rode that one out okay, but the hill's so steep that once the truck started to end-o, there was nothing to stop it. I'm counting five end-for-end flips. Maybe six. He came partially out of the cab on about number three, and all the way on four or maybe five."

Jackie shifted the drawing once more and touched her pencil to an artistically rendered set of rocks. "This is where the driver hit the first time after being thrown out through the passenger window. The truck crushed him up against the rocks right there. His right foot didn't come loose right away, which is why we found his shoe down by the truck. His body came to rest where we found him…. That's forty-one feet from the first bits of blood and cloth to where he ended up on his back."

"There's no evidence that he moved at all after that?"

The deputy shook her head and held both hands up as if in surrender. "Where he landed is where he stayed.

There's a scuff mark that would have been under his left heel. He drew his leg up maybe once or twice, and that's it. Just a reflex." She turned and surveyed the steep, rock-strewn slope behind them. "I didn't find anything until I started combing the hillside right after dawn, Estelle. The flags mark points of interest. Bobby and Tom are moving outward and down from where the victim ended up, seeing if they can find anything else."

"And these?" Estelle indicated the three small numbers drawn on the sketch.

"That's what I wanted to show you. I didn't want to leave 'em lying out in the weather, just in case." She opened the passenger door of the Bronco and in a moment appeared with a small cardboard box. Pulling out the first plastic evidence bag, she laid it on the hood. Estelle took it by the corner of the label. The beer can was crumpled, the sort of crush that a good grip on an empty aluminum can could easily produce.

"A good toss," Jackie said. "Eighty-one feet north-east from the truck, and fifty-six feet from the victim. All the other cans from the six-pack are accounted for. Four cans that would have been full had they not broken open in and around the truck itself, one with its zip-top popped upslope a couple dozen feet right in line with the wreckage path, and this one, way off to the side. Makes for an interesting scenario, don't you think?"

"The force of the truck crashing down the hill isn't going to throw an empty can more than eighty feet off to one side, perpendicular to the line of travel," Estelle said.

"I don't think so. But only fifty feet from the victim?"

The undersheriff scrutinized the drawing, then turned and stepped to the guardrail.

"Look right off to the left, there," Jackie said. "See

the little group of scrub oaks with the juniper in the mid-dle? That's where the can was, just beyond that, down in the rocks. If you step over this way, you can see the flagging."

"The other possibility is that it didn't come from the victim or his truck."

The deputy looked skeptical. "Same brand, a new can? If we check the beer residue inside, it probably still has its fizz."

"And it fits what Perrone says."

"You said last night that the victim had somehow aspirated beer into his lungs. How could he do that?"

"That's a good question. Perrone says a considerable quantity, in fact. At least into his left lung...the one that still worked."

"That's cold, if it happened the way I'm thinking," Jackie said. "One thing's for sure....Chris Marsh didn't toss a can fifty feet, not with his bones all mush." She cocked an arm and imitated a pitch. "Not a whole lot of arm to manage that throw, but not just a weenie toss, either. Not what you'd do with the ends of your broken bones grating together."

Estelle nodded. "What else?" She saw that Jackie was holding another plastic bag and she reached out for it. Inside, the plastic name tag's metal clip was bent as if ripped from the pocket flap. "'Barry Roberts,'" she read, and turned the tag this way and that. "Chris Marsh's face, by any other name. Global Productivity Systems?"

"Sounds nice, but GPS is fictitious, at least in this version," Jackie said. "I checked on my laptop, and can't find any reference to it."

"Where did you find the name tag?"

"Stuck between a couple of rocks right in line with

the wreck. It could have torn off when he was taking a somersault, but if somebody had wanted to recover it, it would have been hard to see in the dark. But I'm thinking that they would have wanted it." Estelle turned the tag this way and that. "Chris Marsh, what were you up to?" she said aloud.

"If what he was up to was down in Regál, it isn't going to be hard to find out," Jackie said. "I spent some more time with the truck, Estelle. I'd be willing to bet that it had magnetic signs on the doors. You can see the marks where they used to be. Want to make bets on what they said?"

Estelle held out the name tag to the deputy. "We'll want to check Marsh's shirt pocket. If he was wearing this, there'll be some tearing of the threads where this was ripped away. We want to make sure of that."

"That's easy enough."

"And you said three things...the marks on the doors?"

"In part," Jackie said. "I went over that truck with everything but a microscope. There's nothing in it."

"Just the beer cans."

"That's true. But nothing else, Estelle. And I mean *nothing* that would do us any good." She nestled the evidence bags back in her briefcase and laid it on top of her sketch pad. "If Global was a real company, I'm thinking that I'd find a cab full of paperwork, right? I mean, those electronic delivery log thingies that they carry where you sign for a package? Nothing like that. No other packages. No paperwork. I mean, *nothing*. And nothing in the back. The camper shell was locked, but torn to pieces by the crash. If there'd been packages in the rear, they'd be spread all over the hillside. Nothing. Just a wrecked truck, some beer cans, and a dead driver."

Estelle stood quietly, looking down the slope. "One of two things, Jackie, and I don't like either one. If the truck was empty when it went over, what was Marsh up to? Perrone is willing to bet someone else was involved, and it looks as if that somebody wanted him really, really dead," she said finally. "And somebody wanted to erase any evidence of what he'd been up to. That opens the door for us."

"Stupid, stupid," Jackie said. "The killer scrambles down the hill after the wreck, and finds this Marsh guy lyin' in the rocks, gasping like a dying fish. It should be obvious that he isn't going to get up and walk out for help. He's too busted up to even use a cell phone, assuming he had one. Why didn't the second guy just leave? I can see clearing out the truck of anything incriminating. But why murder a man who's obviously toast anyway?"

"If Marsh was moaning and whimpering for help, the killer would want to shut him up. Drowning's pretty quiet, especially when the victim's too broken up to move in protest."

The deputy made a face. "I want to meet this guy," she said.

"Another thing is really interesting," Estelle said. "The killer wasn't riding with Marsh. That means he was in another vehicle, or waiting for him somewhere— but close enough that he would know about the wreck." She looked at Jackie. "That's bizarre."

"It is that." She looked down the hill thoughtfully. "One thing is easy," she said finally. "Somebody in Regál knows what Chris Marsh was doing the night he was killed…unless he was just plain lost. Maybe he took a wrong turn somewhere."

"If he did that, he wasn't much good at reading road

signs," Jackie said. "Anything else you want me to do this morning?"

"Take a break," Estelle said. "And keep thinking. We'll have someone work on finding Marsh's family. That might turn something."

"You want me to work on that?"

"No," Estelle laughed. "I want you off-duty for a while. It'd be nice to have at least one fresh face around the joint if things go from bad to worse."

THIRTEEN

ANOTHER TWO HOURS on the hillside produced nothing beyond various bits of debris that had once been a Chevrolet pickup truck and its lone occupant. The truck itself was notable for what it did not contain—any clue as to what cargo it had carried, or what business had prompted Christopher Marsh to dress and drive like a package delivery agent.

Shortly before ten that Saturday morning, Estelle's phone demanded attention. She sat down on a large rock just above the truck wreckage and saw that the call was from Deputy Tony Abeyta.

"What did you find out, Tony?"

"Number one, Chris Marsh was a student at the state university in Las Cruces for three years. He dropped out last year with enough credits to be a sophomore. Anyway, I found out that his parents live in Brookhaven, New York. They're not real interested in coming out, either."

"Really. How touching."

"That's for sure. They said to cremate the body and if we wanted to, we could send the ashes back to them."

"If *we* wanted to?" Estelle asked. "What do *they* want?"

"It didn't sound like they gave a shit one way or another. They claim that they haven't heard from their son since May of last year, after he got himself arrested by the campus police for disorderly conduct. I would guess that they weren't on the best of terms before that, either. I haven't found out yet what that incident was, but he left school shortly after that."

"And that's when the folks wrote him off?"

"Apparently that was the last straw, yes. His dad said that the kid could talk himself out of anything. That's when he said, 'He's made his bed, now he can lie in it.' I told him that it wasn't a question of that—that his son had been *killed*. I almost said the bed he was lyin' in was a pile of rocks, but I didn't."

"All kinds," Estelle said. A meeting between the Marshes and Elliot Parker would be interesting, she thought.

"I told them that you might be calling later today. But I didn't hear any weeping in the background, so I don't hold out much hope that they're going to be of any help. I got the impression that they'd had about all the expense and heartache with this kid that they could stomach."

"That happens, Tony. What else?"

"Not much. I talked to one of the folks in the Dean's Office at the college. She happened to be in catching up on some things on a Saturday morning. I didn't get too far. Marsh didn't make much of an impression on anyone. She gave me the dean's home phone, but no answer. Then I got ahold of Grunt, and he's going to check out Marsh's trailer for us." Las Cruces detective Guenther "Grunt" Nilson wouldn't miss much, Estelle knew.

"The address came back as a trailer over on the southeast side. Grunt says it's a little mobile home park with maybe twenty trailer spaces. They're going to find out who Marsh was living with."

"Did you mention to Nilson that we have other things going on beyond just an MVA?" Estelle asked.

"I told him everything I knew. I didn't want the cops down there walking into something unawares. They're being careful."

"Good man. If you think it would pay off, you might go ahead and drive over there. I'd like to know what you think. I'm certain that there was someone else here with Marsh. Someone wanted to make sure that he never made it out alive after the crash, and then cleaned up afterward. Somebody, sometime, had to have seen Chris Marsh hanging out with a buddy, girlfriend, live-in, or whatever."

"I already told Grunt that I'd probably be down."

"You might give Perrone a call and take along any updates he has."

"Ten-four."

"Keep us posted." She folded the phone and sat quietly for a moment, gazing down past the truck. The sun bounced off the rocks, warm and peaceful, the gray, soggy mist of the night before just faint wisps now through the trees across the canyon. Bob Torrez and Tom Pasquale were working around the truck, and the sheriff stopped, looking up the slope toward her. He raised his voice just enough that it carried upward across the hundred feet of rocks that separated them.

"You seen all you need to see on this thing?" the sheriff asked.

"I think so," Estelle said, funneling her mouth with both hands so she wouldn't have to shout.

"We want to see what's underneath," Torrez said, and made a balling motion with both hands. "Stubby's on his way out."

The cable from Stub Moore's huge wrecker would ball up the battered truck worse than it already was during the drag up the hill. But between herself and Linda Real, the scene had been photographed and rephotographed from every conceivable angle.

"I'm going to take a few minutes and head down to Regál," Estelle said.

"You looked at that envelope of stuff from Catron?"

"Yes, I did. The phone number is Betty's."

"Thought so. You might stop and talk with her. Busy-body like that sees everything. And what the hell...she might have seen Marsh around town. Or his truck. That's what I'm thinkin'."

Maybe. Maybe not, Estelle thought as she made her way back up the slope. Sometimes the small town legend about everyone knowing everyone else's business was just that: legend. If it was more convenient *not* to know, then the ignorance could be legendary in itself.

Her cell phone rang just as she was reaching out to grab the guardrail, and she ignored the phone until she had stepped back onto level ground, the stretch over the railing making the muscles in her right side twang.

"Guzman."

"Are we having fun yet?" Bill Gastner asked.

"You bet," she replied. "What's up, *padrino*?"

"Well, I just dropped Madelyn Bolles off at Rachel's," he said, referring to Rachel Melvin's B and B on 10th Street in Posadas. "Interesting morning."

For a moment Estelle frowned, trying to remember who Madelyn Bolles might be. Catching the hesitation of Estelle's puzzlement, Gastner added, "She of the magazine article, sweetheart. The lady who wants to interview everyone in Posadas County, but in particular, you."

"Ah." Estelle started the walk back toward her car, glancing at her watch as she did so. "She's early. She cornered you, did she?" The undersheriff scrutinized the day-date window of her watch. "I was about to say that we didn't expect her until Saturday, but this *is* Saturday, isn't it."

"Indeed it is," Gastner said. "Anyway, it was interesting. We took a little tour of the county while we talked. She had planned to talk with Leona this morning, but then she heard about what's going on down there, and decided that this would be a stellar time to see you in action. She stopped in and talked with Dispatch."

"I see."

"Yeah, well. She wanted to freshen up a little and rummage through all the notes I gave her. She said she'd make contact with you some time today. I just thought I'd give you a heads-up. Be on the lookout sort of thing. She's driving a bright red rental car. A Buick LaCrosse, I think."

"Did she seem like an okay kind of person?"

Gastner laughed. "I don't know what I was expecting, but 'tweren't her," he said. "She's right behind me on that slippery slope of impending geezerhood. That kinda surprised me. But listen, I don't want to say too much. You'll make up your own mind. I just wanted to pass along a heads-up."

"I appreciate that. I'm headed to Regál at the moment. I need to talk with Betty."

Gastner didn't ask, *About what?* "Give her my regards, please. Anything you want or need me to do?"

"You could come over for dinner tonight. Irma was planning to make enchiladas the last I heard."

"Oh, gosh, no thanks," Gastner said. "I had my heart set on a baloney sandwich and some stale potato chips. What time?"

"You know how that always goes, sir. Irma said that she was going to serve whoever shows up at six *exactamente, ni un momento más o menos.*"

"I'll hold her to it," the old man chuckled. "There would be some benefits to being the only one to show up, you know."

"You're the rock around which we all orbit," Estelle said soberly, and that prompted a loud guffaw.

"I love it," he said. "Be careful."

She folded up the phone and slipped it in her pocket as she reached her sedan. For a few minutes she sat in the car, thumbing through her notes. She looked at the slip of paper that included the Contrerases' home phone number. *How odd, all these little connections*, she thought.

FOURTEEN

A TELEPHONE CALL to Betty Contreras—to the number on
the slip of paper—would have been simple enough, but
Estelle held off. What Betty's connection might be with
a couple of illegal alien woodcutters was just a curiosity
at the moment, a problem more for the Catron County
authorities than Estelle.

More important was tracking the movements of
Christopher Marsh before the violent crash on Regál
Pass. If anyone had seen the white Chevy pickup truck
cruising the dirt lanes of Regál, it would be Betty. Maybe
she had even spoken to Chris Marsh, fresh and neatly
pressed in his deliveryman's garb.

Estelle drove south from Regál Pass, struck as always
by the view of the dry, bleak country of northern Mexico. Forty miles in the distance, she could see the blue
hump of the mesa that loomed on the outskirts of Tres
Santos, the tiny village where she had spent the first
sixteen years of her life. *What a difference forty miles
made,* she thought.

Or even one mile. Sun winked off the razor-wire-
topped border fence where it cut the desert just south of
the graveled parking lot of Iglesia de Nuestra Señora,
the little mission that overlooked the village. Pavement
on the U.S. side of the fence turned abruptly into dirt
in Mexico.

Estelle could remember her first adventure across

that line in the dust. She had been but six years old, the fence was no more than a strand or two of barbed wire, and the Border Patrol had business elsewhere. For those who felt threatened, the new fence was a grand thing, she reflected—and it had made a lot of money for some well-connected contractor.

On a map, the border between the two countries was a straight line, but the San Cristóbal Mountains ignored that. They formed a loose, open arc, the west and east ends dipping into Mexico while the center cradled Regál.

Contractors hadn't extended the border fence any farther than necessary into the rugged mountains to the east and west. The fence made a good show across the port of entry and a few hundred yards of open prairie after that, then disappeared into the hills and rocks.

The system worked all right, since Regál lay on no major north–south route for travelers. Illegal aliens would find no difficulty in avoiding the section of border fence. They could skirt the ends of the fence all right, but then they'd spend days scrambling up the towering, crumbling granite face of the San Cristóbals. And then what? If the travelers didn't die of exposure or snakebite, a view from the peak's summit would reveal another long, dangerous trek down the back side of the mountains—to the open, equally desolate prairie.

As the county car eased down the highway into the village, Estelle saw a familiar figure leave Iglesia de Nuestra Señora, bustling across the parking lot. Betty Contreras carried a small wicker basket, and Estelle guessed that it had contained lunch for Emilio. The undersheriff slowed, lowering the driver's side window. Oncoming traffic forced her to wait before swinging into the church parking lot. It was a Border Patrol vehicle, and as he passed, Estelle raised a hand in salute. Nothing but a hard stare greeted her in return, the young officer looking first at her and then across at Betty, who fluttered her fingers at him.

"Good afternoon, young lady." Betty reached out and rested a free hand against the roof of the patrol car, bending down to look at Estelle.

"How are you and Emilio doing, Betty?" Estelle asked.

"Oh, we're fine. I just fed and watered *mi esposo*, and now it's time for us." She bent down a little farther, looking hard at Estelle. "You look as if you've been up most of the night."

"Actually, not *most*," Estelle replied. "It's just that we have about eighteen different things going on right now, and I'm not sure I feel like doing any of them."

"Oh, *si*. I know how that goes." She watched as Estelle stretched a bit, pushing against the constraints of the shoulder harness. "How about a cup of tea? That's always a good place to start."

"I'd like that." She reached across the car and slid her small briefcase off the seat, balancing it on what remained of the center console. "Jump in."

The ride was a scant two hundred yards, but Betty dutifully fumbled with the seat belt harness. "Don't want to get a ticket," she quipped.

"Speaking of which, do you know that officer who just went by?" The undersheriff pointed after the government SUV, now taking the long ascent up the pass.

"No, I don't. Too many now to keep track of. We just ignore 'em, which isn't the polite thing to do, of course. But they don't smile much. Not what I'd call exactly neighborly."

"Well, it's a tough time for them."

"I suppose. But it's all a problem of their own making. That's my take on it, anyway. I'd like to see them just peel that grand fence down and do away with the border."

"Ay, caramba," Estelle said with amusement. "Wouldn't *that* be interesting." She slowed the car as they bumped off the pavement and swung onto Sanchez Lane, the only thoroughfare in Regál actually wide enough to pass by another vehicle without swinging into the ditch.

"You can park right behind mine," Betty said. Estelle pulled in behind the blue Toyota, snugging up close so that the rear end of the patrol car didn't project out into the narrow lane. Betty watched as the undersheriff pulled the mike off the clip.

"PCS, three-ten is ten-six, Contreras residence in Regál."

"Three-ten, ten-four." Dispatcher Gayle Torrez sounded preoccupied.

"This is an interesting office you have here," Betty said, taking in the computer terminal, the stack of radios, the shotgun, the briefcase…even a Stetson with rain cover and a black baseball cap hooked on the security grill behind the seats.

"So homey, isn't it," Estelle laughed. "How's Emilio getting along these days? I haven't seen him since before Christmas."

"Each day is a source of joy for him," Betty said. She struggled out of the low-slung car. "It's really that simple. Aches and pains don't mean a thing. Not to him. Remind me to show you a photograph when we get inside."

Estelle snapped open her briefcase and pulled the manila envelope out, then followed Betty inside the small house, past a porch littered with children's toys, bikes, and a row of folding chairs stacked neatly against one wall.

"Grandchildren," Betty said as she pushed open the door.

The thick adobe walls muffled the sound, and Estelle felt the atmosphere close in around her. The paint scheme was white with turquoise trim, the white so bright it appeared self-illuminated. A flotilla of inexpensive Mexican rugs protected the floor's polish. Tiny windows, still reflecting the heritage when windows were gun ports first and sources of light and air only secondarily, were all lace curtained and closed.

"Come on into the kitchen," Betty said. "Let's see what goodies I can scare up."

Just before the doorway, they passed a deep *nicho* where a crowded collection of framed photos was displayed. Estelle paused.

"Nineteen is the answer," Betty called. "That's the grand total of grandchildren...so far. And six greatgrandchildren. Sometimes when everyone is here visiting, I'm sure I'll go nutzo. That's why I take so many walks." A clank and clatter were followed by the sound of running water. "Plain tea is your favorite, as I remember?"

"It is. Thank you." Estelle stepped into the kitchen, and Betty saw the envelope for the first time.

"Whatcha got?"

"I wanted to show you a photo, if you'd be willing."

"Is this one of those ghastly things?"

"Well, sort of. Yes." Estelle pulled out the eight-by-ten of Christopher Marsh, not such a bad portrait after all, considering how a tumbling truck had rearranged his body parts.

"Oh, yuck," Betty said, sounding exactly like the elementary school teacher that she had been for thirty years. "Is this the driver of that little truck that crashed up on the pass? I heard about that."

"Yes. His name is Christopher Marsh."

"Oh my. So young, too."

"Twenty-one."

"He wasn't from around Posadas, was he?"

"We think Las Cruces."

Betty took one last look, grimaced, and handed the photo back to Estelle. "Do we know what happened yet?"

"It appears that he swerved to avoid a deer, Betty."

"They need a fence, or *something*, along that stretch of highway. I mean, it's just *lethal*. I've come close to collecting Bambi any number of times…and not always when I'm in a car."

Estelle drew out another photo, this one of the truck. She slid it across the table. "Had you seen this vehicle around the village in the past few days?"

Betty took the photo and scrutinized it carefully. "Is this… Well, no, it's hard to tell…. This looks like it might belong to one of those parcel delivery outfits."

Their eyes met and Estelle let Betty mull over what she had said. It took a moment to ascertain that the crushed vehicle in the photo *was* a truck, rather than a car or SUV, yet something had jarred Betty's memory.

"It's a Chevy S-ten pickup," Estelle said. "This torn metal here was a matching white camper shell. Do you recall seeing a truck like that around the village in the past day or two?"

"I think so." Betty bent forward, leaning on her clasped hands, looking hard at the photograph that rested on the table in front of her. "They're around all the time, you know. More often UPS, though. Who drives these little white ones? Is that FedEx?"

"Not in this case," Estelle said.

"What's the other one? I'm trying to recall. And yes, I think I saw him." She tapped the picture. "I'm quite sure… I can't be positive, of course…that this might be the truck that came with Joe and Lucinda's sweepstakes prize."

FIFTEEN

"Joe and Lucinda Baca?" the undersheriff asked. "You mean when they won the state lottery?"

"Oh, that's ancient history," Betty said. "My goodness, when was that, in November? No…they won this sweepstakes thing just a bit ago. In fact, they won twice, of all things. And they weren't the only ones." She got up as the teakettle started to whistle. "I have some of that Chinese white pear tea," she said. "How does that sound?"

"Wonderful."

After selecting a pair of thin porcelain mugs from a corner cabinet, the older woman concentrated on serving the tea. Estelle watched her, enjoying the fragrance that swept up from the boiling water.

"Now, I have chocolate-chip, and I have butter pecan sandies, and I have fresh banana bread." The list was presented not as a choice but as a fait accompli, and Estelle watched with amusement as Betty loaded a Mexican stoneware platter with the baked goodies. Small wonder that Bill Gastner thought so highly of the Contrerases.

"I didn't hear about this latest sweepstakes," Estelle said. *Curious for Frank Dayan to miss that one,* she thought.

"Oh my, we've had a run, you know. Such good fortune. Twice now. I think someone's computer has a glitch. That's *my* theory, but of course I keep that to myself. Have a cookie."

"And the truck? How was that involved?"

"Oh, the truck. Well, it's my understanding that to collect the sweepstakes check, there's a small charge, sort of like COD? I know that Serafina Roybal won a small amount, even before Joe and Lucinda did. It's some sweepstakes from Canada. Calgary, I think. But *she* won a little bit, and then won *again*. See, that's why I think that there's a computer glitch of some sort."

"So she won twice as well?" Estelle asked. She knew Serafina Roybal even better than she knew Betty, although she saw the elderly woman less frequently. Serafina, now a wrinkled, stooped widow, had taken the sixteen-year-old Estelle Reyes under her wing at Posadas High School, easing the girl's transition into American culture in speech and drama classes and smoothing and extending her language skills in Spanish.

"She did indeed," Betty said. "When the prize check comes, you have to pay the duty, and the taxes, and there's something else...." She fell silent, gazing at the pile of goodies. "What did Serafina tell me, now." She brightened. "Ah...the exchange rate. That was it. Because the sweepstakes originates in Canada." She held up both hands. "You have to pay the piper," she added.

"She... Serafina...paid who, then?"

"Well, she paid via the delivery company. That's how she knew that it was legitimate, you see."

No, I don't see, Estelle wanted to say. "Like if you order something COD, you pay the driver?"

"Yes. That's exactly right. They have those electronic pad gadgets that you sign with the stylus?" Betty made a writing motion over her left palm. "And I suppose that's part of the fee, too."

"Do you know how much she paid?"

"I have no idea. It wasn't all that much. But for it to happen *twice,* and within the space of just a couple of weeks...that's what makes me think someone's computer is all jazzed up."

"You were saying that Joe and Lucinda won. They entered the same sweepstakes?"

"Yes," Betty said, looking skeptical. "And *that's* what *really* made me think someone better check their software. They had already won the state thing, and wasn't that something?"

"I heard about that one," Estelle agreed. Frank Dayan had heard about it as well, since the publicity that fell on state winners' heads was automatic. "I don't remember how much it was for."

"One hundred and sixty thousand dollars," Betty said with satisfaction. "One more number and they would have been millionaires. Just imagine that." She took a bite of a chocolate-chip cookie. "Not that one hundred and sixty thousand is something to sneeze at. I think that they collected a check for about one thirty something after taxes were taken out."

"And then they won the Canadian game, too?"

"Twice. Just like Serafina. When that delivery service brought the first check, the driver told them that it wasn't unusual for someone to win more than once. Serafina told me that. Apparently, once a number tricks the computer, then it's more apt to do it again. That's how he explained it."

And how would a delivery driver know that, Estelle

thought. "So they paid him some amount of money, and collected their winnings?"

"It's—" Betty stopped, staring down into her tea, trying to stir the memory. "Oh, you'd have to ask them. It seems to me that Lucinda told me that they had to pay the percentage, but I can't remember the amount."

"They wrote a check for that amount, then? Some percentage of the prize?"

"Yes. That's the way *I* understand it, but this is all secondhand, and I may just have *everything* all tied in a knot. I *think* that they paid the delivery service, just like a COD, and then they received their check. Right then and there. And sure enough. Twice. I wanted to ask Lucinda how much she and Joe won the second time, but I decided not to be a busybody." She saw the ghost of a smile twitch the corners of Estelle's mouth. "I know, I know," she laughed. "But it was a *lot* more the second time."

"How long ago was this?"

"Well, just a few days. I mean, the check was supposed to arrive like last Monday or some such? There was some holdup, and then I think it actually ended up coming this week sometime. Maybe Tuesday or Wednesday. This past Wednesday?"

"Such fortune," Estelle said. She leaned back in her chair and surveyed the low-ceilinged kitchen. "I wonder how they found out that they'd won?"

"Some notification came in the mail, I think." Betty shrugged. "You know how those things are always popping up. Most of the time it's junk. But not this time. It's got the rest of us checking our mail a whole lot more carefully, let me tell you."

"And not the Nigerian scam thing," Estelle observed.

"Oh, no," Betty said quickly. "The winnings are very,

very real. You just ask Serafina or Lucinda, Estelle. There's no complaint from *them*. It isn't one of those scams where they talk you into sending your money away in the hopes of winning some big super-pot. No, no." She made a seesaw motion with both hands. "You pay a little bit to cover taxes and the Canadian exchange rate, and then the Post Office hands you your check. That's how I understand it."

"Not the Post Office, though."

"Well, no. It's one of the parcel services. But the same idea. How about some more tea?"

"That would be wonderful." She didn't say that the aroma of fresh tea might mask the thick stench of rotting fish. A small window of possibility opened in her mind. There might be good reason why someone would rifle through the wreckage of the crashed truck—even Christopher Marsh's pockets. Someone knew exactly what to look for.

From there it was a simple step to understanding why that same person might want to make sure that young Mr. Marsh would be in no condition to talk to rescuers. In all likelihood, the wreck, an unlucky turn of events, had prompted this particular falling-out among thieves.

When Betty Contreras was once more seated, Estelle reached out and rested her hand on the manila envelope once more. "I need to ask a favor," she said.

"Anything. You know that."

Estelle opened the envelope and drew out the photo of the young woodcutter. He appeared to be sleeping, leaning against the juniper, eyes not quite closed. His face drew the first glance, and it was only a second look that took in the ocean of blood that had pumped from his torn leg and soaked his trousers, his clutching hands, and the ground where he sat.

"I need to know about this young man," Estelle said quietly, and handed the photo to Betty.

A series of emotions slipped across Betty Contreras' face, preceded by a little backward jerk of her head that spoke as clearly as words.

While Betty examined the picture, and recoiled with revulsion when she finally saw the blood and realized that in all likelihood the young man *wasn't* asleep, Estelle drew out a photocopy of the little note that had been found in his pocket. She slid the paper across to Betty.

"This was a woodcutting accident up north, outside of Reserve," Estelle said. "The investigating deputies found this little folded scrap of paper in the victim's pocket."

Betty looked at the paper and then at Estelle. "That's our phone number," she said.

"Yes. It is."

"Why would he have our phone number?" Her question didn't sound altogether convincing.

"That's what we're wondering," Estelle said. She watched Betty's face as the older woman examined the photo.

"Was he working alone?" She laid the picture down thoughtfully. "But of course he wouldn't be. I mean, I assume someone had to have gone for help when this happened. Up by Reserve, you say?"

"Between Reserve and Quemado. They were working on a firewood contract for a rancher up that way."

"The poor boy," Betty murmured. "No, I don't know him. And I can't explain the number."

"Well," Estelle said, "I told the investigators up north

that I'd ask. If you recall something, give me a buzz, will you?"

"Most assuredly."

"And maybe Emilio would know," Estelle added.

"I doubt that," Betty said. "But you're welcome to ask him. You know right where he is."

"That's not his writing, though," Estelle said, picking up the photocopy of the note.

"No. If Emilio had written it, it would look like something from one of those illuminated medieval manuscripts. He has the most beautiful penmanship."

"I remember that he does," Estelle said. "By the way, do you happen to have Joe and Lucinda's number? I'd like to chat with them, but I don't want to just barge in."

"Surely I do." Betty rose, jotted down a number, peeled off the Post-it note, and handed it to Estelle. Her flowing schoolteacher's script favored elegantly swooping curves on the 8s and bold, horizontal strikes for the tops of the 5s, nothing like the choppy block letters on the woodcutter's note. *A perfect match would have been convenient,* Estelle thought. "It's not mine, is it," Betty asked, and Estelle glanced up quickly at her, intrigued at the odd tone in her voice. "The handwriting, I mean."

"No, it's not. I'm just wondering who would have given your telephone number to a woodcutter working one hundred and fifty miles away."

"Maybe someone wrote down a number incorrectly. Our prefix here is so much like so many others. And the last four digits—the eight-four-eight-five—that could be misprinted a dozen ways, too."

"You're right about that." Estelle looked at the wall clock and sighed. "I need to run."

"Take some goodies along for those two boys of

yours," Betty said, and she didn't wait for a response. Collecting a small tin from one of the bottom cupboards, she filled it quickly with a generous collection. "Oh... and I have a picture for you," she said as she handed the tin to Estelle. "I meant to give it to you *months* ago, and it kept slipping my mind." She held up a hand like a tour guide demanding attention, and sailed off into the living room.

A moment's rummaging through a small album by the fireplace and she found the five-by-seven print. She held it fondly, then extended it to Estelle. "I took this of the altar after Emilio finished that night." She didn't bother to explain what "that night" was, and didn't need to. Estelle felt a stab of gratitude mixed with an odd, deep sadness. Centered among a sea of short, white candles on the altar was a family photo—*her family*. The portrait included her and Francis, with the two boys perched on their laps.

"Teresa loaned me that photo," Betty whispered. "Our prayers were all with you that day."

Betty didn't need to explain when *that day* was. "I appreciate that, Betty," Estelle said, and started to hand the photograph back.

"No, you keep it," Betty said. "You keep that." She patted Estelle's arm affectionately. "You and your husband have done a lot for this community. It's only natural that they should hold you in their prayers when something like this happens."

Estelle slipped the photo in the manila envelope, along with the photos of two other people who might have benefited from a few kind thoughts.

SIXTEEN

JOE AND LUCINDA Baca's home was another quarter mile east, and to reach it required a circuitous route through the village, finally reaching a fork in the two-track a quarter mile beyond the abandoned adobe that had once belonged to Joe's late brother. The lane then wound through an old apple orchard much in need of pruning, and forked again.

Estelle slowed the county car, steering onto the left shoulder to avoid the apple limbs that hung over the narrow lane. A large stump marked another turn, the wood scarred barkless from the dozens of times that a bumper had nicked it during the driver's careless or inebriated moments.

The right-hand trail led to Joe and Lucinda's. A portion of their home dated back to the early 1930s, when Joe's father had built a two-room adobe and stone dwelling, its back nestled into a gathering of car-sized boulders that he hoped had finished their tumble down the mountain. Estelle remembered tales about her great-uncle Reuben and Joe as they laid up stones for the fireplace— one batch of mortar, then a wine break. Another batch and beer. That the fireplace finished up more or less vertical and plumb was a testimony to dumb luck.

As the family grew, so did the home. Now, with Joe Baca having already celebrated his seventieth birthday, the place was a rambling ten-room adobe with attached garage and a scattering of outbuildings.

Estelle pulled in behind Joe's pickup and once more keyed the radio.

"PCS, three-ten is ten-six at Joe Baca's in Regál."

"Ten-four, three-ten. Be advised that you have a visitor here in the office," Gayle Torrez said.

Estelle pulled out her phone and touched the auto-dial for Dispatch.

"Who have we got?" she asked when Gayle picked up the phone.

"The lady from the magazine is here," Gayle said. "Madelyn Bolles?"

"It's going to be a while," Estelle said. "I have some loose ends to tie up down here in Regál, and then I'll be back up."

"Just a sec." Gayle didn't bother covering the mouthpiece of her headset, and Estelle could hear her explaining the situation to Ms. Bolles. The discussion continued for a moment, and then Gayle said, "Sorry about that, Estelle. She wants to know if she can meet you in Regál somewhere. She suggests at the mission."

"That's fine. I don't know how long I'll be. Is she still driving the red Buick rental?"

Gayle relayed the question, and the response in the background sounded amused. "She says yes."

"Then I'll keep a lookout for her. It's a pretty small world down here. She shouldn't be hard to find."

Estelle realized that Joe Baca was standing on the front porch of his home, watching her with interest. She waved a greeting. "Oh," Gayle said. "Bobby is back in from the accident site. He said that he wanted to talk with you later today about Deputy Collins."

"We need to do that," Estelle replied.

"I think he's settled down a little," Gayle said. "Bobby, that is."

"I hope so. I'll be back in a little bit," Estelle said. She put the phone away and unbuckled from her office.

"Good afternoon, Joe," she called as she got out of the car.

"Buenas tardes, hija," Baca replied, and stiffly held up a hand as if his shoulder joint was frozen. "How come you don't come around anymore?"

"Here I am," Estelle said, and stretched out a hand to the old man. His grip was warm and light, and she could feel the individual bones in his hand. "We've been so busy that sometimes I don't know which way is up."

He looked at her askance, assessing her from head to toe. "You came out of it okay, then." Joe made it sound as if *it* had been only the week before, not ten months.

"Yes. I'm fine."

He grunted something unintelligible and shook his head. "Nobody," and he accented each syllable carefully, "is fine after something like that, *hija*."

"I was lucky."

"Yes, you were. Very lucky. I saw you stop at Emilio's place just now." He turned, moving toward an old wicker chair. He didn't sit down but rested a hand on it. "I wondered if you were going to stop by."

"Sure," Estelle said.

"You want to sit down? Let's go inside. It's chilly out here."

He turned toward the door. "I thought maybe it would freeze last night. Maybe this year I'll have some peaches."

"They look fine. It's way early yet."

"We'll see." He shuffled inside, more like a man of ninety than someone two decades younger. "Lucinda isn't here just now, *hija*. She had to go to town. Maybe she'll be back before you have to go."

"I'd like to see her," Estelle said.

"There was an accident on the highway last night, I hear. Up on the pass."

"A bad one, Joe."

"Somebody got killed?"

"A young man from Las Cruces. His truck hit a deer and somersaulted over the guardrail just north of the pass."

Joe waved at the living room, as dark and gloomy as Betty Contreras' was light and cheerful. The walls had been plastered a generation or two ago, and then painted a bright green that had faded to hideous. Various magazine pictures of Christ, the Virgin, and the various apostles had been framed and hung here and there. A huge photographic print of the Grand Tetons hung over the TV set.

"You want some cider?"

"No thanks, Joe. Betty wouldn't let me go without tea and cookies."

"She's a good cook," he said, somehow managing to imply that Lucinda wasn't.

Estelle drew one of the photos of Chris Marsh out of the envelope. "*Con permiso,* I want to show you this, Joe," she said. "This is the young man who was killed up on the pass." He took the photo and moved toward one of the windows.

"Ah, *por Dios,*" he whispered.

"You know him, then?"

"He drives for that company," Joe said. "You know."

"The package delivery company, you mean?"

"Yes. He's stopped here before. We saw him this past week." He looked up at Estelle. "He brought the checks."

"The checks?"

"Lucinda won one of those sweepstakes things," Joe said. "In fact, she won twice. Quite the thing, you know."

"Do you recall his name, Joe?"

"No. He had a name tag, but without my glasses…"

"What was he driving, do you remember?"

"Sure I remember. A little white truck. A Chevy, I think. It had one of those camper shells on the back. White, too. A nice little rig."

"Any lettering on it?"

"What do you mean, 'lettering'?" He handed the photo back to Estelle.

"Like the company name. The logo. Something like that."

"The name of the company was on the door," Joe replied. "I'm pretty sure about that."

"Do you remember what the name was?"

"Something 'Global.' That's all. I didn't pay attention. I know it wasn't UPS or anything like that. Not a big van. Just a little truck. That boy had on a uniform with a name tag on the pocket. I remember that. And he had one of those fancy gadgets that you sign. That new stuff. No paper."

"And you say that he gave you a check?"

"He did," Joe said emphatically. "Both times."

"But you gave him a check as well? Do I understand that correctly?"

He nodded. "That's the way it works. The cashier's check that we gave him…he said it was for the taxes and the…what do you call it now…the exchange rate." He moved painfully to one of the chairs and sat down with a popping of joints. "When did the accident happen? Last night?"

"We don't think so, Joe. We're thinking maybe Wednesday or Thursday. We just found him last night."

"I'm surprised that he was ever found, going down in that country."

"So am I, Joe. You're sure this is the same young man, then?"

"Oh, yes."

"When did he drop off the last check?"

"You know, I think it was Wednesday right after dinner." Joe's face lit up a little at the recollection. "That's what it was. I remember him apologizing for being so late, but he said that he'd had a really busy delivery schedule, and that he'd also had some trouble with a flat tire." Joe shook his head sadly. "Too bad. Too bad. A nice young man. These things happen, sometimes." He looked up. "The cashier's check we gave him…maybe he still had it with him in the truck, then? You think that's possible?"

"It's possible." *But he didn't,* Estelle almost added. "Do you have the winning check that he delivered to you?"

"Lucinda took it to the bank on Friday afternoon. That's what happened. Friday."

"How much was it for?" Estelle knew the blunt question about the prize amount would draw Joe up short, and she watched as he struggled with whether to answer or not. He hesitated and looked at the manila envelope again. He shifted uneasily in his chair.

"Is there some kind of problem with the check? If they don't receive the money for the exchange rate... maybe they stop payment. I don't know how these things work."

"I'm not sure yet what problems there are, Joe."

"Lucinda already took the check he gave us to the bank," Joe said with finality.

"Posadas State?"

"Yes."

"And you wrote a check to the driver?"

"No. We had to have a cashier's check. Lucinda got that Wednesday morning. She could tell you the reason why. I don't remember. But that's what we gave to the young man. The cashier's check. Anybody could cash it."

"And when you did that, he handed you the sweepstakes check?"

Joe nodded. "That's how it happened. We won twice, you know. Betty told you that."

"When was the first time?"

"I would have to look in the checkbook. But I think it was about two weeks ago. Maybe three."

"Same deal? You handed over a check, and in return were given the sweepstakes winnings?"

Joe nodded emphatically. "Same exact thing. Only the prize wasn't so big the first time."

"Do you mind me asking how large it was?" she asked gently. This time, he replied without hesitation.

"No, I don't mind," he said with a note of pride. "We won more than eight thousand dollars the first time."

"You were given a check for that amount, then?"

"We had to pay... Wait a minute. This is making my brain go all to mush." He pushed himself out of the chair. "Wait a minute." In a few minutes he returned with a well-worn checkbook. "Now," he said with satisfaction, and settled back in the chair. "Let's see what this is all about." Estelle waited for him to thumb through the records.

"On January: eighteenth, we gave him a cashier's check for $1,402.50." Joe repeated the number while Estelle jotted it in a small notebook. "That was for taxes and all that stuff."

"The exchange rate, you mean?"

"That's it. He said it was up to seventeen percent now."

"And the delivery driver...he was this same young man?"

"Yes. The same man."

"And then?"

"And then what?"

"This last time? The second time you won? What did you give him?"

Joe hesitated and flipped a page. "It was Wednesday. We wrote a check for this much to the bank, so we could have a cashier's check." He turned the book toward her as if embarrassed to say the number.

"Thirty thousand four hundred thirteen," Estelle said, and the jolt of apprehension she felt was palpable. "And you received a check for how much?"

"Here's the copy of the deposit ticket," he said, and handed it to Estelle. "Lucinda went to the bank on Friday afternoon." Estelle looked at the number and blinked—$178,900.

"One hundred and seventy-eight thousand," she said. "And nine hundred."

"That's a lot of money, Joe. That's quite a streak of good fortune you've had. First the state lottery back in November, and now this."

He grinned slyly. "That lottery... I bought the ticket, you know. Good thing, too. Otherwise we wouldn't have had the money to pay for this." He reached out and touched the deposit ticket.

"Was there a particular reason why you and Lucinda waited two days to deposit the check?"

"We had things to do," Joe replied, and smiled. "Maybe we had to give it time to sink in."

"That would take some thinking," Estelle said. *"Caramba."* She sat back, the deposit slip in hand. "Do you have one of the original mailings for the sweepstakes?"

"Lucinda might remember where she put it. I don't know. I can look if you want. There's nothing wrong, is there?"

Other than a dead man? Estelle wanted to say. She looked at the deposit ticket again. The advance payment for a lottery prize was one of the oldest scams, and existed in a myriad of iterations, she knew. The undersheriff had a small folder of solicitations that she had collected over the years, including a Nigerian version, where the mark was told that he had been selected to help a foreign corporation transfer an enormous sum of money to avoid tax penalties, and had only to provide bank account numbers for transfer. Some required wiring advance money to pay various charges. But none offered a check on the spot, delivered in person.

This was simplicity itself. The Bacas had paid a total of just under $32,000 in "fees" and received, on the spot, checks that totaled more than $187,000, for a profit of more than $155,000.

When Estelle didn't respond, Joe tapped the paperwork. "You ask Serafina," he said. "She'll tell you the same story."

"Serafina won from the same contest?"

"Sure, she won before we did. She won twice, too."

"You're kidding." She didn't mention that Betty had already spread the good news.

"No, I'm not kidding, *hija*," he said, and then added, the tone of his voice implying that somehow he and his wife had found the magic formula, "Maybe we shouldn't have... I don't know. The driver told us that he had delivered more than one prize a lot of times. Serafina won twice, I know that. And so did we."

Estelle sat back in the chair. "Fascinating," she said. No complaint, no crime. Joe and Lucinda Baca evidently hadn't been defrauded.... In fact, they'd collected handsomely—maybe. The second, larger check hadn't had time to clear the bank yet. Maybe it would. But there had to be a catch, Estelle knew. The whole "taxes and exchange rate" nonsense was just that, as surely as the sun rose. Somehow, the next step in the scam had been scotched when Chris Marsh had plunged his truck over the mountainside.

She tapped the envelope on her knee thoughtfully. "Joe, let me ask you one more thing." She drew out the photo of the woodcutter and handed it to the old man. She watched his face intently.

"Now this," he said slowly. "What happened?"

"Do you know this man?"

"No...." He shifted uneasily. "Maybe I've seen him around. I don't know his name. What happened to him?" He squinted at the photo.

"An accident while cutting wood—up north near Reserve."

"Who took this picture?"

"One of the investigating officers."

"Who was with him? He was working alone?"

"I'd like to know the answer to that, Joe."

"This is all too bad," Joe Baca said. He handed the photo back, and Estelle handed him the paper with the telephone number. "What's this, then?" he asked.

"You know the number?"

"Well, sure I know it. That's Emilio's phone. Or I guess I should say Betty's. Emilio doesn't answer the phone ever. By the time he gets to it, it's the next day." Joe smiled. "Why do you need that?"

"I don't need that," Estelle said. "It was in the young man's pocket when he was found."

"And he was already dead?"

"Yes. He bled to death."

Joe shook his head slowly. "That's bad, *hija*. That's a bad business. Those chain saws..."

"Is this your handwriting?"

"Why would that be my writing?" he replied. "You already talked with Betty. That's *her* number."

"But she didn't write this note," Estelle said, and slipped the paper back in the envelope.

"I don't know what to tell you," Joe said. "He's not from around here. That much I can tell you."

"But you saw him around the village," Estelle suggested.

Joe shifted, his frown deepening. "Maybe I was mistaken. You know, in this country there are a lot of people. They come and go all the time. I can't be sure."

A lot of people. Regál counted forty-one residents. The border provided a constant trickle, but how many of those travelers—either north or southbound—paused long enough to be noticed?

"It's fortunate that you have recovered from that experience," he said, apparently eager to drop the subject about whom he might, or might not, know. "We all prayed for you, you know."

"I appreciate that, Joe." She was touched that her welfare immediately after the shooting nearly a year ago had been on the minds and in the prayers of so many people.

"So, where are you headed now? Can you wait until Lucinda comes home? She'll just be a few minutes." He had skillfully opened the door for Estelle.

"I wish I could," Estelle replied. "I don't get down here often enough. But maybe next time." She glanced at her watch. "Dispatch tells me that I have a visitor waiting for me, so I'd best be on my way. I appreciate your help, Joe. Give Lucinda my best." She stood and slipped the envelope under her arm, freeing her hands to take the old man's in both of hers. "And I appreciate your thoughts," she said. "It means a lot." He patted the back of her hand.

"I think he was just passing through," Joe said, nodding at the envelope that contained the photos.

"I'm sure you're right." *And I'm sure you know more*

than you're telling me, she thought, and saw the crinkles
around the corners of his eyes deepen a touch as if he
could read her mind.

SEVENTEEN

ESTELLE RECALLED SERAFINA Roybal as a large, imposing woman who could be intimidating when she chose. But that was an image from twenty-four years before, when Mrs. R, as the students universally called her, had taught Spanish, speech, and drama at Posadas High School. Her husband, Octavio, Betty Contreras' oldest brother, had taught history until pancreatic cancer had killed him on his sixtieth birthday.

Those many years before, Mrs. R had taken the darkly gorgeous and equally reticent Mexican teenager from Tres Santos under her generous wing after consultation with Estelle's foster mother, Teresa. Serafina and Teresa had known each other for years, no doubt through Estelle's great-uncle Reuben, who knew everyone along that section of border, especially if that everyone happened to be female.

Teresa was adamant about her adopted daughter's future. Just turned sixteen, Estelle would finish high school in the United States and then attend an appropriate college, collecting her official U.S. citizenship in the process. She would not be left to languish in the dusty poverty of rural northern Mexico. Estelle had accepted that notion with alacrity—she had no desire to languish anywhere—and soon found that Mrs. R was a teacher of enormous imagination and good humor.

Over the years since then, when Estelle would on rare

occasions meet Serafina Roybal in the grocery store or in passing at the bank, their conversations were more often than not in the dignified Castilian Spanish that Mrs. R taught her students. And over the years, Serafina shrank.

The woman who answered Estelle's knock this day was impossibly tiny. This could not be the imposing woman who had stood figuratively—and sometimes literally—between Estelle and the swarms of eager teenaged boys who to their credit recognized beauty when they saw it.

Withering into herself, the now eighty-year-old Serafina was a wrinkled little gnome, only her thick, luxuriant hair—now iron gray—a reminder of the long years past. Her right eye showed the first signs of clouding, but she recognized the undersheriff with a little gasp of delight.

"Estellita!" she cried, and held out both arms. "Oh, it's so good to see you." It was hard to imagine that this tiny bag of bones was the same fearsome woman who had nailed four senior boys for smoking funny tobacco behind the high school's votech building.

Serafina cocked her head as far as her stiff neck allowed and looked up at the undersheriff. "How's that husband of yours?" she asked in Spanish.

"He's too busy," Estelle laughed.

"That's always the case. And the boys?"

"They keep me young."

"The oldest boy…he continues with his studies?" Serafina held out two arthritic hands and played a phantom keyboard.

"More than ever," Estelle replied. "We have discussions about where he wants to study when the time comes."

"And it will come too soon," Serafina said. "Don't be in a rush."

"How is Esmeralda doing these days? It's been years since I've seen her."

Serafina made a wry face at the mention of her daughter. "She doesn't visit much anymore," she said. "Not enough time to bother with an old lady."

"I'm sorry to hear that. Her family is well?" Estelle had a vague recollection that Serafina and Octavio Roybal had raised only the single daughter, Esmeralda, who in turn had moved away to raise her own family.

"I hope so," Serafina said. "That's the big news, you know. You'll come in for a few minutes? I know you're busy today."

Estelle was fascinated that the tiny village's grapevine was flourishing even in the few moments it took the undersheriff to drive from one house to another.

"Thank you."

"I have some coffee," Serafina offered, but Estelle held up a defensive hand.

"No, thanks so much, Mrs. Roybal." Estelle followed the elderly woman as she shuffled inside, one tiny, slow step at a time. The home displayed the much-worn pathways of the very elderly. The large cushioned chair, with back and arms covered with graying, tattered doilies, faced the television across the room. The TV set was one of those cabinet affairs with light maple woodwork, and Estelle saw that the picture would be much brighter if the thick layer of dust was wiped from the screen.

A path worn into the amorphous designs on the carpeting led to the simple kitchen, and another to the bathroom and two bedrooms. Serafina's world was gradually collapsing inward to a few well-worn, predictable routines.

"What's the big news?" Estelle asked.

"Well, now, you won't guess who's visiting tomorrow," Serafina said. "My granddaughter called and said she'd like to stop by. That's Ezzi's oldest, Irene. She's an honor student now, you know. But...," and Serafina lowered her voice as if she didn't want the ghosts to hear, "she's had a crush on that Danny Rivera since I don't know when. Not that it does any good. Mr. Danny doesn't show any signs of wanting any part of the big wide world." She turned and beamed at Estelle. "Irene is going to have to come to him, you know. But that's fashionable these days."

Serafina pointed a crooked finger at the envelope that Estelle had brought inside with her. "You have something for me?"

"I have a photo or two, Mrs. Roybal. A couple of strange faces. I need to know if you've seen either one around the village."

"I don't get out so much, you know. I can't even walk through the orchard anymore. I used to enjoy that. All the birds, you know."

"I understand that." *And it's not an orchard now,* Estelle thought—the gnarled old stumps, tinder dry, hadn't seen irrigation or fruit for ten years. She removed the photo of Christopher Marsh but hesitated. *Maybe life should reach a point of serenity,* she thought. Serafina Roybal had known her share of heartache over the decades. She'd seen prize students go on to enjoy successful lives but suffered the ones who were killed on prom night in a tangle of metal and broken bottles, or those who were expended by their governments. It seemed unfair to inflict Chris Marsh on this gentle woman.

"This young man was killed up on Regál Pass Wednesday night. The crash wasn't discovered until last night," the undersheriff said, still holding the photo. "I apologize for this, Mrs. Roybal. But I need to know if you recognize him."

The old woman took the picture without hesitation and straightened in her chair, holding the photo in both hands down in her lap. Her face took on the same severe expression that she had reserved for student papers that weren't up to snuff.

"Do you recognize this man?" Estelle asked.

"Who is this?" Serafina replied. "His name, I mean."

"His name is Christopher Marsh. We think that he lived in Las Cruces."

"A car accident, you said."

"Yes. His truck hit a deer."

"Oh my." She lifted her eyebrows philosophically. "You know, he impressed me as such a nice, thoughtful young man."

"You recognize him, then?"

"He was a deliveryman," she replied, using the single Spanish word *repartidor*. "I don't remember the name of the company."

"Do you remember the vehicle he was driving?"

"No. I don't pay attention to things like that."

"But you had packages delivered here?"

"I won a drawing by some magazine company. Not so much, but every little bit is a help, no? Such a surprise." Her eyebrows lifted. "Not so much of a surprise as when I won not once, but twice."

"Would you tell me about it?"

"There is nothing to tell, Estellita. It was just one of those sweepstakes that come along. Usually I throw them away, but this was a personal letter, and I read it." She glanced at Estelle. "I didn't have to do a thing, you see. Nothing to fill out. Maybe I'm just foolish, but it turned out all right."

"How much did you win?"

"The first time it was about three thousand dollars," Serafina said. "Of course, I had to pay some fees. That was a nuisance, but this young man made it easy for me."

"How did he do that?"

"He said that his company usually requires a cashier's check from the bank. But it's hard for me to get into town now. He said that his company would accept a personal check, since the amount wasn't so large."

Estelle did a rapid mental calculation, using the 17 percent figure for fees and exchange rate penalties that Joe Baca had mentioned. "You had to pay approximately five hundred dollars?"

"Yes. But they accepted my check."

"And in return?"

"He delivered the official check right then. The check for what they said I had won."

"For more than three thousand dollars."

"Yes."

"Serafina, you said the *first* time. This happened again, then?"

"This young man," and she held up the photo, "said that it wasn't uncommon for someone to win more than once. He had his own theory that maybe it was some kind of computer error." She shrugged. "Maybe so. Anyway, the next time I won twenty-eight hundred dollars. Not so much."

"What did you send in the second time?"

"Nothing. I sent in nothing. Not the first time, either. He came right to the door." She frowned. "I would never send anything off. I know those scams are so common."

"And you paid that time, too? Four or five hundred in fees?"

"Yes. But overall, you see, I came out ahead. Did you talk with Joe? I saw your car over there."

"Yes. He had similar good fortune, it seems."

"I should say so. Only he won much, much more. And on top of the big lottery as well. My heavens, the stars were looking out for us."

"But this man came to your door." Estelle held up Marsh's photo.

"Yes. The two times about which I've told you."

"Was anyone with him?"

"I couldn't tell. I don't see so well anymore, you know. I don't think so."

"Do you happen to have the letters that they sent to you? The magazine company?"

"I save everything," Serafina said with resignation. "An affliction of an old lady. Even if I know it doesn't matter, I save it. The challenge is in the finding." She held up a hand and rose unsteadily from her chair. "Let me see. You're sure you don't want something to drink?"

"No thank you, Serafina."

Estelle watched Serafina make her way toward the bedroom. From where she sat, the undersheriff could see a small yellow nightstand, the corner of the bed, and another door that would lead to the bathroom. After several moments, Serafina reemerged with several papers.

"I'm so pleased that you stopped by," she said. "You know, last year you gave us quite a scare, young lady."

"I scared myself," Estelle said. "That's the letter?"

"I have the first one," Serafina said. "I remember that when it came in the mail, I thought it was a *chanchullo*," and Estelle was surprised to hear her use the colloquial word that had come to mean "scam" or "trickery."

"Too good to be true?"

"Exactly. Here. You read it and tell me what you think. While you do that, I'll see if I can find the second one."

The letter, on heavy, high-quality paper, featured an impressive full-color letterhead from Canadian Publications Limited, located in Calgary, Alberta, Canada. The letterhead included the street address, phone and fax numbers, and e-mail information. It was tri-folded in an equally high-quality envelope, with the same return address printed on the upper left corner. The Canadian stamp was a generic coil issue with perforations on two sides. Estelle held the envelope over toward the lamp to catch more light. The postmark was Canadian, dated December 10 of the previous year.

She held the paper carefully by just the corners and read the text. It was lively, polite, and brief:

Dear Mrs. Serafina Roybal:

We are pleased to announce that your name has been selected as a second level prize winner in the Canadian Publications Limited Reader Awards Sweepstakes. Although you have not been selected for the Grand Prize, your winnings total $3,250.00. This sweepstakes reflects our commitment to generating reader interest in the periodicals distributed by CPL, but requires no purchase on your part.

The check for the winning amount will be de-

livered to your home in Regál, New Mexico. Canadian Publications Limited has contracted exclusively with Global Productivity Systems, Inc., for delivery of prize winnings, with proceeds drawn on First State National Savings Bank of Las Cruces.

As you are no doubt aware, transferring prize winnings from one country to another incurs certain tax charges, along with monetary exchange rate adjustments. At the current time, those charges amount to 16.981% of gross winnings, and by law cannot simply be deducted from the winning amount.

GPS, Inc., a bonded and certified parcel delivery firm that serves your area, has agreed to serve as the monetary transfer agent for your winning check. The driver who calls on you with the prize check will accept a standard cashier's check for the monetary exchange adjustment, a total of $551.88. We regret the inconvenience that personal checks cannot be accepted. As well, GPS, Inc., will not accept cash payments.

A GPS courier will contact you at your home on or about Dec. 14, 2007, to effect the transfer of funds. If this is not possible, feel free to contact our Funds Disbursement Office in Calgary, Alberta, Canada, at the number at the top of this letter.

Again, our best wishes, and congratulations!

Sincerely, E. Everett Walker, Jr.
Vice President, Sweepstakes Coordination Operations

"¡Caramba!" Estelle whispered to herself. "This is a good one." She read the letter several more times. From out of the blue, money. No strings attached. And what was the catch?

She looked up as Serafina shuffled back into the room. "I cannot find the second one, Estellita. But it was much the same. A little different amount, but otherwise, the same."

"Serafina, when the driver delivered the check, did you have to sign something?"

"Oh, yes. One of those new gadgets with the little window. I don't know how they work, but I know they've been using them for some time."

"And you had the cashier's check?"

"The first time, yes. Betty and I did errands, and I stopped in at the bank in Posadas. Not the second time."

Estelle made a passing motion with both hands. "He gave you a check, and in exchange, you handed a cashier's check to him."

"Yes. You sound as if something is wrong, Estellita."

"I hope not, Serafina. But as you said, it all seems too good to be true. The bank accepted the prize check with no problem?"

"Lucinda took it in for me. I didn't hear anything, so I assume it was just fine."

"May I take this with me to make a copy?" Estelle asked, indicating the letter.

"Of course you may, Estellita. And I'll call to let you know when I find the second one. I know I have it." She laughed gently. "Like so many things."

"I have one more thing of interest," Estelle said. *"Con permiso,* another photo. And a sad, sad situation." She slid the photo of the woodcutter from the envelope and handed it to Serafina. The old woman turned and held the photo close to her good eye, adjusting it so that the light bounced off just right.

"Do you know this man? Have you ever seen him around the village?"

"No. This one is a stranger, Estellita. Whatever happened?"

"It was a woodcutting accident. Up in the country around Reserve and Quemado." Serafina looked at her quizzically and Estelle added, "This was found in his pocket." She handed Serafina the copy of Betty Contreras' telephone number.

"This is Emilio and Betty," Serafina said immediately.

"Yes, it is."

"And this was in the poor man's pocket? Whatever for?"

"Yes, and that's the question. Do you recognize the handwriting?"

"A few numbers...not enough even for this old schoolteacher to recognize. I wish I could help you, Estellita. So tell me...this prize thing. I won twice, and Joe and Lucinda won twice, and considerably more than I did. Is something wrong, then? Is that what you think?"

Estelle put the photos and telephone number carefully back in the envelope with the sweepstakes letter that Serafina had given her. "Something is wrong, Serafina. Yes. I don't know what it is, yet. Let me suggest this. You say that both checks were deposited in your account in Posadas?"

"Yes. Both."

"Then don't spend any of the amount. Just let it ride. If somehow this thing is legitimate, fine. If not, you'll be protected—except for the amount you've already given them."

"And that," Serafina said with finality, "is a total of nearly a thousand dollars. I can't afford to see that just fly out the window."

"I know you can't. And I hope I'm wrong. We'll see what happens."

"I could understand a scam that seeks to collect thousands and thousands of dollars from some poor unsuspecting soul. But this seems too petty."

"Let's hope so," Estelle said. She didn't remind the retired teacher that one of her own classmates during her junior year had been killed after an argument that had started over the disputed ownership of thirty-seven cents. Chris Marsh had managed to get himself crosswise with someone over far more than that.

EIGHTEEN

From a small rise just beyond Serafina Roybal's neat little home, Estelle could see Iglesia de Nuestra Señora a thousand yards away and the single vehicle parked near its entrance. Madelyn Bolles couldn't have made the drive south from Posadas so quickly. Bill Gastner had said that the reporter was driving a red Buick—this one didn't have enough color to judge, and it didn't glint in the sun.

Before starting the car, Estelle drew out the letter that Serafina had given to her. Opening her cell phone, she dialed the Canadian number carefully, committing it to the phone's memory. On a Saturday, she didn't expect an answer, and in three rings was rewarded with an answering machine.

"Hello. You have reached the corporate offices of Canadian Publications Limited, your source for the best in leisure, educational, and technical reading. Our regular business hours are Monday through Friday, from nine a.m. to five p.m., Mountain Time. If you know your party's three-digit extension, you may enter that now to leave voice mail. Thank you for calling Canadian Publications."

Estelle sat for a long minute, staring at the phone. "Most strange," she said aloud, and then dialed Dispatch.

"Gayle, I need a favor," she said when Gayle Torrez answered. "Will you give the Calgary Police Department a buzz for me? I need to know what's located at this address." She read the information from the letterhead, including the notation that Canadian Publications operated out of Suite 11-e.

"That shouldn't take more than a few minutes," Gayle said cheerfully. "I'll jump on the Web and get right back to you."

"I'd rather that you call the Calgary police directly," Estelle said. "I want to hear their take on both the address and the company working out of there."

"Copy that." Gayle didn't question the request, odd as it might sound. "Did you meet Ms. Bolles yet?"

"No. I'm clear here for the moment. I'm going to stop at the church to see Emilio, then I'll be heading back in."

Estelle left the envelope on the seat as she headed toward the church, meandering through the village where no single street took command of direction. In many places, she had to slow the Crown Victoria to a walk as she passed between stump and mailbox, or around a front porch, or through yards populated with dogs, cats, goats, and occasionally children.

She reached the main highway just a hundred yards north of the border station. A Border Patrol SUV was parked at the end of the small building beside an unmarked sedan. At the moment there was no traffic, and she pulled across the paved road to the driveway leading up to the church parking lot.

The aging Chevy sedan parked there sported a hood, roof, and trunk lid that were sun bleached to bare metal. The top of the backseat, exposed to the sun by the expanse of the rear window, was tattered, unraveled, and faded, but she knew the priest who owned the car was no slave to fashion. Estelle parked behind Father Bertrand

Anselmo's relic and got out of her car. The Chevy sat low on four tires in varying need of attention, including the left rear that was bald as a racing slick. Remnants of tape held the taillight lenses in place. More duct tape, applied in generous quantities, held the left rear window in its frame. If the windshield acquired any more cracks, it would take more than tape. Estelle paused, admiring the rolling junkyard. She could see that even the plastic steering wheel was cracked in several places, the steel skeleton showing through. There probably weren't many wholesale vehicles that the southbound *burros*, the car dealers who hauled their tandems of long-of-tooth whole-sale vehicles to Mexico, would refuse, but this might be one of them.

Estelle knew that Father Anselmo had been stopped by law enforcement officers from every agency that roamed the county—and probably some visiting ones from out of town. The car *looked* guilty, riding low and battered on its worn-out suspension as if the generous trunk might be full of half a ton of weed or half a dozen illegals. On the good father's behalf, any cop would tes-tify that the car would never be caught speeding, its li-cense and registration were up-to-date, and a current insurance card rode in the remains of the glove box. Anselmo apparently believed that the good Lord would take care of everything else.

Five stone steps led up to the *iglesia's* mammoth front door, five steps that added just a bit more to Emilio Contreras' penance each day. The heavily carved door stood ajar, its rope handle inviting. The door's two-hundred-year-old cottonwood planks were polished to a deep, warm sheen, unscarred by any attempts at illegal entry. It wasn't necessary to try to force the lock. There wasn't one. If the door was closed, one had merely to tug the thick rope, pulling up the beautifully balanced drop latch on the inside.

As she swung the door open, she enjoyed the wave of fragrant comfort that wafted out of the ancient building. Fresh juniper led the bouquet, followed by a hint of lemon oil, latex paint, and overtones of musty books. The door opened so soundlessly that Father Anselmo, standing near the communion railing and facing the front of the church, didn't hear her enter. Emilio Contreras leaned a hip against the railing, both hands resting on top of his aluminum cane. He saw the undersheriff and raised one hand in greeting, and the priest turned.

"Well, now," his voice boomed in the empty church, "what a treat this is." He reached out a hand to touch Emilio on the forearm and then strode down the aisle toward Estelle. Still half a dozen paces away, he extended both hands, and then his huge grip enveloped hers. "It's so good to see you," he said, making the simple word "so" about five syllables long.

A great bear of a man whose casual dress was as unkempt and worn as his Chevrolet, Bertrand Anselmo would have had no trouble fitting into an earlier century. His full black beard accentuated the broad bone structure of a strong face. A pair of tiny frameless half-glasses perched on his generous, wide nose, and he tipped his head to regard Estelle through the lenses, looking at her critically. "How are you doing these days?"

"I'm fine, Bert." He squeezed her hands in response to that. "Or it might be more accurate to say that I'm making good progress toward being fine."

He laughed, showing the need for considerable dental care that he could not afford. Releasing her hands, he nodded at the envelope under her arm. "We're glad to hear that. But you're here on business, unfortunately."

He accepted the photograph of Christopher Marsh, turning so that the light from the nearest window fell over his shoulder. He made a small sign of the cross over the photo. "May the Lord bless you and keep you," he said, and then sighed. "I don't know this unfortunate young man. Should I?"

"I can't imagine why you would, sir. If you had seen him around town, it would be helpful to know when and where."

"I don't think so. Now, Emilio would know more than I...or Betty, the source of all information in the Western Hemisphere. Have you talked to her?"

"Yes."

"Then you already know a good deal more than I do." Anselmo accepted the second photo, and the ritual of blessing was repeated. This time, however, he examined the photo more thoroughly, adjusting it this way and that, bringing it closer to his half-glasses. "Ah," he said, finally. He lowered the photo and looked down the nave toward Emilio Contreras, who was making his way toward them, one slow, painful shuffling step at a time. Emilio used the same kind of cane that Teresa Reyes favored—aluminum with a splayed four-footed base, a sort of mini-walker that would stand by itself.

"How did this happen?" Father Anselmo asked quietly.

"A woodcutting accident, apparently. Up near Reserve."

"'Apparently' implies something else," the priest said, and Estelle nodded.

"We're not sure yet. Actually I should say the Catron County authorities aren't sure."

"They're looking into it and asked your help, then."

"Yes." She pulled out the photocopy of the small note that contained the Contreras telephone number and handed it to Father Anselmo. "He had this in his pocket."

"No ID or anything else?"

"No."

"Well, that makes it more difficult," the priest said, and Estelle wasn't sure whether she heard a note of relief in his tone, or even if the remark had been meant for her to hear.

"Can you tell me anything about him?" the undersheriff asked.

"Like what?" Anselmo asked, pleasantly enough. "Am I supposed to know this chap?"

"That's a good place to start."

"Ah, who he is," Anselmo murmured. "Now you're making demands on a memory that's of no particular use to anyone, including its owner."

Estelle remained silent, regarding the priest. She had known Bertrand Anselmo for thirty years—had listened to more than one guest sermon at the tiny Iglesia de Tres Santos in the Mexican village where she had spent her childhood. She knew, from her mother's frequent reports, that Anselmo was content with his work—that he lived in a tiny four-room adobe house in María with the barest of amenities, and that he offered mass at both the church in María and that in Regál, with frequent visits to Tres Santos, forty miles south in Mexico. She supposed that his bishop was content to leave Bertrand Anselmo in that tiny corner of the world indefinitely, since his isolated pastorate appeared to match Anselmo's needs perfectly.

Regardless of background, training, or even personal inclination, every person had, on some occasion, his own struggle with telling the truth, and Estelle could see that this was such a moment for the priest.

"I don't want to enter into a sparring match with you," he said finally, handing the photograph back to the undersheriff. He removed his half-glasses and rubbed his face, turning to watch Emilio's progress toward them. Halfway down the nave, the old man had stopped in front of the wood-burning potbellied stove, with its towering stovepipe. He opened the door, regarded what was left of the morning fire, and closed it with a clang.

"A sparring match? What does that mean?" Estelle asked.

"Well," Anselmo said with resignation, "I can tell you that his name was Felix Otero."

"From?"

"Down south. But of course, you knew that."

"He's an illegal, then?"

"I suppose some would say so." Anselmo's beard twitched a little as he smiled at Estelle. "But that depends on whose laws you're talking about. Would the absence of that little slip of paper make *you* more or less than you are?"

"As a matter of fact, it would," Estelle replied, and then ignored the bait. She had no desire to settle into an extended dialogue with the priest about the justice or lack thereof along the U.S.–Mexican border. "But you knew Felix Otero somehow?"

"Yes. I knew him. He…" And Anselmo paused, choosing his words carefully. "He passed through here, yes."

"And this?"

"This is a jotted telephone number. If my memory serves me correctly, it's Emilio and Betty's number. Am I right?"

"You're right. Do you know who did the jotting?"

Anselmo chuckled. "I may be many things, Estelle, but psychic I'm not." He reached out a hand toward Emilio Contreras' shoulder. The old man had progressed to the last pew, and he examined the pew's polished armrest critically. A tiny man, he had been graceful, even nimble, until a fall while pruning a crab apple tree had wrecked his hip.

"Emilio, it's good to see you," Estelle said, and took his hand in hers. "Thank you for all you've done."

"We're expecting a crowd tomorrow," he said, nodding. He turned slowly to survey his church.

"A seventy-fifth wedding anniversary," Father Anselmo added. "You know Fernando and Maria Rivera, of course."

"Of course," Estelle said.

"That's what Emilio and I were planning," the priest said.

"The logistics of one hundred people in this tiny place. The reception is afterward, up at the VFW in Posadas. Thank heavens. Betty would like to have it here, and we will have a small gathering…but not the full-blown affair."

"Emilio," Estelle said, "I'm wondering if you know either of these two men." She removed the photos while the old man sat carefully in the pew.

"Why do you have these?" he asked after a moment.

"This young man is the driver of the truck that crashed up on the pass a day or two ago," she said.

"Betty told me about that. I didn't know him."

"Did he ever stop here?"

"Why would he do that?"

"Needing directions, perhaps. Regál isn't the easiest place to find an address if you're a stranger."

"No, he never talked to me." Emilio shuffled the photos, gazing for a long time at the woodcutter.

"That's Felix Otero, isn't it, Emilio?"

"I don't know the names," the old man said. "It could be. But I don't keep track."

That brought a burst of laughter from the priest. He wagged a finger at Estelle like a grade school teacher locking the attention of a recalcitrant student. "You'll find that out when age catches up with you, Estelle Guzman." He pulled his shirtsleeve back and looked at his watch. "I have errands that I've almost forgotten."

"So tell me," Estelle said. "Who is this Felix Otero? You both know his name. You both have seen him before, evidently. Was he just a man looking for work? Does he have relatives here in Regál? Does he have parents down in Mexico, wondering if they're going to see their son again? Does he have a wife? Children? And Emilio, can you tell me why he would be carrying your telephone number in his pocket? No ID, but your number?"

She paused, but neither the priest nor Emilio Contreras spoke, and she tried another tack. "We need to inform his family as soon as possible."

Anselmo's broad face settled into an expression of sad resignation. "I'll see what I can do, Estelle," he said, but didn't explain just what that might be. The sound of a vehicle, its tires crunching on the gravel of the parking lot, interrupted them. As if grateful for the diver-

sion, the priest stepped to the door and pushed it open.
Through the opening, Estelle caught the glint of sun on
bright red paint.

NINETEEN

"Isn't this lovely," Madelyn Bolles said. She had nodded her thanks to Father Anselmo for opening the door, and stepped into Iglesia de Nuestra Señora, halting just inside. She took off her sun-glasses and with a quick, experienced glance surveyed the interior of the church. Then she dismissed the architecture with a curt nod and turned her attention to Estelle.

"And you would be Posadas County undersheriff Estelle Guzman," Madelyn said with a warm smile.

"Good afternoon, Ms. Bolles."

"Madelyn, please." She stepped away from the door as Anselmo's bulk loomed behind her.

"This is Father Bertrand Anselmo," Estelle said. "He offers mass both here and in María." Estelle watched Bolles as the woman turned to offer her hand. At the same time, the reporter's eyes did another quick inventory, this time of the disheveled priest.

"Madelyn Bolles," she said. "I write for *A Woman's World* magazine."

"Well, my pleasure," Anselmo said. "What brings you to this little corner of paradise?"

"Paradise exactly," Bolles said, and turned to survey the *iglesia* again. "This really is fetching, if that's the correct word to describe a mission."

"I'd like you to meet Emilio Contreras," Estelle said. "What you see around you is his work."

"We all do what we can. And where are you from, *señora*?" Emilio asked, his slow, cadenced voice giving full measure to each word as he shook hands with Bolles.

"At the moment, Las Cruces," the reporter said. Easily past fifty, Madelyn Bolles wore her stylish dark blue suit easily, managing to look casual despite the businesslike cut.

"Listen, you folks enjoy a blessed day," Father Anselmo said. "I really do have errands I need to run. Ms. Bolles, it's my pleasure to meet you, and welcome to the parish. If there's anything I can do for you, let me know. Estelle knows how to reach me. And Emilio, of course."

"Nice to meet you, Father," Madelyn said, extending her hand once more. "Perhaps if you'd leave your cell number with me?"

"Ah, cell phone. I don't have one," the priest said. "But I *do* have a phone at home in María." He patted his pockets and Madelyn came to his rescue with a business card and a pen. "Thank you." He turned and rested the card on the daybook of guest signatures, writing the telephone number slowly, as if he had difficulty remembering the seven digits. Then he added a second number below the first. "The top number is mine," he said, "and I took the liberty of giving you Emilio and Betty Contreras' number here in Regál. They always know where I am, if there's need to reach me." He handed the card back to the reporter. "Have a wonderful visit."

"I shall," she said. "I shall. Thank you."

The priest pushed the door open, and said to Emilio, "I'm going to leave this open for a while. Let some fresh air in."

"The dust blows in from the parking lot," Emilio said, and the priest looked surprised.

"Oh. Well, then," the priest said. "Let's keep it closed. Estelle, it was nice to see you again. Don't be such a stranger."

"Have a good day, Father," Estelle said.

"He doesn't pay attention," Emilio said with resignation as the door closed, leaving them in the comfortable dim light. He nodded at Madelyn. "It's nice to meet you. You want to talk with Betty, not me. She'll tell you anything you need to know." Without waiting for an answer, he pushed himself out of the pew, adjusted the cane before putting weight forward, and then began his slow shuffle back up the aisle toward where he had been working before his day was interrupted.

Estelle watched his progress for a moment, at the same time listening as outside Father Bertrand Anselmo's aging Chevrolet grumbled into life. She realized that Madelyn Bolles was studying her.

"You're a little older than I would have guessed after seeing the various photographs," the reporter said.

"Every day," Estelle laughed. "I haven't figured out a way to avoid it."

"Ain't that the truth. I've caught you right in the middle of something, your dispatcher tells me."

"About three things." Estelle tapped the manila envelope on the back of the pew. "That's the way it generally goes. Weeks and weeks of peace and quiet, and then the sky falls on us."

Madelyn cocked her head. "That would be a challenge in itself, putting up with that roller coaster."

"What's your schedule, then?" Estelle asked.

The reporter held up both hands, palms up. "Whatever it takes," she said. "I have an absolutely wonderful room at the Casa de Posadas on Tenth Street, complete with high-speed Internet, yet. Who would have thunk."

"We're wildly progressive around here," Estelle laughed.

"I can see that," Madelyn said, turning in place with her hands thrust in the pockets of her suit coat. "This really is a wonderful place, isn't it. I saw the historical plaque set in the adobe on the outside wall." She took a deep breath, leaning backward to gaze up at the ceiling where the stovepipe vented through the roof. "No lights, a woodstove…one of those places where the baptismal font freezes if you forget to empty it. And I don't see any sign of electricity, either."

"None whatsoever," Estelle agreed.

"Wow." After another moment spent examining the church's simple, almost fortresslike architecture, Madelyn added, "What I really want to do is find a few minutes sometime for a preliminary meeting with you, some time when we can just sit and chat in private—no notes, no recorder, no camera." She turned and regarded Estelle thoughtfully. "I like to do that, you know…kind of sort out the rules we're going to play by."

Estelle found herself liking this woman—Madelyn Bolles was no rookie reporter, that seemed evident. Shorter than Estelle by several inches, Madelyn was ramrod straight, looking as if she'd be equally at home in a New York Wall Street boardroom or the principal's office of an elementary school.

"I'm heading back to Posadas now," the undersheriff said. "If you follow me back, maybe we can find a quiet corner in my office. I don't want to waste your time."

Madelyn frowned and held up a hand. "No, no. This isn't about me, undersheriff. What I want is to do this

right. That's all. Whatever it takes." She held out the
business card with the phone numbers Father Anselmo
had given her, and out of reflex, Estelle took it. "Is there
a chance I can have your cell number? I promise I won't
be a nuisance."

"Not to worry," Estelle said, digging out one of her
own business cards. "If I'm in the middle of something,
I just don't answer the thing. And you can always reach
me through Dispatch."

"I met… Gayle, is it? What an elegant gal *she* is. And
she's the sheriff's wife, I'm told."

"Yes." But Estelle's attention was drawn to the numbers on the back of the reporter's business card. "Excuse
me a moment," she said, and walked to the nearest window, a deep-silled, narrow expanse of stained glass rising
nearly eight feet to an arched top. She laid the business
card on the smooth white sill, and then opened the manila envelope, drawing out the photocopy of the slip of
paper found in Felix Otero's pocket.

"*Ay*, now that's interesting," she whispered to herself.
Even simple digits were tiny windows themselves, opening secrets. The digits 8, 5, and 7 especially invited the
individual strokes of the pen. Estelle slid the two numbers close together. In both cases, the 8 was formed with
not a single graceful stroke, but by joining two some-
what angular circles, one perched atop the other. The 5
included two features, a separate stroke for the bottom
portion that included a tail looping back to cross the
downward stroke, and a second horizontal mark form-
ing the top plane of the letter. The 7 was more generic,
save for the horizontal stroke that crossed the stem in
the European fashion.

She realized that Bolles was standing off to one side,

watching her. She slid the copy back in the envelope, and reached out with the card.

"Thank you."

"You're welcome," Madelyn Bolles said, making no move to accept. "And keep it. I have the numbers."

Estelle slid the card not into her pocket, but into the manila envelope, feeling an odd mixture of emotions. Father Bertrand Anselmo, whom she had known since she was in single digits, hadn't actually lied to her, but nor had he taken her into his confidence. In another time and place, when there were no other ears to hear, perhaps he would. And perhaps not.

That the priest would give the Mexican—if it turned out that indeed that's who Felix Otero was—the telephone number of the village's most accomplished grapevine cultivator, Betty Contreras, was in itself enough to pique curiosity, although that's exactly what he had just done with Madelyn Bolles. Perhaps, in his own amused way, he had intended for Estelle to notice.

"Let's meet in my office," Estelle said. "About an hour?"

"Perfect," the reporter said.

"Emilio, thank you," Estelle called. The old man had returned to his labors, meticulously waxing and polishing the communion rail. He raised a hand in salute.

"Come back and see us," he said. "You're always welcome. You know that."

I'm not sure that will always be the case, Estelle thought as she pushed open the heavy door. As her feet touched the gravel of the parking lot, her cell phone buzzed. "Excuse me a second," she said to the writer, and turned away, walking toward the county car.

"Estelle, the address checks out," Gayle Torrez said.

"I talked with a Calgary city detective who says that CPL operates out of a double suite at that address. He doesn't know anything about them, other than that they're where they say they are. He says that area isn't one of the high-rent places…just a little mini-mall sort of thing."

"That's a help," Estelle said.

"They were supercordial," Gayle added. "If you need any more information, they're pleased to cooperate. Anything we need. I have the officer's name and number when you need it."

"Thanks so much," Estelle said. "You're the best."

She broke the connection and pointed toward the mountain pass behind them. "See you in an hour?"

"That's a date," Madelyn said. She let Estelle leave the parking lot first, and as the undersheriff crested the pass, she saw that the wrecker was finished with its chore of cranking Chris Marsh's crumpled truck up the mountain. Only Jackie Taber's vehicle was parked along the highway. Her shift was long since finished, and she hadn't taken Estelle's suggestion.

Estelle's hand went to the radio mike, but then she thought better of going public. Instead, she pulled off the highway a short distance ahead of Jackie's unit, and auto-dialed 303 on her phone. Jackie would be some-where downslope, seeing what the wrecker might have shaken loose when it bundled the crushed pickup truck back up the hillside.

"Taber."

"Jackie, you were supposed to go home," Estelle said. "What are you finding down there?"

"Rocks, rocks, and more rocks. I don't think we missed much."

Estelle looked up as Madelyn Bolles' red sedan swooshed by, the driver offering a cheery wave.

"Okay," Estelle said. "I just finished up down in Regál with Betty and a few of her neighbors. My gut feeling is that this thing is going to get really messy before we're through."

"Where's it going to take us?" Jackie asked.

"It looks like Marsh was delivering sweepstakes checks to a couple of the village residents."

"No kidding. What are the odds of that, I wonder."

"Of winning?"

"No...of there being more than one winner in such a tiny town. That smells. How much did they lose?"

"That's what's bizarre, Jackie. Nobody has lost anything. They've *won*. Signed, sealed, and delivered. It's just that it was delivered by a bogus courier."

"Now there's a scenario," Jackie said. "I wonder what the bank says. Are you headed back in?"

"Yes. Here's the thing to think about, Jackie. A bogus *courier* doesn't necessarily make the items that he was *delivering* bogus. I mean, Chris Marsh might have passed himself off to Canadian Publications as a legit service."

"A Canadian sweepstakes?"

"So it seems."

"That smells even worse."

"Yes, but the phone and address on the confirmation letter that the folks received checks out, so far. It *exists*, anyway."

"Huh. I don't believe it."

"What would have been the next step for these guys? If Chris Marsh hadn't hit the deer, hadn't been killed here on the pass, what would have been the next step? I just found out that he was carrying a check with him from Joe and Lucinda Baca for more than thirty thousand."

"*That* stinks worser and worser, Estelle. I can think of several ways that little deal could go south. Somebody had to have been waiting for him when the deer got in the way."

"Think on that," Estelle said. "You're about finished out here?"

"I think so. The sun on the rocks is reminding me that it's nap time."

"Go for it." She looked in her rearview mirror as the sound of another vehicle reached her. The rattling, gasping chug was familiar, and in a moment, Father Bertrand Anselmo's Chevy crested the pass and started down the north side, passing her with a faint whiff of very old, very burned, oil. The priest raised a hand in greeting.

The Chevy gained speed until it disappeared around one of the sweeping curves. Estelle pulled back on the highway. By the time she had caught up with Father Anselmo and the blue cloud that trailed his car, they were nearing the Broken Spur Saloon. His speed surprised her. Drawing to within a few hundred yards, she slowed long enough to pace him. The aging sedan thundered along at 71 miles an hour, in flagrant disregard of the speed limit and the condition of its tires.

Suddenly aware that he was being paced by a county car, the priest touched his brakes. One of the brake lights managed a faint flare, and Estelle pulled out and passed him. In the wink of time when their eyes met, Anselmo's expression was guarded. Estelle wondered where the priest had gone after leaving the church, and then felt a pang of regret that his movements might become her business.

In another few miles, as she approached the little ghost town of Moore just beyond the Rio Salinas bridge, she saw flashing lights. Sure enough, the magazine writer's red Buick LaCrosse was pulled off the road, snared by one of the state troopers who liked to park behind the remains of Moore Mercantile, a tumbled-down reminder of half a century ago that now afforded an open radar shot in either direction.

"Oops," Estelle said. The trooper was standing on the passenger side of the Buick, bent down so he could see inside. He heard her county car approaching, itself rocketing along well over the speed limit, and looked up. He was smiling broadly, and Estelle wondered what Madelyn Bolles had used as an excuse.

TWENTY

"THE MAGAZINE writer is in town," Estelle said, and when Sheriff Bob Torrez looked at her blandly as if to say, *So what?* added, "She may want to talk to you at some point."

"People in hell want ice water, too," the sheriff said affably.

"She followed me in from Regál. We're going to meet here after a bit."

Torrez shifted so that he could stretch out both legs past his desk, and Estelle nudged the door closed and then pulled one of the metal folding chairs out of the corner. The sheriff's office was long on function and short on amenities or color. He never spoke of the two years he'd spent in the army decades before, but apparently he'd been impressed with the use of drab as a foundation style.

He opened his desk drawer and took out the same pistol that she had showed Bill Gastner, reached across the desk, and laid it directly in front of Estelle. "I did some studying," Torrez said cryptically, as if that explained everything. She reached out and hefted Deputy Dennis Collins' department sidearm. The slide was locked back, with an empty magazine in place.

"These have inertia firing pins," Torrez said after a moment. "Could be, if that gun is loaded, cocked, and locked, it could fire if it falls and hits the muzzle just right."

"Except it fell against the truck, back sight first," Estelle said. "And not very hard, at that."

"I know it did. I'm just sayin'. If that *don't* happen, it means that either something else was wrong with the gun or it was cocked, locked, and his finger pulled the trigger when he grabbed onto it."

"That's most likely," she agreed.

Torrez leaned forward and folded his hands on his desk. "Not that it matters a whole hell of a lot," and then he sat back abruptly as if he'd caught himself talking too much.

Estelle laid Dennis Collins' gun back on the sheriff's desk. "I suspect that you could pick any gun, made by anybody anywhere in the world, and if you worked hard enough, you could invent a circumstance where it might go off unintentionally."

Torrez nodded once. "And if you take any gun and pull the trigger, it's going to go off…unless there's something wrong with it or the ammo. Collins was too quick gettin' it out of the holster, then he fumbled it, and then he flat ran out of luck."

"I think that's exactly what happened," Estelle said.

"We got to make sure that the fumble don't happen again."

"Any word yet from the boy's father? He impressed me as the sort who won't let go. My impression was that he thinks he can lay the blame for this whole mess right on the deputy's head."

"Don't care about him," Torrez snapped. "He's all mouth. He can do what he wants. If he wants to sue us, let 'im. I could give a shit. I've been thinkin' about what *we* need to do." What he said next surprised Estelle. "I think Collins is a good, solid kid. I don't plan to just throw him away."

"Do you want suggestions and input, or have you already decided?" Estelle said, and she saw the sheriff's left eyebrow edge up a little.

"You can input all you want," he said, and held up both hands, waiting.

"Well, first of all, we need to take a long, hard look at our own training and qualification program," Estelle said. "Dennis went through the academy last summer, and then he had to qualify here. I don't think he's a shooter in his leisure time, and I'm willing to bet that before the other night, he hadn't actually fired a box of ammo through this pistol since he had to go through the department's qualification...and when was that, October?"

"Well, he's going to start," Torrez said. He pointed at the filing cabinet across the room. Resting on top of it was a stack of heavy paper nearly six inches high. "That's a thousand targets," he said. "It's all we had in the vault, and that's what he shoots before he goes back on duty. Each target is a full magazine, starting with the gun holstered. Draw against the clock. He's going to shoot at three, seven, and fifteen yards, and three hundred rounds or whatever it works out to be for each distance." He rose carefully, as if his bones were fragile, and edged around the desk. He slid one of the targets out of the plastic pack. "He puts the date here, the time, the score, and one of us initials it."

"That's an ambitious program," Estelle said, both impressed and relieved that Torrez hadn't taken the simple route and told Dennis Collins to go sell real estate.

"Yep. And by the time he's done, maybe he won't drop the damn gun again. He'll be able to draw and fire in his sleep. He'll be a damn Sundance Kid."

"He needs someone with him for the first few go-arounds to make sure he doesn't have any dangerous habits. You'll do that?"

"Could. Me or Eddie or you. But I was thinkin' of asking Bill to do it. What the hell, that old gunny ain't got nothin' better to do."

"He might just like that."

"Anybody else wants to go along and do the same thing, they can," the sheriff said. "We're requalifyin'," and he paused while he leaned forward to examine the calendar on the wall beside the filing cabinet, "on August second. Everybody. That gives us two and a half months to do what we gotta do to be ready."

"And this is everyone?"

"Every single everyone," Torrez said emphatically. "Includin' me." He turned and frowned at Estelle. "And that's includin' you. And Eddie. And everyone."

"That's ambitious," she said. "Changes in the scoring?" The actual scores needed for police qualifying had always impressed Estelle as abysmal, and cheating the system wasn't unusual, either. She was aware of the standard, budget-saving arguments. Cops were required to make correct decisions that sometimes—although rarely in these far-flung rural areas—required that their weapon be drawn.

But cops weren't required to shoot out a gnat's eye at fifty paces with a handgun. They didn't need to. That's what shotguns or sniper rifles were for. Hitting center mass on a man-sized target at seven yards didn't require the skills of an exhibition shooter. And, she reflected ruefully, an entirely different set of skills was required if the "man-sized target" was shooting back or flailing with a butcher knife. It was almost entirely mind-set, not gun-set.

Torrez smiled, an expression that Estelle thought the sheriff should do more often. "Oh, yeah," he said. "There's changes in the scoring. I'll post 'em as soon as I talk to some folks. A *whole* lot higher scores this time around." He rested back in the chair and changed subjects as effortlessly as a breeze shifted. "What the hell was Marsh up to?"

Estelle took a moment to organize her thoughts. "I talked with Betty, and then visited with Joe Baca and Serafina Roybal. It appears that Chris Marsh was delivering checks from a Canadian sweepstakes."

"You gotta be shittin' me."

"No. Not one of them noticed his name tag enough to read the fake name he was using. But they all remember the face."

"You mean he was doing one of them scam things, like the Nigerian stuff?"

"At first, that's what I thought. But no…there's something going on here that's a little different. The first contact Marsh had with anyone in Regál—that we know of, at least—was a couple of months ago. On December fourteenth, he delivered a check for a little more than three thousand dollars to Serafina Roybal. In exchange, she gave him a cashier's check for five hundred bucks or so. To cover what the sweepstakes company called taxes and exchange rate. I have the original letter." She pulled out her pocket notebook and flipped pages. "Thirty-two fifty in winnings, five fifty-two in fees. She netted twenty-six ninety-eight."

"That's until the check bounces," Torrez said. "Ain't that the way these things work?"

"And that's the catch. The check *didn't* bounce, Bobby. It cleared just fine, and the money is sitting in Serafina's bank account. I had Gayle track down the telephone number and address that was listed on the stationery for the sweepstakes company in Calgary. It's a real place. No one answered because it's the weekend, and I'll pursue it more on Monday. But the business exists. At least it has a storefront. The Calgary PD is willing to cooperate in any way they can, if we feel the need. Anyway, there has been plenty of time for the check to clear, which evidently it did." She leafed through the notebook.

"And then it gets bizarre. Marsh delivered a *second* check, this time for about twenty-eight hundred even. He collected a personal check from her this time for about five hundred. He told her that the company didn't usually do that, but he apparently made the decision so Serafina wouldn't be inconvenienced."

"Go figure. She could have just stopped payment."

"But she didn't. She had no reason to. The winning check was good."

"You're shittin' me. So she won twice, is what you're sayin'."

"Exactly. And Marsh made a point of telling Joe and Lucinda when he delivered *their* first check that multiple winners were common…that he thought it might be some sort of computer glitch."

"Glitch, my ass."

"The multiple wins thing is part of it somehow. I'm sure of it. What better way to sucker somebody in."

"Ain't breakin' the bank, though," Torrez mused. "A few thousand ain't much of a jackpot."

"No, it's not. That's part of the puzzle, I'm sure. The thing we have to remember is that Chris Marsh *wasn't* a legitimate deliveryman. The company on his name tag doesn't exist. Jackie scouted that on the Internet."

"So why's he doin' it? Odd way to play Santa Claus. Unless he's settin' somebody up. Is he cheating the Canadians?"

"That's one possibility, Bobby. I'll follow up on that Monday. But here's what I'm thinking. Serafina won twice, and word of that's going to go through the village like wildfire. A month or more *before* that, the Bacas won a legitimate state lottery jackpot. And that's a *lot* of money."

"Like more than a hundred grand, I heard."

"That's right. After taxes, it's a nice old age pension. Well, then, consider what happens next. A month later, more or less, Serafina wins twice, two nice little nest eggs. She's a bright woman, Bobby. I don't think she'd fall for sending money off into the blue, in hopes of getting a prize."

"People do it all the time."

"I know they do, and maybe she *would* fall for it. But I don't think so. I would hope that she wouldn't. But this way, she is face-to-face with a personable young man who looks the part…uniform, name tag, white truck with a logo on the door. When one of the package delivery folks comes to our door, we trust them, don't we? Just like the mailman."

"I'm wondering now if that's part of it," Torrez said.

"I think it is. Remember COD? You take the parcel, and the postman or delivery agent collects the COD fee. We trust them to do that, right? We're used to it now. We sign the gadget, and take the package, just like Christmas. That's what Serafina did. And the check she received was good. Both times. At least the bank hasn't said otherwise, and it's been weeks—plenty long enough to notice a bogus check. And how long does it take the good news to spread?"

"Minutes, maybe. And then?"

"And then he does it again, this time with Joe and Lucinda. The first time, they won a little bit more than Serafina." She lifted the page. "Eight thousand, two hundred and fifty dollars. They handed over a bank check to the driver—Chris Marsh—for just over fourteen hundred. That means their net winning is almost seven thousand."

"That's enough to make 'em short of breath," Torrez muttered.

"Indeed it is. And the driver delivers, just like with Serafina. And this time, he plays off her experience, telling Joe and Lucinda that it hasn't been unusual for someone to win more than once…maybe it's even a computer glitch back at the home office."

"Oh, sure," Torrez said. He frowned. "But they got the money, am I right? The check was good?"

"It was good. There again, there's been a couple of weeks for it to clear. No problems. But I'm beginning to think that Marsh's making the comment about multiple winnings is enough to get them thinking, *Oh gosh, maybe we'll win twice, you think?* And sure enough. The big one. The letter comes telling them that they've won $178,900, the big one. And what's the risk? They don't have to send money off to Nigeria or someplace like that. The handsome young man will come to their door with his official truck and his official this and that, and trade checks. He gives them a check for $178,900, and they hand over a cashier's check for $30,413. They're ahead $148,487. A nice chunk of change."

"If the check is good," Torrez said. "Don't make no sense to me that it is. I ain't never heard of a sweepstakes working like that. I never understood how those things made money."

"In the legitimate world, I think it's just a different way of spending your advertising budget," Estelle said.

"Any chance of rousting Terri out of his weekend for some answers?" Terri Mears, the identical twin of Sergeant Tom Mears, was chief operating officer of Posadas State Bank.

"He'll cooperate, I'm sure. The problem isn't on this end. No one in some other financial institution is going to be working. We'd have to find someone in Calgary who has computer access after-hours, or at the issuing bank in Las Cruces. That's going to take as long as just waiting a day until Monday morning."

"If we have to, though…"

"If. And all this prompts the question of what Chris Marsh is doing with a fake ID, maybe a fake sign on his truck, and maybe a fake electronic signature board."

"And all of that seventeen percent shit sounds official." Torrez held up the letter that Estelle had handed him. "Listen to that nonsense: 'those charges amount to 16.981 percent…'"

"Very official. And the comment about *'by law'* is convincing."

"We don't know about the second check for the 178 grand, do we. That ain't had time to clear?"

Estelle shook her head. "Lucinda Baca deposited it on Friday afternoon."

"What time?"

"About three thirty or so."

"Well, shit. What'd she wait so long for? She got it, what, Wednesday evening sometime?"

"Exactly. I don't know why she waited, except she just did. Maybe they wanted some time to stare at it some, trying to figure out what to do with it."

"You takin' bets?"

"No. I have a sinking feeling, is what I have," Estelle said.

"If the setup was aiming at Joe and Lucinda all along, it worked pretty well. Counting Serafina's two checks and the first one to the Bacas, that's $11,800 or so invested. They copped a second check from the Bacas for $30,413. But when it shakes all out, that's about twenty grand for profit."

"That's if the last check doesn't go south," Torrez mused.

"Folks have been murdered for a whole lot less."

"Oh, indeed. But maybe all this is just practice," Estelle said.

"Perfecting the system. That's what I've been thinking. The way I see it, there are two roads to investigate. Either Chris Marsh thought he'd found some way to steal checks from this Canadian company—he was just waiting for the big one that he figured was coming—*or* the sweepstakes company itself is a scam, Marsh included. And that's the way I'm thinking right now. If the company was legit, and Marsh was just waiting in the wings, I don't see how he'd know what was coming through the pipeline."

"I can't figure that," the sheriff said. "How'd they get the names, anyways? When Joe and Lucinda won the state thing, it was in the paper. Probably radio and TV, too. But Serafina wasn't on nobody's radar, was she?"

"We don't know the answer to that, Bobby. But there must be dozens of ways. Mailing lists are commodities."

"Well," he said, swinging a foot up to rest it on the desk, "somebody climbed down to the crash site, found this Marsh kid, and then made sure that he wasn't in no condition to talk. Took the paperwork, what there was of it, took the electronic receipt book, took the magnetic signs off the doors. Probably woulda taken Marsh's name tag if it hadn't been ripped off and lost." He shrugged. "Somebody's got something to hide, that's for sure. Nilson and Abeyta are looking to find what they can about Marsh over in Cruces. There's got to be something there. Somebody's got to know something."

"And there's the Canadian connection," Estelle said. "We need to know more about Canadian Publications Limited."

"Sooner rather than later," Torrez grunted. "And first thing, if that big check don't clear? We need to give Baker a call. If the check is bogus, that takes it out of our hands."

John Baker, an old friend and contact in the Albuquerque office of the Federal Bureau of Investigation, would be intrigued, Estelle thought. "I was thinking of having a chat with him anyway," she said. "It would be interesting to hear if he's run across this one—or a variant."

"If the check bounces, whether it came from Canada or Las Cruces, it's their baby anyways," Torrez said. "Bank fraud is either them or the Postal Inspectors, or both. A heads-up won't hurt."

"Oh, one other little thing," Estelle said. "The telephone number in the woodcutter's pocket? It's the Contrerases' number."

Torrez glowered at her for a moment. "And so…"

"And so, I'm just about sure that Bertrand Anselmo wrote it."

"No shit? Why would he do that?"

"Good question. The dead man's name is Felix Otero. Joe Baca recognized him."

For a long minute, Sheriff Robert Torrez stared at Estelle, or rather *through* her, it seemed to her, pondering the possibilities. "Did you just out and ask Anselmo about all this?"

"No. He's spooked. I want to know more before I do that."

"What did Betty have to say?"

"She didn't recognize Otero. Or said she didn't. Joe admitted seeing him around sometime, he doesn't remember when. Anselmo was evasive."

"Ain't that interesting," Torrez said. "This wouldn't be the first time that Betty had a convenient memory lapse."

"Neighbors know what neighbors are doing. Regál is a tiny village," Estelle said.

"Ain't it, though."

TWENTY-ONE

MADELYN BOLLES WAS engaged in animated conversation with Gayle Torrez at the dispatch center as Estelle left the sheriff's office, and wrapped it up by signing the document that lay on the counter in front of her. As Estelle approached, Madelyn smiled broadly at the undersheriff.

"You're all waived," she said, and handed the county attorney's release of liability form to Gayle.

"Then let's go for a ride," Estelle said. "You've already had a tour of sorts with Bill Gastner, I understand?"

"Wonderful," the writer said. "We did a late breakfast—"

"That's not surprising," Gayle interrupted, and Madelyn laughed.

"My impression is that his passions include green chile," she said. "And we're going to talk again. Mr. Gastner has a most interesting perspective on life in general and this country in particular."

"A unique perspective, that's for sure," Estelle said. "Join me in my office for a few minutes?" She held the low gate for the writer, and they walked down the narrow hall to Estelle's office. Madelyn turned in place, surveying the room critically.

"Have a seat," Estelle said, but the reporter's attention had been drawn to the east wall, where a series of twelve framed photographs hung, each an eight-by-ten, some in color, some in spectacular black and white. The photos were displayed in a pleasing, staggered arrangement. "That's last year's calendar," Estelle said.

"Literally, you mean?"

"Yes. It's an idea that our department photographer, Linda Real, had a number of years ago. She started collecting candid shots, and then had the brainstorm to put them together in a calendar. Now she does it every year."

"My word," Bolles breathed. "This is the entire department?"

"That's us. An even dozen."

"Let's see. I saw this deputy down south, at Regál Pass. Jackie Taber. And this is the sheriff's wife. And this is you, of course. That means this must be your department photographer."

"That's Linda."

"Quite a talent. We should hire her away from you." She turned to look at Estelle when the undersheriff made no response. "I would think that happens a lot in a rural setting like this. You train the talent, and then they move on."

"That happens once in a while," Estelle agreed. "We certainly hope it doesn't happen anytime soon with Linda."

"This is the Great Stone Face," Madelyn said, touching the bottom of Sheriff Bob Torrez's portrait, a photo that captured him with one foot up on the front bumper of his pickup, a pair of binoculars in one hand, and a map spread out on the hood.

He was glowering at something, no doubt the shutter of Linda's camera. "He is *so* Mr. Outdoor Life," Madelyn added. "I wonder if he knows just how handsome he really is."

"You'd have to ask him."

Madelyn chuckled at that and then took a step to her right, where she frowned at a wonderful portrait of Captain Eddie Mitchell, kneeling amongst a forest of adult legs, talking to a tiny child wrapped in a soiled white blanket, the head of a teddy bear sticking out from the folds. Estelle remembered that circumstance, a mobile home fire in the middle of the night, and remembered how Linda had dropped to one knee so that the camera wasn't looking down on Mitchell or the child.

"This is a tough-looking hombre," Madelyn observed. "In a soft moment."

"That's Captain Eddie Mitchell. He was the village chief of police before the village dissolved its department and started contracting services from the county."

"Uh-huh. She could sell prints like this," the writer said. "Has she ever tried that?"

"You'd have to ask her, Madelyn."

"Interesting. Interesting organization. So let me ask you something. Who are your dispatchers?"

Estelle stepped closer and touched the three photos of Gayle, Brent Sutherland, and Ernie Wheeler.

"Just the three?"

"Yes. At the moment."

"How do you cover twenty-four/seven with just three people?"

"We swing a road deputy in to cover when we have to."

"And the road deputies are…"

"Sergeant Tom Mears, Tom Pasquale, Jackie Taber, Tony Abeyta, Dennis Collins, and Mike Sisneros." She touched the corner of each photo in order. "We just lost

Sergeant Howard Baker to retirement. We're short-handed, and just starting the hiring process."

"And you, the sheriff, and the captain are the supervisors? That's it?"

"That's it."

"Impossible. That would mean that, more often than not, you only have one officer on the road during some of the shifts. One officer for the entire county."

"That's correct. But we have a good working relationship with the State Police, as you may have noticed. Thankfully, we have long bouts of peace and quiet."

"'Long bouts of peace.' I like that." She turned away from the photographs with a final nod of approval, and her eyes roamed the rest of the small, comfortable office. "So." And she sat down, arranging her jacket and slacks carefully. "There is a wonderful story here for my magazine," she said. "One-third of your department is made up of women. Your background is a story all by itself." She spread both hands. "Born in Mexico?"

"Yes." *Omission was a wonderful convenience,* Estelle thought. She caught a tiny wrinkling around the corners of Madelyn Bolles' eyes, and wondered how much the reporter knew—if anything. She was not poised to take notes, and there was no visible tape recorder. She appeared to be simply surveying the ore load of the mine prior to serious digging.

"Sent to the United States to finish your schooling?"

"Yes."

"Eighteen years old before you became a U.S. citizen?"

"Yes."

At the third monosyllabic response, Madelyn smiled

broadly. "Don't worry. I'll get beyond the yes-or-no questions."

Estelle rested her elbows on her desk, chin comfortable on her cupped hands, and waited.

"Married a medical student who is now a successful family practitioner and general surgeon?"

"Yes."

"And Dr. Guzman is a naturalized U.S. citizen?"

"Yes."

"You have two wonderful children, Francisco, aged eight, and Carlos, now almost six."

"Yes." Madelyn Bolles had obviously done her homework, and more than that…she had committed the demographics to memory. Estelle wondered how much Bill Gastner had told the reporter, although knowing *padrino*'s discretion, she doubted that any of the personal data had come from him.

"You're now thirty-nine years old, which means that you've worked for the Posadas County Sheriff's Department for sixteen years."

Estelle took a deep breath and lifted her head, laying her hands down on the desk. "Yes, and yes. I'm impressed."

"Trivia is easy," Madelyn Bolles said with an offhand wave of her left hand. "Most of the time. But we have to move beyond that. Every single person I've talked to so far, including his wife, Ms. Gayle, tells me that your esteemed movie star of a sheriff is going to be the tough nut to crack."

"Probably true."

"But that's all right," Madelyn said easily. "That'll be fun. Do you ever read our magazine, Estelle?"

"I confess that I don't. I've seen it, of course."

"Let me tell you what we do. We specialize in thorough, probing, tough articles about today's women, Estelle. Not just a superficial profile of some glamorous star, or a page of gratuitous praise for a Nobel or Pulitzer winner. We like to think that we present complete portraits of women who we believe are accomplishing major goals in life, sometimes against considerable odds, women who are inspirations to others in this man's world. We lean heavily on biography as a way to explain why our featured women are taking the paths that they are. Am I making sense?"

"Yes."

"I love that." She regarded Estelle, and the undersheriff could see the assessment going on behind the alert violet eyes. "We're a highly regarded, much-awarded national magazine, Estelle, and I don't tell you that just to blow smoke. We don't take our assignments lightly. We're thorough, as I said, and fair." She reached forward and rested her right index finger on the edge of Estelle's desk, as if the pressure she applied kept the desk from floating off into space. "I have to tell you from the beginning that although sometimes I use a tape recorder, most of the time I don't. I trust my memory, I trust my instincts. I take my own photographs. When all is said and done, I will let you read the rough draft copy of the article, but will accept only corrections where I might have made an error in fact…not impression or interpretation."

"All right. But I don't need to read it. You do what you do."

"Well, fair enough. But really most important is the *way* I work. I'd like to leave an open calendar for this."

"What does that mean?" Estelle asked.

"It means that I won't be flitting off to something that someone says is more important. I won't be interrupted. And I'm also saying that this isn't an afternoon thing, or one or two days. Who knows. I might be in town for two weeks. Maybe more. It depends on how much time we can find to work together—because it really is a collaborative effort, Estelle." She tapped the desk for punctuation and withdrew her hand. "My intent is not to invade your privacy, although a certain amount of that is inevitable. I want to offer a profile of you, your department, even your family, that's inspiring to our readers." She sat back and waited.

"Caramba," Estelle whispered, more to herself than anyone else. "Why would I want to do all this?"

"Because you recognize that this *is* a good story. It's not a question of what you have to gain from it, since I don't really believe you're concerned about that. It's what our readers have to gain. Inspiration is a wonderful gift, Estelle."

"This is all a good deal more than I expected," the undersheriff said.

"I don't want there to be any misunderstanding. But I'll add this, Estelle. It is *so* worthwhile." Madelyn sat patiently, without moving a muscle, while the undersheriff mulled over the proposal.

"I have a couple of concerns," Estelle said. "First of all, I hope you realize that if I agree to all of this, I won't discuss the department employees with you, except in the most general sort of way. Their personnel files are not public record, and it's not up to me to talk about them behind their backs. As I said in my e-mail to you, you're welcome to initiate an interview with whomever you like. Some of the staff will talk with you, some may not." She shrugged. "Bobby, for instance."

"Yes," Madelyn said, and Estelle found herself captivated by this bright woman.

"There's that," Estelle continued. "Some of them, I'm sure, will talk with you. One or two might even seek you out. I've already told all of them that they're welcome to cooperate with you, and that if they do so, they don't have to feel that they have to clear anything with me… or Bobby. They're entitled to their own opinions."

"That's more than fair. Most bosses aren't so secure."

"Most important, though," Estelle said. "I hope you appreciate that the nature of our work, much of the time, is confidential. For instance, at this moment, we're right in the middle of a homicide investigation. That obviously takes priority. I will not discuss that case, or any other case, or release information to you that I would not release to any other journalist. I think that's only fair. You're welcome to watch us work and draw your own conclusions. I'll tell you what I can, when I can, but understand that there are necessary constraints. I'd really take offense at seeing in print a comment that might be made offhandedly concerning an investigation."

"Believe me, I understand the legal issues," Madelyn said. "And rest assured that we are not *Police Gazette*. I'm not here to scoop the *Posadas Register*, either. By the time we publish, the daily details will be ancient history anyway. They don't matter to us, except by way of example." She cocked her head and toyed with the small gold earring in her left ear. "Frank Dayan is an interesting sort, by the way."

"Yes, he is."

"He wants to do more about your son's accomplishments for his paper," Madelyn said. "He cheerfully admits that he doesn't know how. His editor—it's Pam?" Estelle nodded. "I wanted to talk with her, but I understand that her daughter is in the hospital? That's so sad, isn't it."

"Madelyn," Estelle said, with no intention of entering into a discussion of publisher Frank Dayan's relationship with editor/ reporter/photographer/single mom Pam Gardiner, "you need to know from the very beginning that I have reservations about subjecting my family to media exposure. I've had that conversation with Frank a number of times. That's why he *hasn't* had articles about Francisco in the paper."

"We can't very well profile you without talking with your family," the writer said. "And this isn't like being on the front page of the Sunday paper, either. In the first place, we're talking about six months, minimum, before the article even sees the light of day. But your two sons are remarkable boys. I was captivated by that photo of Francisco in concert over in Las Cruces."

"My two sons *are* remarkable little boys, and that's not just their mother talking. They *are* remarkable. Maybe they will talk to you. Maybe not. We'll have to see. I won't tell them that they have to."

"I look forward to the challenge of winning their confidence," Madelyn said. "And yours, if you'll let me. How's this for a deal?… I will never talk to your children when you or your husband aren't present. How's that?"

"It's a place to start."

"There's an interesting question we could address right now, and it might be revealing for both of us." She steepled her fingers, the tips of her index fingers resting on her lips. "I know what *I* want out of this article,

Estelle. What do you want? Why have you agreed to see me? A moment ago, you wondered that very thing. Why didn't you just press the delete key when you saw my initial e-mail?"

"Partly curiosity, I suppose."

"It must be more than that."

"I'm sure it is. I don't know how to put it into words."

"Think on that, then. That gives me an opportunity to do something meaningful for you, Estelle. That's important to me. I don't consider this a one-way street that we're on here." The writer nodded with finality. "Which brings us to mechanics, Estelle. May I be your shadow, then? This is a lot to ask, I know. If you're awake and decent, I'd like to be with you."

Estelle laughed. "*That's* going to get tiresome for you, that's for sure."

"But here again, let's set a ground rule we can work with. When you need privacy, I want you to feel free just to say, 'Go away.' And I will. No questions asked. But if you *don't* tell me to go away, there I'll be."

"We'll see how that works," Estelle said. "That's all I can say."

"Fair enough. Might I make a suggestion, by the way? It's inevitable that you'll feel it necessary to introduce me to someone. Might I suggest that a simple 'this is Madelyn Bolles' is sufficient? No other explanation? It's been my experience that most of the time, people will fill in the blanks to their own satisfaction."

"*Pecados de omisión,*" Estelle said. "Sins of omission are one of law enforcement's favorite tools." The undersheriff glanced at the wall clock. "You're staying over at Mrs. Melvin's B and B, is that right?"

"That's my base ops, yes. Room three, the one with the outside stairway around back."

"Do you need to check in there today, or are we ready for a ride?"

"We're ready," Madelyn Bolles said. "I just need to fetch my laptop and briefcase from my car."

Estelle rolled her chair back and stood up. "Oh… I noticed that you've already become acquainted with one of the state officers. I saw that he had you stopped down by Moore."

Madelyn grimaced. "Ah, that. I wasn't paying attention. He said I was driving eighty-four in a sixty-five zone. I'm sure he was right, radar being what it is. A nice enough young man. I don't recall his name."

"John Allen," Estelle said. "He's new."

"Well, he's also *forgiving*, and that's what is important in this instance," the writer said. "I'll meet you—" Estelle's desk phone interrupted her by buzzing line one.

"By the pumps outside," Estelle finished for Madelyn. "Excuse me a minute." She picked up the phone. "Guzman."

"Estelle, this is Betty. Did I catch you at a bad time?"

"Of course not. What can I do for you?" She pulled a pad of paper close.

"I think there's someone here you should talk to," Betty Contreras said.

TWENTY-TWO

ESTELLE'S PLANS TO give Madelyn Bolles a proper orientation into passenger etiquette in a patrol car were reduced to a quick "buckle up tight." The reporter was still fussing with belt and accoutrements as they charged out of the parking lot and onto Grande Avenue, the main north–south thoroughfare of Posadas. She finally settled for the laptop under her knees, and the soft briefcase clutched in her lap.

By the time they roared under the interstate overpass and took the long curve onto State 56, the speedometer had climbed past 80. Madelyn's right hand crept forward on the door sill, looking for something to clutch, proving that riding fast was very different from *driving* fast.

Waiting until she had dusted past two southbound *burros*, Estelle reached out for the mike.

"Three-oh-three, three-ten."

"Three-oh-three." Jackie Taber didn't sound as tired as she had to be.

"Ten-twenty?"

"Three-oh-three is just comin' up on Victor's place, northbound."

Estelle took a deep breath of relief that Jackie Taber had been slow to call it a day. She was capable of sitting quietly for hours on a warm rock in the shade of a piñon with her pencil and sketch pad. At the same time, Jackie knew as well as anyone else that Tony Abeyta was on his way to Las Cruces and the other denizen of the day shift, Dennis Collins, was stuck firmly in limbo after the dropped-gun incident. What was important at that moment was that Jackie Taber, nearing Victor Sanchez's Broken Spur Saloon, was twenty-five miles closer to Regál than Estelle was.

"Three-oh-three, I'll be ten-twenty-one."

Taking her time, Estelle slowed the car a fraction and opened her cell phone. Madelyn watched closely, not losing her grip on briefcase and door.

"Jackie," Estelle said as the phone connection went through, "Betty Contreras is waiting for us at her house. She says that an illegal who might have been the woodcutter up north just walked past her house."

"Might have been," Jackie said, alert to nuance as always, tired as she might be.

"She says that he's headed toward Joe Baca's."

"Oh, crap," Jackie said. In the background, Estelle could hear the squeal of tires and then hard acceleration. "And here we thought Betty didn't know nuttin' about nobody. All of a sudden she knows the woodcutter and his pal?"

"That's what we're headed to find out, Jackie. I'm southbound, but we're just leaving town. I want the man detained, but as long as he doesn't force his way inside or pose an immediate threat, hang back and wait for us."

"You got it. Joe's the one who's got the money, am I right?"

"Yes, he does. Be careful."

"Roger that."

Estelle auto-dialed Dispatch. "Gayle, we're responding to a complaint in Regál that I think is tied to Catron

County's case with the woodcutter. Has Tony left for Cruces yet?"

"He and John Allen are standing right here," Gayle replied, and, after a moment of hurried conversation off-line, added, "and now they're out the door."

"Thanks. Jackie's responding, and I'll be about fifteen minutes behind her."

"Got it."

Without looking, the undersheriff placed the phone on the car's computer keyboard that took up most of the center console.

Ahead, a county dump truck, its flashers bright, rumbled along the shoulder behind a road grader.

"I have to ask," Madelyn Bolles shouted over the roar of the car and the rushing slipstream. "Why the phone instead of the radio? I thought cops were always ten-fouring on the air."

"Sometimes we are," Estelle replied. "But sometimes, we don't want the whole world listening in, and the phone is more private." She let the county car drift into the oncoming lane so she could give the truck and grader plenty of space.

"Good heavens, who's going to be listening?"

"You'd be amazed," Estelle said. "It's a hobby for some folks, why I couldn't begin to tell you. Bill Gastner calls 'em 'scanner ghouls.' If we have a messy accident in the middle of the night, sometimes there isn't room to park by the time we get there."

"You've got to be kidding."

"I wish I was. The less we can be on the air, the better."

"It's hard to imagine them sitting home in their bathrobes, huddled around the family scanner, waiting to race you to the scene."

The road straightened as they approached Moore, and now past traffic, Estelle held the speed at an even 90. "It's also easier to hear the telephone sometimes. Remind me to tell you a story or two sometime," she said. "By the way, a couple of things, Madelyn," she said, speaking unnaturally loud to be heard. "When we're on the scene of a call, I'm going to require that you stay in the vehicle, unless I specifically say otherwise. Understood?"

"Oh, yes."

"The shotgun by your left knee?" Without taking her eyes off the road, she reached out with her right hand and touched a button on the radio-lights-siren console without pushing it. "This is the electric lock release. Have you ever used a shotgun before?"

"Well, years ago my dad and uncle—" Madelyn stopped short. "No. I haven't."

"Unlock the rack by pushing that button. When you have the gun clear, push the safety button behind the trigger to the left, and watch where you point the muzzle. There are three rounds in the magazine and one in the chamber. Just keep pumping until it goes click."

"You think I'm going to remember all that?"

"Yes, I do. You remember everything."

"I don't think so," Madelyn said fervently.

"Well, you should know it's there."

"I'll sit here quiet as a church mouse," the reporter said.

"Sometimes that's not enough," Estelle said, remembering Linda Real's disastrous ride-along with one of the deputies seven years before, on this very stretch of highway. It was only a matter of time before Madelyn interviewed the photographer, and Linda would not bring up the memory. But Madelyn would see the scars on the photographer's face, and she'd find a way to ask. And then, she might not be so eager for ride-alongs.

In another minute, they crossed the old concrete bridge over the Rio Salinas, and as they swept around the end of the mesa, Estelle saw a wink of lights in her rearview mirror. Deputy Tony Abeyta would be driving one of the Expeditions, and he wouldn't have been gaining on her with that. In a moment, she could see the low, squat shape of one of the new State Police cruisers with the distinctive white pimple of the computer antenna on the roof. Despite her pace, the state car quickly pulled to within a hundred yards of her and then slowed, pacing her as they shot across the Rio Guigarro and headed toward the Broken Spur Saloon and then the intersection with County Road 14.

"PCS all units, three-oh-three."

"PCS. Go ahead, three-oh-three."

"All units ten-twenty-six south of the pass."

"Three-ten copies." In a second, Abeyta also acknowledged Jackie Taber's request that siren and lights not be used.

"Three-ten, Allen on tack two."

Working by feel, her eyes glued to the road as they left the flat prairie behind and took the first dangerous curve up the north flank of the San Cristóbals, Estelle toggled one of the selectors on her radio to match the State Police car-to-car frequency.

"Three-ten."

"What we got?" the State Policeman asked.

"One individual, a possible illegal who may have been

involved with a death that Catron County is currently investigating."

"He's tryin' to skip across the border?"

Estelle braked hard for the first switchback to the right, and her passenger's left hand flew up to slap the dashboard for support. "Maybe," Estelle said. "Right now it appears that he may be paying a visit to one of the residents down there."

"Taber's on it?"

"Ten-four."

"Then there ain't no rush," Allen said. "I'll be behind you. Lemme know what you need. This guy known to be armed?"

"That's negative, but we never know. Thanks, John."

She racked the mike and leaned forward slightly to look uphill through the sparse trees. The road was empty, and on the next, even sharper switchback she used both lanes. For a moment, they were heading due east along the ridge, and had she chosen to do so, she could have looked down and seen the saloon, the county road, and the spread of prairie all the way north to Cat Mesa behind Posadas. The road crumpled back on itself again, and after a switchback followed by a leisurely series of esses, they started up the long grade to the pass.

As they rushed past the sign announcing the pass elevation, Estelle flipped off the emergency lights and slowed her pace.

The south side of the pass was an easier descent, long straights between gentle switchbacks. At one point, Estelle could look down directly into the heart of the village. She saw the white county Bronco just on the highway side of Betty Contreras' house, but she couldn't tell if the deputy's truck was parked or just driving slowly. Joe Baca's home was out of sight, hidden behind the bulk of the water tank.

"Three-oh-three, three-ten is just coming off the pass, ETA three minutes."

"Ten-four. Ten-twenty-one."

Estelle had enough time to hang up the mike and take the phone before it buzzed. "He's sitting under one of the apple trees in front of Sosimo Baca's place," Jackie said. "I'm watchin' him through the trees from just this side of Betty's."

"He's just sitting?" The adobe that had once been home to Joe Baca's older brother had stood empty since the old man's death, the orchard going untended and gnarly as the little house gradually dissolved.

"Yeah, he is. But he's looking up toward the pass. You got a state cruiser behind you?"

"Affirmative."

"He saw it. He's getting up now and headed west. He's joggin'. You want me to intercept?"

"No. Hold off. I want to know where he's going."

"Evidently *he* knows," Jackie said. "He isn't just out for a stroll."

"Just watch him then." Keeping the phone connection open, Estelle slowed the car as they swept down the last stretch behind the water tank and pumping station. The church and its gravel parking lot was a quarter of a mile ahead, with the border crossing just beyond. Right at the bottom of the hill, Sanchez Street met the highway, and as she turned onto the narrow dirt lane, she grimaced in anticipation of the rough jounce.

"He's cutting cross-lots," Jackie said. "That's going to take him right behind Joe's woodpile." And by now, Estelle thought, the man would be able to hear the traffic. Even with engines little more than idling, the tires of three vehicles crunching on gravel carried like gunshots. Betty Contreras was standing in her front yard, hands caught up in her apron. She bustled to meet them, but Estelle slowed only to a walk as she lowered the passenger window.

"We'll be back to talk in a bit," she called. Betty stopped, uncertain, looking first at Madelyn and then back at the State Police cruiser. The expression on Betty's face was one of confusion and apprehension.

"He's still behind the woodpile," Jackie said, voice calm and almost bemused. "Maybe that's where he's staying. If he breaks for the house, he'll be in plain sight." Behind Joe Baca's woodpile, enough piñon, juniper, scrub oak, and mesquite for ten winters, a jumble of boulders formed a giant's necklace along the base of the foothills. Estelle turned the county car off onto the lane to Joe's, and saw that Jackie's vehicle was parked right by the Bacas' mailbox. The man had nowhere to go. He could sprint to the house, a distance of twenty-five yards. He could clamber up into the rocks behind the village. He could dart from cover and try to zigzag through the village, heading for the border and custody.

"There's Joe," Jackie Taber said, but Estelle had already seen him. She pulled past Jackie's unit and drove up the Bacas' driveway.

"Keep watch," Estelle said, and snapped the phone closed. Turning to Madelyn, whose wonderful eyes were now about the size of dinner plates, she said, "Stay in the car."

"Oh, yes."

Estelle had experienced passengers in the past who

had said that very thing, then gotten out and found a way to get in the way.

"Stay *in* the car," she said again, and raised the window.

"I heard and I understand," Madelyn said.

"Thank you."

Joe showed no signs of stepping off the house porch. Estelle unbuckled and took her time getting out of the car. She saw that the driver's doors of both Jackie's vehicle and the State Police cruiser were ajar, but the officers were staying put.

As Estelle walked past the front fender of her car, she reached back and adjusted the bulk of the .45 automatic. "Joe," she said, keeping her voice conversational. *"¿Cómo está?"* As she expected, the old man was uneasy—anyone would be with an army just arrived in his front yard. A quick glance told her that Trooper Allen had gotten out of his car and stood relaxed by the front fender. He held a scoped semiautomatic rifle at high port. Jackie Taber still sat in her unit, ready to dive out or charge the Bronco forward, whatever the need might be.

Estelle could easily imagine the fugitive crouching behind the woodpile, his heart hammering. Did the *policía* know about the death up in Catron County? Were they actually after *him*, or was this some other problem—so close to the border, it could be anything. Better to crouch and wait. Nothing to lose.

The undersheriff took her time as she walked up the mild slope of the yard. She found it interesting that Joe Baca didn't glance toward the woodpile where the fugitive was hidden. Perhaps Joe didn't know the man was there...unless he had been looking out through the kitchen window. If he'd come outside in response to the three police vehicles, then he might not know. She thrust her hands in her jacket pockets, considering what tack to take, keeping the bulk of the woodpile between herself and the hidden man's view.

"Joe, did Betty call you a little bit ago?" she asked in English.

Baca skillfully skirted that one. "We talk all the time," he said. "We're neighbors."

She ambled up closer, still keeping several paces' distance, wondering how fluent the illegal's English was. The undersheriff kept her voice down. "I need to know what you can tell me about the second man. The one who was with Felix Otero up north."

Joe looked puzzled, but he didn't glance at the woodpile.

Estelle continued, "Why would he want to come back here? To your house?"

"My house?"

"Yes."

"I haven't seen him."

Estelle hesitated. "But you know who I'm talking about, no?"

"I don't know *what* you're talking about," Joe said lamely.

"Can you and I go inside for a minute?"

"Sure. The others want something, too? I got coffee."

"No thanks."

He turned toward the door, and Estelle followed for only two steps, then turned abruptly and, with her right hand out of her pocket and sweeping the jacket back, gripped the butt of her automatic. Another step toward the house brought her into view of the corner of the woodpile nearest the house. She could rock back a step, and be protected by the firewood.

The young man, unkempt and clearly fatigued, sat on his rump, his back against the stack, arms clasped around drawn-up knees. His wary expression slowly dissolved to one of resignation as he saw the Posadas County Sheriff's Department badge on Estelle's belt. He didn't move, but his eyes flicked from her as the roar of another vehicle attracted his attention. Deputy Taber had driven her Bronco right up into Joe Baca's front yard, leaped out, and from her position could see both the undersheriff and the fugitive.

"Buenas tardes," Estelle said gently. She could see no weapon, and the man's body language said *cower*, but that could change in a heartbeat. *"Levante las manos por encima de la cabeza."*

"Estoy descansando, nada más," the young man whispered. His arms lifted slowly as if on hydraulics, and his eyes were locked not on Estelle, but on Jackie Taber a dozen yards away. Her threatening stance was obvious, but with the woodpile at his back, the man could move only deeper into her line of fire.

"Slowly now," Estelle continued in English. "I want you to lie forward on your stomach." The man's confusion wasn't at the change of language. To be seated firmly on his rump against the woodpile, with his knees drawn up in front of him, locked him in place. Any movement was awkward. He shouldered forward, moving his legs to one side, and flopped down, eyes still locked on the uniformed deputy.

"One hand behind your back," Estelle said. She slipped her cuffs off her belt and approached quickly, staying close to the pile of fragrant split wood. Jackie had moved off to her left. *"Ahora, la otra,"* the under-sheriff said, and finished cuffing the man. "Get up now," she said. "Take it easy."

"I have…" the man started to say as he struggled to his feet. Estelle turned him in place and pushed him face-first against the woodpile. A pat-down discovered only a meager amount of change, a small pocket utility knife, and a wallet. Keeping her left hand on his shoulder, she thumbed open the billfold. Thirty-two dollars was the extent of his fortune. She nudged the Mexican driver's license far enough out to see his name.

"Señor Ynostroza," she said. "Ricardo Ynostroza. *¿Cómo está?"* She pushed the wallet back into his hip pocket, and the small knife into her own. Deputy Taber had holstered her gun, and now stood with one hand resting on Joe Baca's shoulder. The old man stood just off the front step of the house. Estelle turned the man around and regarded him. She guessed him to be perhaps thirty years old, no more, with a week's sparse stubble of beard and dark circles under his eyes. His blue denim shirt hung loose on his wiry frame. His scuffed work boots hinted at plenty of mileage. He didn't reply to her question but stood silent and watchful. She saw a flicker of apprehension cross his broad face as John Allen's State Police cruiser pulled up beside Jackie's unit.

"Señor Ynostroza," she said, "Señora Contreras was concerned about you."

"I have…" seemed to be the extent of the young man's vocabulary.

"Do you understand English?"

"Yes, I do," he said eagerly this time, nodding vigorously.

"Good, then. Where were you going, *señor?"*

"I thought perhaps…"

"Where is your home, *señor*?"

"I am from Buenaventura," he said. "It is a small town—"

"I know where it is," Estelle said. "Is that where Felix Otero lived as well?"

"I don't know…."

"Yes, *señor*, you do." She turned without taking her eyes off the young man and beckoned for Jackie. "Obviously, we must talk." The young man's eyes flicked toward the approaching deputy, and then to Joe Baca, who hadn't moved but now stood in company with Allen.

"We'll transport this young man in your vehicle," Estelle said to Jackie. "I need to talk with Joe for a little bit." She had been watching the old man, reading the confusion and concern in his posture. Ynostroza started to say something, but she ignored him, leaving the young man in the deputy's custody.

Joe Baca studied the ground in front of his boots as Estelle approached.

"How do you know this man?" she asked without preamble.

"I don't," Baca said, but he wouldn't look at her.

"He was coming to see you," she pressed. "Betty Contreras said that she was worried about that. Why does he want to see you? Is he after money?"

Joe's eyes flicked up at that. "Maybe. Maybe that's it."

"And maybe there's more to it," Estelle said. "It would be much simpler if you would tell me what's going on, Joe."

"He is just…" And his hands waved helplessly. "He is just like any of the others. You know."

"Except you know him, Joe," she said impatiently.

"And so does Betty. And so does Father Anselmo. This man, Ricardo Ynostroza, was with Felix Otero, the young man who died up north. That's what Betty says. Do you want to talk to me about that?"

Another vehicle appeared, and an expression of relief washed across Joe's face. Estelle recognized Lucinda Baca's car. "Maybe she knows," he said.

"Officer Allen, would you take a statement from Mr. Baca?" Estelle asked. "I'll talk with Lucinda." She could see that obviously wasn't what Joe Baca had in mind, but feeling adrift might loosen his tongue a bit.

TWENTY-THREE

"WHY WOULD we know who this guy is?" Lucinda Baca snapped as she led Estelle inside the house. She was as thorny as her husband was mellow, a surprising woman who at first glance looked as soft and compliant as a marshmallow. "And what's that state cop want with Joe, anyway?"

"He's just taking a short statement, Mrs. Baca."

"About what now, may I ask?"

"We have several unanswered questions. I stopped by earlier to talk to Joe about the sweepstakes...." She hesitated. The young Mexican worker in the back of Jackie Taber's Bronco was a separate issue, and if there were any ties between him and the case involving Chris Marsh and the lottery winners, they weren't obvious at the moment—other than the natural attraction that piles of money presented.

Before Estelle could continue, Lucinda interrupted, "Sweepstakes? *Por Dios*, is that the whole county's business now?" She turned to face Estelle, one hand on an ample hip. She punctuated with a wagging finger. "All of a sudden I got a yard full of cops because maybe we won a few dollars?"

"That's not quite it," Estelle said.

"Well, you tell me what *is* it, Estelle Guzman. We've known you since you were this high," and she swept her hand down to her knees. "And now all of a sudden..."

She might as well have just said, *You remember your place, young lady.*

"I stopped by to see if Joe recognized this man." She held out the eight-by-ten glossy morgue photo of Christopher Marsh.

"Oh, my poor soul," Lucinda said, instantly softening. "Isn't that… That's the boy who made the sweepstakes deliveries. Barry something."

"His real name is Christopher Marsh, Lucinda. He was the driver of that truck that went over the side up on the pass."

"Dios mío," Lucinda breathed. "Is this the crash all the cops were at last night?"

"That's when we found it. It happened sometime Wednesday evening. Right after he left you folks."

Lucinda sat down abruptly, still holding the photo. She stared at the image for a long time, and Estelle didn't interrupt her thoughts. The expression on the woman's face was impossible to read. She could have been saying a prayer for the young man who had lost his life, or for the $30,413 check that police might have found in the wreckage.

"Betty said that he hit a deer," Lucinda said finally.

"That appears to be the case, Mrs. Baca. I'm sorry."

"They picked up all his deliveries and things? He'd just left here, you know." A light came on. "Now wait a minute. You said the accident happened *Wednesday* night?"

"That's what we think. You spoke with him sometime early that evening. He was found by a highway department patrol on Friday evening."

"Oh, no," and Lucinda softened again. "You mean this boy just lay out there all that time?"

"It appears that way."

"Was he killed outright? Oh, how awful." A single tear formed in the corner of Lucinda's left eye, and she brushed at it with an index finger.

"Probably," Estelle said. *If you consider drowning in beer outright.*

Some of Lucinda's previous armor hardened again. "And now what does the lottery have to do with the cops?" she asked. "Sit down, at least." She waved toward one of the chairs, and sat back, arms folded over her chest. The photo of Marsh lay on her lap. "The taxes were taken right off the top. We don't owe anyone."

"It's not the state lottery that's of interest," Estelle said. "But the Canadian sweepstakes thing sets off some alarm bells."

Lucinda fell silent, her small eyes assessing. She ran a hand around the crease at the base of her throat where a necklace would have been hidden had she been wearing one.

"Was Marsh alone when he came to your door?" Estelle asked.

"This boy?" She touched the photo. "Yes, he was alone. Both times. Just him and that little truck. You know the ones that they drive."

"Mrs. Baca, when did you deposit the second check— the larger one?"

She bristled and hugged her ample bosom closer. "Who said that I *did* deposit it?"

"Did you, ma'am?"

"And now tell me why that should be the business of the Sheriff's Department?" She lifted her lower jaw as if pointing at the horizon with her chin. "How's your mother, by the way?" *We're all family, remember.*

"She's fine, thank you. If the check is bogus, Lucinda, then it *is our business. Ours, and the Federal Bureau of Investigation's,* and then we can include the Internal Revenue Service, the U.S. Postal Service, and all sorts of other interesting people. We won't know the answer to that until you take the check to the bank."

"Well, I did that… Friday afternoon. We just—we just had things to do on Thursday and Friday morning, and we didn't get to it." She took a slow, deep breath. "Maybe it was partly… Well, it was for a lot of money. It was sitting there on the television set, and each time I walked by, I'd look at it just a little." She smiled. "Like maybe it wasn't real, you know? Like maybe one time I'd look, and it wouldn't be there?"

"Lucinda, we have every reason to believe that Chris Marsh worked for a bogus company…a fake delivery service."

"This boy? I don't believe that," Lucinda said smugly. "He had an ID, and he didn't *want* anything, after all. And listen.…I *cashed* the check that we won the first time, and it cleared just fine. So there's that. And—"

"And both of Serafina's cleared, too," Estelle interrupted. "We know that. But the fact of the matter is that if this fourth check *doesn't* clear—if it's as fake as we think it is—then you'll be out more than thirty thousand dollars."

"But we *won* already," the woman insisted. "I cashed a check for something like eight thousand dollars, *por Dios*… It *cleared.* I *paid* the taxes and fees on that one, just like I did this last time."

"You gave Chris Marsh a cashier's check for thirty thousand this past Wednesday evening."

"Yes. And received a sweepstakes check for more

than $178,000 in return. So I really don't know what you're talking about, Estelle Guzman. Now I've heard of all those scams that are going around. What do they call it…the Niagara thing."

"Nigerian, I think."

"Whatever. Now how ridiculous is that one? Who's going to send money or bank account information to some foreigner. If they're anything like some of the telephone solicitors we get, *por Dios*, you can't even understand a word they're saying."

Lucinda handed the photo of Chris Marsh back to Estelle. "You know, when Joe and I won that state lottery, it was almost as much nuisance as it was a blessing. And then the sweepstakes on top of it all? It takes the breath away."

"What did the courier tell you about the sweepstakes?"

"What did he tell us? What did he *have* to tell us? It was all spelled out in the letters that they sent. We didn't have much time, I know that." She grimaced. "And you know, I think I might have just thrown everything away if it hadn't been for Serafina. She won a little bit.… In fact it's just like you said. She won *twice*. So I thought, *Well, maybe. What will it hurt?* It's a nuisance driving to the bank for the cashier's check, but it all worked out."

"And it had to be a cashier's check," Estelle prodded.

"That's right. He said that the delivery company only accepts cashier's checks. The letter said the same thing. Not personal checks and not cash. Now, that's the first thing, Estelle. If someone won't take cash, doesn't that tell you something?"

"I suppose that it does. Did he mention anything about multiple winners?"

"Yes, he did. He said that it happens often enough that he thinks there's some kind of computer mix-up." She shrugged, evidently sharing her husband's view that if a mistake opened the doors of opportunity, why not walk on through?

"What time of day did he come by?"

"It was afternoon, I suppose. Yes. Midafternoon the first time, but quite late the second visit. I remember the last time—this past week—he said that he was running late. He came just as we were finishing up with supper."

"You signed for the delivery?"

"Of course I signed." She rose, walked to the living room window, and pushed the curtain to one side. "Just what does the State Police want with my husband? And who is that in your car? For heaven's sakes, half the neighborhood is being locked up."

"That's a visitor to the department riding with me," Estelle said. "And the man that we arrested just now, the man sitting in the truck with Deputy Taber—he knew this man." She held out the grisly photo of the wood-cutter as Lucinda walked back to her chair. This time the woman took the picture with a sigh of exasperation.

"Now who is this? He looks hurt."

"Dead, in fact," Estelle said. "It was a woodcutting accident up by Reserve."

"Por Dios, that's the other side of the world."

"It is a ways. We have reason to believe that the man we just took into custody was with him at the time."

Lucinda reached across and turned on the light beside her chair, and reexamined the photo. "What in heaven's name happened?"

"The saw kicked back," Estelle said. "He bled to death. Do you know him?"

"How should I know him?" Lucinda said. "I had a cousin who lived up in Quemado. But he's long dead now."

"We apprehended the young man hiding behind your woodpile. An odd place to hide, don't you think?"

"Behind our *woodpile*? Is he an illegal, or what? What's he doing here?"

"That's what we're trying to find out, Mrs. Baca. We do know that the two men were working together up in Reserve." She handed the photocopy of Betty Contreras' telephone number to the woman without comment.

"What's this?"

"Do you recognize the number?"

"Of course I do. It's Bet's."

"Betty Contreras?"

Lucinda nodded with impatience. "Sure. And now what's this for?"

"Catron County officers found this in the dead man's pocket."

"The woodcutter? What's he have to do with all of this?"

"Mrs. Baca, we don't know who he is. We have a *name*. Felix Otero. But then your husband recognized him, and so did Betty. The phone number means that there's some sort of connection between the dead man and Betty, maybe your husband as well. Maybe others. We don't know any more about him than that." She stabbed a finger toward the window.

"That man, the one we found hiding behind your woodpile, is a young man from Mexico named Ricardo Ynostroza. He was with Otero up north. He ran when the accident happened, leaving his friend to bleed to death. Apparently, he ran back down here. We'll find out the details when we talk to him at length. We'll find out why Felix had a local Regál phone number in his pocket. We'll find out who *wrote* the number, and why. That should all be interesting, no? And most important, Mrs. Baca, we need to inform Felix Otero's family in Mexico. It's going to be a sad day for them."

"*Por Dios*, what a mess. First the car crash up on the pass, and now this."

"We're notifying Chris Marsh's family as well," Estelle said. "If he said anything else to you, anything that might help us in that line, we would appreciate knowing."

Estelle carefully slid the photos back into the envelope. "Mrs. Baca, why do you think that Ricardo Ynostroza came to your house? Why wouldn't he go to Betty's? The men had *her* telephone number, after all."

"I have absolutely *no* idea. How did you all find out that he was here?"

"A telephone call."

"Well, then the first thing to do is ask that person… the one who called you to report him."

"Of course. You have no idea yourself?"

"No. I told you. I have no idea about any of this. Except half the world knows now that we won some money. What, do they all think we keep it in bags around the house?"

Estelle laughed gently. "I hope you don't. I would wonder, though…how would a man like Señor Ynostroza know about your winnings?"

"Your guess is every bit as good as mine," Lucinda said. "When are the cops going to be through with my husband?"

"And you don't know anything about who might have

written this note, or why?" Estelle asked, ignoring the question.

"No. How could I know that?"

Estelle stood up. "I have a feeling," she said, "that the news won't be good about your second check, Lucinda. We'll be able to track that down with the bank on Monday morning."

"What are you going to do if it *is* good? I really think it is, you know."

"Then you'll have my best wishes to spend it in good health," the undersheriff said.

TWENTY-FOUR

As she walked back to her car, Estelle Reyes-Guzman saw that Madelyn Bolles had taken the command to stay in the vehicle in the spirit of the order, if not the letter. The passenger door was open, and the writer was turned sideways in the front seat, feet outside on the ground, fingers dancing over her laptop's keyboard.

"Were you beginning to think you'd been abandoned?" Estelle asked.

"Oh, no," Madelyn replied brightly. "I'm just taking the opportunity to catch up on some notes." She nodded back down the road, the dust of Jackie Taber's Bronco still hanging in the air. "As soon as the deputy and the fugitive left, I figured it was safe to stop paying attention for a few minutes."

Estelle laughed. "I suppose that's one way to look at it. Of course, if he'd been in collusion with someone with a high-powered rifle inside the house..."

Madelyn folded the computer closed and slid it onto the floor in front of her seat. "Then I don't think that you would have approached the way you did, right out in the open." She pulled herself out of the car and stretched, turning in place as she surveyed the small village. "I would think that this would *not* be a hotbed of illegal alien crossings," she observed.

"It isn't."

"I mean there's an official border crossing right here,

with that magnificently homely fence. And even if they climb up into the mountains, where are they going to go?"

"Exactly."

"So what was the young man after?"

"We don't know yet." The undersheriff settled into the driver's seat. She started to put the envelope into her briefcase, and then thought better of it. Slipping out the picture of the dead woodcutter, she handed it to the writer. "This young man died in a woodcutting accident up near the little village of Reserve, a couple hundred miles north of here."

"Yuck." She examined the photo closely. "Femoral artery?"

"It would appear so. That and then some. The young man we just took into custody was with him at the time of his death. It appears that when the accident happened, the young man we just arrested hightailed it out of the woods, never stopping to look back…and never trying to save his friend."

"That would take a miracle of modern medicine, undersheriff."

"True. But he didn't try."

"Under New Mexico law, is he required to?"

"No. But we could hope that the law of decency might kick in."

"What makes you sure that it was an accident, and not a homicide?"

"The Catron deputies haven't said that the nature of the circumstances points to that, or the nature of the wound, either. It doesn't look like someone snuck up behind him and slipped a chain saw between his legs."

"That's gross enough for any grocery store tabloid."

Estelle handed Madelyn the copy of the telephone number. "For whatever reason, this was found in the dead man's pocket. It's a local Regál number—and happens to be that of the woman who tipped us off that Ricardo Ynostroza was in the village, headed toward Joe Baca's house." She pointed at the low adobe. "This one."

"He certainly took his time, then," Madelyn said. "I mean, he wasn't exactly *fleeing* from anything. Could he just walk back through the border checkpoint?"

"Sure." Estelle nodded. "Or he could hike through the hills a bit and skirt the fence. Either way. But he sat and thought things through. Maybe he couldn't decide whether to go to Betty's house.... He walked right by it on the way in, the one back there with the turquoise trim? Now why did he do that? Maybe he doesn't trust her. Maybe he doesn't actually *know* her. We don't know. And then he headed to Joe's."

"Weird."

"Yes."

"What's the woman who called you have to say—the woman whose phone number was on the note?"

"That's Betty Contreras. And that's where we're headed right now."

"Allen to three-ten." The radio was jarringly loud, and Estelle reached out and turned it down.

"Go ahead." Ahead of them, Joe Baca still sat in the front passenger seat of the state car.

"I'm about to go ten-eight. I have Mr. Baca's phone number if there's anything else we need."

"Ten-four. Thanks, John."

The door of the state car opened and Joe struggled out. Estelle knew the old man was embarrassed at being detained, even if informally. But the undersheriff had wanted to talk with Lucinda before the couple had a chance to compare stories. Allen had provided a convenient avenue for that, and he had played the part perfectly. John Allen swung the black-and-white around and drove out the dirt lane.

Estelle got out of the car and called to the old man as he trudged toward the house. "Joe, thanks for your help."

He stopped and raised an uncertain hand. "Let us know," he said.

"Por supuesto," Estelle replied.

"They seem like nice people," Madelyn said as Estelle started the car and turned it around.

"They are." Estelle saw that her passenger had opened her digital camera. She didn't offer to show Estelle the photos on the viewing screen.

"Is it fair to say that you've known these folks for years and years and years?"

"Yes."

"Maybe since you were a kid?"

"Yes."

"That must make it interesting."

"It does."

"Some edgy moments there," Madelyn said after a moment. "I have a good picture of you taken side on, hand on your gun. You would have used it, do you think?"

Estelle glanced at her. "That depends."

"Of course. Forgive a silly question. If he had sprung out from behind that woodpile brandishing a weapon, putting you in jeopardy, you would have used your gun. Is that fair to say?"

"Yes. I can imagine that Deputy Taber would have responded first, since she had a full field of view and was weapon in hand."

"What's that like, Estelle?"

"What's what like?"

"I'm not sure what I mean. *I* never have to make that kind of decision, so I guess I don't understand people who do. Physical confrontation has to be an interesting way of earning a living."

"It's one very small part of the job," Estelle said. "Is this one of those 'why are you a cop' questions?"

"I suppose it is." Madelyn laughed at the good-natured question.

"Then maybe I should just say something outrageous. Actually, the whole object is to try and control the situation so that *no* physical confrontation is necessary. It comes to that and it means that all negotiations are lost."

"Did you think about that when you were shot last year?"

The blunt question caught Estelle off-guard, and she slowed the patrol car to a walk. Her gaze wandered from shadow to shadow, hunting through old buildings, sheds, corrals, and barns for things out of place.

"There wasn't much time to think," she said finally. "We were all *way* beyond the chance for any kind of negotiation. I couldn't tell you exactly what happened that day, step-by-step, moment-by-moment. I think I could tell you what I was *trying* to do, but that's a different story. I have to rely on others to tell me exactly what *did* happen."

"Were you thinking about that incident today? Just now, back there?"

The "does it still haunt you" question, Estelle thought. "No, I don't think so."

"What *were* you thinking?"

"That no one gets hurt. That everyone goes home when it's over."

"Except the felon, of course."

"He's not a felon yet," Estelle said. "And there's every chance that he won't be." She eased the car into the Contreras driveway behind Betty's Toyota. "And if he's not, then he should go home, too. He has family, just like you and me."

"I should stay in the car?"

"Yes. You really should, Madelyn. I want to give Mrs. Contreras the chance to let her guard down."

Betty Contreras was waiting in the doorway to the kitchen as the undersheriff approached. "You have company," Betty said.

"Yes, I do. Every once in a while, we get civilian ride-alongs."

"Talk about too much free time," Betty scoffed. "Come on in. It's been a busy couple of days, no?"

"Indeed."

"I saw Jackie drive by with our friend in custody. I hope there was no problem."

"Everything went fine."

"Who is he?"

"I had the impression that you already knew him," Estelle said.

"I've seen him before, I think. He's been in town."

"When?"

"Oh," Betty backtracked, "I couldn't be sure."

"His name is Ricardo Ynostroza, from Buenaventura. I wanted to ask you what prompted your call to the Sheriff's Department, Betty." Estelle didn't mention that she knew Betty had called the regular office line, not using 911, making sure that Dispatch reached Estelle and not someone else.

"Well, for one thing, strangers stick out like sore thumbs in a little village like this. You certainly know all about that."

"Indeed they do. He was on foot when you first saw him?"

"I heard a car stop out on the highway and looked out the kitchen window here." She stepped to the window, with a view past the vehicles, fence, and small field to the state highway a hundred yards east. "They dropped him off right here at my street, and I thought *that* was odd."

"Why odd? Who was he riding with, do you know?"

"One of the *burros*," Betty said, referring to the tandem car tows that headed, one well-used, battered vehicle towing another, in a regular flow south of the border. "He could have just hitched a ride all the way south, wherever he was headed. Why get out here? That's what made me nervous."

"And then what did he do?"

"At first, I thought he was headed for the church. He walked halfway across the parking lot, and then changed his mind and started to head this way. He crossed the road and came on down our lane, but he didn't stop. He seemed to know where he was going."

"What prompted the call, then?"

"Well," and Betty hesitated. "I thought… I thought he might be after money."

"From Joe and Lucinda?"

"Yes."

"How would he know about them?" Estelle asked.

Betty looked uncomfortable. "Word gets around," she said lamely. "Anyway, that's when I called Gayle. At first it looked like he was going to stop in here, but he didn't, and I thought Lucinda might be home all by herself, so it seemed prudent to let someone know."

"Did you speak to him?" If Ricardo Ynostroza had walked right past the Contreras house, he would have been five feet from the front porch.

"No," Betty replied quickly. "I mean, in this day and age, you just never know. This one seemed unsure of himself, and I have to tell you...he looked *awful*. I knew *something* was wrong, and that's what made me nervous. He wasn't in any hurry, either. He stopped at Sosimo's old place and went inside. It isn't locked, you know. I thought, *Well, he's going to take a nap or something.* There's nothing left in that old place to take, after all."

"The Border Patrol is right over there," Estelle said, nodding in the direction of the border crossing less than a quarter mile away. She already knew the answer before Betty Contreras snapped it out.

"*That's* not necessary," the older woman said. "We have to put up with *those* people too much of the time as it is. I'd rather deal with people I know."

"The end result will be the same," Estelle said. "Ynostroza will go back to his home in Mexico."

"And so it goes," Betty said philosophically. "That's better than getting into trouble. That's what I wanted to avoid."

"Did you think that he posed a threat to Joe or Lucinda?"

"Well, he was headed up that way. Theirs is the only

house at the end of the lane. I kept looking out through the window, watching him. He was obviously trying to figure out what to do. I didn't think it would hurt to have you talk to him."

"Did you call Joe?"

"I did. I mean, I tried to. No one answered the phone. Maybe he was outside."

"Perhaps. Would Felix Otero have stopped here if he was passing through?" Estelle asked. "Did he remember you well enough?"

Betty blinked at her. "And he is…"

"The young man who was killed in the woodcutting accident up north. Also from Buenaventura, I would guess. He and Ricardo worked together. After the accident, Ricardo left him to die."

One of Betty's hands drifted up to her mouth, fingers flat against her lips. "I didn't know that."

"Why would Ricardo head back here, then?" Estelle asked. "If he wanted to go home, he had only to ride with the *burros* through the gate. No one's going to question him going *south*bound."

"I have no idea, Estelle."

"Why did the dead man have your phone number, Betty?"

"I told you before… I don't know. I absolutely do not know." She didn't manage to sound convincing but instead looked pained by it all.

"If Felix had gotten into some kind of trouble and was able to call you—he had your number, after all, and *only* your number—what would you have been able to do?" Estelle held up a hand. "Actually, I should say, what were you prepared to do for him?"

When Betty didn't answer, Estelle added, "If Ricardo

Ynostroza had known that his partner, Felix, had your phone number, if he'd known you lived here, would he have stopped here instead of walking on to Joe's?"

Betty leaned against the counter, looking genuinely distressed. "Estelle, how can I tell you these things?"

The undersheriff regarded her for a time, then said, "Because you know the answers?" She waited, and the silence grew heavy between them. "There are too many unanswered questions, Betty. I don't want to involve Immigration, and I don't think that you do, either."

"Well, I won't be bullied," Betty said.

"No one is bullying you," Estelle said.

"You obviously don't know the feds, then," she said. "What we live with every single day around here."

"I've heard the complaints, believe me. I'm not a fed, and I can tell you that as of now, I don't plan to call them in on any of this. So let me ask you this flat out…do you trust me, then?"

"Yes, I do," Betty responded without hesitation. "I've known you since you were a little tyke," and she held a hand at waist level. "I watched you go through school. Now, *I* never had you in class, but Serafina did, and she used to sing your praises—oh, how much she thought of you. We all still do. You and that husband of yours…" Her face softened as she gazed at Estelle. "So yes… I trust you. Sometimes," and she grinned broadly and waggled a teacherly finger, "you aren't the most forthcoming person I know, but I suppose the job does that to you. A few minutes ago, I asked you who that was that you had riding with you, but you didn't answer me. I thought that was odd."

Estelle cocked her head in puzzlement. "You didn't

ask. You made a statement that I had company riding with me. I agreed that I did."

The woman smiled and shook her head in wonder. "You are a wonder. Bill Gastner had a favorite expression for you, but I can't recall it at the moment."

"No doubt he called me a lot of things," Estelle laughed.

"Always complimentary, always," Betty said. "So, who's your passenger?"

"She's a writer for a national magazine."

"Ah. Would I know the one?"

"*A Woman's World.*"

Betty's eyes grew large. "You're joking. She's doing an article on you?"

"On the department."

"Well, what do you know. That deserves a tip of the hat. Why didn't you bring her in with you?"

"Because I needed to talk to you privately, Betty. And that's where we left off. I asked if you trusted me because I think you're reluctant to tell me what you know."

"And what's that? What am I supposed to know?"

"My question is simple enough, Betty. I need to know not *if—because I'm sure you do—but how you happen to know* Ricardo Ynostroza. And how you happen to know Felix Otero."

"Have you talked with Father Bert?"

"Yes."

Betty waited a moment for the undersheriff to elaborate and, when no elaboration was forthcoming, said, "Let me ask him to call you." She nodded as if that would solve the matter. "He should talk to you."

"Why him and not yourself?"

"Just...just because. I think he should. Can we leave it at that for now?"

Estelle looked at the older woman in silence for a long moment. "All right. For now. You have my number, Betty. Any time, day or night. So does Father Anselmo."

"How about taking some banana bread with you?" Betty said brightly, the conversation finished, at least in her mind. "It's marvelous. Your writer person might like some. What's her name?"

"Madelyn Bolles. And I'm sure she'd love some."

That was all the opening Betty Contreras needed to turn her attention from things unpleasant, and in moments Estelle was settling back in the car with a loaf of fragrant banana bread wrapped in foil. "Madelyn, this is Betty Contreras," the undersheriff said as Betty leaned on the county car's passenger windowsill.

"So nice to meet you," Madelyn said, and offered her hand. "I'm Madelyn Bolles."

Betty eyed the laptop, impressed. "I read your magazine, every single issue. I think it's just wonderful," Betty gushed, then wagged a finger. "You do a good job with that article, now. We all know this young lady, and we'll all be reading between the lines."

Madelyn smiled broadly. "That's the kind of readers we like, Mrs. Contreras. I'll do my best. And your bread smells scrumptious."

"Come back for more."

"I may just do that."

As Estelle backed the car out of the driveway, Madelyn Bolles once more folded up her portable office. She patted the top of the bread loaf.

"Bribery, eh?"

"Absolutely," Estelle replied. "And I hope you didn't mind being introduced. I allowed myself to be trapped."

"That's hard to believe. Was it a productive chat?"

Estelle sighed. "Maybe. Maybe it was."

TWENTY-FIVE

"No," Sheriff Torrez said, with a curt shake of the head. Madelyn Bolles held up both hands in surrender. She had followed Estelle down the hallway behind Dispatch, toward Sheriff Robert Torrez's office, but the sheriff would have none of it. He let the one word suffice, offering no explanation.

"I'll be out in Dispatch," Madelyn said.

"You can wait in my office," Estelle said. "I shouldn't be long."

The reporter shook her head. "I don't want to intrude. I'll be outside."

In the sheriff's minimal office, Ricardo Ynostroza sat on one of the metal folding chairs, his back against the filing cabinet. His hands were still handcuffed behind his back, and he leaned forward uncomfortably. He looked from Estelle to Bob Torrez and then to Deputy Jackie Taber, who had eschewed the hard folding chairs and instead stood with her back against the windowsill, two steps from the young man. As Estelle closed the door, the deputy stepped forward and unlocked the handcuffs, and the young man rubbed his wrists gratefully.

"So," Estelle said, and opened her notebook. "Señor Ynostroza. We're a little confused by your behavior today."

He sat motionless and silent. Deputy Taber had reported that Ynostroza hadn't said a word on the ride from Regál to Posadas. "The authorities in Buenaventura tell us that you had a little trouble last week," Estelle said. He didn't answer but shifted a bit in his chair. "They say that they'd like to talk to you about the theft of a 1987 Chevrolet Caprice," she said. Jackie Taber's notes said that the car had been targeted by the car thief less than a week after its purchase.

"I gave it back," Ynostroza said.

"Well, that's okay, then," Torrez said.

"Not entirely in one piece, however," Estelle added, and Ynostroza hunched his shoulders with contrition. "So, talk to us." She handed him the photograph of his woodcutter companion, and he promptly dropped it as he bent sharply forward, face buried in his hands. "Tell us what happened that day," she said. "This past Thursday."

"That is how I left him," the young man whimpered. "I could do nothing."

"Tell us how it happened."

"We were cutting the wood," he said. "Up the tree, so…" and he straightened up enough to swing his hands back and forth, mimicking the motions of nicking the limbs off the trunk. "It…" and English failed him. He slipped into Spanish, the words a torrent. Estelle let him wind down.

"The saw kicked back," she said for the benefit of the others.

"And then he lost his balance when it was still running. He couldn't get away from the chain." She knew that Jackie Taber didn't speak Spanish and Bob Torrez's facility had grown rusty over the years. "Where were you when it kicked back?" she asked.

"I went… I had went…to the truck for the gasoline. He said he was nearly ready. Then I hear his cry. He… he is *tambaleándose?*"

"He staggered?"

"Yes…he hold himself, but the blood…*madre de Dios.*"

"What did you do?"

"I ran to him and tried… I ran to him and he is this stagger, and I help him away. Nothing he does can hold the blood, *agente,*" he said, looking beseechingly at Estelle. "I want to go to the truck, but he is crying, *presa del pánico*. It is like he is trying to escape? He is trying to escape from this thing. He is all white, and fights like the madman. Finally I am able to make him sit down, and I see what the saw has done."

He bent forward once more, both hands clamped on his mouth.

"Jackie, get a towel. I don't want him pukin' on my floor," Torrez said.

Estelle retrieved the photo of the dead woodcutter as the deputy stepped around her. "And that's where he died, leaning against the tree?"

"Yes." The voice from behind the hands was small and hopeless.

"Why did you run away, Ricardo?" she asked.

"How can I stay? We have no papers. If I stay, when they come, they will ask. And I know that I can do nothing."

"You had no phone, I suppose? No way to call for help."

"No, *agente.*"

"Why didn't you take the truck for help?" Torrez asked.

"I have no papers, and it is not my truck," the young man said again. "I knew there could be trouble."

"We don't mean *steal* the truck, Ricardo. But you could have driven for help."

"But I see Felix is unconscious in just a minute or two. I see...there is nothing that I can do that will help him. Even if the help come that very moment, there would be no time. The hospital is so very far away....I see that it is hopeless. And I cannot move him to the truck by my-self. He cannot walk."

Deputy Taber returned and handed Ynostroza a white towel. He wiped his eyes and then clutched the wadded towel in his lap. "If I take the truck, they will look for me. If I just go..." And he held out a thumb. "Then they won't look."

"So you walked out to the highway and caught a ride?"

"Yes. That is what I did."

"You didn't tell anyone about Felix? That he was lying out there all by himself, bleeding to death?"

Ynostroza flinched as if Estelle had slapped him. "Señor Zamora had says that he was going to stop by, maybe five o'clock?"

"What time did the accident happen?"

"Maybe thirty minutes after four? I am not certain. It was late in the afternoon. We were both tired. Señor Zamora had taken out two full loads with the big truck that day, one just then. We were to fill the pickup, and that would be the end. We had work since Monday afternoon."

"And this was Thursday afternoon?"

"Yes."

"Where did you go, Ricardo? When you left Felix, where did you go?"

"No one came right away. Then I think I hear the sirens, and I went down to the river. I walk along it until dark."

"Which river is this?" Torrez asked.

"I don't know what it is called."

The sheriff reached to the small metal bookcase to the right of his desk, and pulled out a battered paperbound state atlas. In a moment, he spun the open book around on his desk and beckoned Ynostroza to look. "This is Reserve," he said, tapping the map. "You were somewhere in here?"

Ynostroza frowned, bending awkwardly over the desk. "Yes. Now I see what I did." He pointed to a spot on the map.

"So you walked down along the Tularosa," Torrez said. "That ain't easy."

"It was very hard," Ynostroza said fervently, as if his efforts to follow the winding little creek were somehow heroic.

"If you'd stayed along the river, you'd still be up there," the sheriff said. "Where'd you go?"

"I knew where the road was, *agente*, far to the west. So just before dark, I walk to the highway, and then through the town. A woman offered me a ride south, but she was going to Mogollon. I did not want to go there."

"I would guess not," Torrez said. Mogollon nestled high in the Gila, on the way to nowhere.

"She drove me to another town. I don't remember the name."

"Glenwood?"

"That may be it. I slept that night in an abandoned house. I knew that no one would find me there."

"Let's cut this travelogue short," Torrez said. "Why did you come back to Regál?"

"I knew that I could go home to Buenaventura from here," he said, and Torrez scoffed.

"Horseshit. You weren't *headed* to Buenaventura, bud."

"But I was...."

"Then all you had to do was ride across the border with one of the *burros*. He gave you a ride that far. Why did you change your mind?"

Ynostroza fell silent and Estelle watched him closely. Calculation was replacing the earlier trepidation, remorse, and guilt, but he wasn't particularly good at it.

"You have nowhere to go," she said, and Ynostroza's eyes flicked her way. "Immigration will turn you over to the *policia* in Buenaventura," she said. "You are finished here."

"If..." And he stopped, biting his lip.

"Would *padre* Anselmo help you, do you think? Is that what you are hoping?"

"I did not go there," he said quickly. "Maybe you would call him...."

"The *burro* dropped you off at the parking lot of the *iglesia*. You could see that the good father's car was not there. You know the *padre*?"

"Everyone knows the *padre*," he said.

"Is that a fact?" Torrez said. "Why would that be?"

"It is known that he gives mass in Tres Santos. Ever since the old *padre* died there."

"Why did Father Anselmo write down the telephone number of the American woman for Felix? The lady in Regál? We found the paper in his pocket."

"I don't—"

"Yeah, you do," Torrez interrupted.

Ynostroza slumped in resignation. "If we needed someone," he admitted. "That is all. We could use the name as the *referencia*."

"A reference," Estelle provided. "Yes."

"Why did you not go to that house, then?" she asked, taking care to avoid mentioning Betty Contreras by name. If Ricardo Ynostroza hadn't known Betty before, he didn't *need* to know her now. "If you have their telephone number, why not go there?"

"That is where I was going when you found me," he replied.

"Not true," she snapped. "Even if you didn't know where your *referencia* lived, why wander through half the town? You could have stopped at any house, and asked, no?"

"Yes."

"Emilio would help you, no?" She saw no puzzlement at the name, and made a further guess. "And you know that he is at the church most of the time."

"Yes."

Estelle felt a surge of relief at this first small opening. "Why did you not go there? Why did you not seek him out?" She waited while the silence grew, then took a leap into the dark. "Isn't that who Father Anselmo told you to turn to if you needed help? Isn't that why he wrote down Emilio's telephone number for you?"

"Yes, that is true," Ynostroza admitted, and he took

a deep breath, holding it in as if he'd climbed a long, rugged slope.

"Why then were you going to the other house?" she asked.

"We must know this, *señor*."

"You are going to send me back?"

"Yes. Of course."

That brought another look of defeat, an expression at which Ricardo Ynostroza was most adept, Estelle reflected. "There may be some discussion on *how* we choose to return you to Mexico," she said. "If you are cooperative."

Ynostroza chewed on that for a moment, searching through her comment for a promise.

"How many of you were there?"

"What do you mean, *agente*?"

"Exactly that, *señor*."

"It was Felix and myself, *agente*."

"How did you learn about the work up north, by Reserve? How did you learn of the woodcutting with Señor Zamora?"

"Father—" And he bit it off. "There is work everywhere. This Señor Zamora, *nos ha tenido trabajando todo el día*."

"I'm sure he did," Estelle said. "How much did he agree to pay you?"

"He was to give forty dollars for the day," Ynostroza said, and shrugged with resignation. "Is not so much, but…"

"The land of milk and honey," Jackie Taber said, breaking her silence for the first time. "Is that forty for each, or twenty apiece?"

Ynostroza looked as if he'd been slapped. "Twenty, each," he said.

"How did you learn of this job? Did Father Anselmo hook you up?" the sheriff asked.

"I don't—"

"Did he know the Zamoras somehow?" Estelle asked.

"Yes, I think so."

"When you first came to this country to speak with the father, when was that?"

"No. We talk with him in Tres Santos."

"You, Felix, and who else?"

Ynostroza hesitated, obviously well aware of where he was about to step. "Six," he said.

"*¿No más?*"

"No. Only six."

Only, Estelle thought. "All from Buenaventura? Or that area?"

"This time, yes."

"This time? You know of other times?"

"Of course."

Estelle looked at Bob Torrez, and the sheriff's face would have done justice to Rushmore, so devoid was it of expression. *No wonder the good father was spooked,* Estelle thought.

"Where are the others now?"

"I do not know that. I heard Albuquerque," and the name rolled off his tongue with a rhythmic lilt.

"How did you get to Reserve?" she asked. "The truck you were using for wood hauling belonged to the Zamoras, did it not? You and Felix certainly didn't walk from Regál to Reserve."

Hitchhiking would have been the obvious answer.

"The father...he made arrangements for us to go to

Silver City," Ynostroza said. "On Sunday afternoon, after the wedding at the church."

Estelle looked at the young man incredulously. "There was someone at the church who agreed to take you and Felix up north?"

"Yes. But just to Silver City. That is where Señor Zamora met us."

"Who was this? Who gave you the ride?"

"I don't know his name. It was someone that Father knew from Tres Santos."

"And Father Anselmo gave you the telephone number."

"Yes. To find him, if there was trouble. He is driving so much, sometimes it is hard. He said we could always find this person with the phone, and she would reach him."

"So tell me, *señor*...when you returned to Regál today, why did you go to the house where we found you? Did you think he would help?"

"I thought, yes. Maybe yes. Maybe he could help."

"You could have just ridden home with *los burros*, Ricardo."

"That is what I should have done."

"Well, then?"

"I thought that..." He fell silent, thinking hard, brows knit together. "I thought that Señor Baca might help."

"Why would he do that?"

"He had help before."

"Ah, he did. How did he help? Did he help Father Anselmo arrange the work for you?"

Ynostroza's expression turned wary. "No."

"But now you return. I'll ask you again.... What was

Joe Baca going to do for you? What did you *think* he could, or would, do for you? You were headed to his place when we stopped you. What did you want from him?"

Ynostroza held up his hands helplessly. "I just thought…"

"What did you just think, Ricardo?"

"Señor Baca is a wealthy man, *agente*. At the church, Father Anselmo gave each one of us twenty dollars. He said that the money came from the congregation. But Felix said that he had heard about Señor Baca winning the *lotería*."

"So, you knew about that," Estelle said. She let her voice sink to just above a whisper, as if she and Ynostroza were the only ones in the room. "Were you going to try and rob Señor Baca? Is that what you were thinking about?"

"*Agente*, I would never do this."

"Really. An old man, *el viejo,* who you knew to be a wealthy and generous man? The thought never crossed your mind?"

"Never, *agente*."

"Lying sack of shit," Sheriff Torrez said matter-of-factly, and Ynostroza's eyes darted first to Torrez and then back to Estelle.

"When you walked from the highway to Señor Baca's, what were you thinking, then?" she asked. "You did not walk directly to his house. You did not approach as an honorable man, straight to the door to make your request. You went inside the old abandoned house first, then sat and smoked a cigarette in the shade of the orchard…. What were you planning to do?"

"I wasn't sure what he would say," Ynostroza said lamely.

"You were trying to make up your mind," Torrez said. "Trying to decide how you were going to do it."

"No. I was worried."

"Of course you were," Estelle said. "And then you saw the State Police car coming down from the pass."

Torrez added, "An illegal on the wrong side of the fence, a thousand yards from the border crossing, thinkin' about tryin' to rob the same people who'd helped you. That's a lot to be worried about."

"Why didn't you go to the church?" Estelle asked. "You knew that the father would help you."

"I could see that he wasn't there," Ynostroza said. "His car, you know. As you say, it would be by the church if he was there."

"Ay," Estelle whispered. She looked at Torrez, and then heavenward. The sheriff seemed amused at this turn of events. She knew Father Bertrand Anselmo's sympathies, and wasn't the least bit surprised that he shuffled a few workers across the border now and then. The process was simple enough, until something went wrong… like a chain saw kicking back into a leg.

"Do you want to talk to Anselmo, or do you want me to?" Torrez asked.

"I'll talk to him," Estelle said.

"Are you going to give Immigration a heads-up?"

"Eventually, we have to," the undersheriff said quickly. "But just at the moment, muscle isn't going to solve this."

"Ain't that the truth," Torrez said. "And we don't need

to be readin' about this at the checkout stand," he added, nodding at the closed door. It was clear that he wasn't referring to *Posadas Register* publisher Frank Dayan.

TWENTY-SIX

THE FORCE OF Irma Sedillos' organization brought the eight of them to the well-laden table in the Guzmans' home on South 12th Street shortly after six that evening. There had been so much food that even Bill Gastner may have felt overwhelmed, although he had significantly more practice at defeating heaping plates than anyone else at the table.

Estelle, thankful for the respite from the peripatetic day, found herself impressed once again with Madelyn Bolles. She was pleased that the writer had accepted the invitation to dinner without hesitation and without protestations about intruding. By the time Madelyn arrived, neat and fresh in simple black summer-weight slacks and a print cotton blouse, she appeared refreshed and ready for the swing shift.

There was only enough time for introductions before Irma and Estelle began to load the dining table. The eight of them—Irma and Madelyn, Francis and Estelle, little Carlos and Francisco, Teresa Reyes and Bill Gastner—were an easy fit around the large oak table.

Estelle noticed a tiny digital camera in a holster on the writer's belt, but that's where the camera stayed. Madelyn was content to simply soak in the experience, appearing to notice everything…including the seating arrangement. Despite the special occasion of company, Francisco and Carlos cajoled their parents into letting them flank Bill Gastner, the former sheriff of Posadas County. Estelle knew that nothing was more important to them than that. As a safety valve, Estelle sat on Carlos' left, and Dr. Francis took a seat on Francisco's right, trapping the little boys within easy reach should *padrino*, sitting between the two boys, prove to be more than Carlos and Francisco could handle.

The contrast couldn't have been more photogenic: the *padrino*, big, gruff, in the habit of eating with his beefy forearms on the table on either side of his plate as if protecting his food from intruders, and the two little boys, spending as much energy trying to behave as eating. Gastner kept his godchildren quietly entertained during the meal with just enough attention that the talk around the rest of the table wasn't monopolized by children—something that would have brought a cryptic rebuke from Teresa Reyes, Estelle's mother.

"You going to eat that?" Gastner asked at one point, leaning left toward Carlos, the younger of the two boys. Gastner pointed with his fork at a bit of green chile enchilada. The various serving plates and bowls had been reduced to empty wreckage, and the adults were starting to take the long, slow breaths of the well beyond sated.

"You can have it," the child chirped, and watched as Gastner made the transfer.

"So, what have you seen in our fair county that's of interest to the rest of the civilized world?" Gastner said without missing a beat, and looked at Madelyn, who sat directly across the table, flanked by Dr. Francis Guzman on her left and Irma on her right.

"Well," the writer said, and pushed herself back from the table a bit, puffing her cheeks. "First of all, I have *never*, and I mean *never*, tasted anything quite like this.

I'm fantasizing about having the *Inquirer* or *Times* food editors sitting here, trying to figure out what hit them." She patted Irma lightly on the forearm with an obvious affection that said they'd known each other for years.

"Last year was a good year for the chiles," Teresa Reyes croaked, as if that explained everything. "This girl roasts them herself." Teresa reached over to rest a tiny, arthritic hand on Irma's. Irma blushed at the double-barreled attention.

"What do folks do when there's a bad year?" Madelyn asked. "It must be catastrophic. Right up there with qualifying for federal disaster aid."

"The crime rate skyrockets," Gastner quipped.

"The crime rate never needs outside help," Dr. Francis said. "It does just fine on its own."

"So tell me," Gastner said, his heavy brows knitting in a frown. He pushed his empty plate forward a bit, and crossed his forearms on the edge of the table in front of himself. Carlos and Francisco did the same thing, a comical bit of mimicry that was so spontaneous that Estelle had to stifle a laugh. *Padrino* ignored the behavior. "I didn't think to ask you this earlier today when we talked. How did we happen to attract your attention? I can't imagine that the affairs of Posadas County are what fill hours of idle conversation in Philadelphia."

Madelyn laughed. "It's all in who you know," she replied.

"And who do you know that brings you out this way?"

"I have a just wonderful aunt who lives in Las Cruces, who by way of it being a small world also happens to be a talented musician." She leaned toward Francisco and raised an eyebrow.

"She's retired now, of course. Boston is no place for

arthritis, and she had discovered Las Cruces years ago because *her* son is a major in the army, stationed at Fort Bliss."

"You were visiting her, then," Gastner said.

"Exactly. I've done so several times. It's getting to be something of a tradition. Last time I was out, for Thanksgiving this time, I saw the picture of this young man in the newspaper," and she nodded at Francisco again, "taken when he played at the college recital there. Things snowballed from there. No mystery."

"Did you come to the recital?" Francisco asked. "There were a lot of people there." He drew his thin arms off the table and sat up a little straighter.

"No, I'm sorry that I missed it. Can you tell me what you played?"

Can you tell me, Estelle thought. Madelyn Bolles had yet to discover that it wasn't "can" in this case. It was "would."

"Some of this and that," the little boy said, suddenly feeling the eyes on him...especially his grandmother's. Teresa Reyes had deeply ingrained rules about the behavior of children, particularly exuberant little boys who would take over the adult stage without a thought if allowed to do so. She hadn't snapped her fingers yet, that ominous signal practiced over decades in the old mud-walled school in Tres Santos, so Estelle knew that her son was still on safe ground.

"Francisco actually played three pieces," Estelle prompted.

"Yes."

"That's hard work," Madelyn observed, and Francisco looked puzzled, since playing was never hard work for him...not even a day that included five or six hours at

the keyboard tussling with some composer's fascination
with five or six sharps. "What did you play?" she asked.

Francisco looked up at his father, but it was the
elbow from the opposite direction, in his left ribs, that
goaded him on. "You don't remember what you did this
morning, let alone what you played last fall, old guy,"
Gastner scoffed.

"I remember," the little boy said, squirming with delight. "Everybody already knows those stories."

"Ms. Bolles has never heard them," Estelle said.

"Give us some after-dinner music while I see if Irma
remembers how to make decent coffee," Gastner said.

"There's some in the pot from three days ago," Irma
said, knowing full well Bill Gastner's indiscriminant
taste for the brew—freshly ground gourmet beans, or
days old in the steel pot with an oil slick on top, it was
all the same to him.

"And you promised some pie," he said, turning and
craning his neck to see into the kitchen. "Do we have to
wait until this kid finishes stumbling all over the keys,
or is it fair game now?"

Estelle reached out an arm and hugged her mother,
and saw the tight compression of Teresa's lips ease a little. "I was hoping for a peaceful evening," the old woman
said, but she couldn't conceal the pride in her voice.

"I for one don't have any room for dessert," Madelyn
said, and Teresa Reyes, who had been gradually working her way upright, stopped with one hand braced on
the table.

"It's better to wait," she said, and aimed the comment at Gastner. "We don't want an *orchestra* of forks
clanking rhythm."

"I heard that," Gastner said, and held out a hand to-

ward Francisco. "Help me up, old guy. I ate too much."
He allowed both little boys to push, shove, and heave as
he feigned helplessness.

"Be right back," Francisco said, and vanished down
the hall.

"He has to have the right shirt on," Estelle explained
as they maneuvered chairs this way and that…except for
Teresa Reyes' rocker, which sat in a corner by the fireplace. The grand piano had been moved so that during
the day natural light from the large living room window
flooded in from behind the bench. Beyond that adjustment, the piano's location was determined by Francisco's
mood. It had to sit at just the right angle, a cornerstone
into his world.

"If you have cell phones, they go on vibrate or off,"
Francis said. "I can say that, because I'm the primary
offender."

"Mine's on the counter in the kitchen," Estelle said.
She had already captured Carlos, and he sat comfortably
in her lap in the glider. "Would you check it, please?"

Francisco padded into the room, wearing his favorite
plum-colored golf shirt. His soft-soled sneakers had been
replaced by black, leather-soled penny loafers…wonder-
fully out of sync with his grubby blue jeans.

Madelyn Bolles, having chosen one of the padded
straight-backed chairs from the dining room, sat immediately beside Estelle. To the right of the piano, they had
an unobstructed view of the keyboard. Madelyn leaned
close to Estelle and whispered, "Why am *I* nervous?"

Estelle hugged Carlos closer and beamed at the writer.
"Just enjoy. No matter what happens." She meant that
literally, of course, since one of the little boy's quirks

was eschewing the announcement of what he intended to play.

Gastner stretched out on the opposite end of the sofa from Irma, his boots kicked off and feet on the small coffee table. He reached over and patted her knee affectionately. "You do good work, kid," he said. Irma blushed. Dr. Francis settled in the recliner.

The enormously heavy piano lid was already yawning wide, and Francisco used both hands to open the keyboard cover, letting it ease back to its stops. He regarded the keyboard as if suspicious that someone might have rearranged the ivories since his last visit—less than two hours before. As he settled on the bench, Estelle took his measure, seeing that he could now easily reach the pedals with his toes.

"I was looking at this today," he said quietly as if talking to himself. His speech now was so introspective and mature that it gave Estelle a turn. There was no music on the rack, and to Estelle it always seemed as if the little boy had to wait until the music burst from the pathways of his mind to each of his strong, slender fingers. As the generator of that process spooled up, he sat quietly and stared, as if trying to burn a hole in middle C. Then his hands moved to the keyboard.

The piece was clearly Bach, and *el gruñón,* or the Grump, as Francisco had nicknamed the composer, had appealed to the little boy with a prelude that was both playful and melodic. Without a giggle, he managed long passages where the two hands argued back and forth, and despite his rocketing musicianship, Estelle felt a pang of regret that this little boy who in the past would dissolve with helpless laughter at some musical image now performed so flawlessly.

Madelyn Bolles leaned slightly forward, as if she couldn't quite believe that the music rack was empty. Prelude rolled into fugue, and in places Francisco played so softly that the piano hammers seemed to kiss the strings, grazing the notes only enough that their purity was unquestioned.

And it was during one of those magic moments that Estelle heard the car's aging muffler outside as the vehicle chugged down 12th Street and then pulled to a stop along the curb. Although she recognized the sound immediately, for an instant she allowed herself to entertain the fantasy that this might be a visitor for one of the neighbors. She heard a car door thud closed. The living room curtain was drawn, but it sounded as if the car had parked immediately behind Bill Gastner's Blazer. Sure enough, in a moment Estelle heard footsteps coming up the sidewalk. The visitor hesitated at the bottom of the three steps leading to the front door, and Estelle groaned inwardly.

She lowered Carlos to the floor and rose silently, padding to the front door. It opened on silent hinges, and Estelle held up a hand, the backs of her fingers over her mouth, begging for silence. Father Bertrand Anselmo hesitated, then slipped inside.

TWENTY-SEVEN

"CON PERMISO," the priest whispered as the final notes of the fugue died away. "I am so sorry to intrude." He turned to Estelle. "May I?"

"Of course. Come in."

Anselmo entered the living room and crossed first to Teresa Reyes. Estelle's mother beamed. "You're late," she croaked. "My grandson has just started."

"I am so sorry to intrude," Anselmo said again. "You're well, I trust?" He took Teresa's tiny right hand in both of his enormous paws.

"I'm old, is what I am," Teresa said. "But that can't be helped."

"Bless you, Teresa," he said. "And how are you, doctor?" the priest asked, stepping across to Francis, who now stood, bemused, with his hand on Francisco's shoulder. Bill Gastner didn't rise but leaned forward with a grunt and extended a hand to the priest as he passed. "Always good to see you, Bill," Anselmo said.

"And I'm Madelyn Bolles," the writer said as Anselmo turned toward her. "We met down at the *iglesia*."

"Ah. So we did, so we did. I hope you're enjoying your visit."

"Indeed I am."

The priest let a hand on each child's head suffice, and then he turned back to the undersheriff, who hadn't left her position by the front door. "Is there a chance that we might talk?" Anselmo asked. "I realize that it's a terrible intrusion, but it's most important."

There was no point in asking if the conversation could wait. Estelle could see that the affable priest was agitated and worried. "I'm sorry," Anselmo continued. "But if I could have just a few minutes…" It wasn't lost on her that he'd taken the time to change into priestly black, broken only by the hyphen of white at his throat. His worn black shoes had been polished until the black cracks and creases showed like rivers on a map.

"Sure," Estelle said. "*Hijo*, a short intermission," she said to her son, and the little boy nodded good-naturedly.

"Perhaps we could just step outside for a moment," Anselmo suggested.

"We can do that," Estelle said. *"Un momento."* From the hall closet she pulled a light jacket. "Now's a good time for the pie," she said, and Bill Gastner brightened, clapping his hands to break the awkward silence. "Francisco and Carlos, will you help Irma serve?"

"Again, I am most apologetic," Father Anselmo said as he and Estelle stepped out into the cool air. "But I wanted to talk to you before things…" He gestured toward the sidewalk. "Shall we walk a little bit?"

"I don't think so," Estelle said. She leaned comfortably against the front fender of her county car and regarded the priest. In most circumstances, she liked Bertrand Anselmo. She liked his unflinching advocacy of his tiny parishes, and the energy he expended on their behalf. Although Teresa Reyes managed to attend perhaps a single mass each month, each one of those occasions prompted heartfelt stories about how *padre* Anselmo had done this or that, or said this or that. And each time there was the sometimes not-so-veiled suggestion that Estelle should be taking the boys to mass. Now she wondered if Teresa knew of the machinations that had brought Anselmo here this evening.

Clearly, Anselmo was in over his head, and Estelle could see the worry lines touching his face. There was no point in playing cat-and-mouse games with him. "Did you want to talk to me about Ricardo Ynostroza?" she asked, keeping her voice down.

"Yes," Anselmo said without hesitation. "And I am distressed to learn of his arrest, and Felix Otero's death. I hope the two tragedies are in no way connected."

"Do you have any reason to suspect that they might be, Father?"

"No. Certainly not. And you, Estelle?"

"An ugly accident, Father. There is no reason to believe that it was anything other than carelessness at the end of a long day of work. But I'm concerned that Otero's companion chose to leave him to die alone."

"That's what he did?" Anselmo's voice sank to a whisper.

"Yes. He ran. That's as simply as I can put it. He could think of nothing else to do. And maybe he was right. The saw ripped open major arteries, Father. It was a catastrophic wound. If Felix had been sixty seconds from an emergency room, maybe he would have survived, but only maybe."

"They had no vehicle at the work site?"

"Yes, as a matter of fact they did, Father, an old truck that belongs to their employer. The nearest clinic would be half an hour away from where they were working—in the best of circumstances. For a man who bleeds out in two minutes, that's not much help."

"And no phone?"

"No."

"So Ricardo ran away."

"Yes. He avoided authorities, walked and hid, and finally hitchhiked back here. And that's what interests me most, Father. He didn't stay with his dying friend—perhaps because he knew that he could do nothing to help, and didn't want to be apprehended by authorities. It may be that he's looking for a way to inform the victim's family. Maybe that was his intention today. Or maybe he thought he had a chance at stealing some of the Bacas' recent fortune." Estelle let that sink in for a moment. "There were so many things he *could* have done, Father. After the accident, he could have hitchhiked in the other direction, up to Albuquerque, for example. To Socorro. To Cruces. Any number of places. He could have continued south with the *burros* that he was riding with, right back to Mexico. He didn't do that. Instead, he chose to come back to Regál. How much are you willing to tell me about all that, Father Anselmo?"

The ghost of a smile touched the priest's face. "How much do I *have* to tell you, Undersheriff Guzman?" he asked, and his tone held both deference and respect.

"Let's begin with the simple things," Estelle said. "Why did you give the two men Betty Contreras' telephone number?"

"Ah," the priest said, and turned to look out at the street as he considered his answer. "Your perception always amazes me." He turned back and met Estelle's gaze. "I thought it would be helpful for them to have a contact, should they encounter troubles. One can *usually* find a telephone."

"Why Betty? Why not your own?"

"She is always available," Anselmo said. "She is a

most resourceful woman, as you know. She volunteered to serve as a contact person. I do not have a cell phone, although I suppose I should. She agreed to pass messages along to me."

"That's all?"

"That's the extent of it. Betty has done nothing wrong, sheriff."

"Ynostroza tells me that he and Felix were just two of several illegals who came through this past week… came through your church, that is."

"That's true. I'm sure Ricardo didn't use the word 'illegals', however. Nor do I. But I'm sure you're not interested in that debate at the moment."

"No, as a matter of fact I'm not, Father. They all have Betty's number? All half dozen of them, or however many there were?"

"Yes. That is what she agreed to provide in instances like this."

"That leads me to believe that this isn't the first time you've assisted a group of undocumented workers."

"Of course not. But the telephone number is needed only rarely, if at all. In fact, Betty has never mentioned that she's received a call for help. I do think that it provides some comfort and security for these people to know that there is someone to call who can be trusted if the need arises."

"Ynostroza did not call her."

"No, apparently not."

"That's what puzzles me, Father."

"I suppose that you'll turn him over to the authorities? The federal authorities, I mean."

"Yes, in all likelihood. I need to talk first with both our district attorney and the folks up in Catron County, where the woodcutting incident happened. I doubt that anyone is going to bring any sort of charges against Ynostroza other than the usual immigration violations. For that, the feds have the appropriate channels established for the processing and handling of aliens. We don't at the county level."

"Despite the fact that you could simply take him to the Regál crossing and wish him well," Anselmo said.

"We're not a taxi service, Father. And we're not free to invent procedures when the law is already quite clear." She saw the pained look of impatience cross his face. "Why was Ynostroza headed for Joe Baca's place? He *didn't* go to Betty's, Father."

"He may not actually know where Betty lives," Anselmo said. "To my knowledge, they have never actually met. I try to keep contacts to a minimum. In her case, just the telephone number, for use in emergencies."

"Odd that he didn't use it this time—what happened certainly qualifies as an emergency. You all meet at the church every time?"

"Yes."

A handy cover, she thought. "But he knew about Joe and Lucinda. He knew right where *they* lived. Explain that to me."

"There had been some talk about the good fortune that has been enjoyed recently," Anselmo said. "It is not a secret that Joe and Lucinda won a state lottery, and then twice more from some sweepstakes thing, something through the mail. I don't know the details. But I *do* know that they have been most generous to the parish. Both before but especially now. I have no doubt that the young men knew of this good fortune—after all, they had the opportunity to speak with them at the church."

"That didn't make you just a little nervous, Father?"

"Should it?" Anselmo looked genuinely puzzled.

Surely you can't be that naive, Estelle thought. "Ynostroza may have been after money, then."

"But I can't believe it would have been robbery," Anselmo said. "I don't know young Ricardo well, but there was nothing to make me believe that he might..."

"Maybe just a little panhandling," Estelle said.

"You're jumping to unwarranted conclusions," Anselmo said, and he abruptly changed tack. "I think he would want to inform the relatives. Such a sad thing," the priest said. He thrust both hands in his pockets. "Felix was married, you know. Three little ones."

"And Ynostroza?"

"Unmarried."

"Father, what we *do* know is that Ynostroza didn't approach the Bacas' home in a straightforward manner. I can't believe that he didn't know where Betty lived, but he didn't stop there to use *her* phone. Something about his behavior prompted Betty to remain in her home when he walked by on the lane. He didn't call them first. He didn't simply walk to the front door."

"Ah," Anselmo said, "but with police cars converging from all directions, what else would you expect?"

"You heard about that, then."

"Yes."

"The grapevine is most efficient, Father."

"Well, it's no grapevine. Betty called me. She said that she had called you when Ricardo walked by. She said that he seemed distraught."

"*Sin duda*. That's what I'm saying, Father. And yet she didn't speak with him when she had the chance."

Anselmo shrugged. "She is home by herself. Perhaps she felt uneasy."

"That's possible. So tell me, Father Anselmo," Estelle said. "How are the arrangements made?"

"Arrangements?"

"Ynostroza tells me that they started work Monday afternoon, so they traveled through Regál perhaps Sunday? Did they meet at the church on Sunday, perhaps after mass? How was that arranged? You talked with the men down in Tres Santos? Is that where you organize the groups? Or in Buenaventura?"

"Must I tell you all this?"

"Father," Estelle said, unable to keep the impatience out of her voice, "I don't know what you want from me. If you're imagining that we might release Ricardo Ynostroza to you, you're mistaken. I can't do that. If you imagine that somehow I can smooth the way for you, for what you're doing, you're mistaken."

"This young man has committed no crime."

"Ah, well…we might debate that all evening. He's certainly in violation of immigration law. *You're* in violation of immigration law, Father. I don't know what you're doing, but I can guess. The church is a perfect sanctuary, and it apparently works well for the illegals to mix in with the congregation. That's really just one step above using the unlocked church as a stopover at night—*that's* been going on for two hundred years."

She paused, watching his face in the glare of the streetlight. He didn't respond to her comments, and she said, "Is another group coming in during the anniversary celebration tomorrow? Are you bringing some of them north from Tres Santos after your mass there?"

"Can you imagine being married seventy-five years?" Anselmo said. "Remarkable."

She laughed gently at his evasion.

"You must feel some sympathy for these people, Estelle. After all…"

"Of course I do. *Some*. That doesn't mean I'm going to invent my own private version of the law, Father. I'm not in a position to do that. I'm not going to work at cross-purposes to what other agencies are trying to accomplish."

"And what *are* they trying to accomplish?" he asked, and then immediately held up a hand. "No, please. I promised no debate, and I apologize for putting you in that position. I'm sorry."

"Father, let me tell you what I *am* going to do," Estelle said. "If during the course of our investigation we find that Ricardo Ynostroza has committed no crime other than his illegal entry into this country—if neither the D.A. nor the Catron County officials want to press charges of any kind—then he will be turned over to Immigration for processing back across the border in a normal fashion. We had word that there is a problem with car theft in Buenaventura—maybe that's more of a misunderstanding than a crime. Whether the authorities there will pursue that, I don't know. That's Ricardo's problem."

"I can ask no more, I suppose."

"You can always ask, Father," she said with a smile. "I'm sure Bobby will agree that's the most expeditious route. It's really the only one open to us."

"Have you discussed any of…of *this*…with the sheriff?"

"My suspicions about what you're doing, Father? No.

But Bobby isn't stupid, and he knows this county and these people just as well as I do, perhaps better in some ways. I'm fairly sure he knows what's going on."

"That wouldn't surprise me."

Estelle pushed herself away from the car. "You know as well as I do that the legislature is trying to find some kind of solution to this immigration mess."

"No doubt more fence," the priest said, interrupting her.

"Well, no doubt. But maybe more than that, with some time. So what I'm asking is that you just *stop*. You've got a group coming tomorrow, I'm guessing. Call it off."

"I don't know if I can do that."

"Of course you can. You don't want a confrontation with authorities at the church."

"Is that what you're promising?"

"Don't put me in that position, Father. Don't put *us* in that position. Don't put your congregation in that position. Am I going to tip off Immigration? No. But they have their own sources, believe me. So for now, just *stop*."

The priest glanced at his watch, and Estelle pondered how much to press him.

"You bring in small groups," she said. "These are workers who for whatever reason can't find proper documentation, I assume."

"That is correct. They want only work. They have little or no money, and they are willing to work hard. I know each one of them."

"You don't drive across the border with six of them stuffed in the trunk of your wonderful car, Father. How do they reach the church?" He didn't respond and she shook her head in resignation. "Up through the rocks of the San Cristóbals to skirt the fence is foolish, Father. Especially at night." *And then a walk through the village,* she thought, with a rendezvous at the *iglesia.* The whole village would know, and the whole village had to agree to be closemouthed, otherwise the plan wouldn't work. She wondered if Serafina Roybal was serving tea at this very moment to weary hikers. A little village could protect its secrets easily.

"Father," Estelle said, taking a step toward the house. "You do what you think is right. We will do the same."

"Always," Anselmo said. "I'm sorry about all of this."

"It was predictable, Father. You must know that eventually, something was bound to happen. That this would fall back on you."

The priest sighed. "I suppose. The risk is not mine, of course. I wish it could be." He held up both hands in surrender, and smiled, an expression that made him look absolutely beatific. "Will we see you at the anniversary celebration on Sunday afternoon?"

"I don't know what will happen tomorrow," the undersheriff said, and she was surprised by the resignation in her voice.

"Well, if it should work out, consider yourself invited, then," Anselmo replied. He extended a hand, and his grip was firm. "And your guest, as well." He did not release her hand right away.

"You're welcome to come in for some dessert," Estelle said.

"Ah, no. Many thanks. I have several stops to make yet this evening."

"I'm sure you do, Father. Travel safe."

She watched him trudge off toward the sagging Chevrolet, and it started with a geriatric symphony of noises that produced a cloud of blue smoke. The backup lights flashed, and she knew that he had pulled it into gear, but the car hesitated for a moment, then produced a sharp clank before easing away from the curb.

Back inside, Irma and Madelyn were collecting empty pie plates, and Estelle saw that Francisco was in the kitchen, washing his hands.

"Is he okay?" Dr. Francis asked as Estelle slipped out of her jacket.

"For now," she said, and saw that Teresa Reyes was watching her from across the room. *Ay.* Estelle sighed. *What does she know?* Estelle stretched up and kissed her husband on the cheek. "I want to hear music," she said.

"The intermission is about over," Francis said.

She crossed and knelt by Bill Gastner, her arms crossed on the padded sofa's arm cushion. "Afterward, will you have a few minutes? I really need to talk to you."

"Sure, sweetheart. I'll be hungry again in a matter of minutes."

"That's good. Thanks."

"Bert got himself in a box?" Gastner asked, perceptive as ever.

"Oh, yes," Estelle replied, and pushed herself to her feet.

TWENTY-EIGHT

BY THE THIRD selection of music, Madelyn Bolles was leaning forward in her chair, her elbows on her knees, chin resting on her clasped hands. Her chair was no more than five feet from the piano keyboard, but Estelle could see that wasn't close enough. The writer watched the child's every move, and remarkably, Francisco ignored her.

Estelle relaxed and watched her son. It was as if his peripheral vision ended where the keyboard did. Sometimes, when the score required the left hand to soar far up into the treble keys or the right hand to stray deep into the bass clef, Francisco watched his fingers. But Estelle had come to the conclusion that her son watched his own fingers out of amused curiosity as the music captured his hands, rather than the need to see where he was going.

"Oh, wow," Madelyn whispered as the last note faded from a particularly melodic piece whose mood had fascinated the little boy since Sofía Tournál, his great-aunt living in Veracruz, Mexico, had played it for him and then sent him the music. When a new piece crossed Francisco's path, he rapidly absorbed it, conquered whatever technical demands it might make, then experimented with the music, coming to understand it and make it his own. Often when he did that with a new composition, the piece would soon be discarded, never to be played again. But this composition, written by a

twenty-nine-year-old Mozart at the peak of his marital
and artistic contentment, had somehow spoken to the
little boy. Estelle had always been curious what her son
saw when he played the simple Andante movement of the
Concerto no. 21 in C Major, but he wouldn't, or couldn't,
explain that to her. Regardless, it was a piece that stayed
with him, never discarded.

"Oh, wow," Madelyn said again, and touched a finger to the corner of her eye. She twisted in her chair to
look at Estelle, who sat comfortably in the rocker, Carlos
zonked out across her lap. "Francisco," the writer said,
"what's the name of that piece?"

He turned on the piano bench, left hand reaching out
to rest on the keys. "Some number," he said with a laugh.
"They always used dumb names. It's about a prince. He
walks into a forest and gets lost."

"Really?"

The little boy nodded. "They look for him, but then
he decides that he wants to live there, and he hides so
they can't find him."

"Do they ever find him?"

"No."

Madelyn glanced at Estelle. "Hollywood would be
fascinated by that interpretation," she said.

"Hollywood always gets it wrong, anyway," Bill Gastner said. "How about playing the car chase for us?"

"And then I need to put this one to bed," Estelle said,
looking down at Carlos' peaceful repose. "My legs are
going to sleep."

Francisco faced the keyboard once again, pausing
for just a moment, frozen with concentration. "Okay,"
he said, and let that suffice as an explanation of what
was coming. There was no predicting that, of course, for

once the boy strayed into his own world of composition, what emerged was an ever-changing story. In this case, it began with a tiny trill high in the treble, reminding Estelle of a column of dust rising far in the distance, the smallest disturbance on the open sea of prairie. From there, the story grew at a controlled pace, and she could imagine standing on a rise watching a vehicle far in the distance approach across the open prairie. In a moment, the image split, the one plume becoming two, locked in pursuit.

At that point, Carlos kicked and awoke, eyes big. The music had apparently pounded into his dreams, and he sat up. Estelle hugged him, but he squirmed down, standing by her knees as he blinked himself awake. She knew exactly what was coming, since this piece had delighted the boys and *padrino* for weeks. After a moment, Carlos slipped away, to cross behind Madelyn's chair and slide between the front of the piano bench and the keyboard. That put his chin level with the ivories, and Francisco leaned toward him without speaking, acknowledging his presence. After a few seconds, the opportunity presented itself. While Francisco's right hand was busy, he reached out and touched two notes far down in the bass. "Those," he whispered.

Carlos poised an index finger from each hand over the notes, one black, one white. He apparently knew the story well, since he needed no prompting. At the important moment, he began a steady, alternating drumming of the two keys, an unrelenting helicopter in the background.

"I love it," Gastner said. "I have to learn that part." The piece continued as the two cars chased each other over mesa, arroyo, cliff and mountain tops. The helicopter kept pace, pausing now and then at some secret signal from the composer, only to reenter the chase. After a moment, it became clear how the story would end. The vast collision sent up plumes of dust and debris, the discord quite amazing in its careful control.

At the end, what Estelle pictured as a single hubcap spiraled away into the ditch, reducing both boys to convulsive giggles. They looked to *padrino* for approval, and his wide grin was all they needed.

"You have your hands full," Madelyn Bolles observed to Estelle. She extended a hand to Francisco as he slid off the bench. "Thank you, young man. That was a treasure." He accepted the hand and added a courtly bow, head ever so slightly tilted with grace but no deference. "And you, too," she said to Carlos, who mimicked his older brother's response.

"Such noise," Teresa said, her first comment of the concert. But her pride was obvious. "You two help me to bed now." She held out both hands, waiting for her escort.

"And then yourselves," Francis added.

"And I'm off," Irma said. "This has been wonderful. Ms. Bolles, it was so nice to meet you. I hope we'll be seeing you again."

"Oh, most assuredly. Thank you, Irma. It was all so lovely."

Irma bent down and circled an arm around Bill Gastner's shoulders. "There's one more piece of pie, if you want it. And I put on a fresh pot of coffee."

"What a sweetheart," Gastner said.

Madelyn Bolles relaxed in the rocker, watching the various ceremonies of departure. At one point, as Estelle passed close by to retrieve her mother's shawl, the writer leaned forward, reaching out a hand. "I should be heading back," she said. "Are you on call tonight?"

Estelle laughed. "I'm always on call."

"And what happens if your husband is called out at the same time?"

"Without Irma, the whole thing would collapse," Estelle replied. "*She's* on call, too."

"You're most fortunate," Madelyn observed. "She seems like a wonderful girl."

"Indeed she is, and we're *most* fortunate. If she ever leaves, I quit."

"Is she married? A family of her own?"

"Not yet. She has a *lonnnnnnng*-suffering boyfriend who has the market cornered on patience. But the time will come. We'll be happy for her and feel desolate at the same time."

"You'd give up your job?"

"Sure." Estelle surprised herself with how quickly the single word came out. Certainly, the thought had crossed her mind, but it had always been pushed back into some quiet corner, not to be discussed. The ache that still crept in and entwined itself around her right rib cage served as a reminder of how quickly a comfortable life could be disrupted—even destroyed.

Madelyn eased herself out of her chair and stepped to the piano. She opened the keyboard cover and stood for a moment as if counting the keys to make sure they were still all there.

"Do you play?" Estelle asked.

"Not so you'd notice," Madelyn replied. "I know the names of all the notes. On a good day, I can play 'Peter, Peter Pumpkin Eater' without making a mistake. How many hours a day does he practice?"

"I don't know how to count what's practice and what's play," Estelle said. "He's at the keyboard one way or another for five or six hours a day. Sometimes more."

"You're kidding."

"No."

Madelyn bent down and inspected the keyboard. "How does a little kid work here for six hours a day and yet the keys stay so clean?"

"Ah, well," Estelle said, folding the shawl over her arm. "That's one of his little quirks. He never has to be reminded to wash his hands for the piano. For eating, yes. For the piano, no.

It's all the more remarkable since his other passion is grubbing outside in the dirt with his brother. They have an enormous excavation going on out back. I think they're trying to make a scale model of an open-pit copper mine."

"Huh," Madelyn said thoughtfully. She lowered the keyboard cover. "He likes school?"

"He's passionate about it," Estelle said. "For everything except music, if you can imagine. He's not fond of the teacher, but they only meet twice a week, so he endures."

"That must be a trial, perhaps for both," Madelyn mused.

"I'm sure it is, and probably more so for her. Right now, she's trying to teach them to play those little plastic recorders."

"We used to call them tonettes?"

"That's it. Francisco can't abide them." She held up her mother's shawl. "I'll be back out in a minute. Bill and I need to talk, and you're welcome to join us. You might find it interesting."

"If I'm not intruding, although I have to admit I'm pooped."

"You're not intruding. Remember our agreement." Estelle smiled. "I'll tell you when you are."

"Done deal," Madelyn said.

In a few moments, with Irma gone home, the two youngsters and their grandmother in bed, and Francis working in his office in the back bedroom, Estelle, Bill Gastner, and Madelyn Bolles settled once more in the dining room. Only, the former sheriff indulged in more coffee and the remaining piece of dessert, and he focused on it as Estelle reviewed the events of the afternoon.

"You know," he said, placing the empty dish on the table, "in my own cowardly way, I always hoped that Father Anselmo wouldn't muck things up until *after* I retired. He did a pretty good job. It's amazing that he's been able to run in folks for so long without something going wrong."

Estelle looked at the former sheriff with astonishment.

"Well, yes, I knew," Gastner said without waiting to be asked. "Well," he backtracked, "I *sorta* knew, you could say. And I think you did, too. After all, the church is never locked. I know for a fact that the Border Patrol checks once in a while, but they're careful.…They have enough bad press as it is without getting the reputation for raiding churches. Anyway, Regál isn't one of their points of concern. Never has been. The mountain makes a pretty good fence, unless you know how to use it. A little advice from a person who knows the country can be a big help." He shrugged.

"The border fence runs about a mile to the west from the crossing, then that big bluff of rocks crosses the border, kind of on a northeast–southwest line. The fence looks like it goes up and over, but it doesn't. So you can skirt around the end, and follow the trail through the rocks. You come down right behind Joe Baca's place—if you don't get lost."

"They do this at night?" Madelyn asked.

"Most of the time. Late evening, I'm guessing. A little light makes it easy for them, hard for the Border Patrol. You can hear a chopper coming from miles away. It doesn't take much to hide in the rocks. But you know," and he hunched forward, resting his thick forearms on the table, "that's not the issue. *Crossing* the border isn't difficult in a bazillion places." He looked up and grinned. "It's like a dog chasing a goddamn truck.... Chasing a truck isn't hard. But what does he do when he finally catches it? You get across the fence, and then what?" He sipped his coffee. "If they had a place to rest for a bit, and then someplace all arranged to work, and a way to *get* to work, then it's easy."

"But it's starting to look as if he has the whole village involved in this," Estelle said. "They must know what's going on, at the very least. It isn't just providing sanctuary at the *iglesia* once in a while for an illegal or two. They're *sponsoring* illegals, *padrino*. A handful comes in, as far as I can tell, and they mix in during a church ceremony of some kind. This next week—in fact tomorrow—it's Fernando and Maria Rivera's seventy-fifth wedding anniversary. And then I wouldn't be surprised if a few folks agree to drive the illegals to either a place of employment, or at least on up the road where hitchhikers don't raise eyebrows. That's what's happening. They have their own little railroad organized."

"I'm not surprised. You have a whole village working together, you can get a lot done." He grinned and hitched himself sideways in his chair. "That idea isn't original with me, by the way."

He leaned forward, reached out and tilted his cup, then pushed himself away from the table and padded over to the coffeepot. "You know how easy it is to cross to Regál," he said as he returned to the table with a refill. "Anywhere else is a hell of a hike. But climbing up into the hills to skirt the fence, hell, that's not hard. Or hitching a ride through the gate with a willing resident? *That's* not hard, either, especially if the right person is working the crossing on our side. *Their* side isn't the issue."

"Is it fair to say," Madelyn Bolles said, "that not everyone around here is concerned about illegals coming into the country?"

"Very fair," Gastner replied, spreading his hands wide. "And on the other hand, to some folks it's the biggest goddamn threat this side of ten-dollar gasoline. 'You can't let all them damn greasers into this country, or first thing you know, one of 'em will want to marry my sister.'" He shrugged. "Then there's the other extreme, those folks who say anybody should be able to work and live anywhere, without any goddamn fences or border checkpoints, or brown shirts standing around with machine guns asking you, 'Where are your papers?'"

He sipped his coffee thoughtfully. "The most reverend Father Bertrand Anselmo is closer to the latter group."

"And you?" the writer asked with a smile. "May I ask that?"

"I've never been able to figure out what I think," Gastner said cheerfully. "I go with the flow of the moment. I make sure I can make it through this day, and then tomorrow takes care of itself." Gastner looked at Estelle thoughtfully. "What'd you tell Bert?"

"I told him to stop it," Estelle replied. "But I'm not going to organize a raid of a wedding anniversary mass."

Gastner chuckled. "That'd make the news, wouldn't it. No doubt, your young woodcutter will be back next week, working for someone else."

"He's wanted in Buenaventura. The authorities say he borrowed a car."

"Well, then, it'll be two weeks," Gastner laughed. "Until he figures out who to bribe. You can see how optimistic I am about this whole mess."

He stretched hugely, blinking himself alert. "But believe it or not, this is the least of your problems, sweetheart. You've got an inconvenient corpse on your hands. Do you have any theories about this sweepstakes thing?"

"Tony Abeyta is over in Cruces," Estelle said. "There has to be a link between Chris Marsh and *somebody*. Tony's working with Grunt Nilson to see what they can dig up. Marsh wasn't working in a vacuum. I'm sure of that."

"Not to mention the nagging little fact that someone killed him," Gastner said. "Or at least hastened the goddamn dying process a little."

"Exactly." She saw Madelyn's eyebrows pucker a little, but the writer didn't intrude with questions, and Estelle was impressed all the more.

"Well, if you need me, don't hesitate to call," Gastner said, and pushed back his chair. He stood up with a sigh. "Wonderful grub, wonderful company, but I have to go back to my burrow." He extended a hand to Madelyn Bolles. "Pleasure seeing you again. How long are you with us?"

"You never know," she replied.

He laughed. "You have my card," he said. "If you get

stranded, give me a buzz. I'll be delighted to tour you around some more."

"I will most assuredly do that."

Estelle escorted the former sheriff of Posadas County to the front door, where he paused, one hand on the knob. "I'd be interested to know about Serafina," he said. "Joe and Lucinda I can figure, especially with the publicity about their big lottery win earlier this spring. But I worry a little about the old lady."

"Why or how she was picked as the first winner, you mean?"

"Yep. You've had the same thought."

"That's my goal tomorrow," Estelle said with a nod. "We'll see what Tony turns down in Cruces, and go from there." She stretched carefully, and unconsciously pressed her right hand to her ribs.

"You taking care of yourself?" Gastner said, his voice dropping to little more than a gruff whisper.

"Yes," Estelle replied. "Long days are a little tougher, is all."

"Then shorten 'em," Gastner replied. He reached out and circled her shoulders, his hug gentle. "Thanks. We'll see you tomorrow."

As she closed the door behind him, Estelle turned to see Madelyn Bolles shrugging into her light blue jacket.

"I'd best be on my way, too," she said. "If you're called out, will you have time to give me a buzz? Probably not, huh."

"There's never any way to tell. Are you sure that you want that, though?"

"At the moment, no. But I'd feel terrible if I missed something." She extended her hand and held Estelle's for a moment. "I really appreciate being included this evening."

"We all enjoyed your visit," Estelle said. "And Francisco enjoyed showing off for you."

"What an amazing gift," the writer said. "I hope I can hear him play again."

Estelle laughed. "That won't be hard to arrange. He seemed to enjoy having you as an audience." She waited on the front step as Madelyn Bolles made her way out to her car, then switched off the porch light as the taillights of the rental Buick disappeared up the street. Estelle stood in the foyer for a moment, then closed and locked the front door.

TWENTY-NINE

On Sunday morning, Deputy Tony Abeyta sounded pessimistic. It was always gratifying when information jumped right into the investigator's headlights, and frustrating when it remained illusive.

"We talked to every neighbor we could find last night," he said, "but a weekend isn't always the best time." He chuckled and added, "It's amazing how many folks can't even describe what their neighbors look like."

"Or want to," Estelle said, then added, "You're off today, you know." Abeyta glanced across her office toward the wall with the whiteboard and its staff schedule.

"Yeah, and so are you," he laughed. He patted the slender folder in his lap. "Grunt's working today, so I thought I'd go over to Cruces again for a little bit, as long as we have the chance." He opened the folder. "A few of the neighbors in the trailer park are willing to admit that they knew Marsh well enough to talk to him on an occasional basis...small talk stuff. Everyone says that he seemed like an okay guy, and two of 'em remember the truck. They thought that he was a student, and that maybe he worked part-time. As near as anyone can recollect, he's lived in the park for about four months. That's what the park manager's rental records show, too."

"Did anyone recall markings on the truck?" Estelle asked. "No. And the Tylers live right next door. Their kitchen window looks out on his trailer, and he parked the truck in the space between. They'd have seen door plaques." He cocked an eyebrow skeptically. "That doesn't mean they remember diddly, though. They were a little bit of help, but not much."

"What's the manager have to say?"

"Marsh paid his rent on time. No loud music, no obnoxious pets, no wild parties. The manager doesn't ask for references, and rentals are by the month. Mostly minimum wagers, a few students, a few snowbirds without a budget, a few down-and-outers. He said he runs about a third vacancies, so he's eager to get anybody who'll pay. It's a dismal little place, Estelle. I can't believe people live like that. It sure isn't about location, location, location. They get all the noise from the interstate, and the trailer park isn't convenient to much of anywhere."

The deputy stretched out his legs and crossed his boots, slouching farther down in his chair. "One little thing, is all. The Tylers—Mrs. Tyler, that is—says that Marsh had a girlfriend."

"I would think so. Before his truck did a tap dance on top of him, he was a pretty good-looking kid."

"She remembered the girl clearly," Abeyta said. "The manager didn't, but the neighbor did. The girl and Marsh 'smooched' a lot, she said." He looked up from his notes and grinned. "It's been a while since I heard anyone use that word."

"Does this Mrs. Tyler neighbor remember anything other than the smooching? A name would be nice."

"We should be so lucky, Estelle. She described the girl as 'willowy.' That's the term she used. Willowy like a fashion model, she said. Taller than Marsh by a little bit. Always showing lots of midriff. And one time here recently, she was driving a late model Mustang convertible."

"Earning more than a casual glance from the neighbor, I would think," Estelle added. "Just 'one time'? What's that mean?"

"The neighbor thought that the 'kids'—that's what she called 'em—were just trying it out. It had a dealer demo sticker instead of a plate."

"The neighbors were keeping more than a casual watch, apparently," Estelle said.

"Well, you gotta understand. This Tyler woman is on the slide way past fifty-five, and on the upside of two hundred and fifty pounds. She isn't a happy camper. She must have told me five times about how her drunk husband won't fix their '84 Crown Vic and that's why the tags were expired. Mr. Tyler didn't remember anything, by the way…or doesn't want to. Not even the midriff. The missus isn't real happy with the world right now, and she's got these two gorgeous lovebirds next door to watch, with the supermodel driving a fancy-schmancy convertible to rub it all in."

"But she only saw that car once," Estelle added.

"That's what she said. Blue convertible with a white rocker panel stripe."

"It'd be interesting to know where the supermodel lives," Estelle mused. "A low-rent trailer in the middle of a mobile home park doesn't sound like her kind of place—not if she can afford a 'fancy-schmancy' new set of wheels."

"I think that just happens to be where the boyfriend is camped out. Why he's chosen such a dump is the puzzle."

"It might be worth paying a visit to the area Ford dealers tomorrow. Maybe even today if any of them have

Sunday hours," Estelle said. "We might get lucky. Some salesman might remember the circumstances of the test drive, if that's what it was."

"I'll see who's open today," Abeyta said.

"What do we know about the girl, other than the 'willowy midriff'?" Estelle asked. "Did anyone get beyond that?"

"Mrs. Tyler said she was Mexican. Long black hair that she tied back in a ponytail sometimes, and really olive skin." Estelle cocked her head at that, and the deputy shrugged. "It's something. Black hair and olive skin narrows it down to about what, forty-seven percent of the population now?" He regarded the backs of his own olive hands. "More than that in Cruces. Unless you consider the Italians, the Indians, the Spanish, the French, the Moroccans, the Iraqis…" He let the list trail off.

"We need to find her," Estelle said. "Chris Marsh wasn't working in a vacuum, Tony. Someone was in the area when he picked up that last check from the Bacas on Wednesday night, and someone followed him, or was planning to meet him afterward. They were close enough that when he crashed the truck, they were Johnny-on-the-spot while he was still alive…and that's looking like minutes."

She glanced up as Brent Sutherland appeared in the doorway. "Ms. Bolles is here," he said.

"We're just about wrapped up," Estelle said. "You can tell her to come on back."

"Will do."

In a moment the magazine reporter appeared, this time dressed entirely in black save for her off-white, frilly blouse and a modest squash blossom turquoise necklace. Deputy Abeyta snapped out of his slouch and pulled himself to his feet.

"Madelyn, this is Deputy Tony Abeyta," Estelle said. "I don't think you two have had a chance to meet yet. Ms. Bolles is a writer for *A Woman's World* magazine, Tony. She has free run of the department while she's here."

"How do you do, ma'am," he said, extending a hand. Estelle saw that the young man's guard was up, his tone efficient, polite, but clipped and noncommittal.

"Deputy August," Madelyn said, without looking at the framed photos on Estelle's office wall—the "calendar" of employees. Linda Real's portrait of Tony Abeyta showed the deputy standing beside a small dun pony. His right arm with lead rope in hand was draped over the horse's neck as if the two of them were old friends. In his left hand, Abeyta held a small notebook, and it appeared that he was ruffling through the pages with his thumb. "I'd like to hear the story behind that photo some time."

"I was just checking the mileage on my patrol unit," Abeyta said with a straight face. "Nothing more mysterious than that." He flashed a smile as he turned toward the door. "I'll let you know," he said to Estelle. "If we dig anything up, I'll give you a call. Ma'am, nice to meet you."

"My pleasure," Madelyn said warmly. She gazed out into the hall after the deputy had left. "He reminds me of someone," she said after a moment. "I can't remember who." She turned and regarded Deputy August's photo, but that didn't prompt an answer, and she turned back to the undersheriff. "You had a quiet night for a change, I see," she said. "Brent the dispatcher says that it was a long, boring shift."

"That's the way we like it," Estelle said. She reached across her desk and x'd out of the Internet search she'd been exploring when Tony Abeyta had arrived. "You look elegant this morning."

"Well, I don't know about that," Madelyn said. "Shed the squash blossom and change the shoes, and I'm ready to dig ditches."

"How about Regál?"

"I thought that might be the case. We're going to church?"

"Ah, no." She saw the flicker of puzzlement on the writer's face. "I don't want those folks thinking that they're under surveillance," Estelle said. "Because they're not. At least not by us."

"I got the impression yesterday that the relationship with the feds is not always the warmest of friendships for some of those folks."

Estelle laughed. "*That's* an understatement. The problem right now is that everything is in flux. The Border Patrol has an impossible job to do, and that frustration boils over sometimes." She watched the computer blink out. "If you're going to write about that angle, you should spend a bunch of time riding with them. They're in the epicenter, not us."

"That might be on the agenda," Madelyn replied. "But one thing at a time. Where are we headed?"

"I have a naggy little question that needs answering," Estelle said. "And I want to follow up on what might just be an inconsequential coincidence."

"Wow," Madelyn said. "'Inconsequential coincidence.' I like that." She stepped over to the whiteboard schedule. "Estelle, when was the last time you said, 'Oh, to hell with it. It can wait until Monday morning?'"

"All the time, when the *it* doesn't involve murder," Estelle replied.

THIRTY

THE HIGHWAY SOUTHWEST to Regál was empty that Sunday morning. Estelle slowed as they approached Victor Sanchez's Broken Spur Saloon. The parking lot in front was deserted, but Estelle could see Victor's blue pickup truck parked in the back, sandwiched between the saloon and the mobile home where he, his wife, and their son lived.

Madelyn Bolles had been a silent passenger for most of the ride, and as Estelle slowed the car and pulled just off the highway on the verge of the saloon's parking lot, she looked quizzically at the undersheriff. Estelle stopped the car. "If you look ahead toward the pass, you can see the switchback just below where the truck crashed," she said. She leaned forward, both arms folded across the steering wheel. "One of the remaining questions." She didn't complete the thought but sat and gazed out at the rugged San Cristóbals.

After a moment she extended a finger and pointed toward Regál Pass. "Chris Marsh drove over the pass sometime Wednesday night. We don't know exactly what time, but it was after dark. The highway was wet, and he swerved to avoid a deer. He lost control, and his truck flipped over the side, crashing down through the rocks." She spread her hands, framing the mountain in front of them. "That's what we know. There's no spot that I can find, short of immediately at the accident site, where we could watch the highway and see headlights come over the pass." She paused, regarding the mountain. "Not from this side. We could sit right on the pass, where the Forest Service sign is, and see the area."

"If someone climbed down to the wreck immediately after it happened, you're wondering where they were parked," Madelyn said.

"Exactly. They were waiting for Chris Marsh. The pass is as far as he got. Someone was in a position to know what happened—or at least to *guess* what happened. We're sure that someone climbed down to the wreck that night—almost immediately after the crash—and made sure that Marsh was dead. They took whatever documents he might have had with him, right down to the delivery service magnetic signs that were on the truck's doors."

"How could someone do such a thing? The beer down the gullet thing?" the writer asked, and then immediately corrected herself. "Don't answer that," she said. "Every corner of the planet has its share of wackos."

"It seems to me," Estelle said, "that this person was waiting for Chris Marsh somewhere…maybe right where we're sitting now."

"He couldn't see the crash site, though," Madelyn said.

"No. They might have been on the phone with each other. That might have been what distracted his attention so that he didn't see the deer in time. He's on the cell, boasting of what he did. 'You're there, I'm here, and I'm on my way with a fat check.'"

"After the wreck, could he have managed a call for help, then?"

"No, I don't think so. My guess is that he could manage a gurgle. That's the extent of it, if he was conscious at all. We never found a cell phone, but that doesn't mean he didn't have one. In any event, he doesn't show up, and he doesn't ring back. His partner is going to go looking. Sure enough, there's a dead deer, and maybe some skid marks." Estelle surveyed the parking lot. "Whoever it was could have been waiting here, or on down at the intersection of the county road, or at any one of the pullouts. She was close. She had to be."

"She?"

"Could have been," Estelle said. "We know that Chris Marsh had a girlfriend—whether it was just casual or not, we don't know."

"That would be cold," Madelyn said.

"But it fits in some ways," Estelle said, and released the brake.

"That's what Tony Abeyta's been digging into. Marsh lived in Las Cruces. We don't know much about him, other than that he was a part-time student, lived in a low-rent trailer park, and had a girlfriend." She drove out of the lot, the car lurching across the shoulder and onto the pavement.

"What about this guy?" Madelyn turned and surveyed the saloon as they pulled away. "Could he have seen anything?"

"Victor? Unlikely. He has no view of any of that area from inside—he can't even see his own parking lot. And I don't think he'd notice, anyway. And he wouldn't tell us if he did."

"Oh," Madelyn said, her eyes growing large. "Hostile country?"

"Oh, very."

"Even something as nasty as this, he wouldn't talk to you?"

"Oh, he might, between grumbles and growls. But he has an image to uphold, you know."

"What about the boy's parents? Have they been of any help?"

"None. They've given up on their son. Wrote him right off. They live back east, and aren't interested in coming out. Cremate him and ship the ashes back, if we want. Or dispose of them here. Whatever."

"You're kidding," Madelyn said.

"Oh, no."

"Does that ever get to you?"

"Well..."

"I mean some of these people that you find yourself dealing with—just amazing. Every wrong decision that could be made, they make it. I've met people who seem to *thrive* on being miserable. If I had to be around 'em for any length of time, they'd drive me either into a grand funk depression, or to homicide. You must feel that way sometimes, don't you?"

"I'd have to think about that," Estelle replied. "I don't spend a lot of time being depressed, though. Everybody has the opportunity to make choices. What they choose to do is their business. Up to a point, anyway. Most of the time the law is pretty clear-cut."

"But don't you wish that sometimes you could just wave a magic wand and make all the sadness, all the viciousness, all the stupidity, just go away?"

"Then I'd be out of a job," Estelle quipped. "It's all part of what Bill Gastner likes to quote as 'the great human experiment.'"

"I can do without some parts of the experiment," Madelyn said.

"Sure enough," Estelle agreed. "But if we live in the middle of it, we don't get to choose."

The highway up through the pass was dappled here and there as the morning sun warmed through the stands of runty trees, and Estelle slowed the car to 30 miles an hour, the slope steep enough that the car shifted to second gear and then stayed there as they ambled up the flank of the mountain. She lowered the window, the flow of air chilly but lush with innocent fragrance.

They reached the short, straight stretch that rose to the pass itself, and after a glance in the rearview mirror, Estelle stopped the car. "He crests the top of the pass, and almost immediately collides with the deer. He loses it, and you can see right over there," and she pointed at the hump of dirt just uphill of the guardrail, "where his truck vaulted over."

"How fast do you think he was going?"

"Sixty, maybe. I don't think much faster than that. That's enough to do it."

Madelyn turned in her seat, looking back the way they'd come. "And the highway department found him two days later."

"Yes. It was more a misting than a rain. The highway was wet, but there wasn't enough rain to flush away the marks. Linda even managed to take an exposure that shows them."

"That answers my question then. If he called and said, 'I'm leaving now,' she…he…whoever it was would wait a few minutes. Late evening, she'd be looking for his headlights."

"That's right."

"She'd still be waiting. After a few minutes, she'd try to call him to ask where he was. No response and she'd go looking. And that's my question. Were there enough traces of the accident left to mark the site?"

"The answer to that is 'yes,' Madelyn. I can imagine her driving to the top of the pass, and maybe even down into Regál. When Marsh doesn't show up, she would retrace the route. Coming northbound, there are the tracks, the dead deer, and a short section of mangled guardrail."

She pulled the car into gear. "Let me move out of these people's way." She accelerated hard and pulled off near the Forest Service sign announcing the pass. An enormous camper towing a flashy SUV rumbled by, its occupants offering a friendly wave, their vehicle leaving a wake of diesel fumes.

"I wonder if she had a pang of doubt," Madelyn said.

"About?"

"I wonder if there was a moment when she thought that the young man—Marsh was his name? When she thought that he was running with the money."

"That's entirely possible."

"Otherwise, why would she have been in the area in the first place? If she trusted him to make the delivery... He had the cashier's check, am I right?"

"Yes."

"So then why is she dogging his tracks? Is she afraid he's going to split on her?"

"Interesting," Estelle said. "We're going to make a convert out of you yet. While you're considering all those questions, add this one to the list, Madelyn. Why didn't she just ride along with Marsh in the first place?"

"Couriers don't carry passengers?"

Estelle pulled the car back out on the highway. "Good

point, but who's going to think about that?" she said. "When a delivery truck pulls up at your driveway, do you check to make sure the driver is solo?"

"Huh. She could have just ridden with him."

"And we would have found her bashed and broken on the cliff side along with Marsh," Estelle said.

"Could she have known the crash would happen? Some sort of vehicular sabotage?"

"Vehicular sabotage," Estelle repeated with a grin. "What a concept."

"Has anyone thought of that?"

"I don't think so," the undersheriff said. "That's the sort of thing that works really, really well in movies, Madelyn. It's right up there in popularity with the explosive post that makes the car inexplicably flip over on cue. In this case, the most likely scenario is that the young man collected a grillful of venison, and then lost control."

"Which prompts the most interesting question of all, at least for me," Madelyn said. "How do you sleep at night with all these unsolved conundrums floating around in your head? How much of this do you take home?"

"I have a houseful of wonderful distractions," Estelle replied. "And you have to remember that this is the exception, rather than the rule. As *padrino* says, our job is ninety-nine percent boredom, interrupted by one percent panic and mayhem. Most of the time, we're *looking* for something to do."

"You think very highly of him, don't you. The 'godfather.' That's how *padrino* translates, am I right?"

"Roughly. And yes, I do think highly of him. We love him dearly."

"You've known him since the ice ages?"

"About that long. I first met Bill Gastner when I was twelve. He and my great-uncle Reuben visited Tres Santos. That's about forty miles straight ahead south from here."

"You guys don't have jurisdiction over the border, though...."

"No, not in any formal sense. In this case, someone stole several pallets of bricks from a construction site near Posadas. The bricks ended up in Tres Santos. Bill and Reuben went down to negotiate their return without involving the *judiciales*."

"Your uncle stole them? Is that what you're saying?"

"'Informal time payment' might be more accurate," Estelle said. "Anyway, that's when I met Bill Gastner for the first time. Twenty-seven years ago. Sometimes it seems a lifetime away, sometimes like yesterday."

"Memory lanes are like that," Madelyn said. Below them, the village of Regál was still in deep shadow, the buttress of mountains hiding them from the sun until late morning. Despite the promise of a mild February day, with the sky clear of clouds, a few wisps of piñon smoke perfumed the village. "You'd think a place like this would be so far out of the way that nothing would touch them," the writer said.

"These folks argue about immigration and abortion rights and taxes and Iraq like everyone else," Estelle said. "And water rights, and the cost of gasoline, and who's sleeping with whom."

"When's the first mass?" They could see that the *iglesia*'s parking lot was still empty.

"Eleven o'clock," Estelle replied. "First and only. Father Anselmo has mass in María at eight, then comes over here." As they drew closer, Estelle could see a trace of smoke from the church's single stovepipe. Emilio Contreras would be at the *iglesia*, chasing the chill, dabbing the last bit of dust from the furnishings. In the old days, he might have had to rouse a few illegals from their snoozing on the pews.

"Do you ever go?" The question surprised Estelle, and she looked across at Madelyn. "Or does your job make that sort of thing difficult?" When the undersheriff didn't respond immediately, Madelyn added, "Or is that question too personal?"

"No," Estelle said. "And no, I don't go." The response sounded more abrupt than she intended, but the writer accepted the explanation with a nod.

"It would be hard, I guess," she said. "You spend a career working with the most base of human ulterior motives, and it would be a challenge to sit in a group of people, hearing all the hypocrisy."

"I hadn't thought of it like that," Estelle said. "I just don't *think* about it. It's not something that I consider."

"Even last year, when you were hurt?"

"Especially not then."

At the bottom of the hill, Estelle slowed and turned into the dirt lane that first passed by the Contreras home, then meandered through the village.

"What will happen to the young man you apprehended yesterday?" Madelyn asked as they passed by the driveway to Joe and Lucinda Baca's adobe.

"Immigration will return him to Mexican authorities," Estelle said. "From that point it's completely unpredictable."

"That's what I've heard. He'll try again, no doubt."

"No doubt. And that's part of the dilemma with Joe

and Lucinda. They make a tempting target. All that money makes an easy target."

"It's not like they keep it in bundles under the bed," Madelyn said. "At least I hope they don't."

"No matter where it's kept," Estelle said. As she drove around another apple orchard, its irrigation pipe discharging a meager stream into the freshly hoed ditch, she slowed the car to a walk, then eased into Serafina Roybal's narrow driveway. The retired schoolteacher's Jeep Wagoneer had been backed out of the small shed and parked near the rose trellis on the southwest side of the adobe. The entire truck was evenly covered with fine dust and sparrow droppings. The left rear tire was just a couple of pounds above dead flat.

A small station wagon was parked close to the kitchen door, and Estelle pulled in directly behind it.

She keyed the mike. "PCS, three-ten."

"Three-ten, PCS."

"Ten-twenty-eight New Mexico niner-eight-niner Charlie Bravo Nora."

"Ten-four."

She waited, mike in hand.

"This doesn't work?" Madelyn said, tapping the flat computer monitor.

Estelle shook her head. "I don't know what happened. It's scheduled for replacement next week. I'm getting a new car with a whole raft of new gadgets coming on board."

"Three-ten, niner-eight-niner Charlie Bravo Nora should appear on a 2003 Subaru Outback, color green over silver, registered to Irene Merriam Salas, 301 College Lane Circle, Las Cruces. Negative wants or warrants."

"Ten-four. Thanks, Brent." She slid the mike back into
the rack. "It appears that the granddaughter is visiting,"
she said, switching off the car. "Serafina said yesterday
that she was going to. I think it's best if you stay here."

THIRTY-ONE

DRESSED IN A blue robe that touched the floor, her steel gray hair in a single long braid that reached below her waist, Serafina Roybal opened the front door before Estelle reached the single step leading to the porch.

"You're just in time for coffee," Serafina said. Her voice was husky. "My soul, twice in two days. This is a treat, young lady."

"Good morning, Serafina," Estelle said. "Who's that with you?"

"Every once in a while, we have civilian ride-alongs," Estelle replied, and she saw a trace of that wonderful skeptical look that students would have been favored with when they were less than honest with this formidable teacher. Estelle was surprised to hear herself add, "She's a writer for one of the national women's magazines."

"Ah, now," Serafina said. "That's nice. You both come in.... The coffee should be ready by now."

"Serafina, I can't stay," Estelle said. "I just stopped for a minute to ask a couple of questions left over from yesterday." But she was talking to the elderly woman's back, and she followed Serafina inside. The house was dark and musty, and the aroma of coffee was strong along with the rest of the potpourri that a home produces. Across the room, the television was on but muted. Ignoring it, the elderly woman made her way toward the kitchen.

"I'm *so* pleased that you came this morning. Such a surprise, you know." She walked back to the doorway to the living room and held out both hands as if she wanted a hug. "My granddaughter came last night. It's been far too long, I must say."

Estelle stopped near the television, looking at the collection of photos that rested on top of the console—most of them showing Octavio Roybal, including several of him as a young stalwart, smart in his army uniform. Arranged to one side was a group of photos of Serafina's daughter, Esmeralda, and her daughter Irene. In the first, the toddler sat on her mother's knee on the front step of the *iglesia*. The photo showed a pudgy toddler who beamed into the camera. A second snapshot caught Irene at about age eight as she sprayed a compliant dog with a garden hose. Finally, a formal high school graduation photo in a gold frame presented Irene in an elegant pose in cap and gown.

"Your granddaughter has grown up," Estelle said, picking up the latest photo.

"Such a dear," Serafina said. "I can't believe that she's a junior in college already. She manages to break away now and then, and I'm *so* glad that she visits. Young folks don't always have time, you know."

"Time slips away," the undersheriff said. Irene looked like her grandmother—square, almost stout, with a strong jaw, and the same shock of unruly hair that would go first salt-and-pepper and then steel gray as she matured.

Serafina headed back toward the kitchen. "I hope she comes back in time for you to say hello," she called. "She walked over to talk with Danny Rivera for a little bit." She smiled. "He thinks that he wants to buy my old car, and they backed it out of the shed this morning. He needs to find a tire, I know that much."

Estelle reached out for the mug of coffee. "And you know," Serafina continued, "I'm glad that you stopped by. I'm so addled headed these days. If I wanted to sell the Jeep, is there anything special that I have to do?"

"Just fill in the back of the title certificate," Estelle said. "That transfers ownership. Then the buyer needs to add the vehicle to his insurance, and register it with the MVD. They have to have it insured before the MVD will issue the registration. It's pretty simple."

"So I just sign the title?"

"That's correct. If you want a bill of sale, the MVD has blank forms that you can use. I'll be happy to help you with it, if you like. You don't have to have one, but a bill of sale is always a good idea."

"Well, we'll see," Serafina said. "Why Danny would want such a monster, I'm sure I don't know."

"Those were good, rugged trucks," Estelle said. "You drove it over the pass to school for a lot of years."

"It's really like new, you know." Serafina waved a hand in dismissal. "I mean, if you don't consider that it's a filthy mess at the moment, with a flat tire. But really, it's all road miles, you know. They say that's good. None of this stop-and-go. But now I didn't drive much, you see. A big old boat like that isn't worth anything anymore. I'd be just as happy to see it put to use."

She motioned toward the living room. "Let's sit. These old bones don't work like they used to." Estelle followed her out and crossed to the TV console, setting down her coffee cup as she sat in the straight chair near the wall heater. The aroma of the coffee was strong, but now she could smell the fragrance of Serafina's visitor, light perfume, maybe shower potions, that drifted out from one of the bedrooms.

"I can't stay long," Estelle said. "I stopped by because I'm still hung up on this sweepstakes thing."

"You worry me a little bit with all this," Serafina said.

"I'm sorry if I do, but I keep wondering how you heard about the sweepstakes originally, Serafina. You gave me the copy of the first letter that you kept. But in the beginning, did they contact you first, or did you have to send something in? How did that all work?"

Serafina sipped the coffee tentatively, grimaced, and said, "I didn't ask if you take cream or sugar. This is pretty strong. I think I lost count when I was putting the coffee in."

"Neither one, thanks."

Serafina relaxed back in the Morris chair. "Let's see, now. I received a letter, right out of the blue. Just a routine mailing, I think. At least, that's what I *thought* it was, at first. Then I saw that it was from Canada, and I'm something of a stamp fancier, so the *first* thing I did was cut off the postage. I have a grandniece who saves stamps, you see. Then I saw that it was a formal business letter, and that's when I read the whole thing. And land, if I hadn't won a little bit. It was the same the second time."

"Just like that? A letter from out of the blue."

Serafina nodded. "But isn't that the way of it? Those notices from the publishers' thing...*they* just arrive unannounced. Except this time, it wasn't a come-on. It was just a formal letter saying that I had won, and what to do in order to claim the prize. None of the usual folderol with all the bright lights and fanfare."

"It said that the check would be delivered by courier, then."

"Certainly. And that made me feel a little better, too, knowing that I'd be dealing with someone face-to-face."

Estelle reached across and picked up the coffee cup, looking down into the brew thoughtfully.

"I'd like to know how they selected your name," she said finally. "That's the thing I can't stop thinking about."

Serafina chuckled. "Oh, in this day and age? Our names are common fodder, I'm sure. Use a credit card once and that's it. Of course, I don't do that. But buy a set of charity Christmas address labels just once, or send away for a magazine. Our lives are open books, dear. But what difference does it all make? They did just what they said they would do."

"I suppose."

"You don't have to drink that if you don't care for it," Serafina said, and Estelle placed the cup back on the console.

"Coffee and I don't get along too well," she said. "But thanks, Serafina. I really need to run. You said that Irene went over to Danny's?"

"Just a few minutes ago. Now," and she smiled slyly, "*supposedly* to try and find a tire from that mess over there. *But they* cut across the old orchard. I told them they should drive, but they wanted to walk a little. It's such a short ways, and it's such a beautiful day."

"Maybe we'll take a minute and stop by there, then," Estelle said, pushing herself to her feet. As an afterthought, she asked, "At any point, did the sweepstakes company call you on the phone?"

"Oh, no. You know," Serafina said, heaving herself

out of the chair with great effort, "half the time, I don't answer the phone anyway. It always rings when I'm right in the middle of something. Us old ladies don't move so fast anymore. And most of the time, you know, it's one of those recordings. They don't give up easily."

"No, they don't," Estelle agreed.

"How's your mother?"

"She's fine."

"Little old ladies are the favorite target these days," Serafina said. "That's what the news is always saying."

"Did you talk about winning with anyone? Relatives, maybe? Or someone here in town?"

Serafina's eyes twinkled again, and she held a crooked index finger over her lips. "In a little place like this," she said, "you talk to just one person and first thing you know, it's a *secreto a voces* through the whole town. Joe and Lucinda, they know all about that."

"You're wise to be careful," Estelle said affectionately. "But I confess I'm still curious. I can understand Joe and Lucinda's names coming up....There's some notoriety there when they won the state lottery. I'm curious how other names are selected."

"You could ask the company."

"Yes, I could. And I will, tomorrow. Sundays are difficult."

She took her full coffee cup out to the kitchen, a tiny room whose surfaces were under years of enamel paint of various pastel colors, with a kitchen sink so stained by Regál's hard water that it looked more like reddish brown stoneware than white porcelain.

Serafina had settled back in her chair and didn't get up as Estelle returned to the living room. The television remained ignored, and Estelle wondered if it had been on all night. "You should visit more often," the elderly woman said.

"Yes, I should."

"Bring your mother with you next time."

"I think she'd like that."

"Who's that riding with you today?" Serafina asked, and Estelle felt a twinge of sadness at the repetition.

"Her name is Madelyn Bolles," the undersheriff said. "She's in town for just a few days."

"A friend from college?"

"No. She's a writer. She's working on a profile of our department."

"Ah. All right. Well, if you have to go, then you have to go."

She reached out a hand to take Estelle's. "It's always so nice to see you, *querida*." She used the grip to boost her out of the chair and, with more of a hobble than a walk, escorted Estelle to the front step. She stood in the doorway watching as Estelle made her way back through the tall grama grass to the car. The undersheriff passed within half a dozen feet of the Jeep, and could smell the perfume of its sludgy oil and sun-baked paint and rubber.

"You look like something is bothering you," Madelyn Bolles commented as Estelle slid back into the Crown Victoria.

"Lots of things," Estelle said. She made no move to start the car. "It makes sense to me that *if* there's a scam being worked here—and I think there is—the Bacas were the target. They're the ones with the proceeds from an earlier win. They're natural targets with deep pockets."

"You don't know yet that the sweepstakes thing *is*

fraudulent, do you? I mean, didn't you say that this lady won twice? And actually collected money?"

"Yes, she did."

"You're thinking that she was used to soften the other couple up for a bigger hit, aren't you. People would hear about her success, and be suckered in?"

Estelle looked across at Madelyn. "*Sin duda.* That's exactly what's nagging at me. If come tomorrow Joe and Lucinda cash that last check with no problems, then I'm going to be *really* puzzled."

"Just a tidal wave of good fortune? Isn't that possible?"

"No. We know that Chris Marsh and his nifty little truck were fraudulent. He was *posing* as a deliveryman, Madelyn. His supposed delivery company doesn't exist. It *sounds* good, it *sounds* like it should be a real company, but it isn't. That makes the whole thing suspect."

"Is someone trying to rip off the sweepstakes company?"

"That's a possibility, and I've thought about that. But I can't imagine a legitimate publishing house doing business that way. Why would you use an unknown courier company, *especially* when so much money is involved, when you could choose one of the established firms? Anyway, you hit it exactly right. What bothers me is that if someone is trying to scam money out of Joe and Lucinda Baca, it makes sense to start small with a close friend—like Serafina here—to build confidence. *That's* what I can't put behind me."

She looked at the small shed where Serafina's Jeep had been stored.... The big SUV would have been a snug fit. The door had been only partially closed.

"I see smoke," Madelyn said. Estelle turned quickly

to look at her, and the writer quickly amended her remark. "I mean from your ears. You're thinking so hard."

"Sure enough." She started the car and backed out to the dirt lane. "I need to check one thing," she said.

"If you want my opinion," Madelyn said, "so much winning in a tiny village would be enough to spook me, too."

"But when the winner wants to take the money so badly, it's easy to say it's just a freak of statistics," Estelle said. "'It's just good fortune.'"

"What are we after, then?"

"If the sweepstakes thing is a scam, then that leads us down an interesting road. Serafina Roybal was the first one who won. I haven't heard of anyone else…no one in Posadas, as far as we know. No one has called the sheriff's office to complain about a possible scam, and we get calls all the time, complaining about this and that. How did Chris Marsh target Serafina, then? How would he know about her?"

"You could drive through a village like this one, point at any little house, and say, 'Let's start with this one.' That's an easy thing to do."

"You could do that," Estelle agreed. "And maybe that's what happened. Especially after the publicity of Joe and Lucinda winning the state lottery. The snag there is that you don't cruise *through* Regál, not with these little lanes and cow tracks. You can't really see Serafina's house from the main highway. That's assuming that you find the village in the first place."

"That's the new bumper sticker: 'Where the hell is Regál?'" Madelyn quipped.

"Everything else was too well planned, at least until

that deer decided to run across the road. Someone was being very, very clever. Just *very* clever."

"Where to now?"

"Serafina's granddaughter is here for a visit. That's who owns the Subaru."

"You know her?"

"I met her once or twice a dozen years ago."

"What's she going to tell you?"

Estelle looked across at Madelyn and smiled. "The crash victim was from Las Cruces."

"Isn't that a bit like meeting a stranger who says he's from such and such city and you say, 'Oh, I have a friend who lives there. Do you know so and so?' Talk about long shots."

"The granddaughter is not only from Cruces. She's also a student at the university there. So was Chris Marsh. There's always a chance, no matter how slight."

"If that's all you have," Madelyn said philosophically.

"That's all we have. And I've never trusted coincidence."

THIRTY-TWO

THE RIVERAS LIVED in the only home in Regál built after 1960—in this case, long after. The gray and white double-wide mobile home had been purchased on Fernando Rivera's eightieth birthday. They probably wouldn't have considered the snazzy new digs if their hot water heater hadn't ignited the utility room of their historic home, resulting in a fire that burned the old adobe hollow.

The couple, celebrating their seventy-fifth wedding anniversary this Sunday in February, were now both ninety-six years old, and looked seventy-five. Their only concession to advanced years was welcoming their grandson, Danny, to share their home.

A fair collection of vehicles adorned the dirt yard, with a large metal shop building off to the east, its double door rolled all the way to one side. Two scruffy short-haired mutts bounced stiff legged out toward the road, barking frantically as the county car neared the driveway.

"Oh, nice," Madelyn muttered. "You don't have to tell me to stay in the car."

A young man appeared in the door of the shop and whistled sharply. The dogs ignored him. When it became clear that the white county car was actually pulling into his yard rather than passing through, he shook his head and angled across toward the dogs. "Come here," he shouted. The dogs did, ratty tails wagging.

He grabbed the larger female by the collar, and the other dog followed along. In a moment, both were snapped onto a chain run beside the house. "They bite," he said as Estelle got out of the car.

"That's nice to know," she said.

The young man wiped his hands on his jeans, which along with his sleeveless denim shirt were so dirty that they could have stood up by themselves. "What can I do for you, sheriff?" he asked. One green eye drifted out of coordination with the other as he glanced toward her car. With the dogs safely tethered, Madelyn had lowered her window. If the breeze was just right, she would have been able to smell the pungent aroma of grease and perspiration. Danny Rivera looked as if he'd crawled out from under a greasy truck on a hot August afternoon.

"How have you been doing, Danny?" Estelle asked. "Are the folks all ready for their big day?"

"We're all fine," he replied, and glanced at his watch, nestled in a crust of grease and dirt on his right wrist. "I figured to get a couple hours' work done before gettin' cleaned up, and then I got side-tracked." His grandparents' seventy-fifth wedding anniversary was occasion enough to slow down the young workaholic, who managed to put more miles on his county road grader than any other three county employees combined.

"I just stopped by Serafina's," Estelle said.

"She okay?" the young man asked quickly, before Estelle had a chance to continue.

"She's fine, Danny. She mentioned that Irene might be over here."

Daniel Rivera's full blond eyebrows wrinkled with

puzzlement, and his errant left eye drifted a bit, *an altogether fetching expression,* Estelle thought. "Is something wrong?" he asked.

"No. I've known Irene since she was like so." She held her hand three feet off the ground. "I just wanted to say hi. We were passing through, and saw her car at Serafina's. Her grandma said we might catch her over here. You guys were working on the Jeep?"

"Oh, that," the young man said. He thrust his hands in his back pockets and nodded toward the shop. "Irene's inside. Come on in." He peered at the police car. "Your friend there's welcome to come in, too. Grandpop and Grandmamá are in the house, if you want to say hello."

"I may see them this afternoon. My mother may want to come down, too."

"That'd be cool. She don't have to drive all this way, though. There's the main reception at the VFW in Posadas." He turned toward the shop, but the sound of her cell phone stopped Estelle in her tracks.

"Let me catch this, Danny. I'll be along in just a second," she said, and turned back toward the car as she opened the phone. "Guzman."

"Sorry to bother you," Brent Sutherland said. "You clear?"

"For a minute," Estelle said. "I'm with Danny Rivera at his grandparents' place." A long pause followed, and Estelle could picture Brent leaning forward, staring at the huge county map on the wall in Dispatch. She heard a familiar voice in the background, and Sutherland said, "Are you clear for a call?"

"Sure."

"Hang on a second." In a moment County Manager Leona Spears' voice warbled over the air.

"Forgive the interruption," Leona said, "but I wanted to tell you that I had a *long* conversation with, oh, what's his name. Something Parker."

"Elliot Parker?" Estelle asked. It was part of Leona's fetching tact that she had taken the time to check with the Sheriff's Department dispatch before contacting Estelle, even though the undersheriff's personal cell phone number was one of the first on the county manager's speed-dial list.

"That's the one. He with the beer bottle–pitching son. He called me at home, for mercy's sakes. On a Sunday morning. That's dedication to being a real nuisance."

"Well, 'nuisance' is a kind term, Leona," Estelle observed.

"I'm trying, I'm trying," Leona chirped. "He wanted to make sure that we were going to *fire* Deputy Collins. Can you imagine that? We're not going to do that, are we?" Her question raised all kinds of interesting turf questions, Estelle reflected, since the sheriff did his own hiring and firing—his was an elected office, not subject to approval or supervision by the county manager. Still, they had all come to value Leona's input.

"No, we're not."

"Wonderful. Because that's what I told Mr. Parker. That was my understanding after talking with Bobby late last night. Mr. Parker, bless his arrogant little soul, didn't like hearing that. And for some reason, he didn't want to talk to Master Robert. I can't imagine why." A little chuckle followed that. "The more Mr. Parker can deflect things away from his little boy, the better, apparently."

"I don't think Judge Hobart is deflectable," Estelle said. "It's in his hands, not ours. Anyway, as far as Dennis is concerned, the sheriff has a new training program in the works. I think it's the right thing to do. Much more stringent qualifications for all of us."

"I heard about that. It's going to cost us some money, but I think it's worth it, and a *wonderful*, proactive notion. I tried to explain that to *Mr.* Parker, but it went in one ear and out the other. Anyway, to make a long story short, he's threatening to sue us, for what, I don't know. He made it an ultimatum, and *that's* when I lost my patience, I'm afraid. He'll probably call you, too, and I wanted you to hear it from the horse's mouth...what I told him, I mean."

"And what's that, Leona?"

"I told him in no uncertain terms that it was going to be wonderfully entertaining watching this whole mess unfold in public court. I said we've needed to bring this underage drinking thing out in the open for a long time, and then I told him that I hoped he had a really good lawyer, because *we* do. A drunken young man throwing a full bottle of beer at an officer and damaging government property, and the officer injured by flying glass? My goodness."

The glass chip did draw a speck of blood, Estelle thought, but she didn't interrupt Leona's roll.

"*And* selling liquor to minors, and on and on," Leona continued. "Probably more than that. I was really wound up. I told him that it was going to be fun." She sniffed. "I think at the moment I'm feeling a little ashamed of myself for losing my temper."

"Some people bring out the best in all of us, Leona. What did Parker say to all this?"

"Well, now he's angry with me, which is probably a good thing," Leona laughed. "He hung up on me when I said, 'Well, why don't you sue *me*, then. Let's just sue everyone, while we're at it, if that's the only way you can figure out how to make a living.' I probably shouldn't have been so melodramatic, but there it is."

"He'll get over it," Estelle said. "His son will get a slap on the wrist, maybe a little bit of probation, and that'll be it, unless Hobart's in a really foul mood."

"Except for the repair of the vehicle," Leona said. "I plan to pursue that if Judge Hobart doesn't order restitution. Anyway, I just wanted to let you know that I'm his latest target, so not to worry."

"Thanks, Leona. I wasn't worried, but I'm glad that things will work out. For Dennis' sake."

"He'll be the better police officer for it," Leona said. Her voice took on a more serious tone. "He wasn't even scheduled to work, was he? I mean, when the incident happened?"

"No. He was finishing up some paperwork at the end of a long day. He took the call as a matter of convenience. He was headed home that way, and no one else was close. He volunteered, and I okayed it. So chalk it up to my mistake. I was tired, but I knew that *he* was, too. I let him go anyway. But at that moment, with the situation as it was, it seemed the expedient solution."

"Oh my. We are *sooooo* shorthanded, aren't we," Leona said. "Well, that's one of my priorities. We're going to do something about that. But you're busy, and I'm rambling. Are we making progress with that horrible truck crash situation?"

"'Progress' may be too optimistic a word, Leona." She glanced at the shop, but Danny Rivera had disappeared inside.

"Well, that's my nature, dear. If there's anything I can do to facilitate, let me know."

"I will, Leona. Thanks for all you do."

"Is that wonderful magazine reporter with you yet?"

"She is."

"I look forward to having the chance to visit with her, if she wants."

"I'm sure she will, Leona. I'll tell her you called."

"Thanks so much. Well, I'm out of your hair now. Ta, dear." The phone went dead, and Estelle laughed.

"Our county manager," she said to Madelyn. "She's one of a kind. She wants to talk with you sometime."

"She's on my list," Madelyn said. "I've heard so many different stories, I don't know what to expect."

"Expect a charming interview," Estelle said. "I'll be back in a minute."

The sun was already baking the gravel in front of the shop as Estelle walked away from the car. As she neared the shop, she could smell the tang of hot steel. By afternoon, the uninsulated building would be toasty warm, as the February sun baked the expanse of roof and wall. She paused in the doorway. Off to the left, a huge red four-wheel-drive pickup rested on blocks, parts from its brakes and wheel hubs laid neatly on clean rags. A quick glance around the shop revealed another older truck with all of its guts removed, various collections of parts here and there, and, incongruously, a slick fiberglass bass boat on a new, white trailer. The cowling had been removed from the massive outboard motor on the boat's transom.

"We can get that oil changed while you're here," Danny said cheerfully. "County ain't too good at keepin' up with maintenance. I know that for a fact."

"That's true," Estelle said. She stepped carefully toward the four-by-four, mindful of the litter of tools and cords on the floor. Toward the back of the shop was an impressive collection of tires. Three of them were spread out on the floor, and Irene Salas turned from her inspection of them.

Estelle wound her way through the litter, and Irene Salas approached to greet her. Stout-framed and athletic, Irene had poured herself into fresh blue jeans and a denim shirt whose tails were tied at her waist. "Irene, welcome home. I was just over talking with your grandmother, and she said you were visiting."

"Hi," Irene said, clearly confused, even a bit guarded.

"The last time I saw you, you were about like this," Estelle said, indicating a small child. "I'm Estelle Guzman."

A flare of recognition touched Irene's eyes. "Grandma Serafina talks about you all the time," she said, and smiled warmly. "I'm sorry I didn't recognize you when you drove up. That sun's so bright. You're sheriff now?"

"Undersheriff," Estelle said. "Bobby Torrez is sheriff. Remember him?"

"The big scary guy who looks like he belongs in the movies...wow."

Estelle laughed. "That would be the one. Your grandmother is thrilled that you came over. Are you here for the anniversary?"

"Isn't that great?" Irene replied. "They're so cute," and she looked affectionately at Danny Rivera. "I can't even *imagine* seventy-five years together."

"That's a long, long time. Irene, your grandma said you're a junior now?"

"I'll be a senior this fall." She beamed. "*Two* more semesters and I get to be unemployed."

"There's always grad school," Danny offered.

"Yeah, well," Irene said. "There is. But I'm not sure yet."

"What are you majoring in?" Estelle asked.

"Anthropology," Irene said. "I *think*. It's much, much harder than I thought, especially now that we're into statistics and all that sort of thing. But I'm loving it…well, most of it, so it'll work out."

"That's an interesting road," Estelle agreed. "When you're finished, you're headed off to Africa or Peru, or someplace like that?"

"Actually, I don't have to travel that far," Irene laughed. "I'm really drawn to the border country." She turned to look at Danny Rivera with undisguised affection. "People like Fernando and Maria? My grandma? I can't even imagine what this country was like when they were young. No pavement, no RVs pouring through, no *fence*," and she looked out the shop door. "Only the *iglesia* is the same."

"Until Emilio passes on," Danny observed.

"See," Irene said, with a heartfelt intensity that impressed Estelle. For added emphasis, the girl reached out and punched Danny Rivera on the shoulder. "What's going to happen then? You watch. Within a month of Emilio's passing, I bet someone puts an electric light over the doorway. You watch." She made a face. "That's the first step."

"Well, *I'm* not the one who's going to do it," Danny said in self-defense.

"You better not." The pugnacious expression softened. "If I'm not around, you kick over their ladder for me."

"The ethnographics of the border country interest you, then," Estelle said, and Irene Salas nodded vigorously.

"Not the cities, though," she said. "I could care less about the metro areas. But like Fernando and Maria?

Or my grandma? Or *your* mom, Estelle? Serafina talks about her all the time, too. This was such a neat stretch of country before politicians ruined it. All the tiny little villages? I love it." She grinned. "We have some rip-roaring arguments about it all in class," she said.

"Who's the 'we?'" Estelle asked.

"Oh, you know. I have one professor who agrees that I should do an ethnographic study just of Regál, while so many of the *viejos are still alive.*"

"You should," Estelle said. "And don't put it off. Things change quickly."

"I know," Irene said. "I had never realized how fast. I talk with Grandma Serafina and realize how much is lost already. Like I never met Octavio? I hear Serafina or my mom talk about my grandpa, and I miss him *soooo* much…and I never met him! He died a jillion years before I was even born. Is that sad, or what?" She shook her shoulders. "Listen to me. I get all wound up."

"It's delightful that you're passionate about your studies," Estelle said. "Perhaps more people should be." She turned and looked back toward the car, and her patient passenger. "I should be running along. We're up to here this weekend," and she made a slice across her throat. "Your grandma probably told you that we had a nasty accident up on the pass Friday night. The driver was a student…or *used* to be a student…at State."

Irene's open, pleasant countenance crumpled in sympathy. "Oh, I *know.* Both she and Danny were talking about it."

"Did you know him?" Estelle paused as if the memory was slow in coming. "His name was Christopher Marsh."

"I helped Stubby winch that mess back up the hill,"

Danny interrupted before Irene could answer. "What a damn crash that was. He must have been flyin'."

"I think he was. You didn't know him, then?" Estelle repeated.

"There's something about the name that sounds kinda familiar, but you know, there's about a jillion people on campus. Plus, it sounds like one of those names, you know."

"If you have a minute, I'd like to show you something," Estelle said. "Do you have a minute?"

"Sure," Irene said.

"I'll be back in just a second."

Estelle turned and walked quickly back to the Ford. Madelyn watched as the undersheriff took the manila folder of eight-by-ten glossies from her briefcase, but made no comment.

"Slim chances," Estelle said by way of explanation. Walking back toward the shop, she smiled apologetically at the two young people.

"I wouldn't do this, but you get around in Cruces, and there's always a chance you might recognize this individual. As I said, he was a student at State for a while, I think. I'm not sure if he was this past semester." She slipped the photo out and handed it to Irene, who flinched. "Oh, gross," she blurted. The eight-by-ten had been taken at the morgue, with the victim cleaned up and his limbs arranged more or less in proper line. Still, there was no doubt that he'd lost the battle with the truck and the rocks in a big way.

"That's the guy, huh?" Danny said, looking over Irene's shoulder. "I wasn't up there when they dug him out of the truck."

"That's the guy," Estelle said. "We're trying to find

out a little more about him." She reached out but didn't take the picture back from Irene. "No recollection? Did you ever catch sight of him on campus?"

With a pained shake of her head, she handed the photo back, dropping it into the folder held open by the undersheriff. Before Estelle could close the folder, Irene reached out and stopped her. "Wait. Can I look at that again?"

"Certainly."

This time, Irene Salas took the photo and took her time, her face touched by revulsion at the obvious injuries. "Do you have any others?"

"You think you might know him?"

"I don't know."

Estelle hesitated. She looked at the four remaining shots, all taken at the accident site, and slid them out of the folder. Irene took them without comment, but Danny Rivera made a face.

"Man," he said, and let it go at that.

Estelle saw the muscles of Irene's jaw clench. "Oh, God," she whispered. "He doesn't even look like himself anymore."

"You know him?"

"Yes. Oh, my God." She slumped a bit, and Danny Rivera reached out to her, lightly embracing her shoulders. Again, she went back to the morgue photo, turning it this way and that. "Oh, my God," she said again. "Last semester, he used to come and meet my lab partner after class. Can you believe that? I'm sure it's him. Well, *almost* sure. I noticed him because he looked like he ought to be a soap opera star or something. He and CJ were a good match."

"And CJ is?"

"That was my lab partner's name. CJ without the periods Vallejos."

"What kind of class was this?" Estelle asked, working hard to keep her tone casually conversational. The pounding sounded as if someone were trying to make their way through the back wall of the shop, but Estelle knew it was her own pulse in her ears.

"Well, not my most favorite, that's for sure. It was physical anthro, but the professor's idea of a good time was to spend the day in a musty lab, brushing dirt off old bones. That's when I found out that paleo-osteology wasn't my bag."

Estelle accepted the photos and tucked them away. "Actually," Irene continued, "by the time the semester was over, Professor Ulrich had convinced most of us that he had actually died and dried up about the same time as his old bone collection."

"Did you ever have the opportunity to talk to Chris Marsh?" Estelle asked.

"Oh, once, I think. Just in passing. But I did see him now and then. He and CJ were pretty tight. A good match."

"How so?"

"Well, salt and pepper sort of thing, you know." She nodded at the folder. "Before he did that to himself, he was *really* attractive, like some surfer Joe. And CJ is, well, CJ. Dark and gorgeous." Her face went blank. "Oh, my God."

"What?"

"This happened Friday night?"

"That's when the wreck was found."

"Oh, my God," Irene said again, a hand going to her mouth.

"I wonder if CJ even *knows*?" She shook her head. "You know, I haven't seen them since semester break. I mean, she and I weren't roommates or best friends or anything like that. We just shared a lab space in that bones class. She hated the work more than I did. She wasn't sure if she was going to come back for the spring semester. I guess she didn't. But still…"

"Do you happen to know her full name? We'll make sure she's informed."

"CJ Vallejos." Irene's brow furrowed. "She told me once what the 'CJ' stood for, but I don't remember now. She lived off campus. Maybe she and Chris weren't even still going together, I don't know. But still…"

"Did you get to know her pretty well during the course of the semester?"

"Well, you know. She was my lab partner, and we talked about this and that. I didn't cut class as much as she did, but…" And she made a resigned face. "Some of the guys can get away with that. *I* never could."

Estelle took a deep breath, letting her insides settle. A whirl of questions crowded her mind, but the door had been opened. At this early stage, the last thing she wanted was Irene Salas on the cell phone, back to Las Cruces, breaking the tragic news to college friends.

"So, you're going to fix up the Jeep?" Estelle asked Danny, and he brightened at the change of subject.

"I think maybe," he said. "First thing is to find a tire that fits."

"Well, I'll leave you guys to do that," Estelle said. "Irene, it's great that you were able to visit Serafina today. She's so pleased."

"I really like coming back here," Irene said. "I wish I could talk Mom out of her love affair with Phoenix. It'd be so great for her to move back here and just...*relax*, you know?"

"Not everyone shares our enthusiasm for the tiny crossroads," Estelle laughed.

"Thank heavens," Irene said. "Regál doesn't need a box store." She reached out and took Estelle's hand. "Or *any* kind of store, for that matter. I'm glad you stopped by. Say hello to the sheriff. The last time we talked, he was just a deputy, and he was writing me a traffic ticket."

"Lead foot," Danny muttered, and he shook hands with Estelle, his grip firm and grimy.

The undersheriff made her way back to the car, forcing her pace to remain at a casual amble. She could tell by the writer's posture that she was primed with questions, but Estelle held up a hand. "Give me some time to think," she said.

The "time to think" lasted about twelve minutes, just long enough for them to shoot over the pass and take the switchbacks down the back side. As they flashed by the Broken Spur, Estelle reached for her phone. Gayle Torrez answered promptly, having relieved the weary Brent Sutherland.

"Gayle, I'm ETA about twenty minutes. I know it's Sunday, but I need Melinda Torrez to meet me at the MVD office as soon as she can."

"She's home, I think," Gayle replied. "Do you want me to have her give you a call?"

"Actually, no. I really need the MVD computer."

"I'll see what I can do."

"If he's not in the middle of anything, you might have Bobby meet me there as well."

"Right at the MVD office?"

"Yes. Thanks, Gayle." She put the phone down, and

Madelyn Bolles waited for a moment before raising one hand, like an elementary school student asking permission.

"Can I ask now?" she said.

"Sure," Estelle said.

"What happened back there?"

The undersheriff looked at Madelyn for a brief second as they charged northbound.

"I found out how the name of a reclusive widow in a tiny village like Regál gets on the list," the undersheriff said. She didn't need to look at the speedometer to know that the needle was posted close enough to 100 to make any passenger nervous. "Now we see how quickly we can open some other doors."

THIRTY-THREE

"IT TAKES A little bit," Melinda Torrez said cheerfully. She turned away from the screen just far enough that she could see Estelle out of the corner of her eye. "Do I really want to know what's going on? Do I want to have something really creative to tell the computer nerds in Santa Fe when they monitor my system and see that I opened up on a Sunday?"

"This all stems from Friday night's crash down on the pass," Estelle said. "A nasty turn."

"Oh my, that," Melinda said, and shook her head sadly.

"There's a considerable flight risk," the undersheriff said. "Otherwise I'd take the chance and wait for tomorrow morning."

"Ah," Melinda said, and nodded. She smiled and leaned back in her chair, arms folded across her chest as she regarded the magazine writer. There was little extra room in the crowded office, a tiny facility that rented space from the U.S. Post Office, and both Madelyn and Estelle waited at the counter as if they were in line to renew their car registrations.

When she had introduced the writer to the sheriff's sister, Estelle had seen the instant magnetism, that uncommon attraction that occurs when two people meet and instantly like each other.

"How long are you in town for, Madelyn?" Melinda asked.

"You know, I'm not sure. When I drove up here, I had all these visions of pastoral peace and quiet...you know, the aroma of chiles roasting and piñon burning."

Melinda laughed. "And now look at the mess Estelle and my brother have landed you in. What will the rest of the world think of us."

"I may have to go on vacation in some quiet inner city somewhere to recover," Madelyn said.

"Hey, take me with you," Melinda said, raising a black eyebrow. She was obviously her brother's sister, cast in the same Torrez mold, with a family resemblance that had once prompted Bill Gastner to remark, "Yep, they threw away the mold after they made Rafael, Elsa, Bobby, Melinda, Scotty, MaryAnne, Tiffany..." And he could continue on and name all nine of Rafael and Elsa's children—the heart of an enormous extended family that virtually took over MacArthur Street in Posadas when the family had a reunion.

What Melinda lacked, Estelle reflected, was the wonderfully dour, deadpan expression that her older brother had perfected as his substitute for charm. Four years younger than the sheriff, unmarried, dedicated totally to her enormous family, "Auntie Melinda" had always impressed Estelle as the very definition of contentment. As supervisor of the local Motor Vehicle Department office, she was adept at guiding folks through the sometimes frustrating labyrinth of state vehicle laws.

A truck idled to the curb, and Melinda nodded, recognizing her brother's vehicle. "Don't say that I said so, but he was taking a *nap*. Here you all are working and he's *napping*." She leaned forward as something appeared on the screen, then quickly tapped in data. She relaxed back again as the computer went on digesting. "You'll have to turn the key to let him in. I locked it." Estelle stepped to the door and twisted the lock.

"Hey," the sheriff said, and let a nod to Madelyn and his sister suffice.

"How's the nap?" Melinda asked, and Torrez's instant frown was dark.

"How do you know if I was nappin' or not," he said. "'Cause Gayle said you were going to," Melinda shot back. "And if Gayle says it, it's true."

"She said I was *going* to. Don't mean I got to, thanks to you guys."

"Okay," Melinda said, and held up both hands. "We're up and running. Who needs a new license first?" Her expression turned serious. "What do we need to know that doesn't require a court order, which you don't have."

"I have a name," Estelle said. "I need to know what vehicles are registered to her. And I need her last known address. CJ Vallejos." She spelled the name, and both she and Melinda finished at the same time.

"Well, now," Melinda said, leaning back again. "I need something to narrow this down. There's a whole city of Vallejoses in the state, and when I scroll down, let me see," and she ran a finger down the screen. "Not a single CJ. Let's roam a bit farther. How about Constance Vallejos?" She looked up at Estelle.

"Maybe. She would be in her early twenties," Estelle replied. "Certainly no more than thirty. The last residence we know of is in Las Cruces."

"Ah. That helps." Melinda leaned an elbow on the computer console and waited as the cursor searched. "Do we have license photos?"

"Sure we do." Melinda reached out and pivoted the computer screen so Estelle could see it by leaning over the counter. "This is Ms. Constance. Her DOB is five eighty-two. That makes her twenty-five, coming up on twenty-six."

"I don't think so." The photo showed a homely young woman whose fleshy, teardrop-shaped face glared into the camera. The rims of her tiny granny glasses nestled grooves into her heavy cheeks. The photo showed the top swell of wide shoulders.... No stretch of the imagination could call this woman willowy.

"Well, then," Melinda said. "In the same pew, we have Consuela Juanita Vallejos. That's a nice, old-fashioned name, isn't it. Ms. Consuela Juanita..." She looked up at Estelle. "CJ for short, maybe? She shows a DOB of eleven nine eighty-four. That makes her twenty-three come November."

Estelle's heart jumped. It took a special kind of composure to look beautiful in a driver's license photo, but Consuela Juanita Vallejos managed to do it. The young woman had cocked her head at the last moment so her face avoided that pasted-on look of Post Office bulletin board photos. Long black hair pulled back, her face finely sculpted, she had allowed the hint of a smile to touch her full lips.

"I see a light," Melinda said, smiling at Estelle.

"Who the hell is this?" Torrez asked.

"It could be one of Irene Salas' classmates at State," Estelle replied. "A lab partner, in fact."

"Irene give you a description?"

"Of sorts. This one fits enough that I need to run it down to Irene to make sure. Melinda, may I have a copy?"

"Um…" Melinda said, thinking. Then she shrugged. "What the hell. I'll give you the photo without all the personal data. How's that?"

"That'll work as long as we can have her address," Estelle said. "And that," she said, pointing at the phone directory. While the photo printed, she found Serafina Roybal's number and dialed, stepping away from the counter. "Come on," she said, waiting as the ring count mounted. After eighteen, the phone connected with a clatter. Serafina's voice was distant and sounded fragile. "Hello?"

"Serafina? This is Estelle Guzman bothering you again."

"Yes, dear. How nice."

"I need to ask you…has Irene come back from the Riveras' yet?"

"Well, you know, I think they're outside working on my old car. Would you like to speak with her?"

"If that's possible, yes."

"Let me call her."

"Take your time, Serafina."

"Oh," and the old woman chuckled. "*That's* a certainty."

As Estelle waited, she looked across at the others. "We need Irene to make a positive ID before we do anything else," she said. "If this isn't the girl, we're back to square one."

The sheriff raised one hand. "I got some preliminaries from Mears, too," he said. Estelle nodded, and in the background over the phone she could hear voices.

"This is Irene," a strong voice on the phone said.

"Irene, this is Estelle Guzman again. Look, I hate to keep bugging you on your holiday, but I have another photo I need you to look at. Will you be at your grandma's for a while longer?"

"Sure, I guess." She didn't sound overly enthusiastic at the prospect of more morgue shots. "You bet. I wasn't going back to Cruces until morning."

"*Perfecto.* It should be about thirty minutes, then."

"I'll probably be back over at the shop," Irene said. "There or here."

"I'll find you. While I'm at it, do you have a cell?"

"Oh, sure. You want that number?"

"Yes. It's hard for Serafina to get to the phone." Estelle jotted down the number. "Thanks."

She snapped the phone shut. "Okay." She stepped back to the counter. "Bobby, I've been beating this same horse to death. I just keep circling around to the notion of *how* Serafina Roybal's name was chosen for this sweepstakes thing. I know, I know…we're probably all on every list in the world. But Chris Marsh was up to something, and *he* knew where she was—where Joe and Lucinda were, too. This is the first link." She held up the photo. "Almost certainly, Irene would have talked to this girl about Serafina. She and CJ Vallejos were partners in an anthro class during the fall semester."

"You got something else?" Torrez asked, openly dubious.

"We'll see. Irene remembers that Chris Marsh came by that anthro class from time to time to pick up his girlfriend." Melinda handed her a printout of the photo. "Thanks. She describes CJ as looking about like this." She passed the photo to the sheriff.

"And?" Torrez said, still unimpressed.

"Can you tell me what vehicles this one has registered?" Estelle asked.

"Most recent is a 2007 Ford Mustang, color blue. License...oh, this is cute. 'MY PONY.'"

"Ay," Estelle whispered. "There we go. She did buy it."

"'There we go' what?" Torrez said.

"That jibes with what Marsh's neighbors at the trailer park told Tony. This is the girlfriend. She's got to be." She read the address. "Off campus, for sure. I want Irene to confirm this photo," she said.

"Betty Contreras has one of those phone-fax-copier thingies," Melinda said. "Might be quicker than driving all the way back down to Regál."

"That's an idea, but it'd take almost as much time to include Betty in the loop as not. Besides, I need to see Irene Salas face-to-face when she IDs the picture."

"Mears finished dusting the beer can, by the way," the sheriff said. "He was goin' over to the county bone-yard to finish with the truck. I'll give him a heads-up."

"We have to have that," Estelle agreed. "By itself, this is nothing." She looked at the photo. "Just because she was Chris Marsh's girlfriend for a while doesn't mean she had any other connection with what he had going on. But if her prints are on the beer can, then that puts her at the scene of the accident."

"Abeyta's still over there? In Cruces?" Torrez asked.

"Yes. He was scouting car dealers." Estelle leaned toward Melinda. "One more tiny little thing?"

"Oh, here we go," Melinda said. "My retirement out the window." She smiled. "What?"

"Did she buy the Mustang from a local dealer?"

Melinda made a face and scrutinized the computer screen. "Just a sec." In a moment, she sat back. "The dealer code is New Mexico."

"And?"

"Sonoraland Ford, Lincoln, Mercury. You need the address?"

"Sure, why not."

"Why not," Melinda said, and read it off.

"We'll need this down the road, maybe," Estelle said with satisfaction. "Right now, Tony needs to hotfoot it over to the last known address."

"From a distance," Torrez said. "When you talk to him, make sure he don't go runnin' in there by himself. I'll tell him the same thing."

"Nobody does anything, yet," Estelle replied.

"But you're thinkin' that way," Torrez said. He turned to his sister. "Any wants or warrants?"

"Nothing. Not even a parking ticket."

"Okay," the sheriff said. "One step at a time. You're headed back to Regál to ID this picture. If we get a hit there, then we got enough cause to question this Vallejos.... Come up with a print match from something from the crash site and that's it. I'm going to head that way after I talk with Mears and see what else he's got. Lemme know." He rapped the counter with his knuckle. "Thanks," he said to his sister.

"Wow," Madelyn said as she settled into the car once more.

The sheriff had already left, his truck trailing blue smoke. "I was watching your face when the young woman's face came up on the screen."

Estelle didn't reply. She had been calculating the time it would take Bobby Torrez to drive to the boneyard to talk with Sergeant Tom Mears, and then on to Las Cruces, an hour away even flying low. She hadn't told Irene *what* photo needed to be identified, and that was good. Still, there had been enough questions asked about the accident victim, Chris Marsh, and his girlfriend, Consuela Juanita Vallejos, that Irene Salas, a member of the modern cell phone generation, might be prompted to make a quick telephone call. Even if done in compassionate innocence, it would be all the tip-off needed.

If she was home in Las Cruces, CJ Vallejos was half an hour, maybe an hour, from the border crossing at El Paso. It was conceivable that she was already waiting in line.

THIRTY-FOUR

"WHERE ARE YOU NOW?"

The telephone connection was scratchy, and it sounded as if Deputy Tony Abeyta was down in the bottom of a large tank, his voice both faint and echoing.

"I'm at Lawson Brothers Ford," the deputy said. "The sales manager doesn't remember anything about a blue Mustang, but he's checkin' their records for me."

"Don't bother. The MVD says that the car came from Sonoraland Ford. I have a name for you," Estelle said. "Consuela Juanita Vallejos." She spelled the first name. "She goes by 'CJ.'"

"Got it."

Estelle gave the deputy the residence address. "I don't have a clue where that is," she added. "But LCPD will. What we need is a close watch for a little while until we can unsnarl some loose ends. It turns out that Ms. Vallejos is a friend—or at least a classmate acquaintance—of Serafina Roybal's granddaughter, Irene. She says that CJ's boyfriend at one time was Chris Marsh."

"Bingo."

"Well, maybe bingo. We'll see. I'm headed to Regál so Irene can ID a driver's license photo. *That's* going to take a half hour, at least. In the meantime, Bobby's flying your way with whatever Mears has been able to dig out of the wrecked truck. That's going to be at least an hour, so hang tight."

"Got it."

"And Tony… I do *not* want you making contact with Vallejos. You copy that?"

"Absolutely."

"No contact at all. If she's home, I want to know. If not, we need to find her, and LCPD can help with that. Okay? In the meantime, alert the border crossing at Santa Teresa, just to be on the safe side. They can spread the word. The Mustang in question is a 2007 model, color blue, license Mary Yankee Paul Ocean Nora Yankee."

"Cute. That'll be hard to find," Abeyta quipped.

"We hope not. I'll be back to you. No contact, Tony. I don't want her knowing you're there."

"Ten-four."

Estelle dropped the phone in her lap and tried to relax back in the seat.

"Flight risk?" Madelyn asked.

"Oh, absolutely that," Estelle said. "She may be already gone."

"And then what?"

"Then all the rules change," she replied.

"I have to ask…."

"Okay."

"Why doesn't…it's Tony? Why doesn't the deputy just detain her right now, if he finds her at home? I mean, there's a fair chance she has *no* idea you're on her tail, isn't there?"

"Better than fair."

"So…"

"For one thing, other than that a certain CJ Vallejos was once Chris Marsh's girlfriend, we have nothing on her. If Irene Salas makes a positive ID from the driver's license photo, then we can put a face to a name. Irene says that CJ Vallejos and Chris Marsh were a couple. That's a good connection. If Marsh's neighbors also make an ID, then that's good corroboration. But other than that…" Estelle shrugged. "We have nothing that directly ties Ms. Consuela Juanita Vallejos to Chris Marsh's death. To his murder. And we don't arrest people 'just in case.'"

"You're saying that this CJ person might not know a thing about Marsh's escapades."

"On the one hand, that's exactly what I'm saying. Maybe they haven't been seeing each other since last fall. Maybe, maybe, maybe. All the possibilities. That's why we don't just land on someone with both feet…at least before we have probable cause. As our district attorney is fond of telling Grand Juries, 'I'd rather let ten criminals back onto the street than arrest one innocent person.' There are a lot of things that the D.A. and I *don't* see eye to eye on, but that's not one of them."

"So you're trying to close some doors, as you said."

"Yes. And that's not always easy. For one thing, we don't always recognize the doors when we see them."

"Ah." Madelyn fell silent for a few minutes, her right hand straying out to the dash at one point as Estelle drifted out to pass a pickup truck with a livestock trailer in tow. With the highway stretching empty before them for another twelve miles to the saloon, the reporter turned a bit sideways in her seat. "You said 'on the one hand.' What's on the other?"

"Someone climbed down to the wreck shortly after it happened. It's certain that Chris Marsh was still alive. He was so horribly injured that he couldn't move. He just lay there, on his back, bashed down between some rocks, bleeding to death. Someone climbed down, ransacked the truck and his person, and finished him off by drowning him with one of his own cans of beer."

"That's grim."

"Yes, it's grim. Maybe at one point, Marsh spasmed enough that he flailed his left arm…. It was already broken in two places, mind you. The killer *stepped* on his hand. By accident? To keep it away from the victim's face while the killer poured the beer down his throat, choking him to death?"

"Okay," Madelyn said. "It's guaranteed that I won't sleep tonight."

"While you're lying there staring at the ceiling tonight, consider the killer's mind-set, Madelyn. Anyone who would kill like that—watching Chris Marsh choke and gag and then die right before her eyes? Kill once in the most cold-blooded, cruel manner possible, you *know* the killer won't hesitate a second time." Estelle glanced across at the writer. "We don't corner a person like that without holding every card in the deck that we can. Whether it's to a sleepless night or not, we all want to go home when the shift is done."

"Some shift."

"In a manner of speaking."

The writer ruminated on that for a few minutes, and then said, "The sheriff."

Estelle flashed a quick look her way.

Madelyn held up a hand as if to say, *I know, I know.* "The sheriff impresses me as being much more on top of things than he would like us to believe."

That prompted a laugh from Estelle. "That's an observation, not a question."

"Exactly. Is it an accurate one?"

"That's a judgment you'll have to make, Madelyn.

Stick around for a while and then decide. I'd hate to bias you one way or another."

The reporter shook her head in amusement. "Probably the figure is something like 99.99999 percent," she said, more to herself than Estelle.

"What figure is that?"

"The percentage of people who will cheerfully talk about someone behind their back when the occasion presents itself."

"Ah."

"I have to try, you understand."

"I do."

The miles melted behind them, and before long they swept up the north side of the San Cristóbals toward the pass, and then over the top. Minutes later, they eased into Sanchez Lane. Madelyn reached over and patted the top of the computer.

"Tell me something," she said. "I'm puzzled. How do you decide that the girl… Irene? How do you decide that *she* doesn't have anything to do with any of this? Or her sexy grease- and oil-soaked boyfriend, for that matter. How do you know that they're not working together? That she won't call CJ…."

"The same way you do," Estelle said. She slowed the car to an amble as they passed the Contreras adobe. "For one thing, there is no evidence that they are involved— *nada*, zip. Nothing. But you saw them. Neither of them has a thing to hide. Their actions and their faces are open books, Madelyn. It takes practice to be a devious liar, and most of the time, lack of practice shows."

"So, your intuition…"

"Call it that. People with things to hide tend to be either *way* too clever, or they're evasive."

"I'll buy that. Irene certainly didn't strike me as *evasive*. Smitten and madly in love, maybe."

"See? That's why I'm sure. We're in the same business, Madelyn. We're people watchers. It's just the outcome that's different."

A late model pickup truck was pulled into Serafina Roybal's driveway, beside the old Wagoneer. The pickup's tailgate was flopped down, with a toolbox open and in disarray. Estelle pulled in close behind it, and saw Danny Rivera working on the back wheel. The truck was jacked up, and he was spraying some potion on the lug nuts. Irene Salas came out of the house, carrying two bottles of Mexican beer, the distinctive label apparent at a quick glance. She smiled and waved, and detoured first to Danny, giving him one of the bottles.

"You want something to drink?" she said, as Estelle got out of the car. "We got iced tea or Coke. I'm not going to offer you one of these."

"No, thanks, Irene."

Danny Rivera didn't get up but nodded at Estelle.

"What's wrong with it?" she asked.

"One…just *one*…of the damn lug nuts is frozen," he said.

"Always something."

"You said you had another picture for me?" Irene prompted.

"I do," Estelle replied. "I need you to identify this person, if you can." She handed the photocopy of the driver's license photo to Irene. She saw the young woman's face brighten with recognition.

"Sure. That's CJ. It oughta be a crime to be that pretty. I don't think she knows it, though."

Oh, yes, she does, Estelle thought. "Did she ever talk about where she was from?"

"I think Chicago? She doesn't seem like the Chicago type, whatever that is. But I remember her saying that's where her family lived now. I know that she was planning to visit back there at Christmas." Irene looked quizzically at Estelle, and that expression changed to one of slow dawning. "She wasn't riding *with* Chris the other night, was she? Oh, God, that would be awful."

"Chris Marsh was alone in the truck, Irene," Estelle said. "No one else was involved in the accident."

"Thank God for that," she said firmly. "You're going to let CJ know? Is that it?"

"Yes. We'll let her know. But let me ask you something. During the time that you knew Chris Marsh, when he would come to the lab to meet with CJ, did you know what he did for a living?"

"I just thought he was another student," Irene replied. "You know...all of us there *are*, so I just assumed that he was, too." She turned and nodded toward the house. "My grandmamá says that he was working for one of the courier companies. He was the one who actually delivered the two little prize checks that she got." She grinned. "And the *biiiiiig* ones that Joe and Lucinda Baca won. Wow."

Estelle silently watched Danny Rivera for a moment as he slid an enormous cheater bar on the lug wrench and gently bounced his weight on it. The lug nut stubbornly refused to move. "I wouldn't turn down a prize or two like that," he said. "I don't see how they make any money doing that."

He sat back on his haunches, regarding the lug nut.

"Stubby said that he actually crashed Wednesday night. That he wasn't found until Friday."

"My God, is that true?" Irene gasped.

"We think so," Estelle said.

"How double awful, to think he was lying down in those rocks, just waiting for help. And it never came."

Not the kind of help he would have asked for, Estelle thought. "Guys, thanks a lot. We need to run." She slipped a business card from her pocket and handed it to Irene. "If you should happen to think of anything else," she said.

As she slid back into the car, Madelyn lowered her voice. "A hit?"

"A hit."

The reporter looked at her watch. "This is going to be a very long day, isn't it."

THIRTY-FIVE

"THE MUSTANG IS parked in the driveway, along with a hot-rodded '55 Chevy pickup truck," Deputy Abeyta said. "No sign of her yet, but a guy came out of the house a few minutes ago. He's been rootin' around in the trunk of the Mustang."

"What's he look like?" Estelle asked. She kept the county car in the left-hand lane of the interstate, grill wiggle-waggles turned on to herd traffic out of the way.

"White male, maybe twenty-five, six-two, a hundred and eighty pounds. Buzz cut, blue jeans, running shoes, and an NMSU polo shirt. He's fit. Looks like a Marine or something."

"The sheriff should be just ten or fifteen minutes out," Estelle said. "Has he contacted you yet?"

"That's affirmative. We're hangin' tight. It's a pretty quiet neighborhood. I'm parked down at the end of the block next to an elementary school playground. Nilson is stationed down at the other end of the street at a convenience store. There's what looks like an irrigation ditch behind their place, so they aren't slippin' out the back."

"Okay. We're just passing Deming. Gayle gave me directions."

"Ten-four. The sheriff said Mears turned some prints?"

"A couple sets. Most important is a clear set from the beer can."

"Hit?"

"Not yet. Nothing has shown up on the computer. There's a significant scar on what he thinks is the left index finger, so a field match might be possible. Stay in touch."

She closed the phone and took a deep breath. "She has a new boyfriend already," Estelle said to Madelyn Bolles.

"That's not surprising."

"Three-ten, three-oh-eight, three-oh-two."

Less than fifteen seconds had elapsed since Abeyta had been on the phone, and now he was asking for both Torrez and herself on the radio.

"Three-oh-two, go ahead," the sheriff's soft voice said.

"Three-oh-two, three-ten," Estelle radioed, and waited, mike in hand.

"Subject is outside the residence. She appears to be in conversation with male subject. She's got what looks like a videocassette in her hand. And she matches the description both you and the trailer park neighbors gave me."

"Ten-four. Does it look like she's headed out somewhere?"

"Affirmative. She's at the door of the Mustang. They're neckin'. Now she's gettin' in. Advise."

"Three-oh-two, if you can follow at a discreet distance, tail her. Are you on car to car with LCPD?"

"That's affirmative. I have one of their handhelds."

"Have Grunt stay where he is. We don't know anything about the male subject yet."

"Ten-four."

"Three-oh-eight copies. Three-ten, ten-twenty?"

"Three-ten just passed mile marker one-oh-five." That

put them thirty-four miles from the exit onto southbound State Route 28, and another three miles farther to the subject's neighborhood. Estelle kicked the speed up a notch, but even if she flogged the aging Crown Victoria all the way up to its "chipped" speed of 128 miles an hour, the point when the engine's computer said, "Enough," they were sixteen minutes from the city.

She settled on a conservative 90, giving herself plenty of time to judge what other motorists on the four-lane might do.

"Good argument for a helicopter," Madelyn said quietly.

"When you talk to our county manager, you might mention that," Estelle replied.

"Three-oh-eight, ten-twenty?"

"Comin' up on Twenty-eight," Torrez replied, referring to the state highway that headed south from Las Cruces to El Paso, first on the east and then the west side of the Rio Grande.

"Ten-four."

Estelle's phone blipped again and she palmed it without taking her eyes off the road and the upcoming string of tractor trailer trucks running in convoy. She reached down and flipped on the siren, its raucous yelp probably not enough to penetrate through the noisy cabs of the big rigs.

"Guzman."

"Estelle, I think she made me," Deputy Abeyta said. "I did a really dumb thing."

"What?"

"I forgot to take the magnetic shields off my doors. She looked right at me."

"Ay," Estelle breathed, understanding why the dep-

uty didn't want that signal broadcast all over southern New Mexico. "Maybe she didn't have time to read the fine print."

"That's what I'm hoping. She's heading northbound now on Twenty-eight."

"Stick with her…from a distance, Tony."

"Affirmative. If she takes off with that car, I sure ain't keepin' up with her."

"Bobby's just about off the interstate. He'll be headed toward you."

"Just a sec," Abeyta said abruptly.

Estelle waited, phone hard against her ear.

"She's pulling into a little plaza here," Abeyta said. "And right up to the video store."

"Stay back, and go ahead and use the radio, Tony. The sheriff needs to hear what's going on."

"You got it."

"Three-oh-eight, three-ten."

"Three-oh-eight."

"The subject left the house and drove to a video store. Abeyta thinks she made him."

"How'd that happen," Torrez said brusquely, but he didn't wait for an explanation. "I'm just takin' the exit now."

"Ten-four."

She dropped the mike in her lap and glanced at Madelyn, whose silence spoke volumes. Her right hand was vise-gripped on to the door sill, and her left was entwined in her shoulder harness. The radio burst into life, and this time Tony Abeyta's voice had shot up an octave.

"All units, subject is northbound on Twenty-eight. She blew me off. She isn't headed back to the house."

"Three-oh-eight copies," Torrez said, managing to sound bored.

"Three-oh-two, tell LCPD to take the male subject into custody," Estelle radioed.

An uncomfortably long silence followed, and Estelle could feel the tension clamping the muscles of her back hard enough to make them ache. Ahead, a line of traffic obediently queued up in the right-hand lane.

"All units, subject has turned off on one of the county roads east-bound. All I can see is a dust trail," Abeyta said. Even as he spoke, Estelle heard another radio come to life in the background.

"All units, stand by," Abeyta added. In a moment, he was back on the air. "All units, be advised LCPD has one subject in custody."

"Ten-four. Stay on her," Estelle shot back.

"All I got is dust," Abeyta said. "I think she's turned north."

"Ten-four," Torrez said, his voice as casual as a rancher leaning on a fence, straw sucked between his teeth. "I know where she's goin'. Tony, pull a one-eighty and get back to northbound Twenty-eight."

Up ahead, Estelle saw an SUV pulling a rental trailer flick on its turn signal, ready to swing into the left lane. She braked hard, but eventually the piercing wail of the siren broke through the driver's fog of inattention. He swerved back into the right lane so hard he almost dumped the trailer on the shoulder, the tires kicking up a cloud of dust.

"She's headed for the interstate," Estelle said. "She *did* read the fine print."

"Why would she do that?" Madelyn asked, shouting over the roar of the car. "The state highway would take her straight south to El Paso. She could cross over to the interstate at any time, and go straight to the border crossing."

"She could still do that," Estelle replied. "If she heads north to I-Ten, then she could turn eastbound to I-Twenty-five. South from there. Or north. Or anywhere she wants."

"But she's got to know you're after her."

"Actually, all she knows is that big, clumsy Posadas County Sheriff's Department Expedition is trying to catch her. She's got all the confidence in the world she can outrun him. She doesn't necessarily know we're out here."

"How could she not?" the writer asked, rearing back in her seat with an instinctive braking effort as Estelle had to slow for a car carrier determined to pass a bumbling RV.

"You'd be amazed at what some people pass off as logic," Estelle said. "Nobody outruns a radio."

"They think you'll give up the chase?"

"Some might actually think that."

"All units, three-oh-two is comin' up on Twenty-eight. We'll be northbound. Negative contact."

"All units, three-oh-eight." Estelle could hear the squeal of tires in the background. "Subject just turned north on Twenty-eight. Northbound. Don't think she saw me."

"Three-ten copies."

Madelyn leaned forward, straining against her seat belt, as if she could see beyond the miles that remained. "Do you know what she's going to do?"

"We're going to find out here in about two minutes." Consuela Juanita Vallejos would have breathed a sigh of relief that she had shaken her initial pursuer…that he was now wandering vainly about the network of county roads that crisscrossed the farmlands south of the city. If she was smart—and in some ways, she certainly was *clever,* Estelle thought—CJ would slow her pace to avoid attracting attention when she pulled back onto State 28 to join the flow of traffic. "Three-oh-eight, three-ten."

"Eight. She's headin' for the westbound entrance ramp to the interstate."

Westbound? Estelle frowned. "Let her do it," she said.

"Ten-four. I'm a block back. She's stickin' to the speed limit."

"Three-ten is eight miles out. We'll find a spot to join the parade."

"Be interesting to see where she thinks she's goin'," Torrez mused, and Estelle clicked the transmit twice in response.

"Where in heaven's name *is* she going?" Madelyn asked.

"Perfect," Estelle said to herself without answering the question. She braked hard. Across the way, a highway department dump truck was on the shoulder, rumbling along with its flashers on, the crew looking for trash hazards. The center median was a rough pasture, and she kept the car's speed up as they crossed. Back on the pavement and westbound, it took them only a few seconds to overtake the truck, and she pulled far enough in front of it that the highway crew would have time to stop. She pulled the county car to a halt well off the pavement, and got out, trotting back toward the idling orange truck.

Puzzled, the driver looked down at her as he cranked down his window.

"I wasn't speedin'," he said, offering a denture-filled smile at his own joke.

"I need some help," Estelle said. "Can you take a break for a few minutes?"

"That ain't hard. What do we got to do?"

"Just stay parked. We've got a vehicle westbound on the interstate that we're interested in. I need a place to wait."

"Puttin' out spike strips?"

"No. Not yet."

He shrugged. "Lemme know," he said.

"Thanks." Returning to the car, she pulled toward the pavement just enough that she could watch the westbound lanes in her side mirror.

"Three-oh-eight, three-ten."

"Go ahead."

"I'm on the westbound shoulder about seven miles out," she said. "There's a highway department truck working here, and he's good cover."

"Ten-four. She's westbound, sittin' right at an even eighty," Torrez said.

"To where," Estelle mused, dropping the mike in her lap. "CJ, where are you going."

"You can't just pull her over now?" Madelyn asked.

"I think she'll run," Estelle replied. "It worked once before."

"Can she outrun this?" the writer asked, patting the door sill.

"Oh, yes. Besides, we have everything to gain by waiting," Estelle said. "Wait and see what she's going to do. If she thinks that she's away clean, that's a good thing."

"What's your guess? What do you think she knows?"

"That's still part of the puzzle, Madelyn." Estelle watched the traffic approaching from the east. "Before this, we could imagine that maybe she didn't know what happened up on the pass Wednesday night...that she didn't have a clue what Chris Marsh was up to." She hunched her shoulders and held them up in a frozen shrug. "If she's not involved in any way, why would she make the decision to run the *instant* she saw a Posadas County unit parked at the end of her street?" She relaxed and looked across at Madelyn. "If she saw Tony's vehicle, the odds are good that she also saw the detective's unit parked at the other end of the block. So she ran, leaving the new boyfriend to take the heat. That's my guess."

"How far are you going to let her go?"

"We might as well find out all we can," the under-sheriff replied.

"Three-ten, three-oh-eight. She's kickin' up to about eighty-seven, leap-froggin' through traffic. You got about a minute before she passes your location."

"Ten-four." Estelle tugged her belt tighter. "Now we find out."

As the blue sports car shot past, Estelle looked down at her center console, hoping that, to the Mustang's driver, the occupants of the unmarked white state car were just a couple of highway supervisors comparing notes with the workers in the truck parked behind them.

A car hauler, its trailer jangling empty, shot by, also well over the speed limit. "Comin' up," Bob Torrez's disembodied voice said over the radio. A black luxury car shot by and, ten car lengths behind that, Torrez's new silver county Expedition. With a quarter mile clear, Estelle pulled out, tires chirping on the pavement. In three miles, she had passed the sheriff's Expedition, caught the BMW, and pulled in behind the car hauler. A quarter mile ahead, she could see the squat shape of the sports car. Glancing at the speedometer, she saw that the car hauler was holding at 87 on the level, fast enough to earn a ticket.

For the next twenty miles, the car hauler continued, its speed pacing the Mustang's, and then the truck took the first Deming exit. Estelle sucked in a sharp breath, and at the same time her hand darted to the channel selector on the radio console. Running in the left-hand eastbound lane, the sedan that had attracted her attention was identifiable even from a great distance. Squat, black, a white pimple of a computer antenna growing from the aft panel of the roof, the state police cruiser would be running just below the speed limit. Sure enough, its front end dipped, and as Estelle shot by, the state officer pulled over to cross the center median. She didn't have time to read the car number, but the cruiser accelerated hard in pursuit.

"I'll tell 'em to hold back," Torrez radioed, but they weren't the only ones who had spotted the state car, and that it had swung around in pursuit. The Mustang pulled abruptly into the passing lane, flying past two trundling bus-sized RVs.

With the fugitive car now cutting through traffic at more than 100 miles an hour, the driver had forced their hand.

"PCS, three-ten. We have a high-speed pursuit westbound on the interstate. We're coming up on mile marker seventy, ETA Posadas exit about eight minutes. Is anyone close enough to drop a spike strip immediately west of the Posadas exit?"

"Three-ten, we'll work on it."

Estelle's radio scanner picked up Torrez's radio on the state police frequency. "Triple five," he said, "we're going to spike the highway just west of the Posadas exit. We're going to have to clear this traffic."

"You got it." The black state car shot past. The problem was simple enough. In the dozen or so miles between their current position and the Posadas exit, there might be half a hundred vehicles, all traveling in their own private worlds, going who knew where that Sunday afternoon. The Mustang would blow by first, easily outpacing its pursuers.

"Three-ten." Gayle Torrez's voice was tight. "Mitchell and Collins ETA about three minutes. John Allen is coming in from the south. ETA about six."

"Ten-four. Have Allen clear the intersection at the bottom of the Posadas exit ramp."

"Ten-four. Eddie has the spike belt." Somehow, Captain Mitchell would have to deploy the belt in front of the speeding Mustang, avoiding confused civilian traffic that would hopefully be slowing or pulling off as they saw the winking lights of parked police vehicles.

"Sheriff, I clocked her at one forty-one and climbing," the state officer said.

"Ten-four." Estelle's cryptic reply belied the hard knot of apprehension in her gut. A nervous tick of the steering wheel could hurtle a car traveling at that speed into catastrophe. The state car couldn't keep up, and neither could she.

Far ahead, she could see a clutch of traffic, the big rigs nothing but tiny dashes on the line of highway. The interstate entered a series of lazy curves, the roadbed banked ever so slightly so that vehicles tended to follow the highway without any conscious input from the drivers. What the curves did accomplish was blocking an easy view to the rear for the truckers for more than a mile or so.

"She's off," the state officer's voice broke through urgently. At the same time, Estelle saw the enormous dust cloud rising up from the prairie as if a bomb had detonated.

THIRTY-SIX

DUST STILL HUNG thick in the air as Estelle slid her car to a halt. The westbound lanes of the interstate became a kaleidoscope of lights and milling people. Five semis sat motionless, blocking both lanes, their diesel engines muttering quietly. More would line up behind them by the minute, with all the rest of the arterial flow adding to the clot until it stretched for a mile or more.

The ball of junk that had once been the sleek, fashionable sports car rested in the center median. One of the truckers had climbed down from the cab of his rig and trotted over to the car, and he stood helpless, hands pumping up and down as if he were reciting an incantation. Three others were walking cautiously around the wreck, two of them with fire extinguishers in hand.

In the distance, Estelle heard the wail of sirens eastbound.... It would be Eddie Mitchell and Dennis Collins. An EMT rescue squad and ambulance would be en route close behind them.

"He just ticked the left rear of my trailer," the first driver said when he saw Estelle. "Jesus H. Christ, he come out of nowhere." He was an older man, pleasant enough looking, his face white as a sheet. "Musta rolled five or six times. I guess he's still inside."

The car lay on its top facing eastbound, three wheels askew but still attached to the car, the fourth ripped off to join the trail of parts marking the car's path along the me-

dian. Estelle took a few seconds to walk a circle around
it, making sure the area was clear of hazards. She approached the driver's side. As she cut across through the
stumpy desert scrub, Robert Torrez's Expedition pulled
off the interstate, crossing the median well behind where
the first marks of the car's trajectory marked the shoulder. He parked on the median side of the eastbound lane's
shoulder fifty yards beyond the crash site, facing traffic.

Estelle knelt beside the wreck, which now from front
to back appeared to be about six feet long, its extremities
crushed and torn by the impact forces. What remained
of the windshield structure and the roof was slammed
into the ground, crushing inward.

She swept away a small bush, mindful that the desert,
even between lanes of an interstate, hosted all kinds of
interesting critters who didn't care for intrusion. Then,
with her face touching the ground, she tried to see
through a small triangle of side window, shattered inward by the crushed roof post. She could not see past the
fabric of the deployed air bag, and she held her breath,
listening. The ticking of hot metal sounded like an old,
out-of-sync clock.

"CJ?" Estelle called. "Can you hear me?" There was
no response. Hearing Sheriff Torrez's heavy breathing
behind her, she pushed herself away. "I don't know," she
said. "I can't see her. I can't tell what position she's in."
She crawled toward the rear of the car, and tried to see
through the little rear wing window.

"We got rescue comin'," Torrez said. "Cut away that
door and we'll be able to tell."

With the metal twisted and mangled into a puzzle of
interlocked, sharp parts, simply hauling the car upright
with a cable from a wrecker was out of the question. The

driver was already apt to be impaled on sharp objects. A careless movement of the car's carcass could finish the job. Estelle circled to the passenger side, but that had taken a number of smashing hits. The car lay more on its right side than left, and the rising ground made it impossible to see inside. From the rear, the trunk lid and its supporting structure had bashed upward, and then driven into the dirt.

"Don't let it burn!" The four words came from the core of the crushed wreckage, thin and desperate.

Estelle darted back to the driver's side and dropped to her hands and knees. "CJ, can you hear me?"

"Don't let it burn!" the voice repeated, and trailed off into a whimper.

"We're going to get you out of there. Just hold on. How badly are you hurt?"

"I... I don't know. I can't move."

"They're on their way," Estelle said.

The wait was agonizing, even though it was probably no more than a few minutes. By the time the rescue squad arrived, set up a perimeter, made a hasty game plan, and finally fired up the gasoline-powered extraction jaws, Estelle saw what had to be at least sixty-five people standing in the median or beside their vehicles.

Dennis Collins, dressed in blue jeans and a light windbreaker with sheriff's department in huge yellow letters across the back, appeared at her side. "We can open the right westbound lane and get most of these guys out of here," he said. "You want Allen and me to start workin' on that?"

"No, I don't," she said. "Until we talk to everyone who saw this, I don't want anything moved." She turned and looked to the east. "That freight liner there with the double trailers?"

"Got it."

"I want everyone who isn't working this, or who doesn't belong to one of the trucks of this front convoy here, back behind that spot. All the rubberneckers. We're going to need the breathing space. Run a yellow tape across to my car, if you have to."

"Got it."

"After she's out of the car, and after we take some measurements, we can open the right-hand lane." She turned her attention back to the emergency workers. Jerry Buckman, a big, burly hulk of a man who appeared even larger in his bunker gear, worked the nose of the jaws into the door frame by the lower hinge, and it spread and popped the metal as if it were aluminum foil. He worked this way and that, worrying the metal of the door away from the frame, all the way down to what, in the upright vehicle, would be the top hinge, now forced into the dirt.

Shifting his stance deftly, he attacked the rear of the door, working down through the door lock itself. Finally, with the jaws between the lower edge of the door and the rocker panel, he eased the door gently away from the frame, always alert that his actions didn't move the car. Throughout the process, the occupant, crushed into this impossibly small space, kept up a stream of whimpers, cries, and wails, most of them drowned out by the power equipment.

Finally Buckman stopped and shut down the noisy saw. "We can get us a chain right through here," he said to Cliff Herrera. Buckman touched the lower edge of the rocker panel, now drawn four or five inches out.

"Run it right down and out through the window." That opening, where the driver's elbow might rest with the window open, was crushed to within a couple inches of the ground.

Within seconds, the rescue workers threaded the chain down through the narrow opening and dragged it back out, securing it to a hefty come-along attached to the big rescue truck's rear bumper.

With both sides and the bottom can-openered away, the door shifted easily, its crushed top and window frame digging a trough in the dirt. Cliff Herrera, about half Buckman's size, bellied down on the ground and squirmed up close to peer inside. Even with the door peeled aside, the opening was desperately small. Knowing that Buckman would never allow her to approach in the first place, Estelle forced herself to stand well back as the rescue team worked. "You ain't dressed for the dance, young lady," he once had told her years before.

"Can you hear me?" Herrera asked, his voice loud and carefully enunciated. His head and one shoulder were inside the car, and Estelle could see him trying to shift position.

"Yes. Oh, please."

"Okay, just hold still," he said. "We're going to get you out of here."

Estelle moved close enough that she could hear Cliff's insistent voice with a nonstop conversation, none of it making much of an impression on the car's occupant.

"Listen," he said at one point, then repeated himself as if the young woman were *not* listening. "Can you move this hand?" Estelle saw Herrera's body shift as he stretched as far into the wreckage as he could. "Well, sure it hurts. Just try to stay calm. We're with you."

"Don't go. It's going to burn."

"I'm not going away, and it's not going to burn, young lady. I'll be right back to get you out of here. Just hang in there with me."

Cliff squirmed backward with alacrity. He lowered his voice, and Buckman and EMT Matty Finnegan drew close.

"The center console is crushing her against the roof," he said. "Her head and shoulders are on the passenger side, and at least one foot is caught down by the pedals. I can't feel around her neck, but everything is twisted up. Her breathing's ragged." He took a deep breath to calm himself. "Look, if we lift this thing up any, there's a good chance it'll crush her. I think what we need to do is take the seats apart. The roof is actually pretty flat. That's going to help us."

"Let's do it," Buckman said. "We're burnin' daylight."

The words were no sooner out of his mouth than a brief symphony of horns and screeching tires erupted from the eastbound lanes, followed by a single loud crash. Knowing exactly what had happened, Estelle turned slowly in place. Two compact cars immediately behind a tractor trailer and in front of a commercial bus had melded into one as the driver in the rear had diverted his attention from traffic to gawk at the crash. The bus had managed to stop well short of the metal and plastic sandwich.

"Oh, cute," Buckman snapped. One of the state troopers who had been directing traffic on that section of highway was standing frozen in place, hands on his hips in a momentary display of indignation at such stupidity.

Captain Eddie Mitchell strode across the median and intercepted Bob Torrez, who looked as if he were intent on killing someone. "Shut it down," the sheriff snapped. "Goddamn morons." Leaving Mitchell and the State Police to sort out the traffic snarl, Torrez beckoned to Estelle.

"What's the deal?" he asked.

"They're going to have to dismantle the car to get her out," the undersheriff replied. "She's responsive.... They can't tell more than that yet."

"Okay. I was just talkin' to Abeyta. I sent him back to Cruces to work with the cops there," Torrez said. "They got the one in custody, and are securing the house. They've got a warrant comin'. Then we'll see what we can find."

He looked past Estelle's shoulder, and she could see the crow's-feet deepen around his eyes. "Your passenger's gettin' more than she bargained for," he said.

Estelle turned and saw Madelyn Bolles standing beside the patrol car, camera in hand, and realized that she had forgotten all about the writer.

"When all the dust clears, it'll be interesting to hear her view on all of this," Estelle remarked.

"Oh, I can't wait," Torrez remarked. He turned to watch the rescue crew. "They say how long it was going to take?"

"No." CJ Vallejos' "golden hour," that time immediately following an accident when the badly injured victim's life hung on a slender thread, was ticking away, each moment that medical care was delayed lessening her chances of survival. The girl was still conscious, still frightened that she was going to end up burning to death. The sixteen minutes that had passed since her car had ticked the back of one of the semis and gone ballistic must have seemed hours to her.

More than anything else, Estelle wanted to talk with her, to learn the answers to a host of still-puzzling questions. But the crash had changed all the rules. Now the center median of the interstate was full of people who had become skillful, compassionate Samaritans, advocates working relentlessly on behalf of Consuela Juanita Vallejos...advocates who for the moment didn't care what she had done or to whom she had done it.

THIRTY-SEVEN

JACK YOUNG'S EXPRESSION looked as if he'd barely managed to leap out of the way of a speeding bus intent on turning him into paste. There was no cause to be sweating on this cool February afternoon, but the young man flicked at his forehead and dabbed his eyes. He tried to appear controlled, even casual, but it was an effort. More than anything else, he appeared thoroughly confused by this odd turn of events.

When Estelle arrived at the address on Capulin Drive off NM28, he was sitting on the running board of his old pickup truck, both hands between his knees. Deputy Tony Abeyta didn't turn his back on the young man but continued to write on his clipboard. Estelle forced herself to take her time, looking at the house and regarding the young man before getting out of her car.

"There's a frightened puppy," Madelyn Bolles said quietly.

"Maybe with good cause," Estelle said. Down the street, two LCPD units were parked facing the house, but she didn't see Guenther "Grunt" Nilson. One uniformed officer remained in his car, the driver's door open. A second officer appeared from the rear of the tiny house, walking a careful perimeter around the building.

Estelle got out of the car and nodded at her deputy.

"Detective Nilson went to pick up a warrant," Tony said by way of greeting. "I haven't been in the house yet.

No wants or warrants on this vehicle. And this is Jack Young. Mr. Young, this is Posadas County undersheriff Estelle Guzman."

"Mr. Young," Estelle said. "We appreciate your cooperation."

"I'd like to know what's going on, ma'am," he replied, and Estelle noted the cadence of his speech, clipped and efficient.

"May I see your driver's license, sir?" Estelle asked, and Tony slipped it from his clipboard and handed it to her, along with a military ID. John Elliot Young was twenty-three, with a Sunland Park address on Woodcrest Avenue.

"You're at Bliss?"

"No, ma'am," he said. "I'm not stationed anywhere at the moment."

"And how's that?"

"I'm on a medical discharge," he said. He swung his right leg out a bit and pulled up the leg of his jeans. An enormous scar began above his ankle and disappeared upward. "Goes to here," he said, touching his thigh. "That's the good part of it."

"I see." She handed the license and ID back to Abeyta. "So tell me."

"Tell you what, ma'am?"

"What are you doing here, sir?"

"I was visiting a friend who lives here."

"The friend's name?"

He frowned at that. "What's your interest in her? Is that her with you in the car?" He squinted toward the county car, but the sun reflecting on the windows made it impossible to see who was inside.

"And who would that be?" Estelle asked.

"All right, all right. Of course I know her name," Young replied. "Her name's CJ Vallejos. I don't know what the 'CJ' stands for."

"So you don't know her all that well, then."

"I guess I know her well enough."

"When did you meet her?"

"I met her last night at Waylon's," he said, naming a popular nightspot. "We hit it off." He shrugged. "She invited me back here after we closed the place down." He shaded his eyes, looking past Estelle at the county car again. "So where is she?"

"How did you happen to meet her?"

He shrugged again. "I said, we were at Waylon's. There she was, there I was. She asked if I was there for the karaoke, and I thought that was pretty funny. I can play the radio pretty good, but that's the extent of it. One thing led to another."

"And you ended up back here."

"Yes, ma'am. Not sure how. We were both lit."

She looked at him for a long minute, and he returned her gaze without flinch or apology.

"That's the first time you met her? Last night?"

"That's it. So what's the big deal? She wanted for murder or something?" He tried a halfhearted smile.

"What makes you ask that, Mr. Young?"

"Well, you know. This many cops…and a search warrant? You don't do that for shoplifting, do you?" A dawning of realization crossed his face. "She didn't steal that fancy car, did she?"

"Not as far as we know."

"What a machine," he said in wonder. "I figured that was Daddy's car."

"Daddy's?"

"How could she afford something like that? As a college student?"

"When Ms. Vallejos left the house this morning, what did she tell you?"

Young hesitated at the sudden change of subject. "She wanted to return a video that she said was overdue. Just down the street. And she was going to pick up a newspaper."

"You didn't think that was odd?"

He held up both hands. "What's odd about returning a movie? She seemed preoccupied, maybe. I thought maybe she was having some second thoughts about us... maybe that was all it was. I was going to fix us something to eat, and she said she'd be back in just a couple of minutes. That's it. That's the story. I figured that she'd come back and tell me to get lost." He shifted position with a grimace. "Mind if I stand up?"

"No." She watched him push himself up, and for a minute he massaged his right knee with both hands. Then he leaned against the door of the truck. "What's she done? They don't send the cops out when a video is overdue. *I* haven't done anything wrong, so it isn't because of me."

"Where do you work, sir?"

"I don't yet. I'm spending most of my time fighting with the VA. Something will come along."

"Did Ms. Vallejos talk to you about any prospects?"

"No, ma'am," Young said. "She seemed kind of down in the dumps when I first met her last night. But we hit it off. And then this morning... I don't know. Maybe she's having second thoughts."

"That happens."

"Yeah, I guess it does. I was going to make us some

brunch or something, and all of a sudden, she's all agitated about that video."

"What were you looking for in the trunk of her car, Jack?"

"Jesus. What do you have, spyware or something? Christ, what is all this? Look, she said she thought that she had a loose mounting bracket on her CD changer in the trunk, so I looked for her. She didn't. What's she telling you?"

"She's not," Estelle said, and Young heard the implications in her tone. He seemed to slump a little, and leaned his back against the door of the truck.

"What's happened? Is she all right?"

"Ms. Vallejos was involved in a high-speed chase on the interstate a little while ago. She lost control of her car over west of Deming."

Young's eyes grew large. "Are you shitting me? What are you saying?"

"I'm saying just that, sir. She took off westbound, and lost control after her car collided with a semi."

"Just now, you mean?" he asked, incredulous.

"Just now."

"My God, where is she? Is she all right?"

"No, sir, she's not all right. By now she's in Posadas General Hospital. I don't know any more than that."

"I don't believe this. Why would she do that? She was going to return a *video*, for Christ's sakes."

Estelle hesitated, weighing how much to tell the young man. "We had a unit parked at each end of the street this morning," she said. "That's when we saw you opening the trunk of her car. I think she might have seen the officers and that tipped her off. The video thing was just an excuse."

"An excuse?"

"That's what I think."

"You mean you guys had this house under *surveillance*?"

Estelle didn't respond and he fell silent, sliding back down the truck door to land on his rump, both hands beside his hips on the running board.

"What's she done? You're going to tell me at least that much?"

"Let me ask you this," Estelle said. "What did you two talk about?"

"What do you mean *what*," he said with irritation. "Just stuff, you know? We were at a *bar*, for Christ's sakes. You just *talk*."

"About school?"

"Yeah, she mentioned that. She was studying political science, and hated it. She wasn't going back."

"What about her work?"

"I didn't get the impression that she had a job," Young said. "A couple of times, she said that she had plans. She never said what they were."

"Did she ever talk about other friends?"

"No."

"Or where she was from?"

"She said Chicago. She's got a brother up in Canada somewhere. Look, I gotta tell you…we talked a lot about *me*, okay? She saw me limping and she wanted to know all about what I'd done. How this happened," and he patted his leg.

"And how did it happen?"

He fell silent. "I was going to tell her this long heroic tale," he said after a moment. "But I couldn't." He closed his eyes. "God, she's an incredible girl, you know that?"

When Estelle didn't respond, he added, "So I just told her the truth." He straightened up and lifted his shirt. The scar ran down the center of his body, thick and corded, disappearing below his waistline. "Changes your life, you better believe," he said. "What do they call it? The young man's cancer?"

"And the leg?"

"I managed that when I got drunk after I was diagnosed and drove into an arroyo on my way back to the base. Maybe I was trying to kill myself. Who knows. I don't think I was. The shrink thought I was, though. Pretty glamorous, huh?"

"And that's what the two of you talked about?"

"Mostly." He looked off into the distance. "Is she hurt pretty bad?"

"I would guess so. We'll know more here in a little bit."

He looked back at Estelle. "You still haven't told me what she's done." An LCPD patrol car pulled into the street.

"That's Detective Nilson," Abeyta said.

"I told you, you don't need a warrant," Young said.

"This is your house?" Estelle asked.

"No. It's CJ's."

"Then we need a warrant. I'm going to ask that you remain here for a little longer."

"I got all the time in the world," he replied.

She reached out a hand and took his shoulder, giving it a gentle, sympathetic shake. "That's what we always think," she said.

A moment later, Estelle had time to open the front door and step over the threshold, breathing in the light aroma of deodorant and other potions and fragrances that lingered throughout the little house. In time, they'd all fade, leaving this address on Capulin just another empty shell waiting for a family.

As she had that thought, her phone chirped. Hearing Eddie Mitchell's quiet voice, she instantly felt a wave of apprehension.

"You clear?" he asked.

"We're about to go through the house, Eddie. What's the word?"

"I'm not sure yet. Your husband says that it's going to be several hours before we're able to talk with her. Preliminaries show that her spine is busted in two places. Dr. Guzman thinks that she'll be paralyzed from the waist down."

"*Ay.* Is she conscious?"

"Not yet. But he's talking about transporting her to Albuquerque if we can get the medivac down here. But look, her car's over in impound, and Mears, the sheriff, and I were going to head over that way right now. If you have a wrap down there, or if you can leave Tony to do it, you might want to pay a visit at the hospital. Just in case."

"That's a good idea. Leave someone in the room with her when you go over to impound, though. All right?"

"She isn't going anywhere."

"No, I mean just so that…just so someone is with her."

"Yeah, I can do that. Taber came in, so she can swing by there."

"That's good. I'll be there in an hour or so."

"One thing, though," Mitchell said. "You might be interested to know that she didn't have so much as an overnight bag with her. But she had something like twenty-one thousand dollars in her purse."

"Nothing else?"

"Just a newly issued New Mexico driver's license, good for eight years. One or two credit card receipts. And four credit cards and two debit cards. That's it. Oh, and a couple of family photos. One of what I would guess to be parents. Another of a good-looking kid that might be her brother. No names or the like on the back sides."

"Okay. Thanks, Eddie. I'm on my way." Estelle turned in place. "I see she has a computer and a pretty nifty printer. I'll make sure Tony brings those along as well as anything else he might turn up. Maybe there are some answers here."

"Take your time," Mitchell said, still at ease with command, his days as chief of police for the village of Posadas recent history.

"We will." She folded the phone and slid it back into her pocket. Walking through someone else's home was always an odd experience for Estelle, and she took a few moments now to make a quick tour. Detective Nilson, a little wizened man who looked twenty years older than he was, stood outside the door, sucking on a cigarette, staring down at the cement step. Jack Young didn't get up from the running board of his truck.

"I want that," Estelle said to Tony Abeyta, pointing at the computer. "Maybe somewhere around here she'll have an address book, some kind of record. Something. One connection we're looking for is the brother. The boyfriend says that CJ mentioned a brother living in Canada." Estelle lifted a small sheaf of bills from the desk. "Phone records, anything like that."

Putting the paperwork down, she walked the length of the living room to the bedroom. From all appearances, it was temporary quarters—nothing frilly, nothing extra.

"If you want Mr. Young to stay while you go through

the house, that's fine," Estelle said as she headed toward the door. "I don't need to talk to him again. As far as I'm concerned, he's free to go."

"You got it."

She stopped at the door and extended her hand to Nilson. He looked at her with eyes so light blue that the irises appeared transparent. "Thanks, detective."

"Hey, don't mention it," Nilson said. His grip was light and faintly clammy. "How are things over in the land of the free and the brave?"

"Things are interesting."

"Oh, I bet," Nilson laughed. "That's what our life is…interesting."

Intent on her laptop, Madelyn Bolles didn't look up as Estelle approached the car. Estelle eased into the driver's seat, and Madelyn finally glanced over at her.

"Here's a question for you," Madelyn said.

"I hope it's an easy one," Estelle replied.

"It is. As I recollect, I started this day around sixish? Something like that? By nine, we were down in Regál, talking with Mrs. Roybal. And so it goes. It's now about four fifteen. I'm curious about what's next."

Estelle stretched, pushing both hands hard against the steering wheel. "I need to stop by the hospital in Posadas for a few minutes. The deputy will finish up here."

"You think there might be time for me to buy you dinner?"

"Dinner," Estelle repeated, as if it were a foreign concept.

"Let's see how things go."

"Is that a 'yes?'"

Estelle laughed. "That's as close to a 'yes' as I can come at the moment."

Her cell phone rang, and she took her time unfolding it. "Guzman."

"Hey," Bob Torrez said. "Eddie just called you?"

"Yes."

"Okay. Look, Jackie's comin' in to cover at the hospital until you can get up here. We got a match."

A match, Estelle thought, caught off-guard. "A match of what, Bobby?"

"Tom is one hundred percent positive that the print on the beer can belongs to the girl's left index finger. One hundred percent. Ain't no wonder why she ran."

"I'll be up there in an hour," Estelle said. She heard what might have been a groan from Madelyn Bolles.

THIRTY-EIGHT

"SHE'S CONSCIOUS AND LUCID," Deputy Jackie Taber said. She pulled the door closed behind her. "And frightened. How are you doing, ma'am," she said to Madelyn Bolles.

"Keeping up, just barely, thank you."

"The docs are in there now doing whatever it is that they do," the deputy continued. She looked at her watch.

"What does she have to say?" Estelle asked.

Taber made a face of exasperation. "I haven't exchanged more than a few words with her," she said, and held out an arm, tugging at her own uniform sleeve. "She doesn't much like the looks of *this*, is my guess. She doesn't know what we know, and she's worried." The deputy shook her head. "That's all conjecture on my part."

The door of the ICU suite behind her opened, and Jackie stepped to one side to allow the nurse out. "Hi," the young woman said, beaming at Estelle. Moira Torrez, the sheriff's youngest sister, was as petite as her brother was huge. Her dazzling smile included Madelyn but immediately turned sober. "You're going to want to talk with her?"

"If we can."

Moira took a quick step out of the way as the door opened again. Dr. Francis Guzman held the door, blocking the opening. "You want a few minutes?" he asked Estelle.

"Yes."

Still blocking the passage, the physician let the door ease closed behind him. "She'll be pretty loopy," he said. "I knew you'd want to talk with her, and we're keeping the sedation as mild as we can. We're going to transport her to Cruces here in a few minutes. Pete Vaskos is on hand down there, and he's going to do an eval and help us with the crushed hip."

"Spinal damage?"

"Not good, *querida*. That's what took the brunt of it. We have nasty fractures down at T-twelve and L-one, as well as a broken pelvis and femur."

"She's paralyzed?"

"Yes. From the waist down."

"Is she going to stay that way?"

"My guess is that she will." He pushed the door open and held it for Estelle, and as she passed through, she beckoned Madelyn to follow. Dr. Alan Perrone ducked his head in greeting and joined Francis out in the hall, leaving Estelle and Madelyn alone with the patient.

Consuela Juanita Vallejos looked tiny, so buried was she under braces, tubes, and wires. Her eyes were open and a little unfocused as the drugs in her system dulled the edges of consciousness.

Estelle moved close to the left side of the bed and looked down at the girl, trying to imagine this desperately injured creature as the vibrant, confident young woman whose appearance had managed to shine through even in a driver's license photo.

Estelle leaned forward, her right hand resting on the frame near the patient's head. CJ's eyes blinked several times as if she was trying to clear the cobwebs.

"Who are you?" she asked. Her voice was husky, just above a whisper.

"I'm Undersheriff Estelle Guzman," she said. "With the Posadas County Sheriff's Department."

"So, you're a cop?"

"Yes."

"I was going kind of fast, wasn't I," CJ said. She closed her eyes and tried a brave smile.

"*Way, way* too fast," Estelle agreed.

"I don't know what happened."

"You tangled with a truck and then rolled."

"All I could think of was that the car was going to catch on fire," the girl whispered.

"You're lucky."

"I can't feel my feet," the girl said.

Estelle didn't respond but let the girl struggle with that thought for a few seconds. She took CJ's left hand in hers, avoiding the IV feed. "Can you feel my touch?" she asked.

"Yes."

Estelle held CJ's hand a moment longer. "That's good, then."

She turned the fine-boned hand ever so slightly, and saw the scar that began at the corner of the girl's left index fingernail and arched around to the center of the pad.

"I need to ask you some questions, CJ," Estelle said.

"It was just a dumb thing to do," the girl said. Her eyes fixed on Estelle, eyes so dark brown and impenetrable that the undersheriff had no difficulty imagining Chris Marsh and Jack Young being swept away.

"What was?"

"My driving," CJ said. Tears welled up, and one tear

tracked down an elegant cheek to stain the pillow. "I don't know why I did that."

Still holding the girl's hand in her left, Estelle slipped the micro-recorder out of her pocket. She held it, a gadget no larger than a deck of cards, so that the girl could see it, then let her hand and the recorder sink to the gurney beside CJ's head. "I want to ask you some questions, Ms. Vallejos. I know that you're hurting, but it's important that we do this now. You're going to be transferred down to Cruces for surgery here in a few minutes."

"The doctor told me," CJ replied. "Are you and him related?"

"He's my husband."

The girl's lips moved to form an *oh* without actually saying the syllable.

"Tell me about Chris Marsh," Estelle said.

At first, it appeared as if CJ Vallejos hadn't heard her. She turned her head away and closed her eyes, the room full of the gentle hiss and beep of gadgets. When she spoke, her voice was small and distant. She turned and looked at first Estelle and then Madelyn, her gaze wary and at odds with the sick child's voice.

"I haven't seen Chris since before Christmas," she said.

"Is that right."

"I think he went home or something."

"You didn't hear about his accident, then."

"Accident?" The sick child's voice went a note or two higher. "My God, what happened?"

"That's what we're investigating, CJ. His truck crashed on Regál Pass Wednesday evening."

"Oh, no. How…"

"It appears that he hit a deer, CJ."

"Why was he...?" She stopped as Estelle pulled her cell phone from her belt. It took a moment for the under-sheriff to scroll down through the numbers she wanted, and as she did so, CJ whispered, "I don't understand." Estelle waited for the connection.

"Abeyta."

"Deputy Abeyta," Estelle said formally, making no attempt to shield the conversation from CJ, "are you still at the Vallejos residence?"

"Affirmative," Abeyta said. "I was going to call in a few minutes. Gayle said you were over there."

"What have you found?"

"A couple of quick things that maybe you can use. Number one, I let the boyfriend go."

"That's fine. I don't think Jack Young has anything to do with any of this."

"And second of all, we found a bunch of stuff that probably was in Chris Marsh's truck...had to have been. In a black plastic trash bag under the bed."

"Under the bed," Estelle repeated, and as she said just those three words, it looked as if someone had reached into CJ Vallejos' skull and turned the rheostat down for the light in her eyes. "What was in it?"

"For one thing, the electronic signature device," Abeyta replied. "We also have the door plaques...pretty professional-looking job, too. Also a white baseball cap with the Global Productivity Systems logo. There's an empty aluminum clipboard, and an empty manila nine-by-twelve envelope."

"You didn't turn on the computer?"

"That's negative. I'm going to bring it along for Tom to mess with. I don't want to erase anything, which with my enormous computer savvy is exactly what would happen."

"Deputy, I'm going to put CJ Vallejos on the line with you. All I want you to do is run down the same list you just gave me."

"You don't need to do that," CJ whispered.

"Go ahead," Estelle said, and held the phone close to the girl's ear. CJ closed her eyes again, tightly this time, and Estelle watched the water squeeze out from under the girl's elegant eyelashes.

Estelle pulled the phone away. "Thanks, Tony. Keep me posted."

"Is she going to make it?" the deputy asked.

"Probably."

"Such a waste," he said. "She was a good-lookin' kid. I mean, you know what I mean," he finished lamely.

"Yes, I do," Estelle said. "Thanks. Keep in touch."

She slipped the phone back on its belt clip. "And CJ... one more important thing," Estelle said. She reached out and took the girl's left hand again, tracing the index finger scar. "We have your prints on the beer can."

A strangled cry issued from the girl as she jerked her head sideways, and her left hand out of Estelle's light grip. CJ cried freely then, great gulping sobs. The hospital room door opened, and Dr. Guzman slipped in, but he didn't interfere.

"How...how could you know?" the girl sobbed. She raised her right hand and thumped the gurney once in anguished frustration.

"Chris was still alive when you reached him, wasn't he?"

"Oh, God," CJ wailed, and she drew the word out into a multi-syllabic howl.

"Why didn't you help him?" Estelle asked. "Why didn't you call for help? You had a phone."

CJ's mouth contorted as the tears flooded. "He was so *stupid*," she managed. "Oh, God, so stupid. He was going to take the money from me."

"Really," Estelle said, without much sympathy. "And what money was that?"

"You know what money," the girl said with surprising venom.

"How did you know that he was going to take it?"

CJ sniffed back a sob and made a strangling sound. "I just...know. He joked about it all the time. But I knew...."

"You knew he wasn't joking?"

CJ nodded. "Oh, God," she wailed again. "He called and said he was heading up the pass, and when he didn't show, I drove down to meet him. There was this deer... lying in the ditch, all kicking and still alive. I could see the skid marks."

"So you looked down the cliff, saw the truck, and climbed down."

"He was lying in the rocks," CJ whimpered. "Just gurgling and hurt. And I could smell the beer. He drinks all the time."

"You want to tell me why? Why drown him in his own beer?"

"If he went to a hospital, they'd find out. He'd talk. I know he would. He'd been drinking....I figured that's what everyone would think when they found him."

"Why did you step on his hand?"

"I didn't...." And she cut off the protest. "He kept pushing at my hand, and I could hear the bones *grating*." She shrieked the last word, the stuff of her own private nightmares for years to come. "And then he choked, and it seemed like something broke inside him." The girl looked beseechingly at Estelle, eyes now bloodshot from crying. "He would have died anyway, don't you see?"

"Maybe so," Estelle said.

"What will happen to me?" CJ asked. The sobs had subsided to little gulps and spasms.

"You'll receive the best medical care available," Estelle said. She straightened up, reached out, and guided a strand of elegant black hair away from the girl's eyes. Estelle turned to regard the heart monitor that beeped on the wall behind the patient's gurney. "And when you're physically able, you'll be arraigned in district court on a variety of charges. Including murder."

The girl's face crumpled in anguish again, and Estelle found it difficult to determine how much of it was finely honed acting skills.

"But I'm paralyzed," CJ Vallejos pleaded. Her voice sank to a whimper. "I may never walk again."

"That's true," Estelle said. "And the more you cooperate with us, the easier your road will be. You think hard on that during the next few hours, CJ." She turned to Francis, who was tactfully scrutinizing the wall tiles. "Thanks, *querida*."

"I'll keep you posted," Francis said, and she reached out a hand to each cheek, cupping his face. She rocked his head gently and their eyes locked, blocking out the rest of the world.

"Madelyn and I are going to get something to eat," she said after a moment.

They left the hospital via the emergency room, walking the half-dozen steps to where Estelle had parked the county car just outside of the ambulance lane. As if their minds were in sync, they both stopped, one on each side of the car. Estelle leaned against the door, folding her hands together on the roof. She didn't say anything, and for a long moment Madelyn stood silently, watching her.

"Can I ask a question?" the writer said.

"Sure." Estelle pushed away from her trance and opened the car door.

They both settled into the car. "This is the first time you've actually seen this young woman, isn't it? Other than a fleeting glimpse when she blew by us at eighty-five miles an hour on the interstate. And *that* seems like a lifetime ago, I have to say."

"Yes. We have a picture of her. That's it," Estelle replied.

"Is that the way it usually is?"

"Usually?"

"When you have a case like this. You're chasing a stranger?"

"Actually, it's the opposite. Most of the time, we're working with folks we've known for years. Joe Smith down the street makes a mistake, and we become involved. Or someone steals a load of bricks. That sort of thing."

"That's not what happened this time, and it's not what happened last year, is it?" The "last year" didn't need an explanation.

Madelyn used the expression, and right on cue, Estelle's ribs under her right arm twanged.

"No."

"So every once in a while," Madelyn Bolles said, "what happens out there in the real world taints the quiet, pastoral paths of Posadas. How's that for poetic."

"Not bad," Estelle laughed. She started the car and pulled it into gear.

"What happens now?"

"Now, we hope CJ Vallejos makes it through the next week or so. It's going to be rough for her. And I don't mean just the physical injuries. And tomorrow, when the banks are open, we'll get some answers. I hope some information will be forthcoming from Calgary. We'll see what tidbits are in her address book, or in her computer files. We go from there."

"Do you think she'll actually go to jail? When she's all cleaned up and looking gorgeously vulnerable, do you think a jury will be able to send her away?"

"That's not my province," Estelle said. "Thank heavens."

"You don't worry about that happening? Her getting off?"

"No."

"Not even a little bit?"

"Not even a little bit. Not an *iota*, Madelyn." She smiled, starting to relax. "What do you care to eat?"

"Leftovers?"

Estelle frowned, and Madelyn added, "At your house. I know what's there, you know. And you need to go home. That's the fastest way to get you there."

THIRTY-NINE

At 4:10 P.M. on April 10, a Grand Jury returned an indictment against Consuela Juanita Vallejos for second-degree murder, conspiracy, and intent to defraud. By midmorning of April 11, CJ Vallejos agreed to a plea bargain on a lesser charge of involuntary manslaughter in full satisfaction of all charges. However, loath to slap a sentence at that very moment, District Judge Lester Hobart set April 22 for sentencing but continued bail at a quarter of a million cash only, after commenting that "despite the wheelchair, young lady, I consider you a flight risk."

Shortly before two that afternoon, Undersheriff Estelle Reyes-Guzman's office phone rang. For two hours, she had been lost in a grant proposal that County Manager Leona Spears had unearthed, the proposal driven by the current wave of Homeland Security hysteria.

"Guzman," she said.

"I love the way you say that, my dear," Madelyn Bolles said.

Delighted, Estelle leaned back, tossing her pencil on the desk. "Well, good morning, Madelyn. Where are you?"

"Philadelphia. Listen, I just talked with your court clerk. *Involuntary manslaughter*? However does that work?"

"Well…"

"I mean, what, did she *accidentally* pour beer down the poor man's throat?"

"Maybe she was just trying to wash the dirt off his face," Estelle laughed. "These things happen, Madelyn. My favorite was one time when a rock-solid DWI case was reduced to a charge of faulty muffler."

"But that's another story," Madelyn said. "Listen, speaking of stories, I'm going to e-mail you a draft of the article, along with a raft of photos.... We're not sure which ones we'll use just yet, but I wanted you to see what's coming."

"You don't need to do that."

"I know. But I *am* doing that, so there you are. I wanted to double-check a couple of things with you before I put a wrap on this. No other indictments are anticipated?"

"You mean against anyone else? No."

"The brother in Calgary?"

"Not as far as we're concerned. It looks like all he did was mail documents for his sister so that they would have a Canadian postmark. I'm not sure he even had an inkling what was in the envelopes. CJ found Canadian Publications Limited on the Internet, and just used the name and address. They had nothing to do with any of this."

"So it was the young lady's scam from top to bottom. I have to wonder how she hatched the scheme in the first place."

"It started with the DIAD—that's the digital signature gadget. She stole it from a legitimate courier truck during an unguarded moment. The driver had gone into a store with a package, and left the gadget on the console of his truck."

"And she happened by," Madelyn said.

"That's it. Just impulse. Once she had it, the rest of the idea was easy. It's a matter of trust, you see. You surround yourself with the right accoutrements and people accept you."

"So she didn't actually use the thing to access records or anything like that."

"No. It was just a stage prop."

"The poor boyfriend. I bet he didn't have a clue what he was getting into."

"Well, I think he did, Madelyn. At least he played the role convincingly. And by the way, the fourth check was bogus, just as we guessed it would be. The bank in Cruces that issued the first cashier's checks had no record of it. And if you compare the fourth check side by side with one of theirs, you'll see the difference. CJ made a pretty good copy on that computer of hers. Not good enough to fool a bank examiner, but plenty good to fool someone who *wanted* to be fooled."

"And this was the prototype scam," Madelyn said. "I remember you calling it that when we talked earlier. Her first dance."

"That's right. Sucker in the victim by the apparent good fortune of a neighbor. It's an interesting strategy."

"And except for the deer wandering out into the road, the fourth time might have worked," Madelyn said. "Anyway, I may be bothering you from time to time over the weekend, but I don't *think* I have any other questions for you. I need to chat with Leona here in a few minutes, but that's just for fun. And I need to talk with Mr. Hollywood Sheriff for just a moment."

"Leona will love hearing from you, but Bobby is out with Bill Gastner at the moment. Someone hijacked a semi loaded with cattle headed for auction, and the two sheriffs past and present are out talking with Herb Torrance, the rancher involved."

"My God. They still rustle cattle?"

"Oh, yes."

"Will he mind if I reach him on his cell?"

"Sure. But go ahead and do it anyway."

"I have a great quote from him, by the way. I wasn't going to use it, but if he gives me a hard time, I will."

"Dare I ask?"

Madelyn laughed. "Indeed you may. Sheriff Hunk told me that the only thing really wrong with having so many women working for him was that about once a month, you guys tend to use the siren too often."

"Wonderful. I'll remember that he said that. But by all means, use that one. You should talk Jackie Taber into doing a cartoon with that in mind."

Just a tiny, brief hesitation told Estelle what she needed to know. "Ah… I already have," Madelyn said. "My editor just loves it, and wonders why we haven't seen more of her work. So who knows what will develop."

"You hire her away from us and you're toast," Estelle said. "I had no idea that Jackie was so good at keeping secrets."

"And we're using a couple of Linda's photographs, too."

"Ditto more toast."

"Anyway, the real reason I called… I'll be visiting my aunt next month, so beware. May I stop by?"

"Of course. We look forward to it. Bring your aunt with you."

"Well, we'll see. Promise me no ride-alongs," Madelyn said. "My nerves can't take any more. I want one of those wonderful 'long bouts of peace' you spoke about when we first met."

"I'll work on that," Estelle said.

* * * * *

Get 2 Free Books,
Plus 2 Free Gifts—
just for trying the
Reader Service!

I N T R I G U E

YES! Please send me 2 FREE Harlequin® Intrigue novels and my 2 FREE gifts (gifts are worth about $10 retail). After receiving them, if I don't wish to receive any more books, I can return the shipping statement marked "cancel." If I don't cancel, I will receive 6 brand-new novels every month and be billed just $4.99 each for the regular-print edition or $5.74 each for the larger-print edition in the U.S., or $5.74 each for the regular-print edition or $6.49 each for the larger-print edition in Canada. That's a savings of at least 12% off the cover price! It's quite a bargain! Shipping and handling is just 50¢ per book in the U.S. and 75¢ per book in Canada.* I understand that accepting the 2 free books and gifts places me under no obligation to buy anything. I can always return a shipment and cancel at any time. Even if I never buy another book, the two free books and gifts are mine to keep forever.

Please check one: ☐ Harlequin® Intrigue Regular-Print   ☐ Harlequin® Intrigue Larger-Print
                        (182/382 HDN GLP2)   (199/399 HDN GLP3)

Name _____
                   (PLEASE PRINT)

Address _____ Apt. # _____

City _____ State/Prov. _____ Zip/Postal Code _____

Signature (if under 18, a parent or guardian must sign) _____

Mail to the **Reader Service**:
IN U.S.A.: P.O. Box 1867, Buffalo, NY 14240-1867
IN CANADA: P.O. Box 611, Fort Erie, Ontario L2A 9Z9

*Terms and prices subject to change without notice. Prices do not include applicable taxes. Sales tax applicable in N.Y. Canadian residents will be charged applicable taxes. Offer not valid in Quebec. This offer is limited to one order per household. Books received may not be as shown. Not valid for current subscribers to Harlequin Intrigue books. All orders subject to credit approval. Credit or debit balances in a customer's account(s) may be offset by any other outstanding balance owed by or to the customer. Please allow 4 to 6 weeks for delivery. Offer available while quantities last.

Your Privacy—The Reader Service is committed to protecting your privacy. Our Privacy Policy is available online at www.ReaderService.com or upon request from the Reader Service.

We make a portion of our mailing list available to reputable third parties that offer products we believe may interest you. If you prefer that we not exchange your name with third parties, or if you wish to clarify or modify your communication preferences, please visit us at www.ReaderService.com/consumerschoice or write to us at Reader Service Preference Service, P.O. Box 9062, Buffalo, NY 14240-9062. Include your complete name and address.

HI17

Get 2 Free Books,
Plus 2 Free Gifts—
just for trying the Reader Service!

Get 2 Free Books,
Plus 2 Free Gifts -
just for trying the Reader Service!

STRS17

READERSERVICE.COM

Manage your account online!

- Review your order history
- Manage your payments
- Update your address

> ### *We've designed the Reader Service website just for you.*

Enjoy all the features!

- Discover new series available to you, and read excerpts from any series.
- Respond to mailings and special monthly offers.
- Browse the Bonus Bucks catalog and online-only exculsives.
- Share your feedback.

Visit us at:

ReaderService.com

RS16R